MORAL DiLEMMA

LEGENDARY ALI SHABAZZ

Moral Dilemma
Copyright 2017 by Legendary Ali Shabazz

FOR SON

CHAPTER 1

*"Paranoid, sittin' in a deep sweat, thinkin' I got to fuck some-
body before the week ends."*

THE PUNGENT SMELL of nervous perspiration was starting to burn
the inside of his nostrils raw. Bodeen cracked the window of the sleek white
Lincoln Navigator as he drove down the dark streets of L.A.

Bodeen was trying to con himself into believing the jittery feeling he
was experiencing was caused by low blood sugar but in reality it was from
fear and anxiety. He was not accustomed to his emotions responding to an
unknown threat and he didn't like it. Bodeen was a cold-blooded individual that believed emotions should be placed on ice. He has been a magister
of the murder game since the age of 14. This being-scared business was
not even in his DNA. But Bodeen had a strange feeling in the pit of his
stomach tonight. It wasn't that gut feeling that was telling him to abort the
mission because danger was lurking. It was something else bothering him
and it felt really weird. Bodeen's plan always panned out to perfection but
tonight he kept having second thoughts. The irony of the entire thing was
he didn't know what those thoughts were trying to tell him...

"Whew I'm glad you cracked that window. Somebody in this car must
be feeling a little timorous cause I can smell that nervous perspiration,"
said LeRon (pronounced *"Lay-Ron" as he proclaims*) who was seated in the
backseat fanning his hand in front of his nose. Bodeen looked at LeRon

through the rear view mirror with evil intent. He clinched his teeth so tight with anger it sounded like his jawbone was cracking. Bodeen was a man of few words but when he spoke Bodeen expected you to listen with caution. Bodeen had already established a no talking rule when LeRon first accepted the job. Violating that rule showed Bodeen that LeRon didn't take his words seriously. He would be dealt with for that. Bodeen didn't need another reason to kill LeRon. He already had three. For one, Layron was an unclean muthafucka. He kept scratching in places where he shouldn't have been itching. The other reasons were Bodeen just didn't like that muthafucka.... or the way he pronounced his name.

Gerald, the other hired hooligan that was riding shotgun, remembered those instructions well. He could see the light switch go off in Bodeen's yellow eyes soon as LeRon opened his mouth. Gerald knew better not to talk. He was already scared before he got in the car so he didn't say shit. Gerald really didn't want to talk to Bodeen on a regular day so he damn sure wasn't ready to lose his life behind his gums flapping that night.

Bodeen made a left turn on Sartori Blvd. The sign at the intersection welcomed them to The City of Torrance. Torrance is a nice quiet coastal community that's known for its warm temperatures, sea breeze, and the highly regarded reputation as being a safe place to raise a family.

Bodeen continued to drive nice and steady. He kept a tight grip on the steering wheel because his hands were shaking moderately. The demonic thoughts popping in his mind were heavy. He was experiencing shortness of breath. Beads of sweat were bubbling up on his wide black nose like chicken grease in a cast iron skillet. Those nervous elements warned Bodeen he had better put his pistol on safety until they arrived at the destination. Bodeen reached his hand down to remove the pistol from his waistband. Bodeen glanced in the rearview mirror and noticed a police car driving up fast behind the Navigator.

The cops were just running a routine check on the plates. Driving up fast like that added the dramatics and it usually scared the shit out of people. Bodeen knew what the cops were doing but didn't pay it any mind. The last cop to stop Bodeen from completing a job in a timely and efficient manner was given the Award for Valor at his funeral. Bodeen was never charged.

The patrol car sped past the Navigator and went about its way. The hired hooligans riding with Bodeen saw the police car whiz pass them and got spooked. Police cars tend to make felons carrying weapons nervous as hell, even when they are not being stopped.

Bodeen could smell the fear coming out of the two dudes' pores. Bodeen hated weakness. He no longer wanted them in his presence. They were soft. They definitely weren't needed to complete the job but they were great characters. Bodeen was using them for show-not for dough. There was only one thing that saved them from dying at that very moment: Bodeen didn't want to get blood on the upholstery of his new ride.

Bodeen liked to work alone. He completed one job at a time. Bodeen was known as the Man That Got Shit Done. He was a Stone Cold Killer and that alone pretty much sums up all the other shit that he did that came with his profession. His reputation grew over the last twenty years not because of what he did but how he did it. Bodeen painted masterpieces highly detailed in murder. Every hit was delivered execution style and he showed no discrimination. Women, children, priest, or police he didn't give a fuck. If the price was right, you were dying that night.

But recently Bodeen had been changing up his game plan by reinventing himself. Bodeen had figured out a while back that killing every mark in cold blood was not always the answer. In some cases, he felt that killing the victim was giving them the easy way out; some assholes were made to suffer. Bodeen wanted to inflict permanent mental damage on his victims so he created a form of psychological torture he christened "Mental Trickery." This job was one of those cases.

* * *

Mario DePaul was a supplier of pharmaceuticals that did his business in the Valley area. Unlike the stereotypical drug dealer, Mario dealt mainly in the depressed *Rich Peoples* highs like Ketamine, Prozac, and antidepressants with names that's hard to pronounce, your Demerols, Propofols, and all that other prescription shit you don't see on the neighborhood street corners.

Mario always found it funny that his rich clientele didn't condone recreational drug use at all. They frowned upon it, with the exception of a little pure cocaine, of course. But as long as the pharmaceutical drug, no matter how bad, was backed by a doctor's signature, it was perfectly fine.

Mario grew up in Granada Hills and the best way to describe his nationality would be "*Other.*" Mario was the complexion of Cream of Wheat. He was one of those beige muthafuckas comprised of races. If one were to ask one of his family members was what color they were, they would name every race in United Nations but the African. They would still try and sneak it in on you. "Oh my grandfather was German and Irish and my grandmother was Scottish and Portuguese. My mother is French and my father is from Mississippi." That multi-racial façade made Mario very wealthy though. Since he looked like he could be related to anyone on the planet, it made everybody feel comfortable dealing with him. Most of Mario's clientele were either rich housewives or functional junkies with great jobs that required a college degree so the money was always steady.

For the most part, Mario is a pretty cool dude but at the same time he's still a drug dealer. There are certain elements that come with the pharmaceutical business that will cause you to lose that cool on one occasion or another. Mario was not a gangster, per se, but that fool was nothing nice if you crossed him the wrong way. He is what you would call hot tempered. Mario earned a reputation for being brilliant with a knife. He would poke you the fuck up. I guess that was the Mexican part in him. Now Mario was not the type of dealer that dealt in street violence even though he was fascinated by it. Trying to muscle another dealer for territory or cutting his product with baby laxatives to stretch the profit was not his modus operandi. Mario was a man of simple principles: don't tamper with his family or his money. If you crossed that line, he would slice you up like a goddamned wolverine.

Mario sought out Bodeen's services to neutralize a situation. Mario had become a fan of Bodeen's work after hearing about what he did to these sex offenders and pedophiles that moved into a rehabilitation house in a South L.A. neighborhood that was predominately single mothers and children.

The Neighborhood Women formed a Committee to take action. Once the women were informed that the police couldn't force the sex offenders to move, they hired Bodeen to eliminate their problem. For Bodeen, that particular job wasn't about the money, even though he still accepted it; it was personal. Bodeen wasn't a Good Samaritan. Bodeen was a killer and the only thing Bodeen hated more than his mother were child molesters.

So without going through the all the graphic details, Bodeen basically walked through the front door of the rehab center and went to work on everybody in the house. Bodeen's intent was to rid the sex offenders of all pleasures. The rapist that he castrated was reminded of what it might have been like to live in the days of Caligula. And the child molesters received a special treat. Bodeen poured sulfuric acid in the eye sockets of the pedophiles so they would never be able to look at another child again. Legend has that after they were blinded, Bodeen put those perverts in the back of a truck, dropped them off in the middle of nowhere, and told them *feel* their way back. Nobody died, but Bodeen still killed their will to live.

Mario was in awe of Bodeen's persona. Mario didn't need him to get too extreme for the problem he had, but having him apply one of the psychological tactics Bodeen was known for would be just enough to get his point across.

Mario's problem was his first cousin Ricky. Mario thought the world of Ricky. He was the brother he never had and the best friend he always wanted. They were also business partners. Ricky didn't deal drugs but he handled the finances. He kept order. Mario and Ricky's business relationship was built on the "what's mine is yours theory" but it was supposed to be in moderation.

Ricky had expensive taste but not for flash. Mario loved the spot light. Ricky invested money. Mario spent money. Mario bought gold chains; Ricky purchased gold bars along with other precious metals and stones. Ricky was concerned about security for the future; Mario lived in the here and now.

Mario was street smart. He enjoyed the hustle. Cousin Ricky went to school for finance and knew exactly what to do with the money. They were the perfect match. Ricky did an excellent job legitimizing the money but Mario wasn't involved in any of the business ventures set up in his name. It wasn't the fact that he didn't care; he just wasn't interested at that time in his life. Mario was good looking, young, and rich. He loved to spend money and feel free. Mario believed that *investment* was just a fancy word for buying expensive items. He trusted Ricky to make his money legit. That was his job.

Mario might not have been wise in the world of the Fortune 500 but he had knowledge of every single cent they made, and how much they should have before and after expenses. His eyes were always open. They were making so much cash Mario would just turn a blind eye when five thousand here or ten thousand dollars there came up missing. It was no big deal, they were family, and Ricky deserved it. As time moved on, 20 to 40 thousand dollar increments started to come up missing. Mario still let it slide. Since Mario was not the type of man to let drug money come before family, he respectfully brought it to Ricky's attention. He wanted to nip the problem in the bud before it got out of hand. A little simple communication can prevent a lot of foolishness. Mario politely told Ricky he should slow it down a bit because he was spending too much money. The words seemed to fall on deaf ears. Ricky never responded to the accusations and that pissed Mario off. Ricky frowned and just brushed him off like Mario was speaking gibberish.

Less than a week after they had the talk, $250,000 dollars was taken from the emergency stash. Soon after that, a half a million dollars vanished faster than frost on a windshield when the sun comes up. That was too much. It started to bring Mario to his breaking point. The gangster part of Mario wanted to slice Ricky's throat so bad he started dreaming about it while he was awake. Even though he had Lucifer whispering in his ear, Mario could never do that. Ricky was his mother's favorite sister's first-born son. Mario had a moral decision to make. If he eliminated Ricky from the business physically or even financially, it would bring sadness and despair to the entire family and Mario couldn't stomach the sight of seeing his mother and aunt crying. But if Mario continued to let Ricky steal, there won't be any business at all.

As he was gathering the intel at their initial meeting, Bodeen became instantly aware that Mario loved Ricky too much to have him killed or his hand cut off for stealing, which Bodeen would have normally done in this situation. Mario DePaul was hiring Bodeen at a very high price to implement scare tactics to slow down Ricky's spending habits. Mario wanted to handle it but he didn't know how to go about doing it without causing

Cousin Ricky some bodily harm so he called in the expert. Mario asked Bodeen to use his best judgment as long as he didn't kill or maim Ricky.

Bodeen learned in his line of work that 99.9 percent of the time when someone ordered a hit or paid "another man to clean up their shit," which is what Bodeen liked to call it, they acted out of anger, frustration, and emotions. They don't take the time to choose their words carefully, and they usually live the rest of their lives wishing they could take that moment back. Bodeen was a man that took everything literally.

As Mario explained it to Bodeen, "Ricky has been mismanaging the money ever since he shacked up with that foreign bitch...he's losing focus..." Even though it sounded more like jealousy than actual facts, that's all Bodeen needed to hear. Bodeen was a contract killer, not the host of couple's therapy. Bodeen accepted the payment and went to work.

Bodeen reached out to a few contacts until he found the people he needed to complete the job. That's where LeRon and Gerald came in and they fit the description for the job Bodeen wanted to pull off to a tee.

* * *

Bodeen glanced at LeRon in the rearview mirror and was disgusted at what he was looking at. LeRon's itchy unwashed ass sitting on his brand new car seats had been disturbing Bodeen's concentration the entire drive. Bodeen decided to blame the jittery feelings he was suffering from on LeRon and they seemed to go away.

LeRon was the most important player needed for the sick game of Mental Trickey Bodeen was about to play on Cousin Ricky.

* * *

LeRon was a freaky necrophiliac that worked down at the funeral home on 43rd and Lennox. LeRon's looks alone were enough to *Fuck Your Mind Up*. It didn't take anything else. If you wanted to be nice, one may say that LeRon was just not desirable in the company of femininity. If one were trying to be politically correct, one might say that LeRon's innate facial characteristics were not conducive to romance with the opposite sex. If you want the straight up truth, LeRon was an ugly muthafucka. He was a big toaster head nigga with real bad skin. He always looked like he was infected with disease. He was ashey and dusty even with lotion on. His hair was dry and brittle and he wore it in two long matted braids. LeRon's lips were chapped and he had the type of mouth that just looked like it stank. His front tooth was missing and he had dingy gold plated caps on the other ones. LeRon made up for his grotesque facial features in the figure department. LeRon was a 6-foot-3, 220-pound perfect athletic specimen. LeRon's body was so ripped and chiseled he had muscles bulging out of his muscles. LeRon was also hung bigger than a horse. If he dropped his drawers, it would look like he was standing on three legs.

Bodeen didn't feel comfortable around LeRon at all but he was perfect for the job. LeRon's lust for sex with something alive and human was going to make Bodeen's plan that much better.

Bodeen offered to pay LeRon $1000 to advance his lust on Ricky's fiancé. From the information Bodeen gathered from Mario, she was the culprit that Ricky was spending the missing money on. Bodeen figured that once Ricky saw his fiancé being brutally raped by this monkey man, he would want nothing else to do with her and he could get his mind back on business. Mario's orders were not to harm Ricky; he didn't say anything about the fiancé.

* * *

Bodeen made another left turn on El Prado Avenue. Ricky had a nice two-bedroom home that sat in the middle of the block. Even at night, you could tell the landscaping was impeccable. Bodeen parked the truck in a good spot and studied his surroundings. The lights were dim inside of Ricky's home and you could see the fire from the candles flickering behind the lace curtains. Bodeen picked his pistol up off of his lap and attached a GEMTECH Sound Suppressor he retrieved from his inside coat pocket.

Gerald checked to make sure he had the rope, handcuffs, gasoline, and gag. Gerald knew not to speak so he gave Bodeen a nod to let him know he was ready. Bodeen could care less. He only hired Gerald because he looked the part. Gerald was a fat scruffy looking character that had a scar that ran all the way down the center of his face. The scar made him look like a killer, but only a chosen few knew that his beauty mark came from a childhood accident playing on the monkey bars when he was six. LeRon was in the backseat scratching his Jones anxiously, waiting to perform.

The message alert chimed on Bodeen's phone. Bodeen cursed himself for having his phone on in the first place. He had broken one of his own rules. His thoughts were too preoccupied with the events that were about to take place as well as the distractions and jittery feelings that kept occurring. Without bothering to see who it was, Bodeen turned his cell phone off and placed it in the glove compartment. He took a deep breath. They exited the vehicle.

The interior of Ricky's home was a complex mixture of cultural, philosophical, mathematical, astrological, and aesthetic concepts. It could technically be labeled Feng Shui because of the discipline associated with the architectural and decorating themes but that wasn't their intention when they assembled it. When the time came for Ricky and his fiancé to look back on their journey, they wanted each area of the house to have its own memorable story to tell.

The vibe in Ricky's home was so serene you could feel the love in the atmosphere. The visuals were very alluring and the scented candles made the home smell delicious.

Ricky was in his humble abode looking very comfortable sporting some light workout gear, a cut-off tee and some loose sweat pants. He was seated on the floor next to the oval shaped earthtone marble coffee table centered perfectly in the middle of the living room. He was studying the portfolio he held in his hand. Ricky reached out in front without looking and picked up the glass of fresh mango juice he'd been sipping on and put it up to his lips. Ricky's eyes never left the portfolio as he turned the glass up to take a drink. A tiny drop of juice that wouldn't quench a flea's thirst teased his tongue. Ricky looked at the empty glass and called out, "Hey Beautiful, before you come back in here to sign these documents would you mind bringing me some more juice or bottled water? Either one. It doesn't matter."

"I don't mind at all, Big Baba. How else am I going to keep my man healthy and in tune with nature if I don't keep his body hydrated with water at all times?" Angie said as she smiled and walked into the living room. Her Afro-Argentine accent flowed in rhythmic tones when she spoke. Angie's beauty was breathtaking as if she were a descendant of an Angel or Goddess. She had the Look of Love. Angie looked so graceful the way she carried the water you didn't know if she was going to make Ricky drink it or baptize him with it. She was wearing a beautiful fitting Dashiki so full of color it made the room feel warm. Her physical beauty is just the tip of the iceberg. Angie is something special. She is a rare jewel indeed.

* * *

Angie is a descendent of the only pure Black race born in Argentina. Even though Angie's ancestors were born on that soil, they were labeled Black, never Argentine. The word Black was taboo. Angie's complexion is smooth and chocolate like a Hershey bar but on her Argentine birth certificate where it says skin color, it says Wheat.

Angie's family was proud of their rich heritage but the living conditions forced them to swallow some of that pride. Angie's family was not dirt poor but they were still forced to live in the city of Corrientes also known as *Camba Cuá*, meaning "Cave of the Blacks." Angie's father despised being a free and well-learned man still living in slave conditions. Even though Angie's dad cherished his family's independence, he was also wise enough to know a free Black in Argentina had less chance for survival than an enslaved one. Angie's family eventually relocated to the Democratic Republic of Congo where the last of their true descendants were. That's where her dad formed the Argentine group called Africa Vive to help rekindle the African heritage of Argentina so it will never be forgotten.

Ricky was taking classes at West L.A. Community College and was given the opportunity to travel abroad and study in The Congo for a semester. That is when Ricky first laid eyes on Angie and immediately fell in love. Angie was the woman that most men spent their life dreaming about. She was stunning, chaste, intelligent, and had a beautiful spirit. Ricky and Angie connected immediately. Her family history fascinated Ricky. Those three funky semester credits Ricky earned for the class was nothing to the lessons he learned about life, preservation, security, principles, character, and integrity from Angie's family legacy.

Ricky brought Angie back to the States on a student visa shortly after her father passed away. In memory of Angie's father and Ricky's hero, they planned to get married on his next birthday.

* * *

"What I'm doing here, Angie, is diversifying your portfolio. One of the best ways to do that is invest in a few geographic areas like your hometown of Argentina. These equities I've purchased will not only help your family preserve their heritage, they will also be part owners of 25 businesses in that country." Ricky explained to Angie before she signed the necessary paperwork.

"Did you always have a gift for mathematics or just have a great teacher?" Angie asked in her sexy Spanish-African accent as she glanced through her portfolio.

Ricky responded in a humble tone, "I was definitely blessed with the skill. I've been fascinated with numbers since the day my great-grandmother taught me how to count to 100. Over the years through trial and error I eventually learned to apply my gift for math to everyday life."

"Speaking of error," Angie stated with her face frowned up. "I see you don't have the same passion for words as you do for numbers. Your penmanship and spelling is horrible, baby." Angie laughed as she shook her head out of pity.

Ricky started cracking up laughing, "You are right about that, baby. Every teacher I had in school said my writing looked like chicken scratch"

"This looks more like chicken kaka," Angie couldn't stop laughing. "What? Do you write with your knuckles?"

* * *

"Lookin' through her window, now my body is warm. She's naked, and I'm a peepin' tom. Her body is beautiful, so I'm thinkin' rape shouldn't have had her curtains open, so that's her fate"

Bodeen and his hooligans were hidden in the large bushes in front of Ricky's home. Ricky and Angie's Zen for nature provided perfect cover in the still of the night. From where he was positioned, Bodeen could see everything that was going on in the home. The sight of Angie made his heart flutter. She looked angelic even through demon's eyes. Angie's beauty almost had Bodeen in a trance. He had to channel every bit of hate he had in his heart just to stay focused on the job.

"Damn that bitch is fine!" LeRon whispered, breaking the silence, the rules, and Bodeen's concentration. "I think I seen that broad before at the job. She interned with those pathologists a few months back. Boy, oh boy if her corpse ever made it to the job, I would keep that on ice for at least three months." LeRon continued, but his funeral home humor created no laughter except his own.

Bodeen didn't say a word; he just made a mental note of LeRon's insolence.

* * *

"These annuities and mutual funds I invested in have us straight for life, Angie. Do you know how important establishing long term security for the entire family is?" Ricky didn't bother waiting for an answer and continued. "We are already at the point where our grandkids' kids will be financially stable!" Ricky yelled, full of enthusiasm. But just as quick, his attitude became somber. "I just don't understand why Cousin Mario can't see what I'm doing. Sometimes he lets his gangster fascination get the best of him and he loses sight of our goals. And you know what, baby? I honestly think he believes I'm tricking off all his money on bullshit. He's acting like he doesn't trust me. And when he gets like that, he goes into his gangster mode... and I don't even like talking to him or being around him then."

But Angie defended Mario. When she spoke partially in her native tongue, Ricky always took heed and listened intensely as opposed to when she didn't for some reason or another. "No njia, siwezi kuamini kwamba! Mario knows you too well and loves you too much. Did you explain to him clearly what you are doing, with the emphasis on clearly?"

"Baby, I tried. But talking to Mario about hedge funds is like trying to talk astrophysics to a wino."

"That's the problem." Angie said, "Talk to a wino about something he can relate to... like alcohol, not astrophysics. Mario loves money. You have to tell him in a language he understands, baby. He wants to see profits. Mario doesn't want a lecture about Wall Street unless you're talking about the movie. Ricky, you also have to keep in mind that you were raised as an only child and you have a bad habit of not involving everyone in what you are doing. You expect us to just know what is in your head with no type of communication. Even if your way is best, there is still a better way to do it. As an investor, you can't be that way with a cousin or not. "

"You are right baby. I haven't been totally clear but damn, I haven't given him any reason not to trust me... have I?"

"Not telling Mario where his money is that he thinks is missing would cause a little dissension, don't you think?"

"I just wanted to surprise him and make him proud of me. But yeah, I can see where it could cause a little disturbance now looking at it from that perspective," Ricky stated after he thought about it.

"A *little* disturbance?" Angie asked, "You have your cousin thinking he lost over a million dollars; that would be enough to cause a catastrophe! Yesu Kristo."

Angie and Ricky laughed about it and fell into each other's embrace.

* * *

It didn't take long for Bodeen to regain his composure. He was evil by nature and was put on this earth to destroy what was good. That was his job and he loved being the best at it.

Bodeen took his gun off safety. Bodeen rustled the bush to get Gerald and LeRon's attention. Bodeen made a gesture with the hand that held the pistol for them to follow his lead. Their footsteps across the dry leaves scattered on the ground sounded like a busted chain saw in the still of the night. Bodeen and his hired hooligans edged toward the front door. When they reached the steps, the automatic sensor was triggered and the porch light came on. Bodeen immediately lifted his pistol. Gerald and LeRon panicked initially and kind of hid behind Bodeen. Bodeen used a hand signal beckoning the hooligans to move back a few steps away from the sensors. They waited patiently until the light went out. Bodeen located the floor sensor and stepped over it. He walked toward the door and triggered the porch light on once again.

Angie and Ricky noticed the porch light from inside the house. "I think the neighbor's cat is in your rose garden again," Ricky assumed.

"Ooh! Kama kwamba nasty shits paka katika nyumba yangu tena mimi nina kwenda kulisha mbwa!" Angie stated angrily.

"Yeah! That's exactly what I was thinking." Ricky laughed 'cause he had no idea what Angie just said but he knew it wasn't nice.

Ricky got up and headed to the front door. He didn't give a damn about that cat but just to make Angie feel better he said, "I'll take a look outside before I lock us in for the night. If see the cat out there, I'll skin it and make you a coat."

Bodeen could hear feet walking toward the front door from inside the house. Ricky was actually closer to the door than where the sound appeared to be. The sudden movement of the doorknob startled Bodeen but his reaction was quick as lightning. Bodeen shot the doorknob off. He raised his thick leg and kicked the door open with his size 14 shoe. Bodeen was on top of Ricky before he knew what hit him. Bodeen snatched Ricky up off the floor by the back of his tee shirt with one hand. The blast Ricky took to his head from the door being kicked in had him out on his feet. Gerald and LeRon rushed in the house behind Bodeen.

The adrenaline rush was a bit much for Gerald. He fell out of character and bolted to the living room. Gerald wasn't the violent type so he aggressively ran behind Angie but held her delicately by her garb as he pretended to hold her hostage. He tried to get a little gangster and started speaking erratic in Angie's ear and daring her to scream. But really, that nigga just wanted to get close enough to Angie to smell her perfume. That old chubby hard luck dude was catching feelings. The last thing Gerald wanted to do was disobey orders but Angie had such an effect on him, touching her anyway he could was worth dying for.

Ricky looked like a limp noodle as Bodeen held him up by his shirt collar. Ricky was trying desperately to shake of the wooziness as he started to come back into consciousness. Bodeen took the water bottle off of the coffee table and doused Ricky in the face with it. Ricky was slowly gathering his senses and trying to make out the faces that had invaded his home.

LeRon felt he needed to do something violent in order to get in Bodeen's good graces so he stepped up and slapped Ricky hard across his cheek and grunted, "I better not ever catch you reckless eyeballin' me again, boy!"

That slap was just enough to bring Ricky back to reality and he immediately showed LeRon he was all man. Ricky fired on LeRon and caught him with an overhand right to his eye. He followed it up with a left hook to the jaw and flurry of combinations that sent LeRon reeling across the floor. Bodeen was actually getting much pleasure out of watching Ricky beat the shit out of LeRon but he was there for business and stopped it. Bodeen saved LeRon from a knockout by placing the silencer of his pistol to the side of Ricky's head.

Bodeen looked across the room. He gave Gerald a chilling look that said he was about to kill him if he didn't do what he came there for. Gerald got the hint and released his hand from around Angie's throat. Gerald darted over to where Ricky was standing and handcuffed his arms behind his back. LeRon got up off the floor completely embarrassed. His audition for Bodeen didn't go so well. LeRon waited until Ricky was securely hand-cuffed and then cracked him over the head with the butt of his pistol when he wasn't looking. Ricky dropped to one knee on the carpet. LeRon's weak actions were making Bodeen sick. He wondered why he hired that clown in the first place. Once Bodeen remembered why, he was ready to get the party started. He just hoped those weak lames could control their actions long enough to complete the job.

Bodeen grabbed a handful of hair on the top of Ricky's head and lifted it up so he could look at him in the eye. Bodeen held Ricky's face close to his. The sticky spit stuck to his lips like spider webs when Bodeen opened his mouth to speak. "Where's the money?"

Ricky couldn't make sense of what was happening or who these people were. His only real concern was protecting Angie by any means necessary. Ricky looked at his Beautiful Goddess. The terrified look on Angie's face fueled him with anger and revenge. It made him confident and strong. It brought the warrior out of him. Ricky made the decision right then and there that he could care less what happened to him but if those sick savages even looked at Angie wrong everybody in the house was dying.

Bodeen sensed immediately that Ricky did not scare easy. Bodeen's nose was about a half inch away from Ricky's face. Bodeen's hot breath felt like hellfire. He refused to repeat his words. Enough had been said already. Bodeen just stared at Ricky in his eyes thinking it was going to get him deeper inside his soul.

Ricky broke the silence and spoke with malice in his heart. "What is this all about? Are you robbing me or what? All the cash I have is in my wallet right there on the table… now take it and just get the fuck outta here!"

Bodeen shook his head in a way that meant no. Bodeen used sign language this time to get his point across so he wouldn't have to speak. Bodeen rapidly rubbed his thumb across his index and middle fingers. It asked the same question, "Where is the money?"

Ricky was sick of this evil joker breathing in his face. If he knew what Bodeen wanted, he would have been more than happy to give it to him. What money was he referring to? Ricky was trying to put two and two together, the two on the ten, just trying to add it all up but kept coming up with zero. Bodeen made it clear that he wasn't dealing in basic math and laid out the statistics and the probabilities.

"Listen here; if you don't give me that money," with an emphasis on money, "this beastly nigga here," pointing to LeRon, "is going to rip your woman's pussy wide open."

Angie's heart damn near dropped out of her body.

LeRon started getting over-anxious and displaying the actions of a sexual predator. "Is it time to do my part, Bodeen? Is it time for my part? Shit, I didn't know you were going to pay me fuck a couple that looks this damn good. I would have done this shit for free. Which one you want me to do first?"

LeRon started unzipping his pants without waiting for Bodeen's answer. He was not following the script. LeRon was like a demon satiating his incurable lust. LeRon stood in front of Ricky and let his khakis drop to the floor. Ricky closed his eyes and jerked his head to the side. He wasn't trying to see what LeRon wanted to show him. Bodeen grabbed Ricky by the hair and turned his head to the front. He held Ricky's head down and ordered him to look at it or he would hurt Angie. Ricky opened his eyes because of the threat made against his fiancée. LeRon had a huge Mississippi Swamp Dick. But in his case Bigger was definitely not better. Nothing about LeRon's penis looked pleasurable. His dick was coated with so many untreated genital warts, it looked like a shingles rash. Most of the scabs were dry but some of them were open and irritated where LeRon had broken the skin from scratching them. There were a couple of yellowish bumps on the head of his penis that were filled with puss and they were going to pop at any moment.

"Goddamn!" someone said, but everybody in the room was thinking the same thing.

LeRon started grinning and grunting like a wild hyena. The thought of having live sex with something other than an attractive corpse aroused him instantly. LeRon started developing a full powerful erection. When his foreskin started stretching his genital warts started to itch. Out of habit, LeRon started scratching those muthafuckas. Flakes of dead skin were chipping off his balls like dandruff. LeRon started looking in Angie's direction with lust in his eyes. The fear in the pit of her stomach was the only thing that prevented Angie from puking all over the floor.

Ricky was getting sick looking at LeRon and broke down, "Will you please tell me what the fuck you want from me? All your one-liners and sign language is not telling me shit. Just tell me what I need to do to get you and this nasty muthafucka out of my sight."

Until that moment Bodeen had never looked at LeRon's exposed private parts. He had heard about the freakish size and girth but knew nothing about the sores. When LeRon started scratching with both hands, that's when Bodeen finally took notice. He didn't like what he saw at all. He didn't realize it at the time, but Bodeen really didn't like the way LeRon was looking at Angie either. He naturally felt obligated to protect her. Bodeen looked back at LeRon and he was flicking the dead foreskin that accumulated under his fingernails on to the floor. It was just too much nastiness for Bodeen to tolerate. He lifted his pistol and shot that nigga LeRon right between his eyes.

Angie gasped but she didn't scream. Never in a million years would she have dreamed that she would find joy in seeing a man get shot in her living room. Gerald was more shook up about LeRon getting shot than Angie was. He was wondering if Bodeen shot LeRon for talking in the car or just because he didn't like him. Gerald was also having thoughts as to if he would be next for disobeying orders.

Bodeen was never going to allow LeRon to rape Angie in the first place. He was just playing Mind Games with them. Bodeen wanted Ricky to believe Angie was going to be on the receiving end of that nasty ass

Swamp Dick so he would come clean about that money. Bodeen thought he would be able to laugh at his twisted prank after the ordeal was over. It just didn't quite work out that way.

Ricky was showing no emotion whatsoever. As long as no one harmed Angie he was content. Ricky consoled his queen. "Our faith is strong, baby. Just look at this, as the worst part of our journey and it will only get better from here. I guarantee you we will survive."

Ricky's words were comforting to Angie, but they irritated the fuck out of Bodeen. It actually made him jealous, another emotion Bodeen was not accustomed to so he didn't know how to react. He knew Ricky wasn't a weak man. Ricky was actually a real man, a protector and provider. Bodeen glanced down at the portfolios on the coffee table. He picked one up and flipped through it. Bodeen was looking at Mario DePaul's portfolio but didn't even know it. Bodeen couldn't really read or write but he recognized the numbers well. He saw all the deposits made in the same amounts Mario said were missing. Bodeen tied the missing money together with the conversation he heard earlier between Angie and Ricky while they hid in the bushes. Seeing the missing figures on paper just confirmed what Bodeen thought he knew all along. Ricky was stealing Mario's money to make Angie happy.

Bodeen knew a man would do anything to keep a woman like Angie, even steal money from his favorite cousin. And just from being in her presence for those brief moments, Bodeen was truly convinced of his theory. It was getting harder and harder for Bodeen to look at Angie without developing feelings for her. Angie didn't look back at Bodeen the same way at all. Bodeen felt it, too. Over the course of his life Bodeen had been beaten, stabbed, and shot but he had never felt the pain that came from a woman breaking his heart. It felt like his feelings were being tortured. The only way Bodeen knew how to defend his heart was through violence.

"You were in the right place for me at the wrong time!"

Bodeen grabbed Angie by her neck. That immediately put Ricky on point.

"Just like I thought... A sucker for a bitch!" Bodeen growled. Ricky's whole demeanor changed. There was no time to think and he was moving on pure instinct. Bodeen smiled and flashed a yellow toothy grin. "It seems to me that this woman has become a distraction. It has you in world of trouble right now, my friend, and it's making you lose focus and causing you to do things you normally wouldn't." Bodeen was philosophizing but he was so smitten by Angie's presence he didn't realize he was also talking about himself. Bodeen continued, "I say, 'Find the source, eliminate it, and it will make all your problems go away.' What you think about that, Ricky?" But Bodeen didn't wait for an answer from Ricky and decided to speak for him, "Who gives a fuck what you think, punk!"

Ricky's eyes narrowed and he took on the look of a demon spawn. Angie didn't even recognize her man. The rage Bodeen saw in Ricky's eyes warned him that he could easily break out of those handcuffs and kill everybody in the house.

Bodeen tossed Gerald a pistol. "Hold this trick, face down! Understand me? If he moves, kill that nigga!"

Gerald was so scared he was shaking like booty meat. He bobbled the pistol as it was thrown to him and he damn near dropped it. Gerald wasn't a killer; he was just a simple car thief trying to make some extra cash on the side. Gerald was in over his head and got himself into some shit he wanted no parts of. Gerald was ready to take off running out of the door and getting the fuck out of there, but he was too scared of Bodeen. Plus Gerald wasn't in the best shape for sprinting so he had to do what he was told. Gerald put his foot in the small of Ricky's back and held the pistol to the back of his head with a quivering hand.

Ricky still didn't have a clue to what the hell was going on. His mind raced trying to put the pieces together. Ricky wasn't in the life. He didn't have any enemies. The only person Ricky could think of that might have been mad at him at the time was Mario, but his cousin would never stoop this low to get his point across. "*The Money... the money*" Ricky was trying to figure out what money Bodeen was referring to. Bodeen saw the portfolio with Mario DePaul's name and social security number big as the sun written across the top of the page. Every penny that Mario claimed Ricky stole was secured and accumulating interest at that very moment. It just didn't make sense. The whole ordeal was *fucking with his Mind.*

...grabbed the bitch by her mouth, drug her back in, slammed her down

on the couch; Whipped out my knife, said, "If you scream, I'm cuttin'" Opened her legs and commenced the fuckin'

Bodeen turned his attention to Angie. His illiteracy and fucked up way of thinking made him believe that she was the root of the problem.

Bodeen's movements were eerie like a rabid wolf as he crept over to Angie. That nervous feeling came over him again but this time it was more intense than ever. Bodeen kept his eyes to the floor. Angie was too angelic to look at. There were voices in Bodeen's head encouraging him to commit *the ungodly act that he despised the most. Rape?* This wasn't his style. This was the kind of shit he frowned upon. Bodeen had savagely killed many men for rape as if it were a personal vendetta. Now he found his own desires were overpowering him. Bodeen was not in control. It felt like he was being controlled by a negative entity and couldn't do a damn thing about it. It was the strangest feeling Bodeen had ever experienced. The best way to put it would be *it was just one of those damn things that are hard to explain.* Negative thoughts flew rapidly in and out of his mind. He thought of the souls of the rapists he had killed coming back to haunt him. He thought about how life would be if he destroyed the demons in Angie's honor and she fell in love with him for it.

Bodeen shook it off and snapped back to reality. Bodeen might have been a very bad man with the mind of a lunatic but a punk ass rapist he was not. Bodeen kept his eyes to the floor so he wouldn't be caught staring at Angie's beautiful face. Bodeen decided pistol whip the information out of Ricky. Bodeen figured that if he made Ricky look weak in front of Angie, she might go for him. The Alpha Male is supposed to get the girl, right?

Right before Bodeen turned around to pistol whip Ricky, he noticed the blue toe nail polish Angie was wearing… and for a reason only known to Bodeen, it triggered the beast in him. He reached his hand back so far his shoulder blade popped and he backhanded Angie hard across her face. She fell back into a thud.

Ricky saw his woman fall and gained the strength of 20 men. He came up off the floor with enough velocity to slam Gerald into the wall. Ricky's hands may have been restricted but that didn't restrict his rage.

Ricky head-butted Gerald square in the nose bone and shattered it like glass. Blood splattered out like a water sprinkler. As Gerald reeled from the blow, Ricky kneed him viciously in the face until he slumped to the floor. Ricky commenced to stomp his head until he was unconscious. Ricky was so irate he didn't even notice the pistol Gerald dropped. Ricky purposefully dropped on his back and used his athleticism to reverse his cuffed hands to the front. Ricky jumped to his feet and charged Bodeen like a raging bull. Bodeen remained calm. He raised his gun and aimed it at Ricky's heart.

As he raised the gun, Angie kicked Bodeen in his spine hard as she could and caused the gun to fire prematurely. The bullet caught Ricky in the top of his shoulder. He didn't even feel it. Ricky was still coming. Bodeen shot him twice in the stomach. Ricky slowed down but his will to protect Angie and his determination to get his hands on Bodeen kept him coming forward. Bodeen shot Ricky once more in his testicles. That bullet dropped him to his knees. But Bodeen didn't plan to kill him. He wanted Ricky to witness what he was about to do to his fiancée.

Bodeen spun toward Angie and she kicked the shit out of him dead in his throat. Bodeen choked with her strike, like liquid went down the wrong windpipe. Angie clawed at Bodeen's face and tried to scratch his right eye out of the socket. Angie dug her claws in and scratched the other side of his face, too. She went to kick again but Bodeen grabbed at her ankle. Angie was too fast and kicked Bodeen in the chin. Bodeen was caught off balance. His knees buckled. She missed that sweet spot by half an inch or he would have been knocked out. The chin shot dazed him. It gave Angie just enough time to grab a heavy object to crack that muthfucka's skull open. The closest object to Angie that would inflict the most damage was the solid gold urn that held her father's remains. It was perfect. A blow to the head from the weight of the urn would kill Bodeen for sure. Daddy was still there when Angie needed him the most.

But Angie couldn't do it. Religious beliefs and respect for her dad's ashes caused Angie to second-guess what she was supposed to do with that urn. Angie scanned the room quickly for a different heavy object to hit him with.

That slight hesitation was costly for Daddy's little girl. Bodeen grabbed Angie by the back of her hair and snatched her around the room like a rag doll. Bodeen slammed Angie on the huge pillow near the offering table on the right side of the living room. The corner of the table caught Angie when she fell and cut her over the eyebrow. Bodeen yanked on her clothing and tore the beautiful garb off of Angie's body and exposed her nakedness. He snatched her panties down to her ankles.

Angie still had some fight in her. She kicked, scratched, and clawed at Bodeen. Then Bodeen brought all that to a halt. He raised his fist and it came crashing down on her forehead like a sledgehammer. She was dazed and silent.

Bodeen stood over Angie, looking at her flawless body. He shuddered. A woman that beautiful should be cherished. Everything about her represented good. Everything about Bodeen was dark and evil. Bodeen hesitated. His conscience disturbed him. Bodeen knew he was in the wrong but then that negative energy came over him and he had no control. The next thing Bodeen knew, his pants were unzipped and he released the monster in his trousers. Bodeen's erection was so strong it was like it had a mind of its own. Bodeen had never been this frightened yet turned on in his entire life but he wasn't enjoying the feeling at all. Bodeen pried Angie's legs apart. Her vagina was more divine than any he had seen before anywhere. Angie just had her cat waxed so it was bare and smooth. Bodeen stared wide-eyed at her split like he was scared of it. He had never seen a vagina that was hairless before.

A deep guttural noise came forth from him as he thrust himself on her motionless body.

Ricky could vaguely see what was happening through his blurred vision, but he was losing so much blood it was hard for him to stay focused. The room was spinning. Ricky could barely remember why two other bodies were laid out in his living room. Then he saw what his move had to be.

Bodeen was focused on trying to enter Angie. But he couldn't find the hole to her inner sanctum, even though it was staring him right in his face.

The head injury left Angie groggy with a concussion. She was in no condition to fight off this 260-pound beast any longer. Angie decided she was just going get through this nightmare as quickly as possible. But Bodeen was dragging out the whole ordeal with all his fumbling and awkwardness. As he tried to unsuccessfully shove himself into her, Angie thought, "This muthafucka is the worst rapist on the planet Earth."

And Bodeen didn't even notice Ricky sliding across the floor to the abandoned pistol.

Ricky got his hand on the pistol. He was exhausted. The 10 yards he crawled across the floor felt like 10 miles. Protecting Angie was the only thing keeping him alive. Ricky inhaled deeply. He tightened his grip on the pistol.

Bodeen was still struggling trying to poke his dick into Angie's private parts and she wasn't making it easy for him at all as she started to scream. Trying to concentrate on the pussy plus holding Angie's shoulders down to prevent her from squirming was making Bodeen very frustrated. Angie kicked at him, spit in his face, scratched at him, and kept fighting off his unwanted and awkward advance the best she could.

But Bodeen was too strong and determined. He shoved her legs until her knees were touching her forehead. Bodeen finally found Angie's hole but barely got the tip of his shaft in. He was extremely aroused feeling the warmth of her vagina but it wasn't moist at all. Angie was dry as the desert heat.

As his tip tried to enter, she laid there catching her breath. A peculiar look came over her face as she came to realize... Bodeen was still a virgin.

Bodeen was indeed unskilled but that didn't prevent him from getting to her hot dry vagina. With determination, Angie locked her legs around Bodeen and tightened up. Losing his virginity at her expense was going to be enough. Angie was not going to make his first time a pleasurable experience.. Bodeen still melted like butter on top of Angie like she was a stack of pancakes. He was in love.

Ricky watched as anger washed over him and gave him just enough strength to kill Bodeen... but it was useless now. He didn't protect his queen. Hopelessness washed over him. Angie would never look at him the same again. She would never feel safe with him as her man after Ricky allowed her to be violated like that. He was the one to blame. If the husband fails to fulfill the sacred duties owed to his queen, he has forsaken the Lord and His sacred rules, which he has ordained.

Ricky felt less than a man. He could not live the rest of his life as a failure. Ricky knew deep inside that he could have prevented all of this by being open with his cousin Mario. Family or not, Ricky realized that it was not in his best interest to keep secrets about Mario's money regardless if he were investing in lucrative deals or not. We are all human but we are not all the same and we don't all think the same. When Ricky looked at the world from his eyes, he believed he was doing something positive. Mario saw him as a great money launderer that he could trust. Everyone's journey is different.

Ricky's entire world revolved around Angie. She was the air he breathed and his reason for living. Ricky was the type of man that would rather lose his life before he allowed Angie to see him any differently than her strong man that protected her. Ricky raised the pistol, placed it to his temple, and he whispered, "Baby, I'm sorry I failed you," as he pulled the trigger. The bullet stopped his thoughts and his life.

Bodeen prematurely convulsed and over three decades of sexual tension exploded inside of Angie. He was elated and felt a little lightheaded. Bodeen had never experienced a climax in the 36 years he's been on Earth. It was too overwhelming. All that built up pressure being released almost made his heart go out. His back tightened up, his legs started shaking, and the emotions that came over him were meant for tactile people not demons. Bodeen held Angie tight against his massive chest. He wanted to stay clung to Angie for the rest of his life. Bodeen had never even dreamed about a moment like this and wanted to hold on to it. He squeezed Angie even tighter fearing the moment the feeling would come to an end. Angie's delicate body went limp and frigid. He looked at her face and it was expressionless like she was no longer breathing. Angie's eyes rolled up to the back of her head and her temperature became cold.

CHAPTER 2

"BLESS UP TO the MOST HIGH!" were the first words spoken as he opened his eyes at 5:07 am in the morning. Coach felt more control when he woke up on his terms before the alarm clock went off and forced him to get up. It was a psychological thing but it worked. If he started his day off right, he had an excellent chance of having a great one.

Coach had a cool morning routine he'd been following since the day he made his knowledge born. Coach always brushed his teeth as soon as the floor was under his feet. He treated morning breath like it was his enemy and he drowned it with toothpaste and mouthwash until it was dead.

Then he headed to the kitchen and made a nice pot of coffee. Coach was serious about his coffee. He didn't believe in the stuff anybody could purchase on the shelf at the local supermarket, No sir.

Coach ordered beans directly from coffee growers around the world. Coach was excited about his most recent purchase. It was just delivered to his job the day before. The blend was called Talkin' Blues, 100% Jamaica Blue Mountain whole bean coffee. Marley was the brand name so it had to be certified gold. Coach wasn't into coffee for the caffeine kick. He was addicted to the lovely aroma and the flavor. It made him feel vivacious. To make the apartment smell even sweeter, Coach lit a Sasha-Imani incense and placed it in the holder. Coach opened up his kitchen drawer and pulled out some potent indica buds and natural hemp papers. He rolled a nice spliff. Coach waited until the pot was good and hot and then poured some Talkin' Blues in his favorite Baltimore Ravens coffee cup. Coach took a sip of the coffee and lit his spliff. They were both delicious.

As a young kid, Coach remembered hearing soul singer Ray Charles in an interview stating that the best way to start the day off right was with a joint and a good cup of coffee. When Coach became an adult he tested that theory. Ray Charles was right on the money. The Blind Sensation was definitely gifted with a vision.

Coach took another sip of coffee and savored the flavor. It tasted so good, it made him close his eyes and say, "Yes!" Coach sat his Ravens cup down and turned off the lamp. He lit three candles that were placed in opposite corners of the room. Coach had a few light exercise routines he like to do depending on what his body was calling for and that particular day it called for yoga. After a 45-minute session and 15-minute meditation cool down, Coach prepared for his Water Ritual. It was just a basic shower and shave, but when Coach described it as a "custom" or a "water ritual" it made it feel more dynamic, like he was about to purify himself in the waters of Lake Minnetonka.

When Coach stepped out of the shower, he looked in the mirror at the handsome 5'11, 190-pound man staring back at him. He checked himself over. It was never out of vanity. It was just to make sure everything was copasetic. Coach had a nice healthy body but he wasn't muscular enough to be voted for the Ebony Man of the Year Award. He didn't have any flab around his abdomen; he had a nice two-pack. Coach got tired of trying to lose the last 5 pounds that's the hardest to get rid of so he just kept it and learned to live with it. His sturdy frame and nicely built shoulders still made him look extremely good in clothes. Coach was blessed with a natural sex appeal and a charming personality. He had smooth beautiful bronze skin like he could have been from the Islands. He also had a slight accent that came out from time to time to accompany the Island theory. His light brown eyes had a natural sparkle to them every time he smiled. His full lips and perfect set of teeth, and fresh breath made women want to tongue kiss him on the spot. Coach had one deep dimple on the right side of his cheek and he played it to its full advantage when he laid that smile on the ladies.

Coach oiled his hair clippers and manicured his goatee. He put a little jojoba oil in his hands and rubbed it in his hair. Coach sported a low curly Afro top with a tapered fade. Coach checked himself in the mirror one last time to make sure he had that confident look in his eyes before he exited the bathroom.

It felt like it was going to be an irie day so Coach went to his reggae folder on the computer and double clicked the song *"Forever Loving JAH."* Coach lit his spliff and stared out the open window. The sun was rising and Coach was determined to be a reflection of that powerful light. The air was fresh. He took in a deep breath. Coach gave thanks to the MOST HIGH again for another glorious day. The vibes were right. Coach started skank-ing to the reggae music. It was feeling real good to him. He was lifting that one knee real high like the reggae singers do when they walk across the stage. Coach sang the hook as he skanked over to the coffee pot. He filled his Ravens mug. Coach grabbed the newspapers he wanted to read off of the bar top.

Just as Coach was about to take a seat, his cell phone rang. If the reggae music didn't have him feeling so good, he would have copped an instant attitude. He woke up early for a reason. That was the time he used to get his mind ready for a long day without interruption from the outside world.

But it was his cutie pie LaTonya. That was his sunshine. She could do no wrong in his eyes if you let him tell it. She knew how to set Coach's day off in a variety of ways and they were all good. Coach answered the phone but he didn't say hello. He moaned and blew a sexy kiss. LaTonya knew how to speak that language too and blew a sweet kiss in return.

"Hey Strong Lion, I hope I didn't fuck with your morning vibe but I don't have to be to work until ten this morning and I miss you. I was wondering if I could come by after you drop your son off at school and get some of that sweet-sweet back. I've been thinking about it all week. You always tell me I need to get my day started right and that sweet dick is what I need in order to make that happen. I feel the need to relieve a little stress this morning. Can you feel me?"

Coach couldn't deny the morning hard-on he had even if he wanted to. The sound of her voice alone had Coach touching himself and he didn't even know it but Coach played coy to her request. "I don't know, LaTonya. The last time you came over I found insect antennas in the bathroom. I think you brought some roaches with you in your overnight bag."

"Boy, you're so silly. I didn't have any damn roaches in my bag. You make me sick!" LaTonya replied after she stopped laughing. "I can always count on you for a good laugh when I need it the most, baby."

"Why are you so stressed out? Are they putting pressure on you at work again?"

"No, work has been cool compared to what I'm dealing with over here. Well, you know my sanctified grandmother has been staying with me until they finish painting her house, right? Bless her sweet soul, but she is driving me absolutely crazy. She has my room smelling like turpentine oil. She burned up all my cute panties. She said I have the same naughty panties that Eve had on the night Adam got in trouble."

"What did she leave you with to wear? Your period panties?"

"No! She gave me a pair of hers to wear. The booty part was all loose in the back, and the elastic stretched out around the legs, and they smelled like a pill bottle... But lately she has really been trippin'. She tossed out all my scented candles. She threw the chicken out of the freezer, and then just the other day—right after I got my hair done and it was looking cute, too—I walked in the house and Granny jumped out from behind the door and threw some damn communion water in my hair!! She had some of her old bingo buddies with her too, and they started shouting over me...for some reason, they think I've been practicing witchcraft!"

"Oh snap! She went there with it...hahahaha! I'm sorry, baby."

"Oh my God! What did you do, Coach?"

"I stopped by your house the other day after I got my tattoo. Granny saw my arm bandaged up and asked me what happened. I told her that you had been practicing voodoo and you scratched me on my arm with a chicken's foot and put a spell on me so I wouldn't leave you."

"What!? You make me so sick! I had a feeling you had something to do with this but I wasn't quite sure. Now I know! You got these old ladies over here poking me with canes, burning my drawers, and throwing holy water on me every time I come in my house... now you know you better relax me with some good lovin' this morning. You owe me for that one."

"Can't I just pay you in cash?"

"You love to tease me don't you?" LaTonya asked in her sexiest voice.

"Oh yes, I do!"

And you know what happens when you tease me right?" LaTonya asked but not needing to hear the answer.

"Ye, indeed!" Coach stated assuredly.

"I put it on ya!" LaTonya exclaimed.

"Yes, you do and that is why I do it!" Coach's smile could be felt across the phone line.

"I want it and I'm coming to get it."

"Handle your business, mama, and don't let me slow you down!"

"Owww! Let's make it do what it do! I'm not about to let that loving go to waste. Imma be over at 8." LaTonya concluded as she put her stamp on it.

"See you then, Sugar… hey, and don't forget to shake your clothes out first! Don't bring those roaches back in here."

Coach put the phone down still smiling. He got lost in his romantic thoughts as he pictured how good it was going to feel to have LaTonya's warm soft body in his strong arms, while he kissed her slow in that spot that made her melt. He wanted to squeeze her even tighter and then tell her "I love you."

At the 7 o'clock hour, Coach entered his son's room to wake him up for school. Coach looked down at his son resting and smiled. There was no greater feeling in the world than the love a real father has for his son.

"Rise and shine, Jah-Jah! It's time to get up! You shouldn't be sleeping anyway. Black men don't sleep; we rest. That's how you get caught slippin': too much sleepin'!"

Jah stretched as he woke up and wiped the sleep from his eyes. "I'm only eight, Dad. Can I enjoy my childhood a little before we start the revolution?"

"Eight! Man, when I was eight I was married and working two full-time jobs plus I had a part-time on the weekends," Coach boasted as he and Jah laughed. Jah wished he could stayed under those warm blankets for five more minutes but he knew his Father was going to stand over him with 101 reasons why extra sleep would destroy his life on earth until he got out of that bed. Coach gave his son a strong hug and then tensed up. Coach pretended that he stopped breathing and collapsed to the floor.

Jah laughed and said, "What are you doing all that for Dad?"

Coach coughed and gagged like he was wounded and said, "I-I was avoiding that morning breath, but you got me, son!"

While Jah killing off that morning stank, Coach made Jah a nice bowl of assorted fruit for his breakfast and a healthy yet hearty meal for his lunch. Coach loved fatherhood. He treated it like the gospel. Coach was serious about breaking the chains of the absentee father that plagued his family tree over the last century.

Coach finished with his morning meal ritual and sat down at the table with his newspapers. He usually read *The LA Watts Times*, *Liberation Now*, and the *Final Call*. Tabloids got no play in Coach's pad. He liked to read about strong black characters doing interesting things. The other publications only wrote about sensitive Negro-Americans involved in homosexual scandals and studio gangsters with ecstasy and lean possession cases. Coach sipped his coffee while he read an interesting article on the front page. Coach sighed "Oy vey! Bumbaclot!" because the article he was reading didn't all fit on the page. Coach sucked his teeth as he spread the newspaper open and searched for the page where the second part of the story he was reading continued. As Coach was shuffling thru the paper from page 1 to page 19, a headline to another story caught his attention in the Metro section titled "Home Invasion Suicide?"

An apparent home invasion has the Torrance Police and local investigators baffled. Three bodies were found at the 4200 block of El Prado Avenue. Two armed assailants entered the home of financial advisor Richard DePaul and were killed in self defense; one by a gunshot wound to the center of the forehead and the other was stomped to death by the owner of the house. The assailant's DNA matched the bloodstains on the bottom of DePaul's feet. The police and forensic experts are still trying to determine the motive behind DePaul taking his own life. Richard DePaul had no criminal record and no known ties to criminal activities. He is survived...

CHAPTER 3

COACH AND JAH lived on the third floor of a decent apartment building. It was an older complex but the units were spacious. Looking at it from that perspective they were definitely getting more bang for their buck. Coach locked up the house and they took the stairs down. Coach and Jah had lived there for seven years and for no reason in particular they never used the elevator.

"Hi Coach, hey lil Coach," Cassandra from the second floor said as they passed each other on the stairway.

"Good Morning, Coach. Hi Jah, you ready for school? You sure are growing. Your little man is going to be bigger than you in a minute, Coach," said the lady that wore bad wig and always smelled stale. She lived somewhere in the building but Coach didn't know her name or where she resided. Regardless, he spoke to her every time they made eye contact.

"What up, Coach? I see your Ravens won last night. That defense is incredible," said Young Dee that stayed on the first floor.

Coach and Jah thought they were going to make it out of the building before they ran into Lorraine but as soon as they hit the pavement there she was. "Hey Coach, how you doing? Hey Jah! Look at you. Jah, you're getting more handsome like your Daddy every day. I'm just going to wait for you to turn 18 since somebody over here," rolling her eyes at Coach, "won't even give me the time of day. He's acting like I'm not even here Jah, like something is wrong with me—ain't nothin' wrong with me. Do you see anything wrong with me, Jah?" Jah shook his head. "And don't believe what your Daddy be telling you about me either. I'm a good woman. I might not be all natural like the women *he* likes and yes, I eat pork but not all the time and yes this is a weave but I bought it so it's mine and—"

Coach and Jah walked away shaking their heads and laughing at Lorraine's crazy ass. She would have kept talking all day if they had let her. The best way to describe Lorraine is to say she is the one that is different from everybody else in her conservative family. That woman was something else.

"Well, son, at least you know who your Prom date is going to be in a few years." Coach laughed.

Jah sighed, "It's not happening Dad. Lorraine is a hot mess. She has too many problems for me. I'm young. I don't need all that in my life. My honeys have little girl problems like they can't stay up past 8:30 on school nights." Jah expressed with a grown man look on his face.

Coach and Jah reached their automobile. Coach put the key in the car door and some more voices rang out.

"Hey Coach!"

"What up Coach!"

Coach turned around and saw three men coming out of the building across the street. The first two men, Willy and Rock, the neighborhood handy men dressed in oil-stained coveralls and work boots waved and exchanged greetings with Coach and Jah. The third man was the only neighbor that never spoke to Coach or anyone else in the four years he lived on the block. They both made eye contact with each other but once again nothing was said. Coach just opened his car door and continued about his day. Bodeen stared back at Coach for a second longer. He rubbed his chin and then he walked away.

CHAPTER 4

COACH LOVED DRIVING his son to school every morning. Jah's school was only 12 minutes away walking distance but Coach never entertained that thought. It wasn't about being overprotective or shielding Jah from the streets; it was just part of the daily routine that Coach enjoyed immensely.

Jah turned the radio station to Big Boy's Neighborhood so they could hear Abazar Luffeigh pull the "Phone Tap" crank of the day. It was a warm morning so Coach dropped the top on his classic '64 Thunderbird. His ride was clean. Coach cruised about 15 miles per hour until they arrived at the Dr. Naim Akbar Elementary School. Coach parked in the residential area up the block and strolled with Jah inside the school gates.

"Stay focused, Young Lion; I'll pick you up later. Love you, Mon!'"

"Love you, too, Dad! Bless Up!"

Coach and Jah gave each other a hug and said Peace. Jah exited to his right and headed toward his classroom and Coach went left to make his school rounds. Being the *cool dad* at an elementary school is like being stranded on a deserted island with beautiful single mothers and hot teachers little boys fantasize about. Coach liked to bask in the adulation on occasion. Coach tried to stay under the radar but in this nosey society somebody is always watching.

"Hi Jah's Dad!" The little bad schoolgirls sang in a high pitch when they greeted Coach. He liked when the called him "Jah's Dad"; it was cool. Coach didn't look like a *Mister* and his spirit was too free for *Sir*. One of the girls that was much wiser than she should have been at seven years old started giggling and said, "Whoop! I know where you be going, Jah's Dad. You be sneaking in Ms. Rawls' classroom. Your son's classroom is that way!" She pointed in the opposite direction and rolled her eyes when she did it.

The rest of the girls started in, "Whoop—Jah's Dad and Ms. Rawls sitting in a tree k-i-s-s-i-n-g- hee hee hee."

Coach couldn't do nothing but laugh. He was cold busted by some third graders.

"Shouldn't you girls be somewhere playing hopscotch or doing the Double-Dutch or something? You're all up in grown folks business when you should be finger painting and coloring pictures with crayons in a coloring book."

Another one of the school girls made the beat box sound with her lips and rolled her eyes, "Excuse me but I don't play with crayons and finger paint. This is not kindergarten, this is second grade! I know my times tables to 12, thank you." Then she gave her friend a high five and brushed Coach off like he wasted their time.

As Coach made his rounds speaking with administrators, talking with parents, and checking on his players, he became five different people within 20 yards. He was "Mr. Coach" the educator and community activist when he spoke with the principal. He was "Heeyyy Coach" the Playboy to the single mothers. "What up Coach" to his football players, and "Hey Handsome" to the sexy teacher that wanted to keep him after class for private tutoring sessions.

Ms. Rawls was tall, slender, and sexy. She was a track star at USC before she hurt her knee due to an incompetent trainer. She was an inch or two taller than Coach and her slender figure and long legs made Coach want to climb her. He entered her classroom and closed the door. Coach and Ms. Rawls embraced. They gave each other one of those good long hugs. They wanted to kiss each other badly but they never did. They were always attracted to each other but they never hooked up. The timing was never right when it came to availability on their part. Coach was monogamous in his relationships but he still enjoyed being in the company of women. He never crossed the line but he teetered over it a lot.

Coach and Ms. Rawls were a good team and played an active part in community activities. They also helped each other out when it came to a few of the student-athletes they worked with. Coach and Ms. Rawls used the barter system. Ms. Rawls would give Coach's football players private track lessons and teach them proper running techniques and in return Coach offered her track students private tutoring at his work facility.

"How are you doing this morning, Ms. Rawls?"

"I'm feeling good Coach; thanks for asking. You crack me up when you call me Ms. Rawls. How come you never call me by my first name?"

"Well, how come you never call me by my first name?" Coach asked just to be asking.

"I do... I call you... Coach- oh. You know I never thought about it... everybody just calls you Coach. What is your first name?"

"See; now look at you... uh-huh. But that's not what I want to talk about. You already know why I coming to see you this morning because that's why you're laughing. We made a deal Ms. Rawls that I will offer *your student-athletes* private sessions; everybody else has to go at the times tutoring is offered."

"What kid are you referring to?"

"Don't con me, Ms. Rawls. You know I'm talking about that little goofy boy named Quincy. He does not run track. That's your friend's son and he needed to someplace to go after school where he could be supervised until his mother got off work. You aren't slick. The only running he's doing is into walls."

"He doesn't run track, but he's still an athlete," Ms. Rawls protested.

"Yeah, he's an athlete all right. He's damn near fifteen years old and I asked him what sport he played and he says, 'Power Rangers!'"

Before she could protest further, the bell rang and the kids started lining up to enter the classroom. Coach made his exit back to the T-Bird.

* * *

It was a beautiful day to live in Los Angeles. The weather was just right. Coach was feeling good. Keeping within the rules of the day, Coach popped in some reggae music. He was in the mood to hear the Cool Ruler Gregory Isaacs. For the remainder of Coach's life on Earth, he will never be able to listen to Gregory Isaacs without thinking about his relationship with Jah's mother. Coach cruised home enjoying the positive vibrations and thinking about the good times.

* * *

Coach raised Jah by himself pretty much since birth. Jah's beautiful mother Khalilah passed away when he was seven months old, after a short bout with LAM, a rare progressive cystic lung disease that occurs exclusively in women. Coach and Khalilah were very good friends with a slight attraction toward each other. Khalilah knew Coach was going to be a good father because of the way he always treated the kids in the neighborhood when they were growing up together. Even though Coach was young himself he still had the uncanny ability to pass valuable knowledge to the other kids the way they needed to hear it without preaching.

Coach and Khalilah shared a lot of personal conversations about their childhoods over the years and parenting was always the subject they were most passionate about.

Coach and Khalilah were content with being best friends but then one of those good days came around and there was an Outdoor Lovers Rock Reggae Festival Under the Stars. Dennis Brown and the Cool Ruler Gregory Isaacs were performing and they're in rare form. Everybody was feeling irie, sipping on pine and ginger juice, and feeling sexy, and the next thing you know, they were blessed with Jah nine months later.

They were going to get married but before they had a chance to start thinking about building a life together Khalilah started experiencing short-ness of breath and chest pains. She went to the doctor and had a lung biopsy. The results were nothing nice. Khalilah died seven months later, just before her 21st birthday.

* * *

Coach cruised down his block. He had to park on the opposite side of street. It was street cleaning day on his side of the block. Coach pulled up behind a white Navigator. Bodeen was sitting in his ride with the engine running. Coach and Bodeen briefly made eye contact through his side view mirror. Bodeen pulled away from the curb and drove off. Coach pulled his car up in the vacated spot so LaTonya, who drove up right on time, could have a place to park behind him.

CHAPTER 5

BODEEN WAS DRIVING and thinking about the conversation he over-heard while he was walking to his truck earlier that morning. The handy-men Willy and Rock were discussing an article they just read in newspaper about a murder-suicide. Bodeen thought to himself, "Three bodies? Um, punk ass Gerald must have survived that critical beat down." Bodeen pulled up to a stop sign and retrieved his phone from the glove box. He turned it on. His unread messages were at the max.

The first text message was from Mario and it read, "Abort the mission. I was reacting on emotion. You can keep the payment for your time. Hit me back when you get this message."

The next message read the same and so did the next ten.

But none of that mattered because Bodeen couldn't read anyway.

Bodeen thought about Angie and wished he could be with her again. Bodeen was ready to celebrate. After 36 years, he lost of his virginity. This was the first time Bodeen had been in a good mood in a long-long time and he sure hated to ruin it by killing Mario. But if he didn't kill Mario before he found out about Ricky, Bodeen was going to be the headline in tomorrow's Metro section of the newspaper without question.

Crime Scene: Ricky's Home 4:09AM

"I'll be right back!" Detective Grayson stated as he abruptly excused him-self from the crime scene.

"You're the second lead investigator on this one so you can't leave.

Where do you think you are going?" The elder officer with the lower rank sarcastically stated.

"To investigate; so do your job until I get back!"

Detective Keller Grayson was a very good cop. He was the last of a dying breed and he knew it. The stripes he earned meant nothing because he wore a heart on his sleeve. As a rookie, young Officer Grayson arrested a college-bound "A" student with big dreams. The student bummed a ride from a neighborhood friend so he could see his grandmother and say good-bye before he left for school. The problem was the neighborhood friend was driving a car that didn't belong to him. The politicians and powers to be were cracking down on carjacking that year so Officer Grayson was forced to stick a grand theft auto charge on the kid. He messed the kid's life up something awful. From that moment on, Detective Grayson vowed to never put another person in jail for anything less than a heinous killing.

Consumed with a life of high profile cases, Detective Grayson found himself confined to a personal prison. He was working a job with no sense of gratification stemming from it. The politics that came with his profession was making him sick. He felt he deserved more than that. Detective Grayson spent the other part of his life trying to fulfill his true passion of becoming an investor and business owner but money just didn't seem to like him. His other cop friends blew their money gambling, on fast women, cocaine, and expensive lavish toys, but they still had something to show for it even if it was just a good time.

Every legit investment Detective Grayson ever made failed. Detective Grayson made wise calculated decisions and solid investments but for some unforeseeable circumstances they always seemed to go wrong. The bottom line was he just had terrible luck with money.

But all that was about to change. Grayson glanced down at the investment portfolios resting in the passenger seat. He patted them like they were the top of a good kid's head. He smiled and pressed the gas pedal a little harder as he drove down the street looking for the nearest 24-hour copy shop.

* * *

When he arrived at the DePaul house, the bloody murder scene wasn't the least bit shocking to him. It was just another reminder of how badly he wanted out of the profession. Detective Grayson immediately saw some familiarities he wanted no part of. To no one in particular Detective Grayson said, "This is not the way to start a morning." As he stepped over Ricky DePaul's corpse, a feeling of nausea overwhelmed him like never before. The sight of the bloody body had nothing to do with it. It was the commanding officers that already chalked up the investigation as some weird home invasion suicide just to keep the stats in the black.

Detective Grayson had great innate ability to perform real police work. In this particular case, his intuition told him immediately this crime scene was not what his superior was writing it off as. Detective Grayson didn't pay the other dead bodies on the floor any mind. It was what was laying on the floor near a broken table that made Keller Grayson jump like he had a wild hair up his butt. The investment portfolios scattered on the floor looked just like the ones he kept. When he opened them they were nothing like his on the inside.

The Keller Grayson portfolio was filled with negative numbers representing his assets written in red ink. The portfolios Detective Grayson was looking at in amazement were making money as he held them in his hands. Ricky DePaul was a brilliant disciplined investor and mathematician. He was now also Detective Grayson's hero. Those portfolios were the blueprints to his new lease on life. Detective Grayson didn't log the portfolios as evidence. He tucked them under his armpit and made up the first excuse that came to his mind to exit the house. Detective Grayson made it to his car and it felt like the weight of the world was off his back. Keller Grayson took a deep breath and let out a sound similar to a cheer. He had never felt happiness and excitement like that in his life. Keller Grayson was good police so he had no intention of stealing any assets from a dead man or the original portfolios. He just wanted the knowledge of how and what to invest in properly. Ricky DePaul became Keller Grayson's savior. He was able to see everything that he was doing wrong in clear understandable terms.

Detective Grayson felt like he owed Ricky DePaul something for leaving him with those blessings. Detective Grayson looked at the other names on the portfolios. Even with the subtle glance he gave the two intruders at

the crime scene, Detective Grayson knew neither one of those musty bastards looked like an Angie and their last names damn sure weren't DePaul.

After Detective Grayson left King O's Copy House, he walked over to
the phone booth and made an anonymous call to Mario DePaul. Grayson
told Mario that there had been a tragic accident at his cousin Ricky's. He
also told him the name of the person that was responsible for it.

CHAPTER 6

MARIO SLAMMED THE phone down. He was irate and overwhelmed with hate, revenge, and tears. Never once did he blame himself for the terrible accident. It never even crossed his mind. Mario shifted all the blame on Bodeen. Mario paced the floor fussing and cussing, "That evil-black ink spot-voodoo monkey lookin' muthafucka!"

Mario stormed to his bedroom closet and started pulling out enough guns and ammo to kill 40 Bodeens. Adrenaline had Mario changing guns in and out of his waistband like he was getting dressed for his first date. Mario finally settled on two 45s, two 9mms, and a custom knife that would kill a man faster than the guns probably would.

Mario started to button his tear-stained shirt in order to conceal the weapons in his waistband but it was soaked with sweat. There was snot on both sleeves from wiping his runny nose. Mario ripped the wet shirt off and threw it on the floor. He snatched a fresh white dress shirt off the hanger in the closet.

"I'm going to kill that black mole-lookin' muthafucka! He hurt my family! Not my cousin Ricky! You fucked up, you baboon!" Mario muttered as he paced the room, checking himself in the mirror. Mario knew he had an advantage because he was scared, and a scared man will shoot without hesitation when his back is against the wall.

Mario poured a shot of whiskey, downed it, and grabbed the car keys off of the mantel. Mario checked the 45s secured in the back of his waistband and he patted the 9mms resting at his sides. He put his faithful knife in the zebra skin case and placed it under his armpit. Mario looked out of the window before he opened his front door. He always did that out of habit to make sure there weren't any Feds disguised in the area watching him. Mario wasn't worried about Bodeen coming to his home. The way the security cameras were structured it was damn near impossible for a household bug to get in the house before being exterminated. A big black muthafucka like Bodeen wouldn't stand a chance.

Mario continued to check his surroundings for any strange cars or landscapers working on their off day. Everything was cool. Mario stormed out of the front door with murder on his mind. He slammed the door closed behind him with so much force it shook the whole house. Mario gripped his knife like a vice with the thoughts of cutting the heart out of that sucka...

I can't tell you what Mario thought after that. A dead man tells no tales. The shotgun blast blew most of the back of Mario's head off as he crashed face first on the concrete. Mario never even made it off the front porch.

CHAPTER 7

COACH AND LATONYA strolled downstairs holding hands and smiling. They were looking like they shared the type of love you only read about in novels. In reality, they were just a cute couple that had very good chemistry.

Coach needed to change vehicles. He asked LaTonya if she would back his Dodge Challenger out of the stall. Coach moved his Thunderbird off the street and parked it in his spot. Coach draped the car cover over his T-Bird. Coach hopped in the passenger side of his other ride. He kissed LaTonya tenderly.

"What was that for?"

"Cause I love you."

LaTonya was still feeling frisky. They never got to finish what they started. Time flies when you're having fun.

"Am I going to see you later?" LaTonya asked.

"Of course! I want you to stay with me tonight."

"Ohh, I can't wait. But you know me and Jah have plans first tonight." LaTonya explained.

"Is that right? What kind of plans do you guys have without me?" Coach asked.

"Don't worry about it. That is our time. Jah is so sweet. I love that boy." LaTonya answered like she took an oath of secrecy.

"You better not have my son on stage somewhere wearing a cloak and emceeing your Granny's Bingo Night."

"Where do you come up with these crazy scenarios, baby?"

"Me? Who does your granny love the most?" Coach asked with his eyebrows raised.

"White Jesus," LaTonya stated without hesitation.

"Let me flip that… Well, who is she *in* love with?" Coach asked again.

"Reverend Ike," she answered with a laugh.

Coach threw his hands out to the side as if to say, "*I rest my case.*"

"Let me get to work, baby, I'll see you tonight. You love me?"

"You don't even have to ask… Of course I do… Oh, and Coach you might want to put a little lotion on those elbows. They look like you just chalked up two pool sticks," LaTonya said as she got in her car and drove off laughing.

Coach ignited the Dodge Challenger and hit the boulevard. Coach finally upgraded from the Toyota Camry he had since college and bought a new whip. The '64 Thunderbird was for play and not to be driven as an everyday car. Coach didn't have to be to work until 11am so the morning traffic had eased off. Coach was normally a smooth, laid back cat but today he felt the need for speed. What was the purpose of having a muscle car if he couldn't flex?

But Coach forgot he lived in L.A. He didn't make it half way up the block before a Mexican jumped out of nowhere and almost hit his brand new ride. The Mexican made a left turn from the far "right turn only" lane that was two lanes over. Coach slammed on his brakes and by the grace of God he just avoided a collision by a fraction of an inch. The Mexican heard the tires screech. He knew he fucked up and he shouldn't be driving in the first place. His license was suspended in Tijuana so he definitely didn't need to be rolling in L.A. He could barely see over the steering wheel. The little Mexican raised one hand up and in his Spanglish accent he said, "Ei-yi-yi! Lo siento! Sorry, amigo!" Coach was mad as hell but couldn't do anything but shake his head and laugh.

"My brown brother! Please explain the concept of your driving, DAMN!" Coach yelled out jokingly.

It was all green lights for at least two miles. He hit the gas pedal hard. Coach actually reached the speed of 45mph before a Korean lady just stopped in the middle of street. No light, no stop sign, no pedestrians jay walking, no reason to stop other than to give a peaceful man road rage.

Coach had to slam on the brakes and swerve around her. Coach put on some music and just decided to cruise easy the rest of the way.

* * *

Coach was Director of Operations at the Jack Tatum Memorial Stadium Park and Recreation Center, better known as Tatum Park. Coach didn't make it into the parking lot good before the smell of grape blunts and Hennessey hit him in the nose. Coach already knew who it was before he laid eyes on them. Back in the days you had to worry about gang-bangers and winos loitering at the park. Nowadays it's those young lesbians that like to dabble into that thug life.

A couple of days a week Coach allowed Jada, a WNBA hopeful, to work on her game in the gym during the morning hours. Jada always brought a couple of other girls with her that played ball as well. That was cool with Coach but then every blue moon Jada would show up with a bunch of butch broads and young femme turnouts that had nothing to do with the sport of basketball. Coach scanned the scene as he parked his ride. Coach had them bobbing their head to the new Too Short and E-40 song he knew they weren't hip to yet. Coach knew most of the lesbians well but there were a few he wasn't too familiar with. Coach winked at Jada and her crew. They all had braids and wore big basketball shorts and socks with flip-flops. Coach threw the peace sign up to the masculine looking dykes along with his flirtatious smile. It kind of brought the sweet daddy's little girl out from beneath their hard thug exterior. They loved Coach to death because real lesbians aren't man haters. Coach was all man and they felt his righteous magnetic energy.

Coach parked his car. He turned off the engine but kept the music bumping. Coach could see the wide stocky figure of Gangster "G" approaching his car through his side view mirror. She was walking with a slow bop.

OG Geraldine was an old school dyke from back in the days before the term *butch* was even popular. When she came on the scene, lesbians with a tough exterior were called a *Jeff Davis*. Gerry looked hard. Her everyday face was like a mug shot. Her hair was styled in six short murder braids straight back with black beads on the ends. She had a fitted Raiders cap cocked to the side on top of her head. She sported a black sweatshirt, some creased khakis, and some hard-sole men's dress shoes. Coach turned down the music in his ride. "Damn Gerry! Those church shoes clacking against the concrete is drowning out the bass."

"It's a thin line between pimpin' and preachin', homie so don't let my Florsheims fool ya," Gerry responded as she took a long drag off a Camel. "I got a good deal on some smoke straight off the boat."

"You got some what off of a what? Girl, you are straight out of a Donald Goines novel. Do you know what year this is? We are well into the 2000s. You haven't been locked up in jail so my question is where in the hell have you been? We are in California, Geraldine. The Medicinal Era! The Green Cross! You need to click the heels of them church shoes together three times and return yourself to the present day."

"Aw fool, cut that shit out; you crazy as a muthafucka," Gerry said as she took another long drag from her Camel. She closed her eyes and drifted like the Camel was actually taking her for a ride.

"What you doing, Geraldine?" Coach asked curiously

"Smokin' wit' cigawetts," Geraldine laughed as she mimicked the YouTube sensation Latarian Milton.

Coach shook his head. "So how's your son doing?"

"He still up north. He was supposed to get out in three months but he got into it with some niggas up there and they might add an extra 30 days." She sighed. "And hey man, I do appreciate the shit you tried to do for him, but he a hard headed boy."

"That's the hard part about my job, Gerry. I want to save them all." Coach said sincerely.

"But you can't."

"See Gerry? That statement right there is what keeps me motivated cuz I can't stand when somebody that knows how dedicated I am tells me what I can't do. Speak to my strength and motivate me! Tell me you know I can do it. I need encouragement, too, so I can help others."

"You know I've known you all your life and you're still an interesting muthafucka to me, Coach... wait a minute-hold up..."

Gerry's beeper went off- in the modern era. Coach was so confused he actually thought he was dreaming for a second. Gerry looked at the number and said, "See that's money right there. My customers don't like all that new shit with the funny names like Papaya Kush, Bionic Chronic, and Instant Death. It's still a market out there for plain old weed. I don't give a fuck what you talking about Coach, I keeps it OG, youngsta." Gerry popped her collar. She kind of looked liked E-40 when she did so it made it kind of funny. Coach said,

"Oh, so you're just going to pop your shirt on me like that, huh?"

"Aww, fool, cut that out. You know my game is strong. I'm about that life. I get mines jackin' or mackin'… look over there," Gerry nodded her head in the area of the young femme turnouts. Those bitches were looking like they had a mind full of problems. "You see I knocked that sweet young yellow thing from that blood nigga named Mingo from Inglewood."

"Are you talking about the one with the cheap miniskirt exposing her ashy, bullet-riddled legs? And damn what's up with that chipped toe nail polish? That broad looks like she's been kicking trees," Coach clowned

"Naw fool, that bitch you talking about is a straight up hot mess. She's a whole 'nother story. I'm talking 'bout the bitch next to her." Gerry pointed out.

"Mmm. You need to keep your ears to the street, Geraldine, and be careful," Coach said out of love.

"Yeah. I know about Mingo's rep, but that fool just got a 16-year bid so I ain't gots to worry about him gunnin' for me any time soon. So what you think about my new turn-out?"

"I think you need to turn that yella broad back in. You know why Mingo got that 16-year bid, right?" Coach asked.

"I heard it was a dope case or some shit like that."

"Hell no, G! Aggravated assault with intent to do bodily harm. Your girl gave Mingo HIV and he tried to kill her muthafuckin' ass!"

"What? Don't you play me." Gerry was hurt, confused and pissed all at the same time.

"C'mon Gerry. You're the one that schooled me about these young fake dykes experiencing with your lifestyle and bringing messy shit to the game at the same time. That broad is trifling. Everybody knows what she's about. I know you getting older, but you can't get relaxed if you gon' to be in the game. Gerry, stay focused."

"Good lookin' out, Coach. That's real talk. I can't be selling a tainted product. That bitch got to be reprimanded," Gerry stated as she gave Coach a pound.

"You raised me. I love you, girl. You threw me my first football. Ain't that some shit?" Coach said as he and Geraldine reminisced and laughed for a second. But after the information Coach just laid on Gerry, she wouldn't stay happy long. Coach's info brought the Gangster "G" back out of Geraldine. Gerry kissed Coach on the forehead and said "Peace!"

Geraldine walked over to where the chick was standing, cocked her arm back, and slapped the taste out of that girl's mouth. It sounded like a firecracker went off. Gangster "G" snatched her femme by the arm, threw her in the backseat of the Cutlass Supreme, and drove off.

Coach removed his gym bag and briefcase from the trunk of the car and looked over at the non-athletic chicks still loitering in the parking lot. They were sipping on Hennessy and cola at 10 in the morning with their pants sagging and Timberland boots on, looking like they were from the Wu Tang Clan. Coach didn't recognize any of them. They must have been WNBA groupies. As Coach was strolling across the parking lot, he noticed that one of High Yellow Stud's dykes who was sporting braids and a wave cap was looking him up and down like she didn't dig his style. Three other broads with the same attitude surrounded her. High Yellow Stud was one of those fake man-hating lesbians that were in the lifestyle because it was the newest trend. Coach knew she was fraudulent because she was trying too hard. She gave Coach a funky look like he had ruined her day by coming to work. Coach quickly made a mental note of that. Coach got into character.

"Jada!" Coach yelled in a stern voice with a hint of anger in it as he walked toward her. Coach stopped a few feet away from Yellow Stud and her crew. He gave Jada a look that meant he wanted her to meet him the rest of the way. She stepped towards him.

"Jada! Come here and let me speak to you in private!" Coach said loudly and with every intention of making it a public spectacle. He was standing an inch from Jada looking her directly in the eyes. "Listen here, Jada. You and I are tight and you know this. We have a cool arrangement: you and your girls got action in the gym any time... nothing but love between us…" Jada nodded and Coach continued. "But you better tell those bitches over there that this is not Camp Lesbian! This is a Park and Recreational Center. Either those bitches put on some big shorts and Chuck Taylors, and get to working on jump shots or they got to get the fuck outta here."

Coach made the non-athletic Studs and their lipstick lesbian girl-friends very uncomfortable. Coach never took his eyes off of Jada but he could hear feet walking, car doors opening, and engines starting up. Jada, her crew, and the real lesbians that Coach loved like his sisters all followed him to the gym. They were cracking up laughing at the way Coach made those fakers evacuate the parking lot.

"Coach you are a fool, for real, man!" Jada stated

"I was provoked… the bitch with the chipped toe nail looked at me like she wanted to kick me with it."

Coach let Jada and her b-ball crew into the gym and headed to his office to start his daily routine.

Coach had a typical park and recreation office. There was a desk, computer, and office phone. There were trophies, plaques, and awards that dated back 20 years on the dusty shelves. There were autographed pictures of sport celebrities that made guest appearances at the park on one occasion or another hanging on the walls. There was sports equipment and boxes full of cones, jump robes, and free weights on the floor in the corners of the office. It may have been a little cluttered but Coach still kept it in order with enough free space to keep his thoughts clear.

Coach loved his job. He made a pretty decent salary, too. He brought in around $62,000 a year plus annual increases. He had full medical and dental benefits, 10 paid sick days a year, and a two-week vacation. Coach also received a few under the table donations from the neighborhood street hustlers that appreciated the work he was doing with their kids. Due to the so-called budget cuts and being in the inner city, Tatum Park was short staffed. Coach and James the maintenance engineer were the only ones on the County payroll. Coach employed at least seven student/athletes part time out of his own salary, the donations he received from the hustlers, and by making minor adjustments to his yearly budget. Nobody but Coach and Jah knew that he was the one employing the students. They all thought they were working for the Park.

Coach paid them out of a business account he set up for the sports mentoring program he had yet to fully develop. Coach would create job titles and give the young employees the two years of experience and knowledge they needed to get in the door of corporate America. When Coach first started giving back to the community financially, it was out of anger and frustration. He was tired of seeing million dollar athletes and politicians coming to the park, taking photographs for the newspaper, and pretending like they were doing something special for the kids. They never came to the park when the cameras were gone. As Coach got to know some of the celebrities and politicians personally he realized that they weren't qualified to do anything but smile for the camera. It wasn't meant in a disrespectful way, but they just didn't know how to reach the youth. They didn't know how to have a regular conversation about everyday life. It was all scripted.

Coach opened up Excel on his computer. He checked if the order for the basketball trophies he asked one of the student employees to calculate, matched his figures. The young prodigy named Jelani was right and exact. Jelani was the first kid Coach met that took algebra, calculus, and all that other complicated linear shit and actually knew how to apply it to everyday life. Coach and Jelani would debate about morals and money constantly. Jelani felt that Coach should use the big corporate companies to produce the teams' uniforms and trophies because they were cheaper with a faster turnaround. Coach expressed that saving a few bucks couldn't compare to the up close and personal relationships and the sense of freedom and pride one develops doing business with the mom and pop stores.

But from a business point of view, Jelani was right so Coach had to find a way to challenge him. Coach asked Jelani to draw up some stats and probabilities to help the small businesses become a strong presence in the community. Coach also threw something in there about David and Goliath to touch his spirit. From that moment on, they'd been working together on the same page... until they found something else to have a friendly debate about.

Coach was so focused doing his monthly reports for the County, he didn't even notice that a couple of hours had passed by. He heard UPS pulling up out front. Coach was expecting some conditioning equipment and a novel he ordered called *I'm a Bachelor; It's Not by Choice… A Hip Hop Love Story*. Rolland the deliveryman came in with three big boxes and a small one.

"What's up Coach. How you feeling today?"

"I feel with my hands, like I always do, Rolland." Coach grinned.

"Um-hum. There you go. You're always starting something, Coach. By the way, my little cousin wants to play football next year and—"

Coach abruptly cut him off. "Stop. I don't want to hear nothing else. Last year, you had a brother that wasn't even your real brother that wanted to play, what happened to him? And year before that, your baby mama's other baby's daddy had a son that was a killer linebacker but he was soft as Charmin toilet paper. We asked the boy his name and he started crying…. So listen here, Brown," Coach's UPS jokes always irritated Rolland especially when he called him Brown. "Let me tell you what you can do for me. Stop coming in here in those tight brown nut huggers you call short pants telling me about make believe children. Honestly, your brown work shorts make me not even want to believe what you got to say. What are those anyway? Capris?"

"Aw Coach! I thought we went way back… you know, like that hairline you trying to hold on to," Rolland snapped back.

Rolland got ready to leave but Coach stopped him before he reached the door.

"What about the package I was supposed to sign for Rolland?" Coach asked.

Rolland looked at Coach like he was senile and then pointed to the boxes on the floor. "They're right there Coach."

Coach gave Rolland that *"Well, what the fuck you waiting for?"* look.

Rolland gave Coach that *"What the fuck you need? I'm in a hurry,"* look.

Coach waited another minute, "Well, aren't you going to make me sign for it?"

"Why? You are standing right here I know who you are."

"I want what I paid for. That package says Coach- all this other stuff says Tatum Park in c/o Coach. C'mon brother, get it together. Even though it looks like I own this park, I still work for the Man and I have to be accountable for every personal move I make while I'm on his dollar, ya dig? I can live with my own mistakes but I'm not trying to get caught up in somebody else's twist. I know you got to deal with that type of shit every day at UPS."

"Man, shit. You right. I got written up the other day because I didn't let this lady with two killer pit bulls running loose in the yard sign for her package. Those dogs were savage. They were eating and scratching through the fence trying to get me."

"It was that brown suit. They thought you were doo-doo." Coach clowned.

"Shit, they must have because they definitely wanted to bury me in the dirt. I threw that box over the fence as far as I could and ran back to the truck... I just didn't know the damn box was filled with wine glasses."

Coach laughed with crazy ass Rolland until it was time for them to get back to work. They gave each other a pound and said "One Love!"

Since Coach was up he decided to walk the premises and check on James the Maintenance Engineer. James automatically took his lunch at twelve o'clock just because the rest of the world was doing it. Coach didn't believe in taking breaks until the work was done. Coach would take his lunch break at the end of the shift and used that time to take care of personal business.

Coach walked out to the beautifully manicured baseball field with the soft red dirt in the infield and smiled. Coach and James had taken a rundown, drug-plagued, nasty park and turned it into a quality athletic facility. It wasn't state of the art, but they painted a beautiful masterpiece. James and Coach put so much hard work in, they didn't even have to tell the gangs, gamblers, and winos to leave. They did it out of respect. Some even helped out during the clean up process. The drug dealers funded the paint and the turf. There was no graffiti on the walls and they tried hard to keep the pissy smelling public bathrooms clean and fresh. Coach and James did in three years what the city couldn't do in thirty, and that was give the people something they were proud of and truly call it their own. The park catered to the needs of the infants to the elderly. Coach walked across the track as a few of senior citizens were finishing up their workouts. He waved to them and they politely waved back.

James' workstation was just beyond the football field. Coach quietly walked into his lab. James was seated with his eyes closed listening to some jazz music with his new Beats by Dre headphones on. Coach and Jah bought those for him last Christmas. Coach was always amazed by the way James' office looked. According to the job description, James was just a janitor/handyman that could clean the facility, do indoor/outdoor odd jobs, light repairs, lock up the building a few evenings a week, and have adequate strength/stamina to set up and/or take down a room with 65 chairs. Landscaping/maintenance skills are required.

But his office looked more like he was a rocket scientist. He had posters of atoms and electrons on the wall. There were volumetric pipets, beakers, desiccators, incubators, and all kinds of other scientific apparatus neatly placed around the room. Coach didn't call James "the Maintenance Engineer" because it was a fancy name for janitor; James truly earned that title.

James was a brilliant man that made one costly mistake more than 35 years ago that kept him restricted to the job. James was the getaway driver for a botched robbery and ended up getting four years and a strike on his first offense. He did two years and one month and hasn't even received a parking ticket since. James went back to college and graduated *summa cum laude* with a 3.89 grade point average. At the time James was pursuing the jobs he went to school for, his felony was still fresh, only four years old. James would get sick to the stomach every time a job required a background check. Coach knew about James' past and the bad breaks he was getting. Coach also knew that a man that could survive jail and came out better and more focused than he was before he went in was the type of person he needed on his team to get the job done right. Those types of people appreciate life more. They appreciate the smell of fresh air, smiles, and good energy because it was taken from them and they refuse to go back through the revolving door.

Coach gave James that shot he needed. He just didn't give him a job, Coach put James in position to get his own business going so he would never have to answer that question *have you ever been convicted of a felony* on an application ever again. Over the past five years, James has been doing very well financially. Coach always contracted the big jobs that needed to be done at all the parks in LA County out to James but on the contract it read different- so we are just going to leave it at that. James stayed loyal to Coach because he made him feel like he was his own boss.

James didn't hear Coach come into his office. Coach could hear the music pounding out of the headphones and patiently waited for a break in the record. Soon as there was a moment of silence Coach squeezed the air horn he was holding and James damn near jumped out of his skin.

James shrieked, "Awwww Lord! JESUS! Please!" He jumped up in the chair kicking his leg. Coach scared the shit out of poor James.

"Man you almost gave me a heart contusion. I can't even catch my breath right now. Please don't do any shit like that, Coach. Aw, man, my nerves are a mess."

"Well I hope your heart isn't that weak because after I give you this news you might pass out."

"What you mean?"

"Whitey down at the main office told me to write you up over those little trees you got planted in the back," Coach stated and handed James a green slip.

"What the hell is this, Coach?"

"Hey man, it is what it is. You know they're watching you. Matter of fact, I know you're real thick right now."

"Thick? What's that mean?"

"It means that YOU smell like weed and the smell is thick, and you need to do something about it, quick."

"What? Fool, you're the one that gave the weed to me!"

"What the fuck does that mean, James? I didn't give it to you to smoke it!"

"What?" James stated baffled and confused.

Coach could no longer keep a straight face and let James off the hook. James has a sense of relief on his face like he just moved his bowels for the first time in three days. James laughed it off but it wasn't funny to him at all. Coach was a good dude but he just liked to fuck with him.

"What is this? Fuck with James Day or something? Don't you need to be 'Directing the Operations' around here instead of pulling Youtube pranks? Where did you find those green slips anyway? I thought I threw them all away when I cleaned your office five years ago."

Coach had found those warning citations when he was looking through his office desk and knew they would be a good prank for the day. Coach didn't give warnings or fire employees. He let them fire themselves. Coach provided a lovely work atmosphere and if you were fool enough to mess up a good job like that then it was on you.

Coach and James talked for about thirty minutes on current affairs, pretty women, and sports. They parted ways and Coach headed over to the Gym to check on Jada and her B-ball friends.

When Coach got over to the gym Jada and most of her crew was exiting the locker area already showered and fully dressed. Coach smiled at them and asked how the practice was. They all gave him a hug in a respectful yet affectionate way. Coach had a way of weakening their tomboy exterior. For one, his cologne game was off the chain and two, he was just a cool ass brother that manifested sincere love straight from his soul.

"Um, Coach you always smell so good," said Yvette as she pressed her body up against Coach and gave him a good squeeze.

Jada peeped out her crew trying to act ladylike in front of Coach and didn't like what she was seeing. Coach played it cool but he could feel Yvette's sexy body up under those big man shorts and the two 3x white t-shirts she was wearing. If Jada didn't snatch Coach out of her arms, Yvette would have felt his manhood pressed up against her crotch in about two more seconds.

Jada wrapped her arm around Coach's bicep and quickly steered him towards his office. Once they got a few paces away from the vultures, Jada slowed their walk to a normal pace. Coach and Jada chatted about how she was doing over at Cal State Long Beach. Jada is 26 years old. She wasn't a bad girl but she lost her way during high school. She dropped out and started hanging out with all kinds of different cliques, experimenting, searching, and trying to find the hidden mysteries of life. Jada is a cutie pie with a lot of tomboy tendencies. When it comes to sex appeal and sexual preference, Jada has that look that says she could go either way. She kind of favors the female rapper Da Brat. Coach took her up under his wing when she was about 19 or 20. He gave her a job and put some game in her ear. Jada listened to the knowledge Coach gave her and the next thing you know she's was flying on her own all the way to the WNBA.

Coach and Jada continued to talk as they walked through the double doors that lead to the equipment room. As the doors shut closed behind them, Coach and Jada both jumped back and twisted their noses up at the same time. Coach looked at Jada and said, "Did you step in some shit?"

They both checked the floor and the bottoms of their shoes. Jada responded, "It's not me. It must be coming from the bathroom. Somebody blew that muthafucka up!"

"We're the only ones here. You know the kids don't use these restrooms until after three o'clock and they don't even smell like that after eating that nasty cafeteria food all day. I hope that homeless man didn't sneak up in there again."

Before Jada could get her next sentence out, one of the basketball-playing lesbians named Tina walked out of the ladies restroom with a look of embarrassment on her face. Coach was in shock, "Damn Tina! Is that you? I thought my uncle Frank was in that muthafucka. Your stomach lining is full of corruption and poisons, girl! Good grief!"

Jada turned up her nose and said, "Damn Tina you smell like Ike!"

Tina couldn't do nothing but try to play it off. "Damn, I just broke a little wind. Man, a girl can't even poot in peace."

"Pooted? Bitch, you shitted on yourself!" Jada responded.

"I don't fart; I whisper in my panties, thank you very much," Tina stated

"Ain't that a bitch? You talkin' that bullshit," Jada laughed.

Coach and Jada left Tina and kept walking around the corridor and back over to the office. Coach said, "Shittin' is normal but no young woman is supposed to smell like that! Y'all are trying to take this 'being like men' shit too far."

"You're so silly," Jada said and nudged Coach with her shoulder.

Coach and Jada were bobbing their heads to the new Joel Ortiz Mix tape playing from the song list on the computer. Coach was seated behind his desk and Jada moved the chair that usually sat across from him next to him. Jada and Coach were basically really good friends that flirted and teased each other from time to time. If they ever did turn it into a relationship, it would be the type of relationship that would be real cool for that moment, attached with a few good memories but it wouldn't last. They were both free spirits with the desire to explore different planets.

But today was one of those times when Coach's cologne and fly velour North Carolina warm-up suit was bringing the other side out of Jada.

"Coach, you had us rolling this morning... what you say again with your crazy self? *This ain't Camp Lesbian.* You are insane. When are you going to come to Club Peanuts with us again?

"Shiiiiit! It was cool but I was tired of seeing all those 40-year-old dykes fighting out in the parking lot... brawling like wrestlers. Some of those broads are mothers. That didn't make any sense to me at all."

"Yeah, those hoes are crazy up there but it was about to get crazy up in here," Jada said. "I was about to slap that bitch Yvette. She was straight trying to gangster *my* dick," with the emphasis on *my*.

Coach didn't know she had exclusive rights to his manhood like that and said, "Oh, is that right?"

Jada didn't stutter or stumble and said it again, "Yeah! That's my shit."

Coach's eyes popped out, startled once again by her claim. He felt it was best to just hear her out and keep his mouth closed since it was obvious he had no say so in the matter.

"Did you see the way she was trying to press all up on you? You don't want that stinky heifer." Now Jada was telling Coach what he didn't want. Then she continued with more, "See what happened was, me and all the girls was chilling' and talkin' like *you men* do about which man we would do and—"

Coach cut her off right there. "First of all, Miss Thang, you would never catch me or the men I know talking about which man they would *do*. That is absurd!"

"You know what I mean, Coach! Now stop fucking with me and let me finish. So anyway—now you got me all messed up, wait a minute, um. Oh yeah, basically they asked me what man me and my dude would sleep with—well not my dude; she's a girl, but I just call her my dude, you know what I mean?"

"No, I don't know what you mean," Coach said jokingly as he leaned back in his chair, amused with the turn of the conversation.

"Dammit Coach! You know what I mean. Now stop fucking with my mind."

"Is that what you call it?" Coach asked

"What?"

"What?" Coach shrugged his shoulders and responded back like he didn't have a clue either.

"Oh, you drive me crazy. Stop playin', Coach. What do you think about that?"

"Think about what?" Coach asked but really didn't want to know the answer.

"You know, getting busy with me and *my girl*," Jada made sure she didn't say *my dude* and ruin the mood again.

"Which girl are you talking about? I hope you ain't talking about that little short African broad that looks like Lil Wayne."

Jada punched Coach hard in the arm. "You know you are wrong for that. My boo does not look like no damn Lil Wayne. And you know she ain't no damn African. Last week you said she looked like Gary Coleman when was he was working as a security guard at the Hawthorne Mall...'"

Coach smirked.

"Oh you make me sick, Coach! Everybody else says she looks just like Beyoncé."

"Where? Inside her booty crack?" Coach asked and then braced himself for the hard punch he knew was coming. Jada punched Coach in the arm again. Undeterred, Coach continued, "You are my heart, Jada so I keep it real with you at all times. You see your woman more than I do. You know what she looks like. It's not *all good*. She is a peculiar looking little bitch... and what the fuck is up with the arched eyebrows she penciled in? She looks like a little voodoo doll. She got that old man civil rights haircut with those dry ass baby hairs that keep coming unraveled at the temples. Jada, I can't believe you want me to go to bed with a broad that wears a short-sleeved shirt and a tie. Beyoncé? My ass! If you strapped a rifle around your girl's chest, and put her in some sweatpants and tattered dress shoes, that broad would look just like one of those niggas fighting over there in Rwanda," Coach laughed, as he started jogging in place acting like he was holding a rifle and yelling in an African dialect.

"Awww, you make me sick!" Jada said as she playfully attacked Coach. Jada hit Coach on the arm a few more times until he grabbed her wrist. Jada stopped fighting. Coach released her wrist. Jada put her arms around Coach's shoulders. They looked each other in the eyes for a long moment.

But the sound of tennis shoes screeching down the hallway put a stop to that little situation before it even got started. Jada sat down in her seat before the female ballers walked in. Yvette was trying to see if anything was going on between Coach and Jada. Coach gave all the girls hugs as they said their goodbyes. Coach and Jada held on to each other's hand after they hugged for a little while longer. They kept smiling and said goodbye to each other again.

After Jada left, Coach started shadow boxing to clear his mind. On a deeper level though, it symbolized that he was fighting a strong temptation.

CHAPTER 8

COACH ALWAYS MADE it to the school five to seven minutes before the bell rang. As usual, Coach parked his car a few blocks away from the school. After school traffic is worse than being stuck on the 405 Freeway during rush hour. Cars are triple parked with hazard lights flashing for five blocks. Once the children were let out of school and the crossing guards took their post at the intersections, the area became more congested than a chest cold.

Coach strolled from the rear of the school that was surrounded by a 10' chain link fence. Coach could hear the chatter of children near the portables masked behind clouds of chalk dust as they clapped the erasers together to get them clean. Coach smiled when he heard the teacher yelling at the children from the classroom door. "You ladies are supposed to be cleaning erasers, not standing out here socializing! Keep it up and you are going to have two more weeks of eraser duty, you hear?"

It brought back memories, but not necessarily good ones. Coach remembered the days he had to do that ungodly chore for running his mouth too much in class as a youth. Coach had his own philosophy that was better than the teacher's... in his mind, "Once the work is done, it's time to have fun!"

Not much had changed since he was in school. He saw the same tetherball pole and the yellow hopscotch squares painted on the ground. The metal monkey bars were gone. That was another memory that wasn't necessarily a good one for Coach. That one landed him in the hospital with a concussion. Coach could still see his body hitting the black safety mat and feel his head bouncing.

Coach saw one of his former football players Trevino. He was a big fifth grader now. He was coming from the office with another youth that was even taller than Trevino that Coach didn't know. There was also another kid that was about 200 pounds heavier than both of them that Coach didn't know either but he had seen him around. Trevino noticed Coach right away. The look of admiration in his eyes showed the impact Coach had on his young life. "What's up, Coach?"

"Trevino… what's going on, Sun? I see you shining, young lord."

"I'm just reflecting off of your light, Coach. I'm just a star, a mere nuclear fusion," Trevino responded with pure respect. Trevino loved Coach. He was one of the sincere coaches that helped him with life skills and didn't just use him for his football talents. "Hey Coach did you see my game last week?"

Coach was a defensive specialist so even though Trevino had a phenomenal game with over 200 yards rushing and multiple touchdowns on offense, he still teased him like it wasn't anything special. "I saw it. And I didn't see you make one tackle." Coach lied.

The other two kids started laughing at Tre just because that's what little knucklehead boys do to shame the other.

"Aw Coach! I scored three touchdowns!" Trevino defended himself and struck the Heisman Pose.

"What does that mean, young lord? I know you can score a touchdown. I want to know who you hit. How many solo tackles you had. You offensive guys don't want to get physical. You didn't even have any dirt on your uniform after the game," Coach teased.

"That's because we were playing on turf!"

Trevino and Coach gave each other high fives even though the fence separated them before they parted ways.

"Peace Coach, I'll see you up at practice tonight."

"Be safe, you hear? One love!"

As Coach turned away, Trevino and his friends were still in earshot range. Coach heard some words that humbled him. The tall skinny youth asked Trevino, "Is that your father?"

"Naw, that was my junior football clinic coach when I was seven... but man, I sure wish he was my father," Trevino responded the way a child would talk about a dream.

The heavyset kid didn't even know Coach but he added, "I wish he was my Pops, too."

That set it off. Coach had to control the tears of joy welling up in his eyes. It gets no better than that as a coach and mentor. Those are the simple things that gave Coach's life some meaning and purpose. That was the reason he loved waking up to go to work every morning for a salary that was far below his school credentials. Seeing the fruit he bore gave him substance to continue to do what he did. There was no amount of money that can compare to the feeling he just experienced. Coach immediately gave thanks to the MOST HIGH and quickly wiped his eyes with the inside sleeve of his warm-up jacket.

Coach made his way to the front entrance. He got himself together before anybody saw him smiling with tears coming from his eyes. The school bell rang. You could hear the noise erupt as hundreds of children exited the classrooms. You could also hear the sigh of relief coming from the teachers that just had a long ass day dealing with those children.

Jah wasn't hard to notice when he left the class because he toted the biggest backpack in the world on his back. Jah brought every textbook home every day. Jah was smart and got decent grades but he didn't love school like a child prodigy would. Jah's fourth grade teacher's pet peeve was uncleanliness. A student with a messy desk got a week of eraser cleaning duty, trash pickup, and 250 standards that said, 'I will not treat my desk as if it were a pigsty. Swine is an unclean animal and I (say your name) am a clean, righteous human being.'

So with all that punishment coming for one infraction, Jah just avoided storing items in the desk all together and kept everything in his backpack instead.

Coach saw Jah walking across the yard looking like he was giving somebody a piggyback ride. He also saw the third grade teacher Mr. Bardwell walking fast toward Jah holding a leather attaché case, kitchen cleaner, and a whole roll of paper towels. Mr. Bardwell wasn't hard to spot either. He was the only white teacher in the entire school. Coach knew what was about to go down so he posted up against the wall and observed his son.

Jah took the 90 pounds off of his back and unzipped the bag. Jah took out his personal leather attaché case, 409 cleaner, and roll of paper towels. Jah and Mr. Bardwell exchanged greetings as they both sprayed and wiped down two areas of the lunch table until it was clean enough to eat off of. Mr. Bardwell took a white cotton sheet from his case and covered the table. Jah simultaneously did the same thing. Mr. Bardwell took out a smaller white silk sheet, folded it twice, and then laid it on top of the cotton sheet. Jah took out a fresh white silk pillow case still in plastic and laid it on top of his sheet.

Mr. Bardwell was an excellent teacher that was too skilled in his profession to be getting paid the starting salary for a third grade teacher in the LAUSD. Mr. Bardwell was addicted to traveling around the world and tasting expensive vintage wines and 39K a year wasn't going to get him there. But at the same time, Mr. Bardwell wanted to teach kids that deserved a fair shot at life. While the money was good teaching privileged kids, it wasn't gratifying or interesting. For some reason or another, he bonded best with black kids. The passion was there and he enjoyed watching the kids drink up his knowledge. Mr. Bardwell was trained by one of the old legendary black teachers named Ms. Crabtree that was known to hit students (and teachers!) with a long ruler when they got out of line. When Mr. Bardwell first started teaching, he wondered how it would be being the only white guy in a school of color. To try and fit in, Mr. Bardwell used to tell the children and staff that he was mixed and his name Dan was short for Dante. He learned quickly that being himself around black people and succeeding as an educator was more important than faking the funk. Now Mr. Bardwell is one of the best teachers in the district.

"Are you ready for this?" Mr. Bardwell asked Jah as he removed a small key from his wallet and unlocked his attaché case.

"This is the moment of truth. Show me your hand," Jah replied as he removed a small key hidden in his sock and unlocked his own attaché case.

They both looked at each other. Mr. Bardwell unzipped a compartment inside of his case. Jah did the same. They both took out the contents. They looked at each other again and took deep breaths.

Coach was still watching from across the yard. He was smiling proud and thinking to himself, *"That's my son. Look at the discipline. I couldn't have done it better myself."*

Since this potential transaction was Mr. Bardwell's idea, Jah let him show his hand first. Mr. Bardwell carefully unfolded one corner of the cloth at a time until the gem was exposed. Mr. Bardwell slowly set the objects on the table and took a step back to admire what he was seeing for the last time. Jah performed the same ritual. They both stood there looking at the football cards like they were newly-cut diamonds. They very well could have been diamond dealers the way they took out their jeweler loupes to inspect the original border colors, gloss, smooth edges, print spots, and focus imperfections.

They were both pleased with the offerings so it was time to deal. Mr. Bardwell was trying to trade his 1958 Topps Jim Brown rookie card, certified grade 8 mint condition and valued at $1,999 for Jah's 1965 Topps #122 Joe Willy Namath rookie card, certified grade 9 mint condition, valued between $1,250 and $1,500. He also wanted the Adrian Peterson autographed rookie card, grade 10 mint , already valued at $600.

Jah would have easily taken the deal even though he would be losing $200 on paper but Jah had a gut feeling that Mr. Bardwell was trying to get over on him because he was a kid. "I want to make this deal, Mr. Bardwell but you have to put up another card because the value of this Adrian Peterson rookie card is going to continue to rise. It's valued at $600 already and he's only been playing five to six years. That Jim Brown card hasn't moved up in value in over 10 years." Jah stated using the written facts.

The actual fact is you can't really put a value on the Great Jim Brown. There is something about that brother that touches the soul of people generation after generation. Jah is eight years old. Jim Brown was retired from football decades before he was born. Jah had never seen Jim Brown play football but for some reason he knew him at three years old. Jim Brown brings out strength and confidence in young men, addresses social issues, and provides tools needed in life. You can't put a price tag on that.

"Excuse my language, Jah, but that listing price is some racist political bullshit. There are only a few Jim Brown cards officially certified so it's a rare collectible. With that being said, you don't buy a collectible like this on ebay or Craigslist. You make an up close and personal deal with the collector," Mr. Bardwell confidently replied. He didn't feel guilty about it but Mr. Bardwell figured that two cards for one might look odd to an 8-year-old. So Mr. Bardwell offered a cool card to go with the trade. "But if you feel that strongly about it, Jah, I'll throw in this Barry Sanders Rookie Card as well."

Jah loved his hobby too much to fall for that okie-doke.

"Are you serious? You're going to offer me a $9 card? No disrespect, Mr. Bardwell, but we're not out here trading Pokémon cards. We're negotiating thousands of dollars. So let's stay focused and do this because I have to get to my homework, sir."

After another ten minutes of wheeling and dealing, they walked away with a straight up trade. Mr. Bardwell pretended that Jah got the best of him in the deal even though he was about to make a net profit of four grand after he dumped the card on an amateur collector. But Jah had his own personal agenda as well. Jah was going to get his card autographed by Jim Brown, which would raise the value an extra zero—from 1,900 to 19,000.

CHAPTER 9

AS THEY DROVE home, Coach and Jah talked about how their day went. They joked around about Jada as a potential stepmother. Jah said, "I love Jada; she is real cool but I question her child rearing techniques, Dad. I just don't think she's ready to make our cipher complete. She wears the same sneakers I wear. I mean, what is she going to bring to the table?"

"Well, she got a wicked jump shot," Coach stated truthfully.

Jah looked at his father waiting for him to say something else and when he didn't they just fell out laughing.

Coach asked Jah how things went with Mr. Bardwell. Jah said, "I stood on it like a rock just like you taught me. He gave in to a straight up trade kind of easy. I was surprised."

"The economy is rough right now, son. He needs that money. It's a shame, too, because he is a true educator and should be compensated for it. Mrs. Thurman is rolling in the dough. She's been teaching for 25 years with tenure and ain't talking nothing about nothing in the classroom. Dan the Man," Coach gave Mr. Bardwell that nickname because they were cool like that outside of school, "is going to leave the school soon I can feel it. His paycheck is too small for a brain that big."

"Do you think he's uncomfortable being the only white man in a school rich with color, Dad?"

"That is a good question." Coach thought about the question for a minute before he answered. "I'm quite sure it was a challenge in the beginning but Dan is not part of the white power structure that oppresses minorities. I doubt he would jump in front of a bullet to save a brother but he definitely wouldn't hold them back in life because of their skin color. I know that for a fact."

"I kind of figured he needed the money. He's been looking disheveled lately. After we made the deal, I slid him the Adrian Peterson Card any-way…on the strength," Jah confessed.

"You are a good son. That's why people call you the Golden Child."

Coach and Jah decided to swing by the house for a little while. Jah completed his homework while Coach took care of some domestic chores. Coach turned on the NFL Network to see what his Baltimore Ravens had in store for those dreaded Pittsburgh Squealers in the game coming up on Sunday. When Jah finished his lessons he came into the living room and flopped down on the smaller couch. They watched a special called the "Top 10 Most Feared Tacklers" with the intensity like they were playing in the game themselves.

Coach cooked dinner during the commercials. Coach prepared king fish and rice & peas for dinner but waited to steam their vegetables until they returned later that evening after practice.

Before they left, Coach asked Jah to get his checkbook and make one out to the landlord for rent. Jah was young, plus he wasn't using his own money, so he loved making out the checks and paying the bills. He felt like he was doing Big Man's work. Coach let him enjoy the moment because all that was going to change when he got older.

* * *

Everything was running smoothly as usual at the rec center. Jah saw a few of his friends but he decided to hang out with the student employee Jelani in Coach's office and challenge his math skills. Coach strolled around the park making sure everything was clean and safe. Coach saw James and cracked up laughing before he could plot a prank.

"What are you up to, Coach? I can see that mischievous look in your eye. Get on the way from around here, you crazy muthafucka. Go get your whistle and get ready for practice? Go on now!" James said as he was shoo-ing Coach away from his area.

"That's why I came to see you, James. You can cut out early if you want to. Jelani can lock up tonight."

"See, that is exactly what I'm talking about, Coach. Stop fucking with me. You know I am in no hurry to get home to those five loud-ass kids of mine. Work is where I find my peace."

"Damn, Joe Jackson! You got five kids now?" Coach asked.

"Yes, sir. Five kids and not one of them little muthafuckas know how to sing. I got five Latoya's and they all crazy just like her, too."

"How old are they now?"

"Um," James, like most parents with multiple kids, always had to look up in space and think about it. Then James proceeded to count on his fingers, "Two, four, five, seven, and eleven," he stated in wonderment.

"Whew! That is a big bundle of joy you got there, James."

"I love them to death, literally cuz they're going to kill me. So no-no, playboy. I'm cool right here. I got a little bit more landscaping I need to do."

Coach looked around and the park was immaculate. There was nothing left that could be done. "You already got the park looking like the Garden of Eden. What else are you going to do? Import some muthafuckin' peacocks? This park is for Student Athletes, not the Hara Krishna. But go ahead and do what you gon' do. I'm outta here tonight. I'm about to go to Darby Park in Inglewood so I can smell some mud and football helmets."

"Go on, Funk Doctor. And I hope you step in some shit while you're running wind sprints. Now get on outta here, boy and have a good practice. Be safe!" James said as he waved bye to Coach.

"One love!"

* * *

Inglewood football is serious business. They play hard and practice even harder. Most of the players were in their designated practice area divided by teams and ages. Coach took a deep breath. The blood stained grass, musty air, and sour uniforms smelled like fresh pumpkin pie if you let Coach tell it. Youth football is more than just a game. When it is played correctly, kids learn life lessons that aid them for the rest of their journey on Earth.

Coach and Jah took a light jog across the field. Coach loved seeing so many black fathers involved in their sons' lives. It was record-breaking numbers compared to the number of fathers around when Coach was a child. It was so bad back then, Gerry had to coach his team one year.

Coach started blowing his whistle before he reached the practice area completely. The little Inglewood Soldiers knew that first whistle meant it was time to suit up. The majority of the players already had on the bottom half of their uniform so all they had to do was put on their shoulder pads and helmets. Coach rapidly blew his whistle multiple times signaling it was time to take two warm up laps. Coach always did every single exercise with the players. It was a good way to stay in shape plus it left no room for excuses out of his players when the conditioning got tough. They were all in it together. Just before they took off, Coach's star quarterback Kiddy Constantine came trotting across the field with the angry child face. His cute Mother was jogging right on his tail giving him an earful. She didn't give Kiddy time to speak.

"I'm sorry he's late, Coach, but Kiddy was messing around and forgot his cleats in his game bag and we had to go all the way back home to get them," Kiddy's mom stated and then she looked at her son and continued, "And you better finish that homework soon as you get home! You better not even think about that damn PlayStation!"

Coach intervened. Kiddy was a cool little dude so he was smooth with his commands. He didn't even bother talking with the Mother because she should have known better.

"You didn't finish your homework yet?" Coach asked curiously.

"No, sir, Coach. But I only have a few vocabulary words left to do."

"Well, why are you out here?"

"I didn't want to get in trouble for being late to practice," Kiddy explained.

"There is no penalty for being late to practice on this team if you are taking care of serious business. Homework is serious business. You know the rules, Quarterback. Think about it. Why would you want to go home after a hard practice and do homework when your body wants to relax? It's time to chill at the end of the day, Cool Breeze. You're supposed to be able to go home, take a hot bath, eat dinner, and get some PlayStation in. Kiddy, get my keys out of my bag, go sit in my car, and finish your lesson. We'll be right out here waiting for you. Now go handle that, Quarterback."

Kiddy's mother started to say something but Coach blew his whistle again and they all took off running. As Coach ran with his little soldiers, he thought about all the parents that had their children thinking they were about to sign an NFL contract because they had a sensational season as a 10-year-old. But at the same time, there is no guarantee that a child will be successful with a college degree.

Coach thought to himself, "Shit. The way the job market looks today a might have a better shot trying to make it in the NFL because they're not even hiring at Fatburger right now."

After that sobering thought, Coach relaxed his mind and enjoyed the run. The team completed their laps and lined up on the field in uniformed order. Coach led all the conditioning drills. He kept it fun and interesting because he added new exercises every few days that you don't normally see on a youth football field. Coach even implemented tai chi and yoga. The other teams in the organization used to laugh at their techniques until they saw them winning 40-0 every week. Coach and his players were doing pushups with their fingertips. The players loved it because nobody else was taking it to that level. Coach was always crazy with the cadence.

"Up... down!" and the team would sound off, "One!"

"Up... Down! Up... halfway down... hold it! Hold it! Busby! Get up off that ground! Hold it, Busby! Five more because Busby didn't hold it; the grass was holding him! Deep breath—let it out. Halfway down...hold it...Busby! I said halfway, not all the way... breathe...hold it! Hold it!... Five more because Jah was breathing funny!"

"Aw c'mon, Coach!" all the players groaned.

"...Up! Hold it. Hold it Can you feel that burn?...Five more because Reece can't feel the fire!" Coach charged them with pushups for every infraction from not being dirty enough to listening to rappers he didn't like. They only did 25 but Coach made it seem like they did 150.

Once they got back to their feet they stood strong like soldiers. Coach marveled at his well-oiled machine of a team. He still struggled with some of his first-year players.

"Anderson! Get over here on the hop! Anderson, you are the team captain, right?" But he didn't wait for an answer. "Can you tell me why Edwards has his thigh pads where his knee pads are supposed to be? Please go help your teammate before I have to go over there." Anderson hustled over to help his teammate.

"Whitman! Whitman! Why are you the only one not standing straight?" Coach yelled. He waited for an answer this time but got silence. Whitman was a thick kid with a man-sized head. Coach didn't know if he was mentally slow or shy because he was so quiet.

"Can you hear me Whitman?" Coach asked.

Whitman nodded.

"I said, can you hear me, Whitman?" Coach asked again.

Whitman nodded again.

"Whitman, stand up straight and put your feet together."

Whitman poked his chest out a little bit but his feet were still going in opposite directions.

"Your feet, Whitman... straighten your feet, not your shoulders. Make them point straight ahead. No, Whitman, straight! Point your feet not your head!"

Whitman used a classic defense mechanism and looked at Coach with that sad puppydog face that kids do to get him off his back. Coach got frustrated and bent down on a knee to straighten Whitman's feet himself. They didn't move much. Coach looked puzzled. Then he laughed, "Well I'll be damned."

Whitman had his shoes on the wrong feet the whole time.

Football practice was fast and physical. It was almost exciting as an actual game. After two hours of shoulder pads crashing and bodies flying, Head Coach Keith Naylor ended practice with his story about "the Great White Shark," one of his many classics.

Coach, Jah, and three other players that needed a ride home started walking across the field to the car. Coach Harrison from the Pee Wee team stopped Coach in mid stride.

"Hey Coach, I heard what happened to your boy. Is he all right?"

The first person that popped in his mind when he heard "your boy" was Jah. Coach immediately snapped into defensive mode even though his son was right next to him. It wasn't personal, just a natural reaction.

"What boy are you talking about?" Coach asked with a frown on his face.

Harrison snapped his fingers trying to think of the kid's name. "That slick kid you use to coach a few years back that was girl crazy... He's the quarterback over at Dorsey High School now…Peter or Percy, man—you know his name."

"Are you talking about Preston Pompey? Yeah, I heard he got a scholarship to UCLA."

"Yeah, that's him!" Harrison exclaimed.

"I think he's now the starting quarterback at Dorsey. What are they doing over there running the option this year? Preston can't throw the football ten yards but he runs like a cheetah cat."

"Well, he should've used that speed to get away from that fool that put hands on him. My man is in bad shape," Harrison's words turned the mood serious.

"Keep talking," Coach stated concerned.

"I heard Preston was leaning up against some crazy nigga's truck tongue kissing and dry humping on one of his girls in the parking lot… and you know how these youngsters today wear those skinny jeans and those metal studded belts, right? Well, I guess while Preston was grinding against the truck he left some scratch marks on the door. They say homeboy saw it and went upside Preston's head with a bottle."

"What? No. It sounds like it is more to it than that." Coach was shocked but even more concerned. "Did Preston take his woman from him?"

"I don't know, Coach, but maybe so. Preston was always in love even when we coached him as a baby. He was bringing the cheerleaders flowers and love letters when he was seven years old. You remember that shit?"

"Well, is he okay?" Coach asked with urgency because he was not trying to go down memory lane at that moment.

"I don't know. That's why I was seeing if you heard something. You know by the time the story got to me through these kids, it was twisted. One kid said Preston was stabbed in his hand, one kid said he was shot in his hand; somebody else said he lost an eye…so I don't know what to believe. I just know he's hurt. That I know for sure."

"Thanks for the heads up. I'll make some calls and see what went down."

On the ride home, Coach made a few calls to folks and they confirmed Coach Harrison's story. It was fairly accurate, but actually a lot worse than the initial story. Preston did get hit in the head with a Snapple bottle but even worse, a piece of glass got lodged in his eye and he is going to lose

85% of the vision in his right eye. Further, Preston was stabbed in his non-throwing hand, but he also had his Achilles tendon sliced so bad he will never be able to walk straight again. Preston didn't get shot but a gun was pulled on him and placed to his face. That part was most likely a threat of what would happen if Preston told the police.

The girl Preston was kissing was being held at the police station for questioning. She denied knowing the man and having any affiliation with a crazed brokenhearted jealous ex-boyfriend. But at the same time she was too terrified to give a description. Preston refused to give one as well.

Coach shook his head in sadness. Coach mumbled something softly then said a prayer for Preston in silence.

Jah and the other players were cracking jokes about some events that occurred at practice and that brought some cheer to Coach's somber mood because he was starting to have ill thoughts. That information about Preston hit too close to home. The sound of laughter is a better cure than medicine. They all laughed so hard about Whitman wearing his cleats on the wrong feet they got bellyaches. Coach dropped off the children one at a time until it was just him and Jah in the car. Coach looked at his son proudly and told Jah he loved him.

Coach got lucky and found a parking spot right in front of his building. When he got out of the car, he saw Bodeen across the street. Bodeen was cursing under his breath and buffing the door on the driver side of his truck. Coach looked on the ground and saw Bodeen was using a rubbing compound that removed minor scratches from the paint. Coach wondered for a second if Bodeen was the crazy nigga that hurt Preston but he brushed the thought out of his mind. Coach knew Bodeen was a gangster and heard a few of his horror stories on the streets but he didn't think Bodeen was that low down to maim a teenager for dry humping a girl on his truck.

Coach and Bodeen made eye contact. Coach nodded towards him. Bodeen returned the gesture. That was the first time in four years they ever somewhat greeted each other. Coach thought it was interesting but didn't give it too much energy. He and Jah headed upstairs to finish their daily routine before they shut it down for the night. They only had eight hours to rest before they had to start the routine all over again the next day.

CHAPTER 10

"Nigga don't act like a Biatch bitch bitch… that's why I don't got love for a Biatch bitch bitch… that's why Too Short and E-40 says Biatch bitch bitch so homie please don't marry that Biatch bitch bitch… and that's why I'll never be a Biatch bitch bitch…"

BODEEN SAT IN the corner of his dark apartment near the window listening to the ring tone on his phone like it was a high quality CD. A foul smelling Newport cigarette only smoked a quarter of the way down was slowly burning out in the ashtray. Bodeen had his hands folded across his lap. He tapped one index finger to the beat every four bars. Bodeen was far too insane to be influenced by some rap lyrics but he looked to the words coming from his ring tone for encouragement. A significant amount of time had passed since he raped Angie but he could not get her off of his mind. The rookie excitement Bodeen felt after he lost his virginity had been long gone. Thinking of Angie now made him angry. He often wished he could dig her out of her grave and kill her again for leaving him feeling empty, befuddled, and in love. Bodeen snatched the phone up and growled into it.

"Speak!"

"Damn, you a mean muthafucka and I was just calling to bring you some joy," Madison Anderson stated as he pretended not to be moved by Bodeen's attitude.

Madison was one of the many clients Bodeen did jobs for. He was also Bodeen's PCP supplier when he needed to escape to the dark side and hone in on his craft. Outside of being a shady criminal, Madison was an okay dude but Bodeen just didn't trust a man with two last names.

"I have preseason tickets for the game at the Staples Center tonight... In the Owner's Box...Clippers and the Heat," Madison spoke in code. When translated, he said, *"I have an easy job... high priority...low pay but requires a gun."*

To prevent from sticking his arm through the phone and choking Madison for bothering him about a job that paid chump change, Bodeen didn't even bother answering the question. After a moment of silence on the line, Madison got scared. He didn't know if he should hang up or offer Bodeen some money out his pocket for irritating him.

"Um, well the after party is the real shit anyway. You want to roll? My treat," translated as *"I got some PCP that will take you out of this world and I'll give you some no charge."*

Bodeen stayed silent for what seemed like hours. Madison figured he should just be quiet while Bodeen decided if he was going to take the job. But Bodeen was stuck. The effects of the Newport cigarette dipped in embalming fluid have the tendency to do that. During the silence, Bodeen incoherently blurted out "Matata" from his subconscious. He had no idea what it meant or any recollection that he even said it. Madison just hung up the phone after almost ten minutes of dead silence.

CHAPTER 11

FOR THE PAST week Coach and Jah had been sick to their stomachs. They were in a very funky mood. A gray cloud hovered over their apartment. Coach and Jah had barely said a word to each other. The only thing they shared that week was pain. Coach and Jah's Inglewood football team lost in the second round of the playoffs to their Carson rivals that previous weekend. They felt awful. Coach was unshaven and looking scruffy. Jah's head was looking peasy too. They decided to roll to the barbershop.

They arrived at Fly Cuts on Pico and Spaulding early enough to beat that Saturday morning rush. As Coach and Jah approached the glass door to enter the barbershop, Coach grinned for the first time in a week and said, "Wow!...Damn, that is a lot of pressure!"

Jah saw what his father was talking about and cracked up laughing. Shirley the manicurist at the salon had the biggest and widest ass in the western hemisphere and it was blocking the entrance. Shirley was a big girl. She stood about 6 feet tall in some open-toed heels that were worn down and leaning to the side. Shirley had on some big action slacks she got on sale at Lerner's and she wore a sleeveless halter-top. She had titties everywhere. Shirley had long natural beautiful hair, but she still wore a tired-ass burgundy weave. Coach never understood why a woman with good hair would put that nasty weave in. But Shirley's #1 assets were her exotic fingernails. She didn't have ornaments and rhinestones like most women had. Shirley's nails were straight up beautiful and the artwork on them was fascinating to look at.

Coach opened up the door at the same time Shirley was bending over to pick up some emery boards that fell from her workstation. Coach couldn't resist and stuck his hand out and squeezed a chunk of butt. Shirley jumped up and landed on those heels that were leaning to the side. She playfully slapped Coach on the arm and yelled, "You better cut that out, boy. Don't be pinching me on my booty!"

Coach denied her accusations and snitched his own son out, "That wasn't me. Jah did that."

Everybody in the barbershop fell out laughing. Jah just looked at his father and shook his head. As they took their seats, Coach was thinking of how good it felt to have a good laugh after a terrible week.

The good feeling didn't last long at all though. Andrew the Barber and his negative energy messed all that up when he opened his mouth, "I heard y'all lost to Carson last week. That's a damn shame. Y'all were so close. I know you feel terrible after a loss like that. Y'all must be sick losing 7 to 6. I know I would be sick. What happened? How come the coach didn't pass the ball in the fourth quarter? How come the quarterback didn't run it when it was third and one in the second quarter…?"

And it just kept coming: *How come this* and *why y'all didn't do that?*

Coach and Jah were not in a mood to do a post-game press conference so they just ignored Andrew's questions until he finally changed the subject.

Coach continued to skim the latest issue of S.I. Coach was reading an article, minding his own business, and soon as Pops Sanford walked in the door, he started talking. "See son, Joe Paterno's unbelievable plays on the football field kept him alive but his unbelievable play off the field is what killed him… understand me?"

Pops Sanford was a young man but everything about him was old. He was somewhere between 15 and 55 years old but it was hard to detect because he had that young-old face. He was in great shape, but he was always complaining of a bad back and his feet always hurt. Pops Sanford was a 32nd degree Mason from Roanoke, Virginia. Pops was a petite man. He stood about 5'5", depending on what shoes he had on. He wore a Covadis haircut with Murray Waves and a 3-inch part just above his right temple. He wore a thick bow tie and a fresh white dress shirt with heavy starch every day. His slacks were tailored with Harlem Renaissance style cuffs, and he wore these old wingtip shoes that looked like something your grandfather had on in the family photo album.

Pops Sanford talked like was born in the 1940's and everything he did in life was so long ago. As a matter of fact, Pops Sanford just talked... all day long. Anything can get him started. He would make a conversation out of silence. "Y'all hear that? It's called silence. That means absence of sound. The Old French calls it *Stillness* but it means the same thing." The sound of Pops Sanford's voice was very Avery Johnson-esque and he made everybody feel like they were related to him.

Coach was seated in Kenny the Barber's chair and Jah patiently waited for his favorite barber Herman to finish up with his customer. Coach hated to get his haircut once Pops Sanford started talking. Pops Sanford was good for saying something so outlandish that it would cause you to jerk your head from laughing. Many plugs have been cut out of heads because of that fool.

Pops Sanford dusted his chair off with an old whiskbroom that was surely out of production. He placed a booster seat in the empty chair and slapped it with a towel so swift it sounded like a champagne bottle was popped open. Pops looked at Jah and said, "Now step on up here, boy. The squeaky wheel gets the oil first."

Jah gave him that *who me?* look and then said, "No thank you, sir. The last time I sat in your chair, I asked you for a Mohawk and you gave me a haircut that looks like yours."

"Mmm-mm-mm, these youngsters nowadays is something else... Not all beef is created equal -some of it is tough as a bull. I got to school this young pepper squire... this is a real haircut here, young'n. The Mohawk went out with Mr. T years ago. This haircut never goes out of style, and if it does, it always comes back in style. Now what haircut do you know that can do that? No answer... I thought so. The greatest men on the planet Earth wear this same hairstyle that I got. The best dancer to ever put on a pair of tap shoes: Mr. Bojangles Bill Robinson, uh, uh Louis Farrakhan got a haircut like this... and uh what's that boy's name? Uh, the football player that you heathens say looks and sounds like me—oh yeah! Shannon Sharpe. Now that's a real haircut! The Greatest Tight End ever played the position... and it was that haircut that got him in the Hall of Fame."

As Pops rambled on, Herman dusted his barber chair off and motioned Jah to come sit in it.

"Stop trying to misguide my customers. Little man is a fly guy. He's not trying to look like a bean pie peddler. Say Pops, I was wondering, how did you get that old face on a young boy's body anyway Or is it a young face on an old frame? You look like you could be my little brother and my Father... You look like a Junior Mint with a bowtie on."

While everyone was laughing, Pops Sanford just stared at Herman with a straight face. "You could start an argument in an empty house cain't ya boy?"

As Jah leaped into Herman's empty barber chair, Pops Sanford looked over at him and said, "That boy's more slippery than snot on a glass door-knob." Pops turned on his heels like he was in the military and walked slowly back to his barber chair and took a seat. He hadn't been to work five minutes and his feet were killing him already.

Pops' foot condition always made Coach think of Gerry's late Uncle Lonnie. Uncle Lonnie had some bad feet. That nigga's feet was so bad they hurt when walked on soft carpet. Coach remembered as a child when they rushed Uncle Lonnie to the hospital because his feet were in so much pain. They stayed in the emergency room for five hours and all the doctor gave Uncle Lonnie was a prescription for some cotton or wool socks. They had more ventilation than those sour smelling nylon and polyester dress socks he always wore. But watching Uncle Lonnie walk across the carpet was better than going to a Comedy Club. For years, the whole house would stop what they were doing just to look at his feet. That muthafucka grunted and groaned with each step. Coach didn't know what was funnier as a kid, watching Uncle Lonnie grunt while he struggled across the carpet or the grimacing look on everybody's face that was staring at him. Gerry's Aunt Ola would twist her face up like she was the one in pain and say, "Mmmmmmmmmm, mmm... boy, that Lonnie got some bad feet!"

Shirley walked passed Pops and stood in the window. Her ass blocked all the sunlight that was shining through. Pops Sanford stared at her ass for a long time and then he whispered loud enough for everybody to hear, "Well, don't you look prettier than a tablespoon of sweet butter melting on a stack of wheat cakes!"

"That looks like a delicious picture, but can you handle this thickness Pops? I'm a big woman. If you can't hang with all this, making love to me will be like throwing a hot dog down an empty hallway," Shirley flirted back.

"Girl, you got me grinning like a possum licking whipped cream from a light socket."

His Virginia Mack Lines triggered the same question in everybody's mind but Herman was the first to ask, "Hey Pops, do you have a woman?"

"Not anymore, brother. She left me last week for cheating on her. Now ain't that something? That word cheating is too overrated with these black women. I'm gonna have to get me a White Swan cuz these Black Crows treat me like a scarecrow in a corn patch," Pops stated. He struggled to his feet as his customer came in. Pops sat his customer down and wrapped him in a fresh pinstriped cape without ever acknowledging he was there until he finished his speech.

"Let's take a look at this word *cheating*. Cheating is from the root word cheat. In order to be cheated, someone has to obtain goods, services or money from you through deceit, fraud, or trickery. That's how you get cheated…Now women say a man having sex with another woman is cheating but they didn't lose any goods… they didn't lose any services… and they didn't lose any money…so I asked her, 'What the fuck did you get cheated out of?' I brought my peter back home with me. I told her the only thing she got cheated out of was a good time because she didn't come with me and make it a threesome… Yes, sir!!"

Pops Sanford was on a roll now and couldn't be stopped. He pointed to a girl walking down the street minding her own business. "See-see? Look at the skinny girl walking right there… we are in hot ass sunny California and she's wearing a sleeveless sundress and got snow boots on. That broad is an oxymoron. I understand fashion statements but I don't know what she's trying to in express in that."

The patrons in the barbershop got about three minutes of silence to catch their breath from laughing before something triggered Pops Sanford to start talking again. A young Muslim brother was reading an article in a hip hop magazine about Jay Z and other so called rappers accused of being part of the Illuminati. The Muslim brother glanced up at Pops Sanford's Masonic ring then back to the article.

"I know what you thinking, boy. Thoughts are coming all out of your pores," Pops accused the Muslim Brother that wasn't even thinking about him and continued, "If you think I'm part of some devil worshipping bullshit you need to get that out of your mind. Yes, I am a Mason. But I'm a Black Mason and if you think the white man is going to tell me some secrets to control the world you need to get that out your mind, too—it ain't gon' happen. You are the secret. The Original Man. Think about that and we'll build on it later, young pepper squire."

The Muslim Brother was reading his article in peace. He didn't want to talk to Pops about his Masonic Ring or the illuminati. He was just waiting for a haircut. It didn't stop Pops Sanford though. "Everybody looks at my ring and always thinks it's Satan. What kind of shit is that? Let's discuss some real devils like Ronald Reagan, J. Edgar Hoover, crack dealers, the Bush family, and that nigga that lives across the street from you, Coach... uh, Bodeen. Now that evil muthafucka Bodeen should be named Beelzebub."

Everybody that knew of Bodeen's reputation agreed. Pops continued to defend his lodge brothers at Bodeen's expense.

"As Masons, we stand on the square. We believe in the mystic works of King Solomon's Temple—a black prophet's house, and Hiram Abiff—a black working man. We have a brotherhood; we pray together; we eat together. But now look at this picture. Here is this savage Bodeen, who has no morals whatsoever. He killed a church lady on a Sunday and dared God to curse him with hell fire! He's connected to those folks...but y'all don't say shit to him- But you want to think I'm part of the illuminati. That's a damn shame!"

"Shit. From what I heard, Bodeen would make hell worse than what it is," a patron in the barbershop chimed in.

"The truth just set you free brother! Amen. That savage doesn't believe in the codes of the streets. He works with the police. And don't catch him when he's tripping on that water- that's slang for sherm or PCP, if you Californians ain't hip to the jargon they use in the ghettos..." Pops stated.

Two Mexicans seated in the Barbershop that were born and raised in East L.A. looked at Pops Sanford like he was either a fool or a tourist.

Pops kept teaching, "…When he's on that Water he starts acting crazier than a sprayed cockroach. See, the side effect to PCP is violent aggressiveness…I don't see how you let him live across the street from you, Coach. I would have burned that whole muthafuckin' building down as soon as he moved in there. Then I would have removed the dirt and dropped in new soil to make sure he didn't return in any form or fashion. Fucks that. Have you ever invited Bodeen to your apartment to watch a pay-per-view boxing event, Coach?"

"I don't know homeboy like that. I just see him coming and going. He never gave me any problems. You cats put too much on that dude like he's a damn vampire or a jackal. He's probably the same dude that used to be the school bully. He's just grown up now doing gangster shit," Coach replied.

"Flarn what you talking about Coach? Boy, you living across the street from Lucifer's bastard child, you better keep a silver bullet with garlic on it ready to pump in that fool's heart. I know what your problem is, Coach. Your last name got you fucked up. You have too much *Love* for everybody. It is okay to like and dislike."

Coach got out of the barber chair. He was groomed and looking extra fly again. Jah was looking slick again as well. Coach paid both barbers. He looked at Pops Sanford and said, "I'm going to keep that silver bullet in mind… because if you ever cut my son's hair again to make it look like yours with that funny looking part, I'm going to put it right in your ass. I was mad as a mule chewing on bumblebees that day."

Everybody laughed at Coach cracking on Pops Sanford as he and Jah left the barbershop smelling like sweet Afro Sheen.

Ten minutes later Bodeen walked into the barbershop. He sat down next to the two Mexicans from East L.A. Within moments, the customers all got up and headed out of the barbershop except Bodeen. He decided he wanted a haircut. Bodeen sat down in Pops' chair.

CHAPTER 12

"THIS PACKAGE FEELS kind of light." Detective Andy Moretti stated as he curled the envelope in one hand like it was a dumbbell.

"That's because you've been in the gym hitting those weights. I can see those 12-inch biceps bulging out of your shirt right now," clowned Sticky. California Sticky was an amateur level man of leisure that pimped two goat-mouth hookers out of the Mustang Motel on Western and 43rd. "And that package is the same as last month's, no more, no less. You're deflating my finances as it is, Detective. We're in a recession. Tricks are unemployed. They don't have the desire or money for pussy under these broke condi-tions. Man, I have to resort to selling them baby oil to jack off with just to keep a couple of dollars in my pocket."

The look Detective Moretti gave Sticky made him feel more pitiful than his pimp game actually was. Det. Moretti got back in his gray Ford and drove up the block to the Southwest Police Station on King Boulevard.

Instead of pulling into the employees' parking lot, Detective Moretti circled the block and pulled in to the Taco Bell next door to the station. He turned off the engine and took a deep breath. Detective Moretti opened the envelope and counted two grand. At one time, Andy Moretti could wipe his ass with two grand and flush it down the toilet like used toilet paper. He used to pull ten grand a week easy from the kingpins of the underworld and that was on a bad week; now here he was shaking down a low level clown for 2K a month. That wasn't going to cut it. He looked out of the window of his car at the huge billboard hanging over Chess Bail Bonds that read: Crime Doesn't Pay.

* * *

Andy Moretti was the typical All-American golden boy born and raised in Palisades, California. He stood around 6'2" and was very fit. Andy's body was chiseled and it could really be seen when he wore his tight nylon short-sleeve crew neck shirts that cops find so fashionable. Andy had dark black hair he cropped close on the sides and back and he wore it spiked up on the top. Andy was 47 years old and he aged well considering all the cocaine and 18-year-old girls gone wild he consumed over the course of his 22-year police career. Andy Moretti was the typical good-looking hot shot cop who drove a Porsche and played harder than he worked.

Andy grew up fairly rich. His father Joseph was an engineer that also taught Algebra II at Pierce College as a hobby. Joseph Moretti also did fairly well in the stock market game. Andy's mother Mary Ellen was a preschool teacher until she became pregnant with Andy. His brother Jody and sister Maureen followed over the next couple of years and Mary Ellen became content being a mother and housewife. Mary Ellen was a dreamer and the extra time on her hands often put her in the world of make-believe.

Andy was named after the man of Mary Ellen's teenage fantasies and alleged one-night-stand, American singer Andy Williams. The first time Andy's parents decided to consummate the relationship Mary Ellen refused to partake in it until Joseph purchased a copy of "Moon River." Mary Ellen fantasized she was in the American singer's embrace while she made love to Joseph for the first time as well as the second and third. Mary Ellen never told anyone her secret. When asked where she came up with that name Mary Ellen would simply say, Andy was a character in her favorite children's book.

Andy Moretti didn't decide to become a cop until he was around 23 years old. He wanted to become a professional surfer but his strict father told him that he would cut his allowance and cut him out of the will if he didn't get a real job. Andy and a couple of his radical friends signed up for the police academy as a joke to please their parents. The adrenaline rush they got during basic training was almost equivalent to the surfing rush minus the spiritual aspect, positive energy, and being one with nature. Andy shot to the top of his class and scored in the 99th percentile on his exam.

When he graduated from the academy, he was placed in the Rampart Division years before it became infamous. Andy was actually one of the early pioneers that gave the Rampart Station its dirty reputation. (But that part of the story is in another book—*wink*.)

Officer Morretti got turned out his first week as a rookie. It started with a routine traffic stop. A Puerto Rican drug dealer from New York was making his way to Alvarado Park to drop off a package. He was driving cool for your average New Yorker, but in Los Angeles his aggressive and erratic style of operating a moving vehicle looked very dangerous. The Puerto Rican only knew how to handle this delay one way. He was a hustler from the Bronx and paying off dirty cops was a daily routine like brushing your teeth where he was from. When Officer Morretti approached the window, the Puerto Rican told him he was in a hurry and he knew the routine.

There are dirty cops everywhere, but dirty L.A. cops take their handouts under the radar, not on the corner. But the Puerto Rican didn't have time to bother with the cultural differences. Dirty was dirty so he called Officer Morretti a pig (in a polite way) and placed five grand wrapped in a rubber band in the palm of his hand and drove off.

From that day forward, Officer Morretti kept a hidden agenda. Over the years, he perfected it to a tee. Officer Morretti kept his image of a model officer up to par. He got married, had a few kids, bought a nice house with a picket fence, and a dog. Officer Morretti moved up the ranks fast and made Detective in the Vice Unit. The Vice Unit was a whole different animal, but Andy Moretti was quickly becoming a beast.

The temptation in the Vice Unit is overwhelming. Money, sex, and drugs flowed freely in the underworld cesspool. Some officers would go undercover and never want to come back. Those square-looking white officers in that division were some of the best burglars, pimps, and drug dealers in the city. They had the perfect façade to pull off the job.

Moretti was actually a very good policeman when he chose to be. He could collar some of the most elusive crime figures without the help of an informant, more commonly known as a snitch. He had his finger on the pulse of the streets. Detective Moretti was young, wild, and willing to adapt to change as the game became more violent.

When powder cocaine was a rich man's high, getting a payoff from a doctor or lawyer in exchange for freedom was smooth and simple. When gangs took over the drug trade, it flat lined. Rock cocaine hit the streets rough and aggressive. The gang bangers controlling it acted like animals so Detective Moretti started recruiting his own young wolves that were willing to attack. After a while, other detectives followed suit and thus the Rampart Division became like a modern day Babylon.

Andy Moretti was smart. He wasn't a psychic but he could see that the good thing he had was not going to last. But the flow of tax-free money wouldn't allow Andy to just quit. He decided he had to put himself in a position to collect without being too involved hands-on. So Andy's new role was similar to a preacher. In church, you have to pay to pray. In the streets, you have to pay to play.

His young wolves were like ushers collecting his tithes. When the game was good, Andy was averaging 50k a month steady. With that money came power and toys: a new Porsche every year, condos for concubines, beach houses for play, the best nose candy, extravagant vacations, a yacht, college girls... and with those indiscretions, came a devastating California divorce garnishing 64% of his wages, a pregnant ex-wife that he can't stand with a bad prescription drug habit, child support, and a lot of other expensive habits that were taking a toll on his happiness.

The divorce and child support payments weren't a problem in the beginning. Andy was making so much cash on the street, it was no different from a utility bill. There were millions of dollars flowing through the underworld in L.A., but it still wasn't enough to quench the thirst of certain individuals. Most of the gangsters that Andy extorted started setting up shop in other states and left him behind with no severance pay. The other ones were either getting shot or catching cases far outside of his jurisdiction and he couldn't get them out of jail. The young wolves that were protecting Andy's jungle were quickly becoming an endangered species. Detective Andy Moretti's cash flow dried up quicker than virgin vagina filled with vinegar and cinnamon.

On one particular day back when Andy still lived at home with his family, he had to collect from one of his crooks. He was pissed because the crook was already delinquent with his payment. Andy was driving angrily when his cell phone rang. It was the principal from his daughter's school and he informed Andy that he was needed right away. Andy was agitated by the call for two reasons. For one, the principal was talking in riddles. The principal said that his daughter Colleen wasn't physically hurt but she seems a bit traumatized as well as the other student involved. The second reason Andy was hot was because since he was a cop, the teachers would use his name as a means of discipline, and it made the kids terrified of him. A kid could poot in class and the teacher would threaten to call Detective Moretti to take him to jail for disturbing the peace. *"Whoever gets in trouble in class today, I'm going to call Detective Moretti and he's going to take you to jail."*

When Andy arrived at the school the ambulance was there and the medics were sedating the bullying kid that assaulted his daughter Colleen. The kid was hyperventilating and going over the top with his dramatics Andy thought.

Apparently after school, the bully was chasing Andy's little girl Colleen up and down the street with a lizard he found scampering in the bushes. Andy's little girl was crying and becoming more frightened as the bully cornered her between a house and a fence. The bully kept poking the lizard in her face. Those beady eyes and that lizard tongue protruding out every few seconds were horrifying to that 6-year-old girl. The bully kept telling Colleen to kiss the lizard when he put it inches from her face. The bully grabbed a handful of Colleen's hair to keep her head still while he forced the lizard's tongue in Colleen's mouth.

The pain of getting her hair yanked only lasted a few seconds because the bully quickly let go of his grip. The terrified little girl looked up and saw a massive black hand around the throat of the bully and it was choking the shit out of him. The bully's feet were five feet off the ground with nothing but a hand around his throat crushing his larynx holding him up. Bodeen didn't say a word. He grabbed the bully by the wrist that was holding the live lizard and forced it in his mouth. Bodeen covered the bully's mouth with his massive hand and said, "Eat it!" The kid wouldn't be able to breathe if he didn't start chewing and swallowing so he had no choice.

Bodeen held the kid by his neck until he swallowed the entire lizard. Bodeen pushed the kid down on the ground next to Colleen and walked to his car. Bodeen didn't give a fuck about the bully or Colleen's thank you. He didn't do it to the bully to protect Colleen. Bodeen just felt like putting his two cents in somebody else's business that day. It kept him sharp.

Colleen pretended to be too traumatized to give a description to the school authorities when they asked what happened. She wasn't going to snitch on her savior. When her father arrived, Colleen gave Andy a better description. Colleen was only hesitant because she didn't know how her Dad would react to the way she was going to express her truth. It wasn't a detailed description at all but it was very blunt. She just told it like she saw it. When Andy asked Colleen what he looked like, the six-year-old paused and then expressed it the way she saw it, "Dad, *he was a big black mutha-fucker!*" That was all she could say. But Colleen did give Bodeen's license plate number to her father when they got to the car. It was one of those moments that make a Cop Dad so proud.

Andy didn't bother getting a statement from the bully. Andy felt he got what was coming to him for messing with his baby girl. The bully was lucky all he had was lizard soufflé is what Andy thought. The way Andy was feeling that day he probably would have beaten the kid to death. Whatever occurred, Andy saw that the bully was scared shitless.

The last they heard of the bully was he transferred to one of those special schools for kids with special needs.

Andy didn't seek out Bodeen right away. It wasn't until he noticed the drastic change in Colleen's confidence over the next few weeks that made him curious about this man. Colleen didn't scare easy anymore. Her big brothers teasing and scare tactics were nothing to her. At one time, she ran to Daddy's arms when her brothers picked on her. Now it seemed like she was waiting for that big black muthafucka to appear again and be her hero. Now Detective Andy Moretti was curious about this fellow.

A few more days passed before Andy looked up the license plate and put a name to a face. Colleen was right. That was a big black mean looking muthafucka. His measurements were 6'5" and 275 pounds of all muscle. Andy looked up his criminal record but it was sealed. He had the authority to get past that but he didn't pry. Andy had no intention on harassing the man that saved his daughter other than to thank him.

Later that day, Detective Andy Moretti drove to the inner city to collect his rents. He was in a relaxed mood that particular day. His pleasantries even caught the dealer Javier off guard. Javier had been late on his payments for three months straight. The last time Andy met with Javier, he had to threaten him with violence to get paid. Andy acted like that day never happened and nonchalantly asked Javier, "Hey Havi. I'm curious about someone that has come to my attention recently. Have you ever heard of man named Bodeen?"

"Oh! It's like that now?" Javier exclaimed with fear in his voice.

"What?" Andy asked oblivious to Javier's response.

"I know I'm late with my dues sometimes, Detective Moretti, but damn, it ain't no need to take extreme action like that for a few punk ass dollars. Here's your money, man! All of it! You proved your point," Javier stated as he turned his pockets inside out to show he didn't have any more money hidden.

Andy didn't inquire about Bodeen further. He just used the leverage to his advantage and took his back pay from Javier. Andy was surprised by this turn of events but he folded the money and stuffed it in his pocket.

The next morning, Andy Moretti decided to see what this Bodeen character was really about. Andy looked on the stove and saw some bacon and eggs covered in foil. He made some toast and a cup of tea. Andy heard some voices outside. It was the gardener telling his helpers something in Spanish. They all sounded very happy like it was payday. Andy looked at the calendar on the fridge and saw that it was the last Thursday of the month indeed. Andy put his breakfast on the table and went to the bedroom to get his checkbook. He knew the gardener would be knocking on the door at any minute for his payment.

By the time Andy signed his name on the check, there was a knock at the door. Andy walked to the door. He opened it. His eyes almost popped out of his skull. The gardener's wife was standing there looking gorgeous. She asked for the payment using the best English words in her vocabulary. Andy didn't understand a word she said. She just held her hand out and kept smiling until she had the check in hand. Andy closed the door and returned to the kitchen. Bodeen was sitting at the table. He was eating a piece of bacon off of Andy's plate. Word on the street was Andy was inquiring about him so Bodeen decided to give him what he wanted and let him meet the source up close and personal. Andy sat down at the table. They studied each other for a short period of time. Then they had a brief conversation and after that, they just clicked.

Andy was intrigued by the way Bodeen handled his business. He began to adopt the method for himself. He began to move more cautiously. Andy cut off all the low-level hustlers he extorted and made deals with more serious veteran crime figures that considered their hustle *"a business."* These new habits Andy helped him see things very clearly. That's why he had the discipline to leave good money behind when he transferred from the Rampart Station years before it became involved in controversy.

Detective Andy Moretti transferred to the Southwest Police Station and he's been here ever since. He gave up a lot when he made that move and it has been going downhill ever since. On top of his domestic life taking a toll on his happiness, he had to deal with the stress that was coming from the job.

It was election time in the city and the police were being pressed to fatten the stats. Detective Moretti hadn't made a high profile arrest in years and he needed something that was going to stick soon.

CHAPTER 13

It's Spring again...

THE SUN IS shining, the weather is sweet, and the birds are singing to a hip-hop beat. God did an excellent job on his end but as Coach walked outside to enjoy the beautiful spring day he saw that Man and his best friend still ruined everything beautiful. Coach despised the new K-9 fad everyone seemed to be involved in because there was dog shit everywhere! For centuries, dogs have pissed on trees and defecated in the dirt. Now all of a sudden every dog wants to take a shit on the concrete. Walking to the car was worse than trying to cross a field full of land mines. Coach looked to his left and saw his neighbor that just left the building from his own apartment and was now pissing in the corner of parking structure. It made no sense.

Spring is the time to fall in love. At least that's what the song says and Biz Markie seems to be credible when it comes to the topic of love. Coach took the cover off of his 64 Thunderbird. His classic automobile was gleaming. Coach was fitted for the occasion as well. He wore a fly white linen piece and his shirt, shoes, and sunglasses were the same color blue as his ride. Coach grabbed his DJ Daz "Good Groove" CD out of the trunk. He wanted to hear some of that smooth shit while he was rollin', ya dig. DJ Daz doesn't make ordinary mix tapes; he creates the soundtrack to your life. *"...folks get down in the sunshine, everybody needs the sunshine- my life my life my life my life-In the sunshine..."*

Coach hit the 90 Freeway and made his way to Marina Del Rey to meet LaTonya for a late lunch. Coach really wanted to make LaTonya his main lady but he had this gut feeling that she wouldn't stay committed to the team if life ever got tough. Coach didn't want to judge her but if he lost his job or three toes due to diabetes, LaTonya just didn't seem like the type that would stick around and stay down for the game. Matter o' fact, Coach didn't know any cute young girls that wanted a man with no job and two toes on his feet.

Coach entered Hal's Bar and Grill. He greeted everybody, even though he didn't know anyone there personally but that's how it is at Hal's, friendly and fly. Coach had Table 7 reserved and he sat down and waited for LaTonya to arrive. She walked in two minutes later but Coach pretended to be waiting for hours. Coach didn't even speak or greet LaTonya with a kiss. He just started talking shit.

"I see punctuality is not part of your precious program."

"I had to find a place to park," LaTonya explained.

"Uh-huh. And you also have a man to tend to," Coach expressed with conceit.

"Excuse me?" LaTonya asked with a little attitude in her voice.

"I didn't stutter or stumble. What's the problem? English not your home language? Well, then, let me correct myself. Suiei suru kemushi," Coach answered.

"You want to go swimming with a caterpillar? Uh huh I watch Kung Fu theater, too, nigga. You ain't no international playa," LaTonya had bruised his ego by laughing at his bilingual skills.

Coach had to let her know he was serious when he needed to be and she wasn't that slick. "Usted tiene un hombre y yo soy el número uno -ichiban toshi ga ookii. Now come here close to me and let me kisu shite mo ii."

"Now that is a language I can understand," LaTonya answered and started kissing Coach…for a long, long time.

The five-piece band was cranking out a cool jazz tune. Coach and LaTonya sat side by side instead of across from each other. Coach put his left arm around LaTonya and moved her a little closer so he could put his lyrics in her.

"So baby, how are you doing?" Coach said as he switched from his crazy antics and got into serious mode.

"You are something else. I'm doing wonderful. This is a nice place. How did you find out about this?" LaTonya replied with sneaky curiosity.

Her slick way of asking how many other women he had brought there before didn't bother Coach. He stopped trying to figure out why women do what they do long ago. It was still irritating that she couldn't just sit down and have a good time but it is what it is.

Coach told her the truth. "This is where the players play. Look around your environment. Everybody in here is fly. Look at that white man over there in the grey fitted suit. You have never seen a white dude with that much style in your life. That's *a Man*- not *The Man*, ya feel me?"

"Oh yes," LaTonya replied as she snuggled up closer to Coach and got a little more comfortable. "And I do like what I'm feeling."

The waiter approached and Coach ordered two glasses of wine. Coach then leaned over and put some words in LaTonya's ear that put her in sexy mood. He reached into his pocket and pulled out a cute little diamond bracelet. It was nothing spectacular, but it was perfect and right on time for the occasion.

"Aw! Thank you, baby! This is so nice!" LaTonya said as she held out her wrist so Coach could put it on. She kissed him real sweet and thanked him again.

"You got that coming to you, my love. It's a beautiful day and we haven't chilled like this together for a long time. So I just wanted take you somewhere special, buy you something nice, and eat your pussy real good. No extras on it. I know what's on your mind because your eyes are narrating the story."

LaTonya giggled because she knew he wasn't lying. The waiter brought over the wine. Coach and LaTonya made a toast. The waiter was standing there to take their food order but they didn't even notice him. He eventually walked away when they started kissing again. LaTonya got a cute sparkle in her eye when the buzz kicked in from the wine. She was so beautiful. Coach was in love with her dimples, her soft sexy voice, and with her style. She reminded him of a sister from the 1940's with her style of dress, class, and sex appeal.

Coach was in love with everything about LaTonya except the person beneath her character because Coach didn't know that part of LaTonya yet. Now they'd been together for a couple of years but had yet to weather a storm. The only disagreement they ever had was over East Coast versus West Coast rap. Coach saw LaTonya as a blessing and the ultimate prize that complemented him well. And she was one of the finest sisters he had seen in L.A. in a long time. Coach was ready to get serious with LaTonya but there was still a question mark in the back of his head. Coach felt she was perfect for *him* but he also had Jah to think about.

LaTonya must have felt the energy in the air or knew what Coach was thinking and decided to speak on it.

"We have a lovely chemistry Coach," she said as she took another sip of wine. She set down her glass and flashed a shy smile at Coach. "Do you ever think about taking our relationship to the next level… like as in wedding bells?"

"I think about it all the time, baby. One of my best joys in life is loving you. We look good together. We have everything in common that we need to live in righteous matrimony," Coach said as he reached her for hand. "But sometimes I wonder if you really love me like you say you do. We haven't even been tested yet. I just need to know if you will stand by our side and not fold under the pressure after our first real argument. To be true, I want to build a nation with you, LaTonya. You are the wife I've always envisioned. You are perfection."

LaTonya loved Coach. He was the husband that she had envisioned. LaTonya wasn't a mother yet but she felt like she would be good for Jah. That was her only hurdle and she was confident she would clear it with ease. LaTonya wanted her future husband to feel assured. LaTonya asked Coach, "So how does Jah feel about us?"

"He's digging' our vibe. He really likes you a lot. He thinks you look like a modern day Dorothy Dandridge."

"Oh yeah? I really like him, too. He's so mature for his age and so cute."

Coach and LaTonya got distracted from their conversation when the band went into a rendition of "I Want You."

"See baby? There's a message in good music," Coach mused. "But back to this family bond we were discussing. You know Jah is not looking for someone to replace his mother. He's content with the hand that life dealt him. But he does enjoy your company. Now I know you love Jah and I don't question that. But hypothetically speaking, what happens if we don't work—"

LaTonya gently placed her finger across Coach's lips and cut off his sentence. "Sshhhh, baby. I love both of you guys dearly and that is something you never have to worry about. I'm laying it on the line. *We* are in this together... and that means forever."

Coach looked into LaTonya's eyes and knew this was true and right. He loved that woman. If he had had a ring in his pocket, Coach would have proposed to LaTonya at that very moment. Their fate was sealed. Coach imagined how good it was going to feel having a wife to complete him and to build a future with.

Coach had even thought about having more kids with LaTonya and building that nation they were discussing earlier. This was very important to Coach. He and Jah were basically on Earth alone. Coach and Jah had no other immediate family. They had never been invited to a holiday dinner by a blood relative. They didn't know what it was like to have a funny uncle or a wise grandmother to tell them old stories and folk tales. They always wondered what that would be like. Well, Coach and Jah wouldn't have to wonder about experiencing those feelings anymore. They were going to finally have a full family now.

CHAPTER 14

NO HANDSHAKES WERE exchanged after Detective Moretti and Bodeen concluded their business underneath the 6th Street Bridge in downtown Los Angeles. They rarely talked on the phone other than to code speak where to meet, preferring to meet face to face. Sometimes when they needed to make quick contact, Detective Moretti would pull up fast in his Ford, flash his police lights and pull Bodeen's truck over to make it look like a routine traffic stop. Detective Moretti would hand Bodeen a ticket with his job objectives typed on it. But today they were dealing with an entirely different animal.

Detective Moretti had major problems. The pressure from his divorce and job was wearing Andy out to the point where he was ready to snap. His ex-wife Mia started out as a thorn in his side but now she was a pain in his ass. Andy partially blamed himself for the problem but he planned on fixing it the best way he knew how: by eliminating it.

A few months back, Andy Moretti fucked up and dropped by his old house, which belonged to the ex-wife now, to give her some money he was already three months late paying to get her off of his back. The kids were gone at the babysitter's even though Mia didn't work or do a damn thing that he could see other than get high. Mia was high as a Georgia Pine off of vodka and amphetamines. Andy himself was high and horny and he thought that if he gave her some good dick she would keep the Child Support Enforcement from garnishing his check. But he ended up fucking Mia too good and got her pregnant again. Mia was already bordering on being an unfit mother to the children they already had. She was in no condition mentally or physically to have another baby but she decided to keep it just to fuck with Andy. Mia actually didn't even tell Andy she was pregnant until the second trimester so he couldn't talk her into an abortion. Andy's finances were going diminish rapidly with the addition of the extra mouth to feed and that was only the half of it. Mia's treachery and use of prescription drugs as well as the hard recreational drugs put the unborn child in harm's way.

By a mere coincidence, Andy bumped Into her OB/GYN at the market. Her OB/GYN was one of the nose candy guys who got busted by Andy and the doc had paid him to hush it up so they'd known each other a long time. Andy was shocked to hear for the first time that his child was going to be born with multiple birth defects. The child was going to suffer from abnormalities like cardiac malformation, low birth weight, deformed limbs, poor muscle control, brain damage, and withdrawal syndrome because of Mia's poor choices. The doctor informed Andy that the child would most probably be in and out of the hospital most of his life.

The medical bills were going to wipe him out, not to mention the stress of having a kid who wouldn't be able to care for himself or live a normal life. Andy Moretti knew he had to kill the bitch. It was going to be simple and painless. Andy was going to force Mia's supplier to give her a hot dose so she would O'D.

But before he could make contact with her dealer, her dealer was found dead with a shotgun blast to the back of the head on his front porch.

Andy was trying to make himself believe that there was a slight chance that the baby might not be his. Andy thought about waiting until after the birth to be 100% sure but he couldn't take that risk. Detective Moretti made the call.

When Bodeen showed up, he knew Detective Moretti was stressed out. Andy Moretti looked disheveled even though he was clean with a nice suit on. Bodeen didn't bother to inform Detective Moretti that he was the one that eliminated his ex-wife's supplier. It was none of his business, plus it would have just complicated things. Detective Moretti put a lot of money in Bodeen's pockets over the years as well as a license to kill. He didn't want to mess a deal like that up.

Bodeen casually suggested that he become Mia's new supplier so they could stick to Detective Moretti's original plan. Bodeen already had her drugs of choice since the day he had cleaned out Mario's house after he murdered him. Mia's drug abuse was already in her medical records so by no means would Andy be implicated. For a moment, Detective Moretti became suspicious about Bodeen already having access to the specific prescription drugs Mia was hooked on. They were not that accessible. But then reason took over and he remembered who Bodeen was and figured a person with Bodeen's reputation surely had access to whatever the fuck he wanted.. And frankly, Andy Moretti needed to get rid of the bitch so the other 99 problems he had would at least be manageable.

Detective Moretti could only offer Bodeen a small down payment with a promise to pay him the rest after he collected the money from Mia's life insurance policy. But Bodeen didn't work for partial payments. He felt disrespected that Detective Moretti wasted his time carrying chump change in his pocket. Detective Moretti was one of his business partners but Bodeen didn't owe him anything. This was a murder business, not a payday loan contract. Bodeen stared at him as he was getting the urge to kill him for showing a sign of weakness.

But Detective Moretti was no punk-ass street dealer. He knew what was up. For the first time in a long time, he was completely focused. He knew Bodeen was physically stronger but he suspected Bodeen couldn't out-think him.

"*If* you decide to take this job, here is a little pocket change to play with while you do your recon work," Andy said as he handed an envelope to Bodeen. "Give me a decision by Friday. If you accept the job, I'll pay you half up front and the rest when you execute the plan. Cool?"

Bodeen really wanted to kill him now for lying to him but he needed Detective Moretti alive more than dead. Bodeen nodded, shoved the money in his pocket, and left without another word.

And with that settled, Detective Moretti still had another major problem. Ever since he transferred to the Southwest Police Department, Detective Moretti hadn't brought in a case worth mentioning. His superiors were threatening to transfer Detective Moretti to Administrative Vice where he would take on less prestigious assignments like bicycle theft or busting up illegal bingo games. That would damage his ego as well as his respect in the streets. The wheels started turning in his head. Detective Moretti needed to collar a major criminal. It needed to be something big that would stick and make him look like a hero so when his ex-wife met her untimely death he would get sympathy from the department.

CHAPTER 15

CORDEDIUS MONTGOMERY, THE notorious kingpin from Detroit, had a little problem. He put in a call to the Problem Solver. Cordedius always liked the way Bodeen handled his business but he wasn't in awe by his legend like most folks. Detroit produced some of the most ruthless killers in America and he had seen some of the best during his 40-year tenure in the crime world. Bodeen himself was no stranger to the Motor City. That's where he hit his prime and earned major stripes. He buried quite a few bodies while he was working for Cordedius' organization. Bodeen even learned a few new tricks to use in his trade while working in Detroit a few years back.

Cordedius Montgomery was connected up high and well respected. Cordedius was an old muthafucka and he got that way from being smart and playing by the rules. But we all know in this game we call the underworld that is still not enough. Even a known crime figure with political connections like Cordedius Montgomery was still subject to being charged with a life sentence for operating a continuing criminal enterprise.

Cordedius and his people treated Bodeen well when he was coming up as a youth. The only reason Bodeen stayed clear of the whole team thing was because he was honest enough with himself to know he lacked loyalty. A fucked up past will do that to a person.

Bodeen worked as an independent contractor, if you will, but if he were to join a crew it would definitely be with Cordedius Montgomery and his organization. So be that as it may, Bodeen was always the best choice when a team needed a free agent.

"Black ass Bodeen! Damn that muthafucka's mean!" was how Cordedius Montgomery greeted Bodeen when he answered the phone.

Bodeen was excited when he heard Cordedius Montgomery's voice on the line. For one, he respected him and two, he knew how to put some real money in a nigga's pocket. Bodeen really showed his enthusiasm when he replied, "Hhmmmmmm!"

Cordedius Montgomery knew Bodeen had no passion for engaging in conversation so he cut straight to the chase. "I need your services, big man. You remember my man Alonzo? You know the one in charge of the drop and load? Well, he found out that the Feds have their nose in his butt and he's spooked. Alonzo saw the assholes taking pictures on the roof after he picked up our last load. Now, the way it sounds I believe they are after our supplier, not him. I told Alonzo to lay low first and then get out of town for a while until our peoples on the inside give me a heads up, but I didn't mean for him to leave right at that moment... and I damn sho' didn't mean for him to leave with ten bricks of the Raw Hoppy in his possession. I'm talkin' about ten muthafuckin' bricks of those wicked Kangaroos, ya dig? I'm talking about that raw uncut that got the country a war!... From the hoppy fields of Afghanistan, ya dig? I can step on each one ten times and still flat line every fiend in the state. Alonzo doesn't know what he's holding. He thinks it is our regular batch ready for distro. The nervous muthafucka even tossed his phone so I can't even talk to him. That scary sum'o'bitch done lost his goddamn mind. Knowing his dumb ass, he's going to dump those bricks at the wholesale price and bring back the money thinking he did us a favor. He does not even know he's killing us! But on the good side, Alonzo can't go nowhere east of Detroit and dump those bricks without drawing suspicion from our connections. The only other folks that can even handle that amount of bricks are those Vietcongs out there in Alhambra. So I know he's heading west to the cut house. We have a little hideaway spot that we use for situations like this in Pomona or Pacoima—one of those muthafuckas—you know, the one off the 60 Freeway. I can guarantee that's where he's headed. Now listen, I'm going to send my Heavy Hitters out there to handle this business with you. It will be like a reunion. You savage muthafuckas are kindred spirits and need

to be around each other to share the sick things y'all have in common."
Cordedius Montgomery laughed at his last statement.

Predictably, Bodeen found no humor in it at all. Bodeen had worked
for Cordedius before and he knew how he operated. If he was sending The
Heavy Hitters, meaning Abdullah Joe and Bobby Boyd, they were coming
for more than just bricks of raw heroin. It was either some big money
involved or Alonzo sang a song for the Feds.

Abdullah Joe and Bobby Boyd are pure executioners. That's what they
do. Their reputations demanded you refer to them by their first and last
name like Al Capone. They don't pick up packages; they don't do drops.
They just kill muthafuckas. Bodeen knew them very well. They showed
him the business aspect of killing when Bodeen became serious about his
art. It would be hard to compare levels of ruthlessness as far as who were
better killers but Abdullah Joe and Bobby Boyd definitely had more bodies
than Bodeen.

Whatever area Abdullah Joe and Bobby Boyd worked in, that state
became the Murder Capital for that year. One year, DC was the Murder
Capital, the next year it was Virginia, then it was Maryland, the year after
that it was Detroit, Michigan, and Detroit seems to have held the title for
the last few years. Cordedius Montgomery controlled all those areas and
a few more due in part to the carnage Abdullah Joe and Bobby Boyd left
behind. Weak hustlers and soft punks weren't supposed to have shit as far
as Abdullah Joe and Bobby Boyd was concerned so they cleaned niggas
out. They were ruthless individuals on their own, but when they worked
together? They left more dead bodies than the troops in the Middle East.

Back when Bodeen worked with them, they had niggas on the street so
scared, regular working citizens refused to buy nice cars because they didn't
want Bodeen, Abdullah, and Bobby to think they were getting money from
hustling. Most of the hustlers that Cordedius Montgomery wholesales to,
buy from him to this very day out of fear of what the Three Diablos would
do to them.

Cordedius Montgomery confirmed Bodeen's theory when he continued, "So I need you and The Hitters to go see Alonzo and get my bricks
before he gives my shit to those Vietnamese for less than what they are
worth. Now he'll probably have some traveling money lying around so you

can slap him up, take that, and divide that money amongst yourselves as a bonus... if you choose to. But I want The Hitters to deal solely with Alonzo while you get the bricks. Nothing else! You get fifty racks for your services. They are going to be flying in tonight on the red eye. They'll holla at you when they touch down. Easy!"

"If I got to choose a coast, I got to choose the East I live out there, so don't go there

But that don't mean a nigga can't rest in the Wes-t See some nice breasts in the West

Smoke some nice sess in the West..."

It wasn't hard spotting Abdullah Joe and Bobby Boyd coming through the LAX terminal. Only some country cats from Detroit would come to Los Angeles on a nice spring morning wearing Steve Harvey suits and long trench coats. Bodeen looked down at their feet and shook his head. He always wondered why out-of-towners' idea of blending in with the California Culture was wearing shoes with no socks. It always disturbed him. The Diablos greeted each other. They were happy to see one another but didn't show it. They didn't waste time hugging and reminiscing. They just performed a unique handshake they only knew the meaning of. They hopped in Bodeen's truck and hit the freeway.

Abdullah Joe said, "Turn on the radio so I can get into the groove."

Bodeen knew the code. Bodeen pressed the number 4 on his CD player and it opened the secret compartment on the floor in the back-seat. Abdullah Joe peered inside the secret spot. There was a .44 Magnum semi-automatic pistol loaded with exploding bullets, a .357 Magnum, a .45 caliber semi-automatic not loaded, a .38 caliber revolver, a .32 caliber semi-automatic, and something that appeared to be a ballpoint pen, but it was actually a pen gun that fires a single .22 caliber bullet.

"Man, you got some sweet heat. You brought the right shit, too, cuz you know it's a possibility we might have to get those bricks back from them Gooks if Alonzo dumped them already... but I doubt it. He's driving from Detroit so if my mathematics ain't off we should get to the cut house a few hours before he arrives."

"Good, that gives us time to stop by the hotel so we could change. Two thug lookin' niggas wearing trench coats in sunny California makes us kind of obvious don't ya think, *man?*", Bobby Boyd chimed in, pronouncing man as *mayne*.

Bodeen caught Bobby Boyd's eye through the rear view mirror—that was his way of saying he agreed.

Abdullah Joe and Bobby Boyd checked themselves into the hotel and Bodeen stayed in the ride. He wanted to get his mind right.

Within minutes, Abdullah Joe and Bobby Boyd returned. If they wanted to avoid looking like tourists, they surely didn't try too hard. Bobby Boyd had on a mint green linen short set and white dress shoes with no socks. Abdullah Joe had on a royal blue short set, powder blue loafers with no socks, and a powder blue cap. Since they were both in their early forties, they looked like two uncles that were visiting from down south. Unlike Bodeen, Bobby Boyd and Abdullah Joe didn't look menacing on sight. They were both some thick dudes that stood over 6 feet tall, not strikingly handsome but they wouldn't have a problem getting a prom date. They didn't possess brute strength but underneath those goofy short sets, they were pure muscle with brutal tactics. They had the ability to kill with guns, knives, or bare hands because that's what they did and they were great at it.

The Three Diablos pulled up to the hideaway. It was a nice modest house in a well-kept neighborhood. The police definitely wouldn't come here looking for a fugitive from Detroit without the help of a snitch.

Alonzo's Cadillac was already in the driveway. Bodeen found that peculiar. Unless Alonzo's Cadillac had wings and ran on jet fuel, there was no way he could get to L.A. from Detroit that fast. Bodeen also noticed The Hitters weren't taken by surprise by Alonzo's early arrival. Bodeen knew right then and there that Alonzo must have violated a rule internal within the organization. He was going to get punished for that. Bodeen wasn't the least bit bothered that they were keeping information from him. He wasn't a soldier in Cordedius Montgomery's organization and truthfully it wasn't any of his business. The less he knew, the better off he would be. He was there to do the job he was paid to do, nothing more, nothing less.

Bodeen and the Heavy Hitters exited the truck. Bodeen grabbed a large suitcase from the back. Abdullah Joe and Bobby Boyd gave Bodeen that *what the fuck is that* look. Bodeen closed the back of the SUV and said nothing. Finally, Bobby Boyd had to ask. "What the fuck are you going to do with that?"

"Damage." Bodeen said.

As they walked up to the house, Bodeen felt the hood of Alonzo's car. It was cold. Abdullah Joe knocked on the door three times. There was no answer. The funky scent of bacon and eggs cooking in old grease were seeping through the cracks of the door. Abdullah Joe knocked again but twice this time. He reached into his pocket and took out the keys. They let themselves in. Alonzo was in the kitchen in his pajamas with a doo rag on his head, standing over the stove, frying his breakfast in a cast iron skillet.

Alonzo looked up without surprise and said, "You big burly niggas always seem to show up when you smell food cooking... and lookee here, Bodeen. Damn, it's been a long time. You must be getting some money cuz you ain't ugly as you use to be... Damn, Bobby Boyd where'd you cop that light green suit and white shoes? Nigga, you look like a slice of key lime pie."

"How come you light-skinned assholes think y'all so cute? You the same color as sperm. You ol' recessive-gene-having ass niggas make me sick. I thought that ugly plaid shirt that you're wearing was a bedspread," Bobby Boyd roasted Alonzo.

Abdullah Joe was still laughing when he said, "Grab your grub Alonzo and come on in the living room. We need to have a little talk about your little situation."

Realizing what was about to happen, Alonzo was no longer hungry but he grabbed his plate anyway and carried it to the front room. Bodeen stayed in the kitchen so he could search the cabinets for the bricks of raw. Bodeen searched the cupboards and didn't see anything but a few dishes and some old canned goods. Bodeen concentrated on his job only but he couldn't help but hear Alonzo trying to explain himself because his voice went up about ten octaves.

Abdullah Joe popped on Alonzo for raising his voice and hit him dead in the center of his forehead with brass knuckles. The blow didn't drop him but Alonzo was dizzy as a muthafucka. Bobby Boyd grabbed Alonzo by the arm and guided him to the dining room table chair where his breakfast was getting cold.

Bodeen didn't find anything in the kitchen so he moved to the other rooms of the house. Bodeen walked past the Heavy Hitters without paying them the least bit of attention. What they were doing was as normal to Bodeen as the sun rising every morning. Bodeen went into one of the bedrooms. He searched the closet. He didn't see anything in there. He checked under the bed and under the mattress. Nothing. Bodeen proceeded to go into the other bedroom. He heard Alonzo lying under the pressure. Bodeen didn't even know what Alonzo was lying about. The way Alonzo was stuttering and he didn't even have a gun pointed at his head was a dead giveaway. Bodeen was excellent at interpreting body language and voice inflictions.

Abdullah Joe was talking to Alonzo more like a friend than a soon-to-be dead man. "Lonzo, Lonzo, Lonzo," he said in a placating tone. "We go too far back for you to be acting like this. It is more disappointing than anything. We're connected! You're set for life! I mean, damn! How much more do you want?

"I-I-I fucked up. I just fucked up," Alonzo pleaded but it wasn't enough. There was no reason for Alonzo to have fucked up so he had no excuses that were justifiable for his actions.

"Go 'head and get some breakfast in you, Alonzo. You look sluggish. You want some cheese to go on those eggs? Bobby Boyd, go get my man Lonzo some of that Parmee-zee-an cheese out the cupboard," Abdullah Joe suggested.

"Listen man, I ain't no rat if that's what your insinuating. I didn't give up anybody from our organization—" Alonzo defended his position but Abdullah Joe cut him off.

"We know you didn't snitch on us. We know everything that happened already. But we just want to hear it from you."

Bodeen hit pay dirt in the second bedroom. He found eight bricks of the Raw in the dresser drawer. But there was supposed to be ten. He opened Alonzo's smaller suitcase and found the other two. Bodeen dumped out the clothes in the suitcase and put the rest of the Raw in it. He rolled the suitcase in to the living room and said, "Ten's in there."

Alonzo tried to use it for leverage. "See? Look! I didn't touch one brick. I wouldn't fuck y'all over!"

"See what? I don't see shit," Abdullah Joe nonchalantly replied.

"C'mon Abdullah Joe! Why are you fucking with my head... Ten bricks of the big bad boy! Count 'em!" Alonzo pleaded.

"Talk to me Lonzo and give me the real, man. Like I said, we go too far back for this silly shit. Man up, nigga," said Abdullah Joe as he gave Alonzo one last chance to come clean.

"All right man, all right. Remember that run I made last month to New York?" Alonzo began to confess.

"No, I don't. But finish your story."

As Alonzo was fessing up, Bodeen turnbed back into the bedroom to continue his search. Alonzo saw him return to the room and tried to stop him without drawing too much suspicion.

"Slow your roll, Bodeen. You got what you came here for. Respect mines, youngster, ain't nothing left in there but my personal shit. This is CMO business, son. Play your position now," Alonzo checked the free agent Bodeen like he was the same 18-year-old kid he met years earlier.

Bodeen acted like he didn't hear Alonzo talking to him but his ears were wide open.

Abdullah Joe played the Good Cop and made Alonzo feel comfortable by agreeing with him. "Yeah Bodeen, we good in here... let that man's personal belongings be. I'm quite sure Lonzo will offer a cash donation for sparing his life after he tells us the truth. There's no need to rob him. Ain't that right, Lonzo?"

Alonzo nodded yes, but Bodeen moved towards the bedroom. Bodeen gave Bobby Boyd a hand signal that he wasn't finished tossing the room and he was going to find whatever else might be there. Bobby Boyd nodded in approval.

As Bodeen inspected the bedroom, Alonzo came clean with his story but it seemed like he was more worried about what Bodeen was doing in the room.

"When I made that trip up to New York... I-I took Stacy with me."

"What the fuck you want to do that for, mayne? And who the fuck is Stacy?" Bobby Boyd asked.

"Pastor Bryant's daughter," Alonzo stated with shame on his face.

"That young triflin' bitch? Out of all the dumb bitches in Detroit, you take the most scandalous one in the city on a heroin run? What in the fuck were you thinking? Pastor Bryant, the Councilman! The only man that won't take bribes from street cats, even with the entire city falling apart. Boy, oh boy! That was an asinine move. Lord have mercy, you sure know how to pick em'… so what else happened?" Abdullah Joe asked.

"Are you sure, man? It gets worse," Alonzo asked. He didn't get an answer from The Hitters so he continued. "Well, we get pulled over by this cop and the muthafucka is a friend of her father."

"Awww shit! Please go on. This is better than television, mayne." Bobby Boyd encouraged.

"Well, then this shit is about to win an Emmy. That punk ass cop is fuckin' Stacy… yeah, ain't that a bitch? He started going off calling her all kinds of sluts and hoes and threatening to charge me with the Mann Act and transporting an underage girl across state lines. Then the muthafucka tells her that if she gets out of my car and leaves with him, he won't hamper her father's chances for re-election… well, I get ready to let her out of the car, and then that crazy bitch goes off saying she ain't going nowhere with him cuz she's too young to be tending to some old man cop that's always constipated. She needs a man that's regular…."

"You got to be bullshittin' me Lonzo," Abdullah Joe stated more out of shock and not because he didn't believe his story.

"Man, I can't make no shit like that up."

Meanwhile, Bodeen was checking the room for loose cash so he and The Heavy Hitters could have something to blow at the strip clubs later on. Bodeen checked the inside pocket of the jacket that was hanging on the chair. He reached in and pulled out about 4,000 bucks. That was a little over 1,300 each. That seemed fair. But he wasn't done. That suspicious look Alonzo had in his eye when Bodeen walked toward the room let him know there was more. Bodeen stood in the corner of the room and used his eyes. He checked the ceiling to see if there were any openings. He scanned the floor.

Bingo! The pattern of the heavy dresser drawer was indented in the carpet two inches from where it was stationed. The dust particles in the deep pattern showed it probably hadn't been moved in years until recently. Bodeen moved the dresser out from the wall. The back panel made out of thin plywood wasn't secure. Bodeen opened it expecting to find about 50 to 100K but it was like a damn fully-funded IRA account in cash. About three million dollars neatly stacked and packed in plastic wrap. Bodeen, the man of few words and with ice water in his veins wished he could have kept his mouth shut but he was overwhelmed by the sight of the money and blurted out, "Damn!"

It got the attention of Abdullah Joe and Bobby Boyd because if Bodeen spoke with emotion, they knew it was something serious. Abdullah Joe shouted into the room.

"What you find, big man?"

Bodeen walked to the door and tossed Bobby Boyd the 4,000 dollars wrapped in a rubber band. Bodeen stepped back and stashed the cash in his suitcase with the false bottom. It barely fit. Bobby Boyd crept silently across the carpet and peeked into the bedroom. He saw Bodeen bent over packing something that was wrapped in plastic but he couldn't make out what it was. Bodeen grabbed his case and returned to the living room. He posted up on the wall. Alonzo was still telling his story.

"...That fool calls for backup and they found some blow in my pocket and my pistol. They take me down and tell me that even if they drop the pimping and pandering charges to save face for Pastor Bryant, I would still have to register as a sex offender. Then they said if didn't take the dope charge and give up somebody I was fucked. I can't go home to my wife and kids with a Sex Offender Jacket. How is that going to look? If I took no deal at all, they were talking about stacking each count and running wild—160 years... I damn sure can't go back inside... another jolt would crack me. So I gave up that new connect. He's just a new punk in the game. It ain't going to hurt us none and I know our insiders at the police department confirmed I didn't mention anything that had to do with our organization. Now that I won't do under any circumstance and you know that about me. I've been there and done ten years straight on that," Alonzo finished.

"Well, that connect you snitched on was connected, Lonzo. He was connected to those police down in Flint that sell that stepped-on bullshit. His people were testing him. They were up on the bust before it even went down. Those bricks right there are packed with pure laxative. They put the word out that if we didn't give you up to them or take care of you in house, we lose our protection and privileges in Flint. Now we will never give you up to those crackers so get that shit out your mind, that's not happening..." Abdullah Joe paused and pulled a Tech 9 from his waistband. Alonzo farted soon as he saw that barrel come up.

He immediately tried to bargain for his life. "Listen, I'll give y'all a million dollars to let me disappear and I promise to never be heard from again."

"No, no man! We need three million, mayne!" Bobby Boyd laughed as he made up the number but the joke was on him.

"Then I won't have enough to live on!" Alonzo whined, pissed at Bobby Boyd's greed.

Abdullah Joe interrupted them, "Stop all that bickering and let me think on this. Eat your food and relax your nerves."

Alonzo started to nibble on the bacon. The sight of those plain eggs getting cold on the plate started to make Bobby Boyd sick.

"You ain't gon' put no seasoning on those eggs, mayne? That's how them powdered eggs look in the county jail. Sprinkle some of that Parmesan on there and liven those shits up or something."

Alonzo looked down at the lukewarm eggs and Bobby Boyd did have a point. He crumbled up his bacon into bits and let them fall on the eggs. He doused it with the Parmesan cheese. He began to eat. It wasn't half bad. Alonzo relaxed a bit more when Abdullah Joe put his gun back in his waistband.

Abdullah Joe and Bobby Boyd stared out of the window and didn't say a word until Alonzo finished his last bite.

"All right Lonzo... I've been thinking here long and hard. We've been contracted to kill you and we are supposed to do it because that is our job. But we like you, Lonzo, and we don't want it to come to that," Abdullah Joe paused when Alonzo started coughing. When Alonzo stopped coughing Abdullah continued. "You fucked up, Lonzo, and put yourself in a terrible situation so that's on you. We're family. We ain't gon' kill you... we are going to let you just kill yourself."

Alonzo started coughing violently. He couldn't get a word out. Sweat started pouring down his face like a fat man full of sodium. Alonzo was trying to vomit, but it wouldn't come out and felt like his throat was closing.

Alonzo began to convulse before he blacked out. Alonzo's body went limp. He was done.

Bobby Boyd started a tune, "If you want to catch a rat…"

Abdullah Joe joined in, "…put-the-cheese-on-the-trap!"

Bobby Boyd grabbed the green can of Parmesan cheese mixed with rat poison and cyanide and destroyed the evidence.

Abdullah Joe and Bobby Boyd started scanning the house looking for the money Alonzo said he had. They figured if he was offering a million to let him live, then he had to be sitting on two or more. And knowing Alonzo, he had it with him. He loved his family but not enough to leave his life savings with them unattended. Alonzo didn't have the type of wife that would stay down for him. If she had ever found out about that young hoe Stacy, she would have broke north with all that dirty money with the kids in tow and never looked back.

Bodeen kicked back on the couch and let The Hitters do their thing. When they entered the bedroom where Alonzo had had everything stashed, Bodeen didn't panic. He knew he lined the dresser drawer up perfectly over the dented carpet. But he was hoping they didn't see the unattached plywood on the back. Bobby Boyd's aggressiveness camouflaged the loose plywood when he flipped the dresser drawers over.

"Damn Bobby, you don't have to break the shit. This pad does belong to our organization… the furniture, too." Abdullah Joe yelled as he bent over to help Bobby Boyd lift the dresser back upright. Abdullah Joe and Bobby Boyd checked under the bed and flipped the mattress over. The plastic cover on the mattress reminded Bobby Boyd of the plastic he saw Bodeen place in his suitcase. He played it cool until they finished the search. Bobby Boyd went into his pocket and pulled out the 4,000 dollars Bodeen tossed him earlier. He divided it up three ways.

"Well, we have $1,360 apiece to fuck off tonight at the clubs." Bobby Boyd tossed Bodeen his cut. Bodeen almost didn't accept it but he knew it would draw suspicion. Bobby Boyd was testing him, too, to see if he would bite. Bodeen passed that test, but Bobby Boyd didn't let up.

"Now what are we going to do with Alonzo? I'm not trying to drive this fool nowhere, mayne. I wish we could wrap him up and bury him in the backyard. Say Bodeen, you got any plastic in your damage kit?"

"Mm-hmm." Bodeen opened up his suitcase for the Heavy Hitters to see. He pulled out a small plastic bag for the head. He pulled out another sheet of plastic big enough to cover the body. Bodeen took out a five-pound bag of lime and tossed it near Alonzo's dead corpse. Bodeen casually kept the suitcase open long enough for Bobby Boyd to scan all the contents that were visible to his eyes. Bobby Boyd was satisfied for the moment. He was actually impressed by Bodeen's instruments of death he carried in his bag. They taught him well.

Bobby Boyd acknowledged it, "Killing is your business, Bodeen and business is looking good, mayne. Where in the hell did you get that Falun Gong Chinese torture instrument? I've been trying to cop one of those for the last two years."

Bodeen pulled out two Falun Gong instruments and tossed him one. Bodeen hit his chest twice and gave Bobby Boyd the peace sign. Bobby Body returned the gesture.

After Bodeen and The Hitters buried Alonzo, they straightened up the house and locked it good. They hit the 60 Freeway west and headed back to Los Angeles.

Bodeen put on some of that Bumpy Knuckles… yeah, that real gangsta shit. The booming system was on blast. Bodeen was driving smooth and steady, but in fact, truth be told, he was downright giddy like a schoolgirl. He couldn't wait to get home and count that money. This was the lick he's been waiting to hit. Bodeen was ready to celebrate. He planned to get his second piece of pussy too. Glimmers of light were starting to shine on the dark side.

CHAPTER 16

AFTER THEY RETURNED from the Alonzo job, Abdullah Joe and Bobby Boyd stayed with Bodeen for another five days and partied hard.

Bodeen even had real sexual intercourse with a beautiful woman that actually liked him, enjoyed being with him, and desired to have him on his second go-around but it didn't compare to the feelings he still had for Angie that haunted him often. The pretty woman was truly ideal for him and I call her that not just for her cute facial features, but Bodeen could only dream of Angie and he didn't even bother remembering her name.

* * *

No pleasurable thoughts were roaming in Detective Andy Moretti's head. He couldn't think straight. His life was getting progressively worse. A month had passed and he hadn't heard a word from Bodeen. Andy was getting desperate. Some of his ATF friends he was in cahoots with were resorting to sticking bogus cases on civilians and first-time offenders that was oblivious to the law to keep their numbers up. They gave an 18 year-old kid that was just the driver in a fast food chain robbery 165 years on his first offense. The actual robbers with priors only got two years. They cut a deal and fingered the kid. It was a cold game in the streets and the police and the criminals was playing hardball.

Matter of fact, Bodeen had forgotten all about Detective Moretti's problem. That was the last thing on his mind. Bodeen was doing big things. The three million dollars he got from Alonzo, plus the two he had already saved put him on easy street. He purchased the apartment building he lived in and a laundromat in full for 3.5 million. Bodeen kept two apartments for himself. He had one on the first floor and the one he already lived in on the second. He remodeled them so he could have access to both apartments without being seen. Nobody knew he occupied the apartment on the first floor. Being cautious and staying one step ahead of the wolves is a virtue in Bodeen's business. Bodeen's antennas had been up ever since Bobby Boyd saw his wall safe open as he was passing by heading into the guest room upstairs. Bodeen wasn't sure if Bobby Boyd saw anything but he wasn't taking any chances.

After Bodeen purchased the laundromat, he moved the safe over there and placed it in the floor under the dryers. He owned two income properties and had a few dollars short of two million in cash to sit on. Bodeen was going to be set for a minute. He turned down all jobs over the next couple of months. Bodeen also vowed to himself that he wouldn't even take a job unless it netted more than his combined monthly income he was making with his legit businesses. But do realize that by no means was Bodeen retiring; his price just went up.

CHAPTER 17

THE 4TH OF July fireworks were nothing compared to Detective Andy Moretti's explosion when he found out that his ex-wife was about to go into labor. She was barely seven months pregnant but the doctor warned him this could happen because of her drug use. Andy tried calling Bodeen one last time. He answered.

"Christ man, where in the fuck have you been? I've been calling you for fucking two months now. You are really fucking me over! You know who I talked to today? I talked to my ex-wife today. How is that possible? I found it strange because the last conversation I had with the cunt three months ago should have been the last. Now the fuckin' evil bitch just went into labor. You got to fix this shit, Bodeen. I don't give a fuck how you do it at this point, just get it done. Episcopalian Hospital, 8th floor room 806… premium pay!"

Fifty thousand dollars was premium pay for that type of hit. Bodeen informed Andy that his ex-wife was pregnant and that counted for two bodies. They settled on 70k. Bodeen didn't even want the job. He didn't need the money but he still needed Detective Moretti. Detective Moretti had enough dirt on Bodeen that would automatically get him the death penalty with no deal to negotiate. Bodeen would rather die in the streets and meet with the devil face to face than wait in a jail cell for years before he was allowed to die in a gas chamber.

Executing a hit in a hospital posed a challenge but it wasn't as difficult as it may seem. If the job were planned to perfection it would work to his advantage. There are thousands of people that walk through a hospital on a daily basis. Anybody could be a suspect. Bodeen got two syringes out of his damage case. He filled them with a poison he concocted that killed instantly. It was far more sophisticated than that shit The Hitters fed Alonzo. This was the stuff the CIA used on the terrorists overseas. Bodeen also added a high dose of Mia's drugs of choice so when the toxicology reports came back, Andy would be in the clear of any funny business. Then Bodeen packed his pistol with the silencer, just in case he needed to adjust on the fly.

Bodeen entered the employee's entrance of Episcopalian Hospital. Bodeen was wearing a pair of gray dress slacks, a white collared shirt with a striped tie, and long white lab coat like the ones that doctors wear. He had a clipboard in his hand and a stethoscope around his neck. The only odd thing that stood out on Bodeen was the name on his badge. It read Dr. Abram Goldsmith MD. Bodeen was a professional and had all areas covered. Bodeen wore a Star of David necklace around his neck just in case some nosey asshole questioned his Jewish attribute.

Bodeen made his way to the west wing virtually unnoticed, until an elderly Jewish woman that lost her way in the huge hospital stopped him. Her vision wasn't the best but it wasn't hard to spot a big black man in a long white coat.

"Hi uh, Dr Goldsmith." The old lady checked her glasses, looked at Bodeen, looked at the nametag, and then looked up at Bodeen again confused.

Bodeen really threw the old lady off of her game when he replied, "Ma koreh?" (*What's up?*)

"Ahh, atah medaber 'ivrit? (*do you speak Hebrew*) My Hebrew is not as good as it use to be. I was born here but my parents are from Jerusalem. Do you know where that is? Um, meayin ata?" (*where are you from*)

"Azov oti be-sheket, lady!" (*leave me alone*) Bodeen replied as politely as he could.

"I don't understand your accent, son. My Hebrew is kind of rusty I haven't used it in many years. My Hebrew is probably just as bad as your English. Hahahahaha! Oh boy, those words are rolling off your tongue so fast. Uh, efshar ledaber yoter le-at?" (*could you speak more slowly*)

"Bitch! Get-the-fuck-out-of-my face!"

Bodeen took the stairs to the eighth floor. That was a close call. He was lucky that old lady was half blind. Bodeen impressed himself by the way he was able to dazzle her with the Hebrew dialect he picked up. He was sure glad he watched that episode of Seinfeld.

When Bodeen got to the floor, he took a quick peek from behind the door to get a feel for the environment. Bodeen needed to create a simple diversion, slip into the room, and give Mia the hot shot. Bodeen put on a surgical mask and some reading glasses. He opened the door and eased out onto the main floor. Bodeen started at room 801. He walked up to the door, glanced at the chart, and looked in on each patient like he was making his rounds. He was actually looking for an unoccupied room near Mia's. The first three rooms were all occupied with pregnant women looking bloated and feeling miserable. All the beautiful Ethiopian and Haitian nurses talking in their thick accents were all starting to look like Angie. It was getting hard for Bodeen to keep focus. Bodeen got dizzy for a second and broke out into a light sweat. He found relief when he hit pay dirt at room 805. Bodeen walked into the bathroom. He took off his surgical mask and eyeglasses and threw cold water on his face. Bodeen cupped his huge hands and let them fill with the cold water. He placed his face inside the pool and just held it there for a few seconds.

Suddenly the door opened. Bodeen lifted his head up but his eyes were squinted from the water falling down his face. The nurse was startled by Bodeen's massive figure in the room as well and she let out a scream. She said something in a foreign dialect and quickly dispersed. Bodeen wiped his eyes with the sleeve of his jacket and tried to get a good look at the lady. He only got a glimpse of her profile and once again he could only see images of Angie. But he did make a mental note of the unique style of braids the Nurse wore her hair in. She had on a teal short sleeve top with matching drawstring bottoms. She was also carrying a baby. Bodeen knew she got a full look at him. He wasn't too worried about being seen by a witness at this point but he never took chances. Bodeen was quite sure she worked there because of her attire so he would be back to pay her a visit at the end of her shift.

Bodeen pulled out a pack of basic smoke bombs that anybody could cop from your local ice cream truck. He lit two of the smoke bombs and placed them in the wastebasket. Bodeen slipped out of the room and headed back to the staircase where he saw the fire alarm. He waited until he saw the smoke seeping out from the room. A Haitian nurse sounded the first alarm when she screamed after she smelled and spotted the smoke coming from the room. She did exactly what Bodeen was hoping for. She opened the door and enough smoke filtered the hallways to impair everyone's vision. Bodeen pulled the fire alarm. He eased back out into the confusion. He pretended to help evacuate the patients. The stinky smell of the smoke bombs had all those pregnant women nauseated like a muthafucka. They didn't know if they wanted to vomit or shit. While they were all waddling to the emergency exits as the nurses ushered them to safety, Bodeen slipped into room 806 with syringe in hand. He was going to inject the hot shot in the same vein the IV was in so there would be no new needle marks. It would have been a good plan if it had worked. When Bodeen pulled the curtain back nobody was there.

This plan wasn't going to be as simple as he thought.

Bodeen came out of the room aggravated. One of the nurses that were rushing past asked Bodeen if all the rooms were clear. Bodeen nodded his head yes. He pointed to Mia Moretti's chart inquiring where she was. The nurse was too preoccupied with the drama that was happening around her to give him a solid answer. Bodeen took the chart off the door. He started showing it to every nurse until he got the answer he was looking for.

"Oh I remember her. They rushed her into the emergency room about ten minutes ago. She is about to have the baby. Are you the specialist they were sending over from Cedars?" The Nurse inquired. Bodeen nodded his head yes and she continued. The nurse pointed to her right and said, "Go down to the elevators—" She stopped herself. She briefly forgot they could only use the stairs in emergency situations. She apologized to Dr. Bodeen Goldsmith and informed him that he would have to take the stairs to the sixth floor.

Bodeen was cool with it until she said, "Follow the signs that say Maternity Emergency... and when you get to the help desk in that area, just tell the nurse who you are and they will escort you to the emergency room."

Bodeen took the stairs down to the sixth floor. He didn't know where to begin. He felt a little ashamed of himself that he was a grown ass man that didn't know how to read. But he also felt that going to school all your life to get a job that didn't pay shit wasn't too smart either so let the chips fall where they may. Bodeen couldn't read but he wasn't a total idiot. He didn't let his inability to read hinder his progress. He knew Maternity started with an M. He sounded out the next part and that was enough for him to move on. There were two M words posted with arrows pointing next to them. They were Maternity and Medical Emergency. Since there was no D in maternity, Bodeen felt he was headed in the right direction.

Bodeen had his hands raised like he just washed them. He had the clipboard with Mia's information on it under his armpit. When Bodeen reached the nurses' station he let it drop on the desk in front of the young nurse's aide. She read it and pointed to the room. Bodeen eased into the room. He saw more than he was looking for. Mia Moretti's legs were wide open on the table giving birth at that very minute. The Doctor was sitting on a stool with his back to Bodeen. There was a Nurse but she was preoccupied with her duties. They were going to pose a problem but not difficult enough for him to solve.

Bodeen slid all the way in the room and positioned himself behind the curtain. He pulled out the syringe. The Doctor was encouraging Mia to breathe and push. Mia was yelling to the top of her lungs. Bodeen had seen too much in his life to be disturbed by the sight of the childbirth but he did find it interesting to see it live up close and personal. Blood and amniotic fluids started oozing from Mia's vagina. The nurse hustled to get more sterilized towels. Mia's vagina started to bulge. The baby's head was starting to make its way out. The doctor continued to coach Mia. "You are doing good, Mrs. Moretti. Give me another deep breath and one good push."

Mia complied and the baby started making his way through the canal. Bodeen put the syringe back in his pocket and eased his pistol out from the small of his back.

"Here it comes!"

Bodeen came from behind the curtain and hit the doctor in the back of the head with the butt of his gun. He was knocked out cold. The baby kept making his way out naturally. Bodeen lifted his pistol and let off two shots. He blew the baby's head right back into the embryonic sac. Bodeen raised his pistol again. He shot Mia in the mouth as she opened it to scream. He put two more bullets into the center of her forehead. Bodeen got up out of there before the screaming nurse exited the supply room and saw the horrific murder scene.

CHAPTER 18

"YOU JUST GOT burnt!"

"Sizzled!"

"Toast!"

Jah and a few of his football buddies, Alley Al, Juju, Kendrick, and Busby were outside working on technique skills. They didn't look like your ordinary 8- and 9-year-old youth football players just running around passing the ball. They were out there conducting themselves like true professionals. Instead of clowning, Alley Al allowed Kendrick to correct his own mistake.

"What happened on that last play, Kendrick? How did you let the receiver get behind you?

"I didn't swing my head around fast enough on the break," Kendrick admitted.

Jah offered some advice, "You got to open up your hips a little more, too. Juju's speed is deceptive. Let's line up and run that play again."

Alley Al was quarterbacking the drill. "Down… Set… Hold up. What are you doing back there, Busby?"

"I'm playing safety!" Busby yelled back.

"But you're a defensive lineman," Juju said.

"I'm a nose guard that plays like a safety. You ain't never seen nothin' like that before. Don't sweat the technique—just run the play."

As crazy as Busby's logic sounded, they couldn't deny his play on the field. He was the only nose guard in the league that had twenty sacks and five interceptions in a season.

"You kids be careful with that ball around my flowers. I just planted those trees the other day!" Mother Taylor yelled from the window.

"No need to worry, Mother Taylor. We are just waiting for my Dad to take us to the park," Jah answered politely.

"Well, then wait over there in the street by your Dad's car and stay away from my trees."

Jah just sighed and smiled politely. They were already in the streets fifty yards from Mother Taylor's flowerbed.

* * *

"Your actions speak louder than your words, LaTonya. You tell me you want to settle down and then I don't hear from ya in three days—" Coach was having fun on the phone with LaTonya and her contradictions as he was looking for the house keys.

"You know I had to work overtime all week. I called you Tuesday and you didn't answer."

Coach's other line clicked. When he came back on the line, he said, "Now what were you telling me, player?"

"You got your nerve, Coach. That was probably one of your other women that just called. Who was that on the other line?" LaTonya asked.

"The girlfriend of the dude you were out with on Tuesday."

"Hardy har har...don't play Jedi mind tricks on me... who was that?"

"Mother Taylor. She wants to be my Cougar. She's downstairs drinking jackrabbit juice and purring like Eartha Kitt getting ready for me."

"Now you know you are not right for that, Coach!"

"You're the one that needed to know who it was. Now let me get downstairs so I can workout with my soldiers. Hit me tonight, beautiful," Coach concluded.

"Sounds good, Mr. Man."

* * *

When Coach got downstairs, he saw the classic ghetto child superstar named Lamont interrupting Jah and his friends' workout with stories about how great of a running back he was back in the day. The stories are good until they get to the part of why they stopped playing. Those stories always end in a ghetto tragedy.

The kids were doing agility drills through the orange cones on the grass in front of the apartment building regardless of what Mother Taylor had to say. The sight of the modern techniques used by the children just sent Lamont into a frenzy.

"Cones? What is that? We didn't need cones to help us with our footwork. We dodged parked cars. That's how we got those shakes." Lamont demonstrated by shaking his shoulders and creating the sound effect with his mouth that went with the move. "Sha shaah—sha shaah... look at those quick reflex skills, boooyyyyy. I got you mesmerized. You kids today ain't tough at all. When I was coming up back in the day, we played tackle in the street straight on concrete... light pole to light pole."

"Why? You didn't have a bus pass to get to the park?" Busby asked and everybody started laughing.

Jah didn't agree with his logic either. "The way these Mexicans be driving out here, I ain't about to be playing no football in the street. I play on a team on a football field."

Coach blocked Lamont out and got the kids back focused on their drills.

"What's up, Dad?"

"What's up, Coach?"

"Hey Coach."

"Why y'all speaking to me like you just seeing me for the first time this morning. Y'all spent the night. I just saw you jive turkeys 30 minutes ago. You must be up to something. Drop down and give me 25 push-ups for acting suspicious," Coach joked with the kids. It wasn't football season. Coach wasn't even in Coach Mode yet, but they still wanted to get that Spring Training in. Coach knew he had some real football players. Anytime you can get eight-year-old kids volunteering to work out instead of playing video games in the house all day is going to lead to a championship. And that's what they had their eye on since that 7-6 loss the season before.

Coach saw something different in their eyes. If that look and their new attitude was any indication of how they were going to play in the forth coming season, a lot of teams were going to be in trouble. As they took a quick break, Coach asked, "What was that fool Lamont flapping his gums about?"

"He was talking about how he used to tackle parked cars. Or something," Busby answered and made the rest of the kids laugh

"And his Running Back Shakes..." Juju added.

"His what?" Coach asked with a laugh.

"His shakes... you know, his moves. What was that noise he was making? Ching Ching?

"No it wasn't. It was Ka kaa ka kaa," Jah made everybody laugh.

Lamont overheard them clowning him and defended his ego. "I'm 38 years old and I bet I can outrun everybody out here, including you Coach. Yeah! Believe that."

"You'll get broke up out here and that's about it," Killa Kendrick spoke truth.

"You got to catch me first. You can't hit what your eyes can't see." Lamont said with cockiness as he demonstrated his Shoulder Shakes again, "Sha shaah-sha shaa!"

Coach and the kids got back to work, not paying Lamont any more attention.

* * *

He was groovin' and that was when he coulda sworn the room was movin'

But that was only in his mind

He was sailin'

He never really seemed to notice vision failin' cause that was all part of the high

Sweat was pourin' —he couldn't take it...

The room was exploding —he might not make it...

Bodeen was in his apartment on the second floor. He was looking out the window at Coach working out with the kids through the telescope lens on his sniper rifle. Bodeen aimed his rifle at each kid.

Pow...pow...pow... Bodeen was using his mouth to simulate the sound of the gunshots. Bodeen was so zooted off of that angel dust, it was truly a blessing from God that the gun wasn't loaded. That shit Bodeen was on was making him crazy for real. He was experiencing adverse reactions to the dust and becoming psychotic to the point where his symptoms were identical to those of schizophrenia. Bodeen was questioning himself and answering back. He had the gun pointed on Busby.

Should I kill that muthafucka?

Naw, man, that's just a kid. You eliminate bad men. You are a killer for hire, not a murderer, you damn fool. There's a difference.

What about that muthafucka George Bush?

That would be nice, but Beelzebub won't be pleased.

Now look at that grown ass man playing with those kids. He should be somewhere fuckin' with some bitches. He's probably a fag just like the rest of them. Go back to Penn State and get the fuck off my street before I kill you, nigga…

* * *

"You guys are looking gooooood! It feels like this is going to be one of those special seasons," Coach said as he admired the work ethic those kids had at such a young age.

"Y'all still want to go to the park or to the movies?" Jah asked his teammates.

"Both. Let's go to the park and then to the movies," Alley Al suggested.

"When are we going to eat? I'm hungry." Busby asked.

Coach and the kids walked toward the Dodge Challenger. Coach had that feeling someone was staring at him so he looked around and then up and saw Bodeen stuck in the second floor window. Coach gave him the *what up* nod with his head and then paid him no mind.

"Don't leave… where you going? Don't get scared now!" Lamont yelled from up the block. Lamont was carrying some cleats in his hand. He was walking with some kids that lived around the corner. They were older kids around 13 or 14. They were coming up the street hard tossing a football in the air like they wanted to do something. They were just the typical neighborhood kids looking for some excitement and direction. Lamont was leading them on the right journey but they just took the wrong path.

"Aren't those the dudes that were Krump Dancing at local talent show that time?" Juju asked.

"I'm going to break his Stanky Leg if they come over here acting like they want to play us in some football," Killer said with conviction.

Coach looked at the foes for potential first. He was always looking for raw talent to groom. He had seen them around the neighborhood from time to time. One week they were jerk dancers, the next week they were R&B singers, and the week after that they wanted to be like Allen Iverson. Coach could tell by their swag they never played organized sports before. But according to Lamont they were better than the Dallas Cowboys.

"These are real football players from the streets. These are my boys. I raised them from the time they was yay big. I'm they Coach. You guys up for a game or are you gettin' scared?" Lamont boasted.

"You don't want to do that. Now is not the time, sir, seriously," Jah said.

Lamont started ranting and raving about how scared and weak Jah and his friends were and he even let the word 'punks' slip out of his mouth. Jah and his friends were already on the grass before Coach could even respond.

"Line it up!" was all Killer had to say.

The teens were noticeably bigger than Jah and his crew but their hearts weren't. They kicked the ball off to Jah's team and Juju ran it all the way back for a touchdown on the first play of the game. Lamont was talking down and cursing his kids out for not making the tackle.

Coach got tired of Lamont's mouth and suggested that they play as well. Lamont got his bluff called but his ego was so out of whack at this point he had to step up.

"Don't blink 'cuz I'm fast."

The home team kicked off and Stanky Leg got the ball. Jah hit him in the ribs with a nice shot. The ball squirted out. Killer picked up the fumble and ran it in for a touchdown. Stanky Leg was out on the ground. He couldn't breathe. He thought he was dying. Kendrick got mad at Jah because he wanted to knock Stanky Leg out first. He was really upset about it, too. The touchdown he just scored meant nothing to him. Play after play, another kid would get smacked and it ended in the same result, fumble-touchdown. Lamont was still talking shit though.

Lamont was telling the wounded kids what he would have done if he were them and he ran the ball. "Put those shakes on 'em. Those fools are slow they can't match your speed. I can't believe some 8-year-old babies are whipping up on y'all. Fuck that. Throw me the ball and watch me shake these fools!"

The next play, they kicked the ball off to Lamont. He takes off running. His blockers are getting dropped on sight. Lamont wanted to run out of bounds to safety but Kendrick was coming up the sideline hard and fast. Lamont changed directions and cut back inside. Coach came up from a 45-degree angle and hit Lamont so hard nobody wanted to play anymore. Coach dropped the whole load on his ass.

Coach could have easily just leveled Lamont with a nice shot and dropped him to the turf but that wasn't dramatic enough. Coach drove his shoulder into Lamont with so much power and speed the momentum carried them out of bounds and Lamont went flying into the mulberry bushes. Coach fucked that nigga up and just destroyed all the poor little trees Mother Taylor just planted in the yard.

Lamont was laid out with one leg bent back so far his heel was touching the back of his head. His fresh white tee shirt had a big ass grass stain on his shoulder blade. He had a hole in his pants where his kneecap was bleeding. The muthafucka had leaves and twigs stuck all in his hair. Lamont was embarrassed and had a little attitude. He felt like Coach took it too far. Coach was just trying to inspire his players by showing them what he meant when he coaches them to run through the ball carrier. It worked. Coach had his players fired up for the season.

The children looked down at Lamont to see if he was all right.

"What happened to your shakes?".

"Where's your sha-shah?"

Lamont finally got up and limped back to his apartment without talking to anybody. They didn't bother to tell him that his back was covered in dirt. Coach just said, "Let's get up out of here before Mother Taylor sees her flower bed looking like this."

And they all just took off running and laughing and hopped in the car like the police was on their tail........ they didn't know it at the time, but they will all reminisce and laugh about that memory for the rest of their lives.

CHAPTER 19

BODEEN WAS STILL in the window when Coach and the kids returned a few hours later. Fortunately, he had come down from his high and put the sniper rifle down. Bodeen was an entirely different person. He had no recollection of the sick thoughts that had churned in his mind. PCP users tend to experience a disassociation of time and space from where and when they are at the current moment.

Bodeen watched Jah and his friends congregate. They conducted themselves like grown men. They used their hands when they talked. Bodeen was moved to see five children that had a fair chance at life. They were not going to have to suffer the same fate he was dealt.

Andy and Mia Moretti's daughter would have been born into miserable surroundings. The child would have started suffering from the moment of its first breath. That's why Bodeen executed it. It was definitely a mercy killing. That baby girl didn't have a shot at life. Killing that infant was doing it a favor. The odds of the kid becoming the next Helen Keller, Rain Man, or Forrest Gump were stacked up against her. Bodeen wished for many years that someone had ended his life like little baby Moretti. He would have been better off.

Bodeen couldn't grasp the concept of what it meant to nurture a child. That was one of life's mysteries he didn't even know existed. The childhood memories he looked back on were a tainted blur. There were no amusement parks, video games, or Christmas presents. Bodeen never had a football thrown to him, much less seen a game. He had no contact with his family and the only friends he ever had was Bobby Boyd and Abdullah Joe, if that's what you want to call them. Bodeen often wondered what was his reason for being. *What was the purpose of coming into this world with no reason to smile?* Not knowing what it feels like to be held or cared for. Bodeen was tired of waking up every morning knowing he has never been loved by anyone a day in his life.

Bodeen stared at Coach interacting with the children for a long time, but this time it was out of admiration. Bodeen couldn't help but respect a black man raising his son on his own and still have the time to care for other kids with the same level of passion. Bodeen started to wonder how different his childhood would have been if he had a father like Coach...

THE BOOK OF CHARLESETTA

"C'MON NIGGA! DIG that shit out, cuzz!"

"Cuzz ain't gon' make it!"

"Here he goes… ONE! Twooo! Threeeee! Fo—"

"Ugh."

"Awwww, shit. He chocked at four. I told you he didn't know what to do with that pootang!"

"Get the fuck outta here, Bosco!"

"Cuzz you make us look bad…"

"Let the homie Otis go… he's next."

"One, twoooo, three…"

"Uh ugh."

"Aww! Three? Three? This nigga is weak!"

The loud chatter and cheering of the Triple 6 Crips echoed through Clarence Thomas Park. It was 3am and pitch black dark out there. Smoky clouds from seeded dirt weed dipped in dust hovered over the rowdy crowd. The stench of musty sweat, malt liquor, and toxic pussy was too thick to be overpowered by the fresh morning air.

Charlesetta was asshole naked on the damp grass with her legs wide open getting a train ran on her by select members of the Triple 6 Crips. It was her initiation in to the gang. Three dudes in a row had to ram pipe in Charlesetta six times, as hard as they could hump, in order for her to be put on the set. The first three dudes—Black Ass Bosco, Otis, and Darryl—didn't reach their quota and came all up in her before they hit the six count. Instead of admitting they were quick shooters, they filled

Charlesetta's ignorant head with murmurs of how good her pussy was. It made her feel so good about herself she was proud of getting dug out by half the set. The next Crips up were Errol, E-Mack, and Nayville. They hit their mark and stamped the 666 all over that bitch.

Charlesetta laid on the ground proud with her pussy sore, ass stinkin', and drippin' cum from six different men. Charlesetta stood up while her big long titties dropped to her waistline and threw up her set, "Triple 6 Ca-Riiiip!"

Charlesetta was a hot mess. Come to think of it, that phrase was probably invented just for her. A scandalous hood rat bitch and I'm not even going to try to sugarcoat it. She was only 15 years old but her ignorance, ornery attitude, bad diet, Newport cigarettes-sometimes wet, and malt liquor consumption made her look like she was 59. Charlesetta was a big girl. She stood about 5'10" and was on the verge of losing the last little bit of cute shape she had left. Her titties were already saggin' and resting on her buckshot belly and the cellulite forming on her butt made her ass look like a bowl of chocolate cottage cheese. We're not even going to discuss the heels of her feet right now because I'm not ready to go there.

Now don't get it twisted, Charlesetta may not have looked as good as a Soul Train Dancer in the 80s, but she never had a problem getting a man. Most times she kept two or three hooligans with their nose up her snatch. Charlesetta did possess the good qualities that were required in the life she chose. She had hustle in her and she stayed down, dirty, and dedicated to no-good niggas. She was good for putting the downtrodden with no education, skills, or the desire to work, back on their feet when they got out of jail. I guess it was her way of giving back to the community.

Charlesetta was born in Texas to Charles and Loretta Brown. Charles was killed in a bank robbery just before she was born. Loretta, who was only14 at the time she had Charlesetta, was sent with her baby to Rialto, California, to live with an elderly aunt they called Sister Auntie that was christened as a saint by the family just because she attended church every Sunday.

Loretta was fine as silk and she was what you would consider one of those little fast tail girls. It didn't take her any time to get the attention of this slick cat named North Star making his rounds looking for runaways getting off the Greyhound. She didn't know he was a pimp at first but she knew he had to be something extraordinary because that nigga was unreal. He got the name North Star from lost bitches looking for direction and he helped them find their way. He knocked Loretta and turned her out before she made it out of the bus station.

A few hours later, Loretta dropped that baby off with Sister Auntie and told her that if she needed to find her just follow the North Star.

Sister Auntie was around 60 years old then and she did the best she could to raise that infant child. Charlesetta wasn't a bad baby but she showed early signs of defiance and a propensity for talking back. Over the first five years of Charlesetta's life, Loretta came home once or twice a month to check on her baby and give Sister Auntie Money for food and shelter. Loretta took care of the clothes, too. One of Loretta's stable mates was a professional booster so Charlesetta stayed in nice outfits. The clothes were a little risqué for her age but nonetheless she didn't hurt for anything.

As Charlesetta got a little older, she got to spend more time with her mom and North Star. Contrary to what some people might believe, they led a normal family life just like anyone else. Charlesetta was expected to do her schoolwork; she did ballet, and played with dolls. Charlesetta and North Star would even dress up every Sunday and have tea parties. As much as it was needed for Loretta to spend time with her child and take some pressure off of her aging Aunt, it wasn't necessarily the greatest idea because Charlesetta was exposed to some things at an early age that she really didn't need to see.

North Star was decent pimp. He always had at least two hoes in his stable. When he reached the top of his game, he had five. North Star didn't like to have an odd number of hoes because he believed in working in pairs. But since Loretta turned out to be such good Bottom Bitch, she was allowed to stay with North Star while the other hoes shared a two-bedroom apartment.

When she was around eight years old, Charlesetta started to become aware of her surroundings and what her mother and North Star did for a living. She began to resent it, but for all the wrong reasons. Charlesetta wasn't born with her Mother's looks. She looked more like her Dad Charles.

It bothered her that she was the least attractive in the family. She really wasn't a bad looking girl, but her defiant attitude made her ugly.

At nine years old, Charlesetta hit a growth spurt. She grew tall and started to fill out everywhere. Unfortunately, her body had hit its peak and that would be the last year she would enjoy having a cute shape. After that, she just became a big bitch. But that didn't hold her back. She learned to use her size as intimidation. North Star's other hoes that had kids Charlesetta's age couldn't stand her ass. Charlesetta use to talk down to them because she got to stay in the big house with North Star and her mom on the days she was allowed to visit. She would call the kids *trick baby* and other nasty names to purposely lower their self-esteem. Charlesetta tortured and beat them whenever she felt the need. It was mainly out of jealousy. For one, they were all cuter than she was and two, they got to stay with their moms year 'round.

North Star was a pimp and his job was managing hoes. They say a good pimp in tune with his hoe should be able to detect if her shit smelled different than it did the day before and figure out why it was so. So on that note, North Star would never allow a person like Charlesetta to stick around and wreck his stable with her treacherous ways, even though she was only a child. To be truthful, North Star knew Charlesetta was a bad seed when he first laid eyes on her as an infant in the Greyhound bus station.

Charlesetta's height and over-developed body was starting to catch the attention of a few of the older guys in the neighborhood. Charlesetta started getting full on herself. She virtually went unnoticed by the person she had her eye on. During one particular summer when Charlesetta came to visit, Loretta was several months pregnant with North Star's son.

Charlesetta became extremely jealous. She knew Loretta having another baby—especially a boy in a house full of women—was going to delete her from the family picture.

North Star was thrilled to be having a son, like most men. As soon as he got the news, he worked his hoes extra hard in order to build a future for his little man. North Star invested in a couple of gentlemen's clubs and bought a few properties in Nevada. Since Loretta was in no condition to be on the track, he put her in charge of the clubs he invested in.

Business was good and North Star decided to move the stable to Vegas.

Charlesetta wasn't invited. First, she tried to seduce North Star by flashing her titties in front of him one morning as she came out of the shower. She had the towel covering her lower half. North Star looked at the young tender virgin girl that desired to have him. He reached out and pulled off her towel and let it drop to the floor. Her soft body was still damp.

North Star undid his buckle. He pulled his belt off slow and sexy. And then North Star proceeded to whip Charlesetta's fast 9-year-old ass. North Star made Charlesetta tell her mother what she did and Loretta whipped her ass again. Charlesetta was embarrassed more than physically hurt. She learned from two vicious ass whippings in a row that she was impervious to pain but dishing it out was becoming her specialty.

The day of the big move finally arrived. The movers were tracking in and out of the house, securing boxes, and loading them into the truck. Loretta's stomach was so huge she couldn't even see her feet. She was trying to help to movers but it was best she sat down. Loretta asked Charlesetta to help her out like a good girl. First Charlesetta helped her mother's diamond necklace and earrings out of the jewelry box and into her pocket. She also helped North Star's Rolex watch and some petty cash into her other pocket. She resealed the box and took it out to the truck like a nice little girl. Charlesetta wasn't worried about getting caught because she knew the movers were going to have to catch the heat for that. Charlesetta's thirst for revenge still wasn't satisfied. She was going to make North Star and Loretta hurt for leaving her behind.

Right before they shut the house down for good, Charlesetta got her chance. The entire house was empty except for Loretta and the reclining chair she sat in. Two of the movers had to help Loretta to her feet. Her balance was a little off when she stood up. One of the movers asked Charlesetta to help her Mother outside. Charlesetta mumbled something under her breath to the nature of *you ain't my daddy*. The mover overheard her and he didn't bite is tongue when he replied, "Thank God."

Loretta used Charlesetta like a crutch as she moved slowly through the front door. Every slow wide-legged step was irritating Charlesetta. She was making all the obvious wind and sigh sounds that were clearly translating *I wish this fat bitch would walk faster.* Loretta picked up on it and told

Charlesetta to fix her attitude. Loretta said it loud enough for the movers to hear and that infuriated Charlesetta even more.

When they got to the front porch, there were three steps they had to go down. Just below the last step, the flat wood four-wheel dolly the movers used to roll the big appliances and heavy objects was partially in the walkway. Technically, it was a potential hazard but there was plenty of room to avoid it. It wasn't like it was sitting in a blind spot unless you were pregnant and having trouble seeing the ground below you.

Charlesetta guided her mother down the first step. On the second step, Loretta stopped to take a deep breath. Charlesetta used her long leg and eased the dolly under the last step with her big toe. It lined up perfectly. They made it to the third step and Charlesetta loosened her grip around Loretta's arm. Loretta stepped on the edge of the dolly and her weight immediately caused it to tilt up and the wheels shoot out from underneath her. Loretta locked her nails into Charlesetta's bicep to help break the fall. Loretta screamed as she lost her balance and saw the ground coming up to meet her fall.

Loretta crashed right into the arms of one of the movers that saw the whole scene unfold. He was standing in the doorway behind Loretta and Charlesetta the whole time, waiting for them to clear the path so he could get the dolly to move the last chair Loretta had been sitting in. The mover looked at Charlesetta like he wanted to kill her as he hollered for someone to bring over a chair.

He didn't want to shake up Loretta anymore than what she was so he sat Loretta in the chair and called North Star to inform him on what happened immediately. He didn't call to snitch but rather to save his own ass. He knew if Charlesetta was evil enough to try and make her pregnant mother fall with the intention of causing her to lose the baby, there was no telling what else she might have done and leave them to take the blame.

Even at 9 years old, Charlesetta was smart enough to know that her failed attempt was a dumb move. North Star was going to beat her to within an inch of her life when he got back and he was already on his way with those exact intentions in mind. Charlesetta ran down the street and found her own way back to Sister Auntie's house.

It would be a long time before Charlesetta saw her mother again and it was best she kept her distance.

* * *

After that fateful day, Charlesetta started to rebel in a big way. The boredom that comes from living in a dead town like Rialto will lead you down the wrong path. Rialto is a town where low-income families can actually purchase a nice affordable home and live a better life. But it defeats the purpose when there are no jobs or opportunities available to keep your home within of 50 miles. The pioneers that commute to work maintain, but the children they raise in Rialto tend to struggle. There is nothing there for them to do. There is no guidance. The only thing they have immediate access to is drugs and idle time and that's a fucked up combination. It kind of gives you a gut feeling that the Rialto Commute Program was designed as a trap.

Charlesetta's bad attitude, filthy mouth, and knack for violence got her suspended from school on numerous occasions. Charlesetta knew she wouldn't be disciplined for her actions at home so it was impossible to change with no direction. Sister Auntie was 75 now and getting senile. To her credit, Charlesetta didn't mistreat Sister Auntie, but she didn't have the type of patience needed to deal with her ailing health so Charlesetta stayed in the streets a lot. The only options were to hang with the *get high crews* or the gangbangers.

Charlesetta gravitated toward that thug element. She bounced around the Inland Empire drinking, fucking, talking shit, and starting fights until she ran up on a crew of niggas from the Triple 6 Crips that didn't fold up like those other weak crews she rolled on. The Triple 6 Crips were grimy and gully. They were her A-Alikes. In order for Charlesetta to join the gang, she would have to take a ride on that Triple 6 train... and she showed and proved she was down for the game.

"Triple 6 Ca-Riiiip!!!"

It didn't take Charlesetta long to figure out somebody got her pregnant that night. She was hoping the father was either Black Ass Bosco because he was the toughest in the gang or E-Mack because he had money, pretty eyes, and fucked the best. The requirements needed to be Charlesetta's baby's daddy didn't involve parenting.

Charlesetta actively participated in abusive relationships with Black Ass Bosco, E-Mack, and another cat from a rival gang until an unknown bitch from Triple 6 Crip mysteriously had him set up and shot during a botched robbery. Every thug that dropped a load of semen in Charlesetta with the exception of Black Ass Bosco abruptly stopped fucking with her once her pregnancy started to show. Nobody wanted to wear that Baby Daddy Jacket.

Charlesetta's prenatal care was definitely not what the doctor prescribed. Her diet consisted of McDonalds, malt liquor, pork rinds, Kool-Aid, and candy. She had no water or vegetable intake whatsoever. For exercise, she got into fights. She beat bitches up and held her own against her boyfriends. Instead of Lamaze classes, Charlesetta did a lot of yelling brought up from the esophagus. But Charlesetta didn't really fuck with drugs on a regular basis during the pregnancy. Black Ass Bosco had enough sense to check her about that. It led to a brutal fight because Charlesetta felt that he couldn't be telling her what to do if he wasn't going to be a man and take responsibility as the father of the baby. She did experiment with a little angel dust to help ease her nerves when she went on her first drive-by shooting and a little bit more to help her forget about it but that was about it. I know you're probably thinking, "Well shit, that was enough!"

A few of the older hood rat bitches schooled Charlesetta on how to come up off the paltry county checks and food stamps since she was going to be a single mother. They even advised her to have more than one kid so she could really come up. They educated her that it was best not to put the father's name on the birth certificate because the state would make him pay child support and cut into her money. That wouldn't be a problem. Charlesetta really had no idea of who the father was. She only knew it was one of the Triple 6 Crips that initiated her.

Charlesetta thought about her mother more often now that she was 15 and pregnant with her own child. She was just a year older than when Loretta had her. Charlesetta wished she could see the look on her Loretta's cute face when she found out she was going to be a grandmother at 29.

The birth of Bodeen was so difficult and painful Charlesetta went out of her way to make him pay for it when he finally arrived. Charlesetta was

In labor for 82 hours. Bodeen did not want to face the world he was being forced into.

Looking at her new infant son didn't help her figure out who the daddy was. Bodeen was the same complexion as Black Ass Bosco, Darryl, and Errol, so that didn't help to narrow it down one bit, and he looked exactly like Charlesetta.

BODEEN (THE EARLY YEARS)

BODEEN CAME INTO the world weighing 10 pounds and 15 ounces. Legend has it that the name Bodeen is a modified street name for *Cockstrong*, meaning a man that is unusually physically strong for his size because of lack of sexual activity. Others say it was some shit Charlesetta made up using the initials of the Crips that initiated her. Sister Auntie said he was named after Jethro Bodine from *The Beverly Hillbillies*, not realizing it wasn't spelled the same. Some people thought his first name was Bo and his last name was Deen. But shit, after he grew into the Notorious Bodeen the Killer, people didn't have time to ask him what his name meant or where he got it. It didn't matter anymore anyway.

During his infancy, Sister Auntie cared for Bodeen for the most part. Charlesetta would lie and say she was going to school, but she was hanging in the hood and up to no good. The only places Charlesetta ever took Bodeen to was the county building to get him verified and to the hood when the other rats had their kids out. It was pitiful. Charlesetta would be caressing a 40-ounce of malt liquor comfortably in one hand while the baby would be slippin' and hanging off of her hip in the other arm. The hood rats would take their babies' hands and form Crip signs with it. Then they would take pictures, post them on gang websites, and tell stories about how hard the kids were going to be. Charlesetta styled Bodeen's hair in two pigtails with blue barrettes. She even got his ear pierced when he wasn't more than a month old.

Around the time Bodeen was six months old, Charlesetta took him to the tattoo shop with her where she got *Bosco* tatted on her ankle.

"Now you have finished mine, I want you to put Triple 6 Crip on my son's chest in block letters."

"Are you serious? I can't put a tat like that on a baby," Pedro, the tattoo artist, said in shock.

"Bullshit, bitch. The sign right there says nobody under 18 without the consent of the parent and I'm his parent so you do what the fuck I say," Charlesetta retorted back.

"Well, the sign right here," Pedro pointed behind her, "states that I have the Right to Refuse Service and I refuse to put the mark of the beast on that child for any price!"

"You best lower your tone talkin' to me and you best open them ears. I didn't say shit about no beast. I said Triple 6 Crip... like the same one you did for E-Mack."

"E-Mack's a beast! I went to school with him. I know what he's capable of. This is a baby. And 666 is the sign of the devil."

"I know that, nigga. I ain't want no the three number sixes, jackass. I want it spelled out T-R-I-P-L-"

Pedro cut her off. "Look. I know how to spell, ma'am, but it's the same thing. You can yell all you want, but I'm not putting that bullshit on no baby."

"What you mean *bullshit*?" Charlesetta asked with an attitude that you could smell.

Pedro stood up and walked behind the counter just staring at her, not saying a word.

"Okay. I see who you really are. But your dumb ass is really gon' see when the homies find out," Charlesetta said as she grabbed Bodeen and sashayed out of the shop.

Later on that night, Charlesetta pumped the Triple Six Crips' heads with lies and bullshit. Black Ass Bosco, Darryl, Errol, and Otis beat Pedro inside the tattoo parlor and robbed him.

But Pedro didn't even have to snitch or press charges. It was caught on tape. The state picked up the case. Four of Bodeen's potential fathers got locked up in Youth Authority for the next two years...over a silly hood rat bitch.

If Sister Auntie weren't alive, Bodeen probably would have been dead by the time he turned three. The few moments Charlesetta did spend with Bodeen were horrific. He was not allowed to do things that babies do like cry, shit, and drool without getting punished for it. Charlesetta was a mean and ignorant bitch. She would always tell Bodeen how black and ugly he was. But he looked exactly like her, just much darker in complexion. As little Bodeen's cognitive skills started to develop, it didn't take him long to figure out it was best to avoid his mother and latch on to Sister Auntie. Charlesetta had the gall to get an attitude about it. That's when the name-calling started. Bodeen was called so many *Nana's Boys* and *punk bitches* by the time he was three years old he thought those were his nicknames.

Matter of fact, Bodeen's first word was *bitch*. Charlesetta thought that was the funniest thing she ever heard and was so proud she kept making him say it all day. People with the foulest mouths didn't think that was funny or cool at all. Charlesetta's homies would even tell her she was an unfit mother. It always ended in the same shouting match.

"You don't tell me how to raise my son! That is my son! Fuck what you think. I do what I want to do!" That was Charlesetta's defense mechanism. Every time she was wrong she used aggression and loud talk to keep people from pointing out her flaws. She had the ability to get you to that point where you didn't even want to deal with it to avoid her mouth.

Bodeen stuck to Sister Auntie like static cling. For an old woman, she did the best she could. All she really saw was a beautiful little child that needed to be cared for. She wasn't coherent enough to know that was Charlesetta's baby and her great nephew. Her natural instincts took over. She would sit Bodeen on her lap and sing songs like *Old McDonald had a Farm* and play pattycake with him all day until she was worn out. Sister Auntie was cold with the Hand Bone, too. Bodeen would leap out Sister Auntie's lap and start dancing up a storm as she rhythmically slapped her hip and shoulder into a funky beat.

Bodeen was still a little too young to remember those good innocent times in his life, but he would never forget the day he went to a church fair with Sister Auntie. The congregation would donate items to the church and then sell them in the parking lot to raise money for the daycare center they'd been trying to build for 40 years. They sold stuff like used books and records for a dollar, secondhand clothing, toys, and furniture. Bodeen didn't run around and play because according to Charlesetta he looked like a black booger bear and he might scare all the little kids away.

Fortunately the kids weren't ignorant like his mama and they invited Bodeen to play with them. Bodeen wasn't social but he participated in all the reindeer games. At first, the other kids thought he was a little slow because he was the same size as the seven-year-olds and still had on Huggies under his church slacks. The kids gave him a pass when they found out his real age, but not ol' Lenny Green. He never missed a Sunday service. Lenny Green kept a flask of good liquor in the inside pocket of his double-breasted suit jacket and had been rolling like that for over 50 years. He was never drunk or loud. He was always extra mellow but quick to point something out on a person that he thought needed fixing.

He saw Bodeen's diaper and spoke his mind, "Say young lad, what kind of drawers you got on under those church slacks? They look all bunched up in that back like you got a pile of shit back there."

Bodeen stood there, not sure of what he should say so Lenny called him over to where he was sitting. Lenny took a whiff of Bodeen and said, "That IS a pile of shit in your drawers. How old are you, boy?"

Bodeen held up four fingers. Lenny said, "Damn, I thought your big ass was about ten. Well, four is still too old to be walking around in some Huggies. Here, take this five-dollar bill over to Sister Betty and tell her you want to buy some real drawers. When you get them come back over here and I'll show you how to put them on. Go on now."

Lenny potty trained Bodeen and had him wearing real underwear in less than an hour.

Later in the day, Sister Auntie won a gift box filled with assorted donation items playing bingo. She told Bodeen he could open it when they got back home. He couldn't wait. When they arrived home, Bodeen tore into the box immediately. There were little plastic toys, crayons, a Jesus Loves Me coloring book, a set of jacks, and a Fisher-Price tape player equipped with a microphone. There were two cassette tapes. One was Michael Jackson *Thriller* and the other was Colonel Abrams *Greatest Hits*. Even though there were more toys in the box than Bodeen ever had, he was captivated by MJ's picture. He just stared at the *Thriller* cassette for a long time. He didn't know what to do with it at first. He lined it up on the floor with his Hot Wheels and scooted it across the carpet while making truck sounds.

A couple of days later, Bodeen and Sister Auntie were watching TV and a Michael Jackson video came on the screen. Bodeen was mesmerized. When it ended, Bodeen bolted to Sister Auntie's room and got his *Thriller* cassette tape and Fisher-Price microphone. Once Sister Auntie figured out how the cassette player worked, the music morphed Bodeen into a whole different child. His world consisted of nothing but Michael Jackson music and his dance steps. Bodeen performed for Sister Auntie every day for the next year. Old McDonald wasn't as funky as Billie Jean. For a big kid, Bodeen was light on his feet. He could moonwalk across carpet just like it was a slick stage.

One night, Sister Auntie wasn't feeling too good and Charlesetta was pissed that she had to stay in the house and look after her and Bodeen. Sister Auntie asked Bodeen to do the Michael Jackson steps and make her feel better. Bodeen went into his routine like he was performing on the Motown 25th Anniversary Special. Bodeen started to moonwalk and glided across the floor like he was on air. A gust of strong wind blowing in the same direction hit Bodeen like a tornado and he went flying across the room until his back came crashing against the wall.

Charlesetta was peeking in Sister Auntie's room to see what she was so happy about. She watched Bodeen performing from behind the door. His talent impressed her, but it wasn't gangster enough. While Bodeen was moonwalking, she burst in to the room and snatched him by the back of his collar and slammed him against the wall. She slapped him hard across his face two times.

"What the fuck you doin', punk bitch? Gangsters don't dance like that! You ain't gon' be in my house shaking your ass like a little faggot. Fuck a moonwalk. You better get to Crip walkin' up in this bitch. If I catch you dancing to this shit again, Mama is going to beat your ass until it's raw. You understand me? Plus you too goddamn ugly to be Michael Jackson...he's cute. You a big black ass nigga like Barry White. Now get the fuck outta here and let Sister Auntie Rest!"

Sister Auntie had the saddest look on her face. The brightest part of her day was violently taken away. The world didn't look beautiful to her anymore. Sister Auntie looked over at Charlesetta with shame in her eyes. She was too weak to speak but she had enough energy to lift her hand and give Charlesetta the middle finger.

The next morning Sister Auntie was gone and so was Bodeen's *Thriller* cassette.

* * *

Once Sister Auntie died, her home turned into the loitering spot for all of Charlesetta's grimy no-good friends. Charlesetta stepped her hustle game up to supplement Sister Auntie's Social Security check she would no longer be receiving. She peddled a little reefer and meth. Charlesetta had some hustle about herself but she was constantly giving her money to the no-good lames she was attracted to. She loved herself a down-and-out, probation-violating hard luck man. Truthfully, I suspect it was a control thing. Charlesetta had a few dudes that were papered up, too, but they did as they pleased. A fool with no car or place of residence tends to stay for a little while longer. Ultimately, they were useless. They had no hustle and couldn't offer Bodeen guidance of any kind.

But I guess the best thing about having a hustlin' gangster for a mother was Bodeen was kept in all the latest Jordan sneakers. He was limited on fashion because if it wasn't gangster he couldn't wear it. Bodeen wanted to be like Mike, but not the one with the basketball. He wanted to be like Mike in the penny loafers and glitter on his socks. A pair of Air Jordans wasn't worth the abuse Bodeen had to take to get them. He'd rather have a pair of Pro Keds than put up with Charlesetta's shit.

Bodeen was starting to get too big and thick for those slaps and that skinny broken purse strap that Charlesetta would use to snap on him. His Michael Jackson dance moves also made him elusive as well. One day, Charlesetta tried to go upside of Bodeen's head for some silly reason or another and she missed every time she tried to strike him. Bodeen would have been better off taking that little ass whooping as Charlesetta was too ornery to be made a fool of. From that day forward, Charlesetta would wrap the purse strap around Bodeen's neck as tight as she could while she kept a tight grip on the end. Charlesetta would then punch Bodeen repeatedly in the forehead with a hard, closed fist. Over the next year, Bodeen blacked out and suffered more concussions than a football player in the NFL.

The loss of oxygen from the strap around his neck and repeated blows to the head proved to be costly once Bodeen started going to school. Bodeen had difficulty adapting to the curriculum. Bodeen understood what the teacher was saying but whenever she wrote something on the chalkboard it looked more foreign than Chinese arithmetic. Bodeen could ace an oral exam with ease, but unfortunately the decent teachers that recognized his potential weren't going to put in the extra time needed to get him up to speed on the money they were making. They also knew from the first open house meeting with Charlesetta that she was immune to suggestions. So instead of dealing with Bodeen's issues head on, the school system just moved him along.

The first couple of years of elementary school were okay. Bodeen was christened King of the Class every year without actually having a schoolyard fight. His complexion and large physique automatically gave him the crown. Bodeen was always picked first to play sports and he shocked the entire staff and student body with his performances at the school assembly. At the Christmas show, Bodeen's class performed a funky version of "Jingle Bell Rock." Bodeen put the Michael Jackson touch on it and rocked the house. He was so good the musical director wanted to give him a dance solo in the show they were going to do for the parents. Bodeen remembered Charlesetta's threats and the beatings he took for dancing in the house and declined. Mrs. Wellington, the music teacher, was disappointed but she understood where Bodeen was coming from. Mrs. Wellington wanted to do something special for Bodeen so she bought him a new *Thriller* cassette and told him he could listen to it at school any time he wanted. Bodeen mastered every song and move on that album from top to bottom.

The first seven years of a child's life is crucial. Then when they reach that seven-year mark, they begin to see and hear things that will have an impact on their lives. In the Christmas show, Bodeen also played one of the three wise men. He was the one that brought Baby Jesus frankincense and myrrh. After the performance, everything that came out of Charlesetta's mouth was negative.

"Who that fat girl up on stage trying to dance? Those costumes look stupid. Your teacher makes me sick. I do not like her funky ass attitude... and how did your dumb ass become a wise man? Shiieeeet, the real ones wasn't no better. If the wise men were so goddamn intelligent, they would have brought Jesus a piece. If they were hiding Jesus that meant somebody was looking for him to kill him; right? So what the fuck they bringing incense and lentil for? The Jews used myrrh as an ointment for dead people. You mean to tell me them wise men walked they asses all the way across that hot ass desert following a damn star that was supposed to lead them to see the big-ass baby Jesus just to bring him some curds and whey? But not one of them wise bastards had Jesus' back when the shit went down. If they was real about it, they would have told him, 'If you ain't got no money in yo' pocket, don't be fuckin' around with them Jews.' Yeah. That's that real shit. I don't believe in no *turn the other cheek* shit. Bodeen, listen to me good. If you hear somebody threaten to fuck up one of yo' homeboys, you best ride on they ass quick. And if anybody ever thinks about putting they hands on you, you best kill 'em or make 'em wish they hadn't been born up in this world. You understand me, boy?"

Bodeen just nodded his head yes. Even though he was trying not to hear what Charlesetta was telling him, her rambling lesson stuck with Bodeen for the rest of his life.

Bodeen didn't like Charlesetta's child rearing techniques but that was all he really knew so he had to tolerate it. Dealing with Charlesetta's bullshit was enough on his plate. Bodeen had to start consuming extra shit when Black Ass Bosco came home from the joint. Bosco did his time but he looked like time had done him. Bodeen, as well as the rest of the hood, often wondered if Bosco was his Father because of the dark complexion. However, as Bodeen started growing older, you could tell they had no other similarities except hue. *"So Black Ass Bosco... you are not the father!"*

But unlike the lames Charlesetta were used to dealing with, Black Ass Bosco had a little hustle about himself. He spent a little time with Bodeen as well, but not enough to get emotionally attached. He taught Bodeen how to box and count money. He would even put a few extra dollars in his pocket occasionally.

Charlesetta and Black Ass Bosco was an entirely different story. They fought verbally and physically all the time. They would really get into it when she abused Bodeen. Most women wanted a man around to teach their son a thing or two, but Charlesetta wanted it to be all about her.

"When everybody thought that was yo' son, your black ass didn't want no parts of being a daddy. Now that you know Bodeen ain't yours, you wanna be Super Daddy and shit. Nigga, get the fuck outta here! You worry about handling this," pointing to her private area, "and let me worry about Bodeen's dumb ass," Charlesetta barked on more than one occasion.

Bosco could handle Charlesetta for the most part as long as he ruled with a hard dick and an iron fist. The nights he had to go upside her head was a different ball game though. Charlesetta is not the type of woman you go to sleep first on after you put your hands on her unless you want to be awakened by some hot grease or a pistol in your mouth. On those bad days, Bosco would sleep on the floor in Bodeen's room with the door locked. That made Charlesetta furious.

Black Ass Bosco was getting tired of Charlesetta anyway. The free rent wasn't worth all the bullshit he had to endure. He had been saving his money and planned to leave soon. A few days before he made that move, Black Ass Bosco took Bodeen shopping and purchased him some farewell gifts. Bosco bought Bodeen a new Walkman to replace that old Fisher-Price radio he still listened to. Bosco asked Bodeen what kind of music he liked. Bodeen was hesitant to answer. Finally, Bodeen looked up at Bosco and asked, "Is it true that Wicked Will got kicked off the set for listening to Michael Jackson?"

Bosco looked at Bodeen like he was crazy. " What? Where in hell did you hear some silly shit like that? Your dumb ass mama? Oh, I'm sorry to be talking about your mama like that but shit, you live with her… you might be young but you ain't dumb… and to answer your question: hell no! Gangsters love Michael Jackson. Those niggas in that *Beat It* video are real hood muthafuckas. Wicked Will was a buster. That's why he was removed from the hood. He had to be dealt with. But trust me, little man, it had nothing to do with the music he listened to. MJ is gangster."

Then Black Ass Bosco proceeded to buy Bodeen some straight leg jeans two inches too short, some penny loafers, a v-neck t-shirt, and an official red and black leather Michael Jackson *Thriller* jacket.

Bodeen kept his outfit hidden from Charlesetta. It was easy to do that because it wasn't like Charlesetta was up in his room cleaning or anything. He only pulled it out on the days she was away from the house for long periods at a time. Bodeen would take a toothbrush and dip it in Vaseline and water and style his baby hair just like MJ. Bodeen would perform up a storm. It was the only time he was at peace.

One day, Bodeen was working on his routine and Charlesetta came home early. Bodeen snatched the clothes off and hid them under his mattress just before Charlesetta entered the house. Bodeen still had the suspicious look on his face children have when they are guilty about something. Charlesetta saw the look on his face but it was the baby hairs she saw pasted down his temples is what made her lose it. Charlesetta made Bodeen strip naked. She went into the kitchen and filled the Kool-Aid pitcher with hot water. She came back into the room and threw the water on Bodeen. Charlesetta snatched an extension cord out of the wall and beat Bodeen with it like he was a slave. She was breaking the skin with every blow. Bodeen tried to run when he could no longer bear the pain and Charlesetta tripped him. Charlesetta wrapped the cord around Bodeen's neck like she would with the purse strap, but this time she tied the other end to the bed leg so she could have both hands free. She beat Bodeen in the head with closed fist until he was completely unconscious. Bodeen's dead weight made the cord around his neck even tighter.

Bodeen would have been dead from a lack of oxygen if Black Ass Bosco hadn't come through the door when he did. Bosco cracked Charlesetta in the back of the head with the 40-ounce bottle of beer he was bringing home to her. She started cussin' about him wasting good malt liquor. Bosco paid her wailing no mind as he tried to unwrap the cord from around Bodeen's neck but it was too tight. Bosco lifted Bodeen's nude limp body to create some slack in the cord and unwrapped the cord.

Bosco wanted to call 911 but being on parole had him scared. Charlesetta would blame him without question. Bosco carried Bodeen to the bathroom and cleaned off his face. Bodeen's skin was tough as leather from the previous beatings. But still it was swollen and bruised and there should have been more blood. The cool water Bosco poured on his face brought Bodeen to consciousness. Bosco carried Bodeen to his room and laid him on the bed. Bosco knew he needed to be checked on periodically because of the blows to the head. Bosco lay down next to Bodeen in the twin bed to monitor him during the night.

Even though it was the right thing to do, it was a bad decision. Bodeen's health was priority number one. Staying out of jail over this mess was a close two. But coming home drunk and helping Bodeen more than he should have was the worst thing he could have done.

Hours passed before Charlesetta made an attempt to check on Bodeen. Since Bodeen's door was left open, she figured Bosco left because he knew better than to go to sleep after he hit her with that bottle. Charlesetta barely had a scratch so you know that's a hardheaded bitch. She walked into the room and saw Black Ass Bosco partially dressed sleeping in the bed with her naked son wrapped in his arms. This was worst than catching him in the bed with a white woman by far. Charlesetta had it in her mind to kill them both, but Charlesetta is a devious bitch, first and foremost. Bosco hadn't awakened. Torturing someone was more gratifying than killing them right away. So Charlesetta videotaped Black Ass Bosco in the bed holding Bodeen's naked body from behind. She was going to use that tape against both of them.

Charlesetta left the room. She took out the tape and hid it. She put in another blank tape and got her 45-caliber pistol out of the drawer. She walked back into room, made a few adjustments to make the scene even more incriminating, and videotaped them some more as a backup. She left the camera recording and placed it on the nightstand. Charlesetta cracked Bosco with the butt of the 45 right over his eyebrow. The skin split immediately. Bosco leaped up but that gun in his face put him right back down on the bed. Charlesetta was pressing the gun down hard on the bridge of Bosco's nose.

"What the fuck is this? Is this the reason why you don't sleep in our bed every night, you nasty-ass perverted bastard? You like little boys, Bosco? Is that why you came home from jail acting all funny? Yeah, nigga, I see it in you now. You's a bitch," Charlesetta took some of the pressure of gun off of his face and continued, "Look up and smile for the camera, you sick faggot!"

Bosco looked up and saw the camera and then turned his head in shame. Charlesetta was spitting words deadlier than venom. "Yeah, rump rouser, you cold busted. I got your dumb black ass on tape. Wait until the homies see this fucked up shit! You is done in this hood. And by the way, that money you thought you had secretly saved up to leave me, huh-uh. You need to go ahead and put that paper in my hand or yo' parole officer is going to get a copy of this tape, too."

Bodeen had laid perfectly still with his eyes shut but they fluttered open. Charlesetta started in on him immediately. "Oh, sissy boy wants to wake up now. How did it feel to take a dick up yo' ass?"

It took a minute before Bodeen could even see clear but when he realized that he was naked in the bed with a grown man, he was shocked. He couldn't believe that Bosco raped him in his sleep. Bodeen was hurt, confused, and feeling used.

"Now I see you been using my Vaseline for other things besides laying your baby hair down, huh, you little punk bitch. You doing booty favors for a gay-ass jacket now, you little faggot? I put food in your belly and clothes on your black ass back! I give you everything you need and this is how you repay your mama? You had to take my man, too? All this is going to come back on you, Bodeen. You can count on that! I found all those bitch made clothes and tight jeans you be hidin' under your mattress, too, you little freak. Since you want to act like a faggot so much, Bodeen, that is the exact way I'm gon' to treat ya black faggot ass from now on until you grow some balls and man up. Now go put some of my panties on 'cuz I'm tired of looking at your naked black ass," Charlesetta barked as she fired a gun shot in the pillow right in between Bosco and Bodeen. At such close range, the pillowcase caught on fire. Bosco flipped the pillow over and smothered the fire. She kept the pistol pointed at him with smoke still coming from the barrel.

"Get the money out yo' stash and get the fuck out of my house. And if you don't want this tape to get out in the hood, half of yo' profits best be in my hand every muthafuckin' week. If you make a nickel, yo' sorry faggot ass better be handing me two and a half pennies. Now get the fuck out of my face before I castrate yo' rapist ass."

There wasn't too much Bosco could do with a 45 in his face. Bosco knew he came home a little drunk but he would never touch any child in that way. It was bothering him because he couldn't remember. How was he going to explain that to a bunch of crazy fools in the hood if they saw the tape? Charlesetta had Black Ass Bosco by the balls but if she ever slipped and lost her grip, he was going to dead her for sure.

After a few months of extortion, Black Ass Bosco got lucky and got arrested again. He was let off the hook for the next six years.

But little Bodeen wasn't so lucky. Charlesetta called Bodeen every homosexual name in the book plus some extra shit she made up. This was her strategy to make him tough. Bodeen was just a kid. He didn't understand the psychology of it. He really loved his mother. He wanted to please her but he didn't know what she expected him to do.

Since Charlesetta wanted him to model himself after her friends, Bodeen watched the gangsters from Triple 6 Crips when they came to the house. All they did was drink, get high, and talk shit about what they would do if so and so from this set or that punk from that gang stepped to them. These dudes were not the real things. Bodeen didn't want to be that. Charlesetta never gave Bodeen *the choice to be anything he wanted to be in this world with a little hard work* like most kids trying to achieve the American Dream. Shit, Charlesetta had the ability to shatter the dreams you had in your sleep. She destroyed Bodeen's fantasy of becoming the next Michael Jackson right along with his brand new Thriller jacket and cassette tapes Charlesetta found. She let him keep the tight straight leg jeans but she took some scissors and cut the ass out. Charlesetta made Bodeen wear them around the house while she forced him to do stuff so feminine, it was a miracle he didn't turn into one of those fun boys. She made him brush her hair. She sent him to the store for tampons even when she wasn't on her period.

And at least twice a week, she made Bodeen perform an act that scarred him for life. Bodeen had to paint Charlesetta's fingernails and toe nails with this Crip Blue nail polish. He hated that more than anything because Charlesetta had the nastiest looking feet and roughest hands ever placed on a woman. Crip Blue nail polish was the only color she ever wore. It was so traumatic that in Bodeen's later years, the sight of blue fingernails would cause him to snap in an instant.

But through all this torture and bullshit, Bodeen was getting bigger, thicker, and stronger. As he grew, he was able to withstand the abuse his mother delivered. His neck muscles became stronger. Those straps his mother wrapped around his neck started to feel like a tight necktie. The punches to his face were losing power also. Bodeen developed an iron jaw and rock solid chin and it became extremely hard to knock him out with bare fist. The anger in Bodeen was burning deeper and hotter. He became more aggressive when he played with the kids from the neighborhood. He didn't fight them, but just a simple game of tag would leave kids bruised and sore after Bodeen tagged them with his strong mitts.

Bodeen was still managing to squeak by in school. He made it all the way to the fourth grade without ever having to pass a written test. Bodeen was only scared at the beginning of the school year when he had a new teacher that wasn't aware of his learning disabilities. Unbeknownst to him, teachers talk about students in the staff meetings so they were long aware of Bodeen's issue. They often talked about Charlesetta in the teachers lounge, where they could discuss how they truly felt.

One day before class started, all the kids were lined up outside waiting for the teacher to open the door. After the bell rang all the other classes filtered in except Bodeen's. The kids started to get restless and began to make a lot of noise out there on the yard unsupervised. It was sort of a pre-celebration because the regular teacher, whom was never late, hadn't arrived so they were hoping they sent a substitute in her place, preferably the old librarian who let them play games all day.

The noise level outside sounded like a riot was going on and then all the sudden, you could hear pin drop. The principal was walking across the yard with a young well-dressed, clean-shaven black guy. The principal started calling out the names of the kids she spotted acting up and they were told to come see her in the office later on that day. The rest of the kids stiffened up in line like model students.

"Good morning, class. This is your substitute teacher Mr. Miguel. Mrs. Paine is out today and maybe tomorrow with the flu. I want you to be on your best behavior. Do not look at this as a free day to play. Mr. Miguel has Mrs. Paine's lesson plan for today. Mr. Miguel has been told to send any student with boisterous behavior straight to my office. I want you to give him the same respect as your regular teacher. Do you all understand?"

As soon as she was out of earshot, the noise erupted all over again. The kids bolted in the classroom when Mr. Miguel opened the door. Bodeen and a few other kids raced to the pencil sharpener. They were thumping each other's ears and horsing around. The little girls were on the other side of the classroom gossiping about some girl in another class that bought the same Hello Kitty purse they had and trying to be like them.

Mr. Miguel was not trying to start his morning off like that. He was just there to collect an honest day's pay. Mr. Miguel was also aware from experience that if he didn't get control of the madness early, it was going to be a long day. Mrs. Paine didn't leave a lesson plan. That was just a weak ploy substitute teachers used to try and maintain order. Mr. Miguel did what most substitute teachers do when they don't have a curriculum to teach.

"Settle down class and take your seats. I'm Mr. Miguel and I'll start the class with telling you a little bit about my background."

The generation of kids today can't be fooled with those old school house tactics. Tiffany raised her hand and interrupted Mr. Miguel before he even got started.

"Excuse me, but how come all you substitute teachers have to narrate your life and we're never going to see you again? All you're doing is trying to make time go by. You ain't fooling anybody. Then after we hear your long boring story, we have to go around the classroom, stand up and introduce ourselves—we all know each other already..."

Mr. Miguel was stuck. That lesson plan was sure to get him to the recess break. Mr. Miguel was young and arrogant and loved to talk about himself so he had a little attitude that he just got put in check by a fourth grader. Fortunately, before he had to come up with a retort or plan, a student named John-John was interested in Mr. Miguel's name.

"Hey teacher, how'd you get the name Mr. Miguel, your Daddy Mexican?"

All the kids started laughing. Mr. Miguel's ego was getting bruised. He used the good-looking black man with a Spanish name and curly hair persona to his advantage. Women found it sexy but the fourth graders thought it was hilarious. They knew Mr. Miguel was a lame.

"My grandfather told me to never trust a black man with no facial hairs or a man with two first names," said Gina.

Mr. Miguel got defensive. "Well your old grandfather doesn't know what he's talking about. And as for you boy, I don't have a daddy, I have a father. I know most of you can't comprehend what that is… and yes, my father is Mexican."

"Oh! So you're a Blaxican?" yelled the class clown from the back of the class and that caused everybody to laugh again."

Mr. Miguel tried the stern approach. "Okay, okay. That's enough, class. I need you to settle down and focus your attention up here…I said focus!"

"Focus on these nuts!" an anonymous voice yelled from somewhere in the classroom.

The kids lost it. They fell out laughing. Mr. Miguel had to turn his back to the class to conceal his laughter as well because the timing was impeccable.

But with that remark, they left him with no other choice. He turned back to the class. "All right, that's enough. I want you, you, and you to pack your things and go to the principal's office right now."

"Awwww, Mr. Miguel! We didn't even do nothin'!" The kids in trouble sang in harmony.

After the kids left the room, Mr. Miguel regained control of the class for about the next thirty seconds. Evelyn, the smartest girl in the class who took her education very seriously, politely raised her hand and said, "No disrespect to you, Mr. Miguel but do you really want to be a teacher? I mean, this is not even an inner city school. This is a fourth grade class in Rialto and you can't even get it under control. You can send me to the principal's office so at least I can get some work done."

Mr. Miguel had the fork stuck in him; he was already done. He didn't know how to respond to the question. His anger had already got the best of him. He started to belittle the students to make him feel like a big man.

"Fourth grade? Did you say this was fourth grade? I thought this was a kindergarten class by the way you kids act. My daughter has more sense than you all and she's just two years old. Until you show me you can act like fourth graders, I'm going to treat you like the babies in kindergarten," Mr. Miguel stated. He had no idea what his plan was but he had to think quick on his feet. He saw a dusty Dr. Seuss book on the shelf and picked it up.

"Since you want to act like little babies, I'm going to read you a story and then I want you to put your head on the desk and take a nap."

The class roared with disapproval. Mr. Miguel countered it with, "Either take a nap or do 500 standards! Make your choice..." He waited a moment. "So judging by the silence, I knew you would see it my way. Matter of fact, we are going to pass the book around the class. Each child read one paragraph; you all know what a paragraph is, don't you?" Mr. Miguel stated sarcastically. "...you little girl, start reading and then I want you to pass the book to the next person seated behind you until everybody has a turn."

Mr. Miguel gave the book to the child seated up front in the first row. She started to read with an extreme attitude. The literature was far beneath her standards.

"...I do not like them in a tree. I do not like them with a bee. I don't like them on my cat. I don't like them with my rat... This is some bullshit!" the Hispanic girl shouted as she slammed the book down on the desk of the student behind her. The book went down the row with each kid reading angrier than the last.

"I would not like them here or there. I would not like them anywhere..." The little white girl read and then she looked at Mr. Miguel and said, "I don't like you either!" She rolled her eyes, twisted her head around and gave Mr. Miguel the hand.

She passed the book to Bodeen. She pointed to the spot where she left off before she rolled her eyes at Mr. Miguel again and sat down in her seat. Bodeen looked at the words on the page for a long time. Mr. Miguel had run out of patience when he first arrived at the school so Bodeen's silence aggravated him. He yelled at Bodeen. "Go on boy we don't have all day and sit up straight."

Bodeen sat up and remembered what his previous teachers taught him about phonetics. Bodeen began to sound the words out.

"Sssss-ssssss-A-aaa-aaim-aim-SaaAamme-Same-I-I-AIM-AIM... AIM...I duh...duh...-O- DOE- DOE... Nnnnn—"

Kids have no compassion for feelings in situations like that no matter what your problem is and they will accept no excuses. It just takes one kid to say the right thing at the wrong time to set the crowd off.

"That black ass muthafucka cain't even read."

The kids fell out on the floor laughing hysterically. It was that contagious laughter. I'm talking about tears rolling down the face and ribs hurting laughter.

"...this-this dumb ass nigga can't read Sam in the fourth grade. He was going Sssssss! Ssssssss!" The kid mimicking Bodeen couldn't even finish his sentence without bursting out in more laughter.

"I wanted to say- Sam! Muthafucka Sam! I do not like green eggs and ham. DAMN!" yelled the class clown from the back of the class. He even caused the teacher to laugh out loud.

"Same I Aim... now that's a damn shame," Mr. Miguel stated. He truly didn't intend for his statement to rhyme and it caused more laughter but the damage was already done.

Bodeen knew he would have to face his fear eventually but he never thought he would be ridiculed in the process. Evelyn, the class valedictorian, didn't find it funny one bit. She demanded respect by the way she carried herself and she got it. Evelyn spoke to the class but she was really directing her anger toward the school system.

"I don't see what is so funny. The same teachers that have been passing Bodeen along and letting him slide are the same ones that are teaching us. And they are the first ones with a picket sign crying for more money. First off, Bodeen, I want to commend you for having the courage to stand up and face your fears. This half of a Mexican that calls himself a teacher should have told you this. If he knew what he was doing he would be helping you instead of putting you down in front of the class. You have to speak to the child's strength, Mr. Miguel, not make fun of them."

Embarrassed, Mr. Miguel answered Evelyn like the chump substitute teacher he was, "I am not his daddy. That is not my job. He should have known how to read before I got here."

A tear rolled down Bodeen's cheek. The other kids had stopped laughing and teasing Bodeen once Evelyn spoke. They started giving him words of encouragement instead.

"Man, Bodeen, you alright. He jus' a sucka who don't have a real job."

"We know you just clownin' him."

"This whole lesson is stupid anyway."

Mr. Miguel had no sympathy.

"Oh did I hurt your feelings? If I bought you some milk and cookies, would it make you feel better? How about if I came over there and gave you a hug and kiss on the forehead and told you everything was going to be all right, sweetie pie?" Mr. Miguel teased.

Mr. Miguel started walking toward Bodeen with his arms extended open like a gay priest. Mr. Miguel wasn't really going to hug him but by that point Bodeen didn't care what his intentions were. Bodeen had two freshly sharpened #2 pencils on his desk. Throughout history every kid turned killer seemed to always get his introduction to the dark side by stabbing someone with a #2 pencil. But Bodeen dared to be different even early on in his career so he stabbed Mr. Miguel in the chest with his Papermate pen instead. Letting out all that pinned up frustration from dealing with Charlesetta's bullshit at home felt so good to Bodeen, he stabbed Mr. Miguel three more times in the gut to make sure he got his point across. Mr Miguel fell and curled up on the floor. Bodeen stood over him as he winced in pain. Bodeen dropped the book on top of Mr. Miguel's wounded body and from memory he sarcastically exclaimed, "Yes Sam I am, I do like scrambled eggs and ham!"

"It's green eggs, muthafucka! Green!" yelled the class clown in the back of the class.

So that's how the Legend of Bodeen began. He became greater every time the story was told. His name was ringing all through the neighborhood. Even though thought was put into the dastardly act, the story still came out the same.

"Bodeen stabbed a teacher with a #2 pencil!"

"You hear what happened at the school? Some teacher tried to kiss Bodeen and he stabbed him in the neck with a #2 pencil and a screwdriver. Blood was everywhere!"

"Man, some shit jumped off at the school today. Bodeen laid about five teachers out. I heard he had like ten #2 pencils in his pocket, and a Bic pen. Teachers was coming at him from everywhere and he just started pokin' 'em until they dropped like flies. They had #2 pencils stickin' out their face. Man, it was crazy. I was right there when it happened, I was like, *Oh my God!*"

Over the years the story that most people latched on to was, *"Bodeen got his start early. He killed his teacher with a #2 pencil when he was just eight years old."*

Mr. Miguel didn't die but he was scared to death that he was going to get ink poisoning. The tip of the pin from the first stab wound did break off deep into the tissue. It wasn't enough to cause him any harm. The second and third were more like puncture wounds that left nasty bruises on his stomach. Mr. Miguel wanted to file a complaint but in every statement from the witnesses, they all said Mr. Miguel provoked it when he came toward Bodeen with his arms stretched out asking Bodeen if he wanted a kiss on the forehead. The teacher was fired. Bodeen was wasn't charged in the stabbing. Nevertheless, Bodeen was still expelled from school.

Charlesetta even gave Bodeen a little praise at home for stabbing Mr. Miguel, but not without warning him of what she would have done to him if he didn't take matters into his own hands.

Even though he could have been transferred to a different school, Bodeen had no intentions of ever returning to any school after suffering from the public humiliation of not being able to read or write. He would not be able to keep the façade going even though the school system was willing to pass him. Some nitwit from the school board with a masters degree in sociology recommended that Bodeen be home-schooled under Charlesetta's supervision.

* * *

Bodeen's newfound celebrity didn't go to his head. It wasn't like he made new friends or had a bunch of groupies trying to rip his clothes off. People were leery of Bodeen so they'd rather talk about him than have a conversation with him. In a strange way it helped form something like a bond with his mother. Charlesetta enjoyed being known for having the toughest son in the neighborhood.

Now I wouldn't say Charlesetta lightened up on Bodeen, but it would be safe to say she channeled her negative energy in a different way. She didn't talk down on him and abuse him like before but she did start to use him. Bodeen's home schooling consisted of bagging up narcotics for Charlesetta, making deliveries, doing chores around the house, and swimming at the indoor public pool. Charlesetta stopped punking Bodeen and making him paint her nails but she still sent him the beauty supply shop to buy her that ugly blue polish.

But every so often, Charlesetta would bring up the videotape incident as a means of control. Bodeen was getting too big to rule with an iron fist. The one thing that weakened Bodeen was when his mother would accuse him of having sex with her boyfriend. He would do anything Charlsetta would tell him so she wouldn't tell anybody about his dark secret. The flip side of that thought for Bodeen was revenge. Bodeen counted the days to when Black Ass Bosco would return to the streets. He couldn't wait.

A couple of years passed and it was the same old shit: just business as usual. Bodeen had grown up fast. He was just twelve years old but was already driving. He looked eighteen. Bodeen never drove with kids his age in the car so he never gave the police a reason to pull him over like they do with most teenagers. Bodeen was just a natural loner. He still refused to join his mother's gang. The Triple Six Crips just weren't serious enough for him. The most valuable education they gave Bodeen was nothing. Any knowledge they would have given Bodeen about life would have hurt him more than it would have helped him.

Bodeen paid attention to everything. He studied his surroundings, watched people and their body language, and all the other intricacies that came with street life. Bodeen had an excellent memory and knew how to speak articulately when he needed to do that.

"Bodeen, drop this off at Smokes' house for me. That muthafucka still owes me money from that last package and he think I forgot. If he don't have my two grand on top of what he's going to give you for this, don't give that muthafucka shit. I don't care what excuse, lie, or whatever slick shit he comes up with. Don't give him this package without that back pay! Oh yeah, and on the way back, stop by the beauty supply and get your mama some Opi Blue Polish #32... and hey, don't bring back that Revlon shit off the cheap nail polish rack from Wal-Mart! I know you trying to keep some extra change, you little slick black nigga."

Bodeen laughed at Charlesetta's last statement because he was guilty as charged. As Charlesetta started to focus more on her hustle than gang bangin', her attitude became progressively better. She had to deal with people that were about making money and not drinking malt liquor on the corner telling drive-by stories. Charlesetta was starting to make some good money. Not enough to buy some class, mind you, but she was making more money than she needed.

Bodeen drove over to Smokes' apartment. It was a well-kept unit with a lot of rubber trees in different areas of the building. There was a pool in the middle of the courtyard. Smokes lived on the first floor. Bodeen pressed #108 and got buzzed in. He walked past the unoccupied pool wishing he had time to take a quick dip. Smokes opened the door before Bodeen had a chance to knock. Smokes was maybe a quarter shade lighter than Bodeen, if that, and always had the nerve to tease him about his dark complexion. I guess it made him feel light skin to see someone a shade darker than he was.

"Triple Darkness! Damn boy! You so black you done put out the afternoon sun. I opened the door and thought it was midnight. I was about to go put my pajamas back on and go to bed," Smokes stated and he and Bodeen slapped five and closed the door behind them. Smokes continued, "You want a beer or something to drink? I got scotch, too."

Bodeen gave Smokes that *C'mon man* look and then declined by shaking his head no.

"How's your mama? She don't come through as often since she had to do that thang, to uh, you know—to old boy around the way," Smokes gave Bodeen that *we don't need to go into details* look and then continued. "But she safe to come around here. Believe me those young fools don't want no more problems with your mama... You know even though your Mama is mean as a muthafucka, she's better company than your non-sociable, funeral suit colored ass."

"Smokes, you're just as burnt as me except for yo' yellow ass teeth. Every time you smile, your face looks like a cheeseburger."

"Ain't that some shit... put your arm out!" They stuck their arms out to compare skin tones. They were damn near the exact same color but Smokes didn't see it that way.

"Look at that! You are twenty shades darker than me," Smokes insisted.

That foolishness went on for another ten minutes before they got down to business.

"I'm glad you came when you did, Onyx, because I am bone dry over here." Smokes pulled out a stack of money from under the couch. "There you go. Eighteen large. Count that up."

"It should be twenty."

"Bullshit! You ain't gonna run game on me. The price was already agreed upon. I'm paying up front," Smokes ranted as his voice began to rise.

Bodeen spoke slow to him so he wouldn't get confused. "The eighteen is straight. But you still owe two grand from the last time."

"What? I know Charlesetta ain't still trippin' off a lousy two grand after all that business I brought her."

"20 or nuttin's happenin'." Bodeen put the stamp on it.

"You're serious, huh?"

Bodeen just looked at him without saying a word.

"Man, tell Charlesetta I'll get it to her after this run. I'm a little short right now."

"Well, get that two together and it'll be here when you get back."

"Man, this is some bullshit for real." Smokes went into his pocket and pulled out a roll of hundred dollar bills. "All I got is 1,600. I know I'm good for that four."

"Get the four and I'll be back," Bodeen replied.

"Get Charlesetta on the phone!"

"You're speaking to her," Bodeen calmly replied.

"You know what? Fuck this! Give me my bread back and I'll take my business elsewhere."

Bodeen gave Smokes all his money back minus two grand. Smokes got an instant attitude.

"What you doing with that two grand?"

"You owe this. Debt paid. I'm gone."

"You better give me that money before you get your young ass hurt. And your mama knows how I get down. I won't fold up like them bitch ass niggas around the corner if she comes waving her pistol up in here. Now give me my money, son, and we'll take care of that later."

Bodeen turned on his heels and started walking toward the door. Bodeen felt Smokes coming up from behind him fast. Bodeen turned and threw a punch that landed in the center of Smokes muscular chest. It was a pretty good punch for a 12-year-old but it just wasn't powerful enough to budge a 34-year-old gangster in great shape. Smokes didn't want to hurt the kid so he just grabbed Bodeen and took him down to the floor. Bodeen was strong for his age. Smokes put his knee in Bodeen's chest. He took his money back from him.

"Man, I thought we were tighter than this, youngster. My feelings are more hurt than anything. If it's that serious, take this grand and tell Charlesetta I'll give her the other one later on tonight. As far as the other business goes, like I said I'll go elsewhere."

Smokes took his knee out of Bodeen's chest and helped him to his feet. Bodeen spit in his face. Smokes clocked him right in the eye. He didn't want to hit Bodeen but he had to. It was a natural reaction. Bodeen's eye got swollen like a fat woman's feet that had tight shoes on all day.

Bodeen drove home and sat the original package and the thousand dollars down in front of Charlesetta.

"What the fuck is this, Bodeen? And where is my nail polish?" Charlesetta asked without looking at him. Bodeen didn't answer and that's what got her attention. She raised her voice, "Do you hear me talking to your black ass? Where is my—damn boy what the fuck happened to you?"

Bodeen explained what went down between him and Smokes.

She listened carefully. When he finished, Bodeen had gained Charlesetta's respect for the way handled himself. His shrewd no nonsense-no breaks approach showed her something about her son. Charlesetta didn't have discipline like that. She would have let Smokes slide on his debt. She would have cursed him out and threatened to cut off his supply, but she wouldn't have left eighteen grand on the table for that old two stack.

"Go get my shit, Bodeen; we're going to see Smokes!"

Bodeen drove Charlesetta back over to Smokes' pad. They waited outside of the car until they saw someone leaving the building. Charlesetta stopped the security door from closing so they could enter without using the code. Charlesetta waited behind a rubber tree while Bodeen knocked on the door. Smokes opened it, but he didn't let Bodeen in.

"What's up, Oil Spot? Listen man, I didn't want to hit you like that but I ain't apologizing either. You should never spit in another black man's face, young soldier. That is the worst form of disrespect. That's deep rooted from those slavery days. I almost snapped and killed your ass... so what you want, Deep Space? It ain't even been an hour. I told you I would have that money for you later tonight. If your mother got a problem with that, tell her she can call me."

"Hello? This is Charlesetta. Can I speak to Smokes?" Charlesetta said from behind the bush.

"This is him speaking. I'm glad you here so we can clear this misunderstanding. Now I know you are a down-ass bitch and that shit you did to those niggas around the corner made a statement that we all had to take to heart. But listen. We made some good money this year, girl, and I know you ain't trippin' off of a couple of funky ass dollars."

"You know I ain't here for that, Smokes. What the fuck you doin' putting your hands on my son? He ain't nothin' but twelve years old... Look at his eye, Smokes. You hit him like he was a grown ass man. You are not supposed to hit a child like that."

"He spit on me. And as ignorant as you are, Charlesetta, I know you had enough sense to teach him not to do no shit like that."

"You better watch your tone talking to me, Smokes. I'm the only bitch that will be able to pull the Triple 6 Crips off your ass after they see what you did to they little homie."

"Listen here, bitch. I AM a grown ass man. And if those little half of thugs come over here and put their hands on me they will not be coming back to the hood the same." Smokes stopped talking and looked toward the rubber plant. He got paranoid like he heard something behind the bush. It was just the wind blowing but he wasn't taking a chance to find out. Smokes grabbed Bodeen in a headlock and pulled his pistol out. He raised it high in the air for Charlesetta to see and anyone else trying to ambush him from behind the trees.

"What the fuck is wrong with you, Smokes? Have you lost your damn mind?"

It was a shame that something like this had to occur before Charlesetta's motherly instincts finally kicked in. She became more protective than a lioness fighting off hungry hyenas trying to attack her cubs.

"You better tell whoever that is behind the bush to stand down or Bodeen's little black ass is going to be bleeding coffee up in this bitch."

Smokes was so convincing Charlesetta had to turn around and make sure nobody was behind her. Charlesetta put her hands up and took a step back. She assured Smokes that nobody was hiding. Smokes scanned the scene. The coast was clear. He let Bodeen loose from his grip.

"Go wait in the car, baby. Smokes and your mama need to discuss some grown folks' business."

Bodeen was hesitant but he followed his mother's orders. Charlesetta returned to the car ten minutes later and they rolled out. Charlesetta didn't say anything, but Bodeen noticed she had tiny drops of blood splattered on her blouse. Charlesetta put her pistol under the seat and she counted out the 18,000.

When they returned home, Charlesetta got out of the car but stopped Bodeen before he turned off the engine. "Now wait a minute, baby. I still need you to hurry up and go get my Blue #32 before the beauty supply closes."

Bodeen was so mad he just hit the gas and drove off while Charlsetta was still standing in the street yelling his name and more items on her checklist to bring back.

Bodeen brought the Blue #32 back home three and a half years later.

BODEEN (THE GRIGORI)

THE CALIFORNIA YOUTH Authority earned a reputation as a dangerous place for children. The CYA houses individuals between the ages of 12-25 depending on the nature of the crime. The CYA was not set up to house first-time juvenile offenders arrested for minor offenses. It was loaded with vicious gang members, sexual offenders, and other violent and repeat offenders. It was worst than most adult prisons. It was common for a child or a CYA staff member to become victims of violent attacks by others while at the California Youth Authority.

The cops that brought him in teased Bodeen for having bought a bottle of blue nail polish. The pistol they found under the seat that was still smoking from the bullets being discharged from it was no joking matter. Bodeen kept his mouth closed and took a 6-year deal for possession of a concealed weapon and driving underage without a license. When the sound of the metal cage door closed on Bodeen, it became clear why Charlesetta was yelling at him in the street and running after the car when he sped off. She was telling him to come back and dispose of that pistol. The first time Bodeen decided to defy his mother was the day she finally said something that was worth listening to. Ain't life a bitch!

The officers put the word out in the jail that Bodeen had blue nail polish in his possession at the time of his arrest as a punishment to him for not giving up the real owner of the gun. But it didn't matter if they spread the rumor or not because your knuckle game is going to be tested in Youth Authority on day one. There is no way around it. CYA was nicknamed the Gladiator School for a reason. You have just enough time to set your state issued blankets and clothing down on the bed before you have to square off against another kid.

Bodeen had a pretty good knuckle game. He hit hard like Ernie Shavers, but his stamina was questionable in the beginning. By the time he left CYA, Bodeen had a record of 10-2-1 with seven knockouts. He lost twice to the same dude. The Spanish kid was projected to be the next Golden Glove Boxing Champion, but he came to the facility with the typical story that seems to plague the Hispanic community. His favorite cousin that kept him off the street and in the gym got killed partaking in gang activity. Hispanics are very protective of their family so we know how that story ended.

The Spanish kid was talented with his hands. He was lightning quick and he hit very hard. Bodeen was brawler. The Spanish kid was a boxer. Bodeen's thick body type wasn't agile enough to thwart off the beautiful combinations. Bodeen learned two things from the first loss. He had trouble with small guys with tremendous speed, but he also discovered he was blessed with an immoveable chin that was rock solid. Bodeen fought him again a few months later, just to see how much he improved. He did better that time around but it still resulted in a loss. Bodeen started training more seriously after the second defeat and became a pretty good student of the sweet science.

There were some tough cats in CYA, but Bodeen held his own. He didn't like the racial politics. Bodeen favored the strong against the weak. Bodeen would rather ride with a tough white racist from the Aryan Nation over most of the weaker blacks he was forced to associate with. It had nothing to do with color. Bodeen wanted to be associated with power.

Bodeen adapted to his environment on the moment he got locked up. The same couldn't be said for a lot of the other youth in CYA. In Bodeen's first year in there, sixteen children committed suicide. Some of them weren't even physically weak but they could no longer tolerate the horrible day-to-day routine at the California Youth Authority. They were found hanging dead in their cells.

Prison activists and politicians were often quoted in the media stating that the children were often treated like animals in a zoo. It sounded good but they obviously had never been to jail or a zoo. They treated the kids in CYA like wild savages. If they had an infraction for fighting or talking back, the kids were locked in little individualized cages as punishment where they were frequently drugged and improperly cared for. The proper term for it is *chemical restraint*. Bodeen was put in the cage four times, but never for fighting. He refused to attend the mandatory school program they offered.

Bodeen saw a lot of sick shit while he was in CYA. Fights and knife play were common, but the things beyond that could mentally scar a person for a long time. Once, while out on work duty, Bodeen watched a low risk non-violent inmate who was only thirteen years old (and with only 30 days left on his sentence) murder a female prison guard. The inmate beat, stabbed, and strangled the guard then placed her body in a trash dumpster. The dead body was found in Riverside County two days later.

The guards in CYA were not soft either. Bodeen saw one juvenile suffer from multiple bite wounds to his lower leg when a CYA guard allowed his dog to attack the juvenile who was actually following orders and already lying on the floor.

Bodeen saw raped victims flip the script and become the rapist themselves. He saw kids cut up the rats in the kitchen and put it in the guards' food. Bodeen absorbed the negative energy and became a part of it. He didn't want to fight it. He was at peace there. Nobody bothered him. And Black Ass Bosco was right; gangsters really did love Michael Jackson. Every killer in that muthafucka had a *Thriller* tape.

As awful as it was to be in those conditions, according to Bodeen it was still better than living with Charlesetta.

* * *

Bodeen was released after 3 and a half years, reinvented. Bodeen stepped out of CYA looking down on the world. It wasn't because he felt like he was on top; he just grew faster than a beanstalk over those last 39 months. Bodeen stood tall at 6'3", but he was no longer thick and stocky. He was long, lean, and chiseled like a young Tommy Hearns. Training in the boxing program, the fast growth spurt, and refusing to eat whatever that was they were serving that looked like meat put him in that type of shape. It had nothing to do with Bodeen getting in tune with himself, having discipline, and following a strict diet. He couldn't wait to sink his teeth in some greasy pork chops, greens, and fatback.

Bodeen had to take a charter bus back home. Charlesetta was still leery about coming near a jail since it was her pistol that got Bodeen locked up in the first place. Needless to say, she never visited Bodeen one time. She did however put more money on his books than he would ever need. The bus dropped Bodeen off near LAX Airport. Bodeen walked to the nearest phone booth. There were different colored cabs lined up on the street. Before Bodeen went to jail, all the cabs he ever saw were yellow. Bodeen called Charlesetta from the pay phone. A recording came on saying the number had been changed and "...*the new number is...*"

The Los Angeles area code the operator recited made Bodeen feel better about coming home. He had no desire to go back to that trap called Rialto. Bodeen called the new number. He took a deep breath and prepared for the worst. Charlesetta answered the phone and her voice was actually pleasant. Bodeen had so much bass in his voice now it rocked Charlesetta's eardrum.

"Hey, Ma."

"Damn! Your voice sounds sexy, who is this?" Charlesetta answered as she rubbed her erect nipples.

"Ma?" Bodeen wasn't hip that Ma was a name dudes called their ladies but not their mothers now.

It took Charlesetta a minute but finally she said, "Bo baby?"

"Mmm-hmm," was Bodeen's way of saying, "Yes, it's me! I'm home. What's the new address? And have some pork chops ready!"

Bodeen was embarrassed when Charlesetta told him to write the address down to the new house. He played it off and told her he had to get a pen. He actually waved a cab driver out of his car with a $50 dollar bill and put him on the phone with Charlesetta to get the address.

The cabbie asked Bodeen which route he wanted to take. He had a choice of three. Bodeen didn't answer. He already gave him a $50 dollar tip just to write down an address. The cabbie took the long route. He wanted to milk Bodeen for as much money as he could. They rode down Century to LaBrea. After they passed all the airport hotels, things started to look different. A lot had changed in a short period of time. There were a lot of corporate shopping centers and fewer and fewer Mom and Pop shops. The cab made a left on LaBrea. As they cruised through Inglewood, Bodeen saw a few Blood members here and there. He could tell by their demeanor they were way more serious than the fools he grew up with in Rialto.

As they continued north, the houses started to get nicer and nicer. The cabbie took a right on Slauson and then a left on Overhill. They were in a city called Windsor Hills. Bodeen looked out the window and thought that either Charlesetta was a kingpin or she robbed a lot of banks to live in that area. These weren't average houses. They were million dollar homes.

The cab turned onto a cul-de-sac called Don Diablo Way and pulled up to a driveway. It was a nice two-story house with a manicured lawn. There were two Mercedes parked in the driveway. The meter on the cab showed $53.65. Bodeen pulled out a wad of cash. The cabbie's eyes lit up like a Christmas ornament. Bodeen gave him $3.75 and waited for his dime in change. The cab driver had the saddest look on his face and his poor heart just sank. He had been just certain that $50 dollars was a tip. He already had the money spent in his head. The entire time the cabbie was driving, he was thinking, "Oh yeah! Soon as I get off work I'm going to get a bottle of drank and buy me a little weed and call the lady over and watch a couple of movies…" And that muthafucka Bodeen wouldn't even let him keep the dime. The menacing look Bodeen gave the cab driver that he developed in the joint translated just as well on the streets. It said *don't fuck with me* and the cabbie had no quarrels with that.

Bodeen heard a voice coming from the house. "Hey Charlesetta somebody is getting out of a cab in front of your house, it looks like Squeeze. What happen to his car?"

Bodeen strolled up the long walkway that leads to the front door. Even though they saw Bodeen coming, he still had to ring the doorbell. The voice that spoke before said, "Who is it?"

"Bo."

"Who are you looking for?"

Bodeen stared into the peephole.

"Charlesetta do you know somebody named Bo? I don't like the way he's looking at me; you need to tell him about himself."

"Bo? Girl, that's my son open up that goddamn door you dumb ass bitch," Charlesetta voice rang loudly from a distance. Now that was the voice of the dragon lady Bodeen remembered, not that sweet-talking one he heard on the phone.

The dumb bitch that was told to open the door was Cassandra. She looked like a hot mess, just like Bodeen figured one of Charlesetta's friends would look. Those ratchet bitches run in packs. But you can't tell them that because they think they are fine as hell. Cassandra gave Bodeen a sexy look up and down that he wasn't accustomed to getting. He was kind of flattered but Cassandra was far from his type. There were two other broads seated in the living room drinking gin and grapefruit juice as Bodeen walked in the spacious and beautiful home. They started cat calling when they saw his lean chiseled 6'3 frame.

"Oh shit! Who is that tall fine chocolate nigga right there?"

"Hey Chocolate Drop...what is your name? You gonna be dancing at the club?"

A lot of things had changed since Bodeen had been gone. Before he was locked up, he was the blackest, most ugly spook the world had ever seen. He thought his skin was a curse. But all that changed once the leader of the black pack, a cat named Wesley Snipes, made that hit movie. It was a change in the guard. Dark skin was in. Now all of a sudden, Bodeen was the finest and sexiest man on the streets.

"Don't let me slice one of you ratchet, crab carrying bitches for trying to get with my son," Charlesetta said as she stepped in to the living room.

She was shocked at the sight of how tall Bodeen had grown. She looked him up and down with a sick lustful look in her eye like she had the hots for him. It made Bodeen uncomfortable.

But he was just as shocked to see her transformation. Charlesetta upgraded from a nasty hood rat to a hot ass mess. Her hair was long, I mean, down past her shoulders long and real soft and silky. Before he left, that shit was so coarse, when she combed it, it sounded like a bowl of Rice Krispies cracklin' up in that muthafucka. *POP! POP! POP!* You had to take cover around that bitch. She used to leave bee-bee shots and the kink-a-bugs that fell out of her comb all in the bathroom sink looking like a bunch of nappy chest hair.

Charlsetta had these long thick painted-on eyebrows that made it look like she had a caterpillar walking across her forehead. She wore heavy makeup now, too. She honestly looked like a jail house tranny with a weave. Charlesetta had on a tight halter-top that made her drooping titties look humongous. She had on a short hoochie skirt exposing her long ashy pockmarked legs and three ugly toes colored with blue nail polish protruding out of some $1,500 Fendi shoes. She had a Fendi purse to match the shoes and a pair of Fendi sunglasses on in the house, too. Bodeen didn't know what Fendi was, but he knew Charlesetta and her friends was not the market they were targeting.

"Hey Baby I'm so glad you're home. Let me show you the new house," Charlesetta said in her new sexy voice while she was chewing on bubble gum.

The pad was laid out. Fly furniture, big screen televisions, and all the latest electronics and appliances. Bodeen had his own room. There was even a poster of NWA on the wall. Just before they got to the master bedroom Charlesetta said, "I got a surprise for you Bo in here. There's somebody I want you to meet."

Charlesetta opened the door and said, "Bo, this here is your grandmother Loretta."

Loretta turned around and Bodeen's jaw dropped to the floor. She looked ten years younger than Charlesetta and she was beautiful. She had the same exact Fendi ensemble Charlesetta had on, but it looked totally different on her. Loretta wore it with class. Her hair was styled flawless. The hard look in her otherwise radiant eyes was the only indication that showed she came up in the street life.

Shortly after Loretta gave birth to North Star's first son, she had two more boys back to back. They became the shining light in North Star's eye. He found fatherhood far more fascinating than pimping. North Star was able to do what most underworld figures can't: leave the game in his prime with all of his money. The family businesses were doing well enough to keep them comfortable so there was no reason to risk everything trying to turn out some young hoe or being crossed by an old bitter one. Two of North Star's former hoes even went back to college and got their degrees. North Star was still going through his transition period at that time so he still conducted his life like a pimp. He sent the hoes to college in pairs just like when he would send them to the track. He made them compete to see who brought home the best grades. It worked. One became CEO and the other was the CFO for his Subway franchises. Loretta was put in charge of the The Guiding Light Gentlemen Clubs. Watching North Star's passion for fatherhood rubbed off on Loretta, just like the game he gave her when she was in the streets.

But when Loretta rolled back up on Charlesetta a year prior, Loretta didn't come back to repair her relationship with her or apologize for leaving. Her intensions upon returning were strictly to throw Charlesetta a bone and get her on her feet. To Loretta's surprise, she was thoroughly impressed to see Charlesetta holding down Sister Auntie's house alone. It showed Loretta that her daughter had some hustle about herself. She was still too violent to be around the girls at the strip club, but Loretta saw that Charlesetta had control over a lot of men that she employed. Since Loretta was seasoned in the business she suggested that Charlesetta open up a male strip club. She was already one of those big thirsty women that went to strip clubs with a fistful of dollar bills so she took to the idea like a fish to water. They started off as partners but Charlesetta bought out her mother's share within months.

Loretta had flown down from Vegas just to meet her grandson for the first time.

"You can call me Mama Lo-Lo, baby. Now come on over and give me a hug," Loretta said as she held her arms open. She gave Bodeen a beautiful Rolex and a little coming home cash for his pockets. Loretta was far too young and beautiful to be the *big mama* grandmother that is typical in most black families. She didn't have any meat on her body for a grandchild to rest his head on when he was feeling down. Loretta's shoulders were too hard and her arms were too skinny. She didn't show Bodeen the extra love that he expected to feel from a grandmother but it was pleasant to see someone in the family that was nice and polite.

Bodeen checked out the rest of the house. He ignored the ratchet rats that whistled when he walked by and said he reminded them of some fool named Squeeze.

"He really does look like Squeeze, but without the blue hair and cocky ass attitude."

"He sure does but when I looked at the crease in his sweatpants I knew for sure it wasn't Squeeze. He was packin' kind of light," the other ratchet replied.

"Girl, Squeeze ain't packin nuttin' but a suitcase full of money. That fool got game with his cocky fine ass."

"I wanna rub that magic lamp underneath those genie pants!" They both fell out laughing and gave each other a high five.

The smell of fresh Pine Sol was coming out of the kitchen and he knew Charlesetta didn't cook. He was hungry as a muthafucka, too. Charlesetta must have heard his stomach grumbling because she sent one of the ratchet rats up the block to La Louisiana Creole Cuisine to get Bodeen some food. Bodeen kicked his feet up in the den and watched TV. That would be his program for the next few weeks. Bodeen practiced and memorized words, phrases, and dialog he learned on TV. Even though he wasn't the social type, he liked to listen to what other people had to say and how they reacted in certain situations.

Bodeen was flipping through the channels and a Michael Jackson video was on MTV. He heard Charlesetta walking toward the den. He quickly changed the station. He cursed himself for still showing weakness from the fear Charlesetta had instilled in him. Charlesetta came in and sat down next to him.

"Well, I see it didn't take you long to get comfortable. You gots your feet all kicked up and shit like King Farouk. It's all good. You stood up like a soldier when you took that charge for me and I ain't gonna forget that. You don't have to worry about checking in to your parole officer every month 'cuz he's a friend of mine. Let's just say I caught him in a tight squeeze," with the emphasis on *squeeze,* along with a sarcastic giggle "and he owes me a favor. Just sign your name on these slips right here and mail them in. The paperwork says you're employed as a day janitor at my club. Now since you still underage and not going to school we had to find a way to get around that but you straight now so don't worry about it. I'm gonna to give you a few weeks to get up on your feet but you a man now, Bodeen, so you gonna have to make your own way. You can work as a bouncer for me at the club to pay for your rent here or you got to find a hustle. I don't sell wholesale dope like I used to since I opened the club but I still serve coke to those fat bitches at my joint that want to trick with my dancers. I don't have too many other options for you unless you want to be a dancer or a…"

Bodeen looked up at Charlesetta as she said it like *"what the fuck are you talking about?"*

Charlesetta caught his eye and looked back at Bodeen. Charlesetta rolled her eyes while she lit a cigarette and said, "Shit, I don't know why you looking at me crazy. You used to like shaking your ass for Sister Auntie and Black Ass Bosco for free so why not put those moves to good use now? My dancers don't make nothing less than a thousand cash money a day. You're tall, dark, and handsome; your body is cut up good with all them muscles, and the way those little bitches in the front room was flipping over you, you could make some good money. How big your dick is?"

* * *

For the next few months, Bodeen worked at Charlesetta's strip club. It was called Sweet Pete's Male Exotic Strip Club. Bodeen chose the security guard position.

Sweet Pete's generated good business. It wasn't because Charlesetta was some hellava entrepreneur but she had a product that nobody else had at that time: African-American Thug Studs. The patrons were a nice balance of thirsty heavyset women that paid what they weighed, ashy legged hood rats, cool working girls with a little freak in them, and there were always a couple of nice girls that were coming to a strip club for the first time after being persuaded by their friends or for a bachelorette party.

The male dancers were a strange group of characters. Most of them were boyfriends of the fat chicks that came to the club. A high percentage of them were bisexual but a few were straight up homosexual. They were easy to detect by the way they danced on stage. The studs would face the women and swing the swipe they were blessed with. The fun boys would turn their backs to the women and jiggle their greasy asses the whole damn time. As long as you had muscles and a dick that measured in the double digits, Charlesetta gave you a job.

Charlesetta worked them boys hard, too. Since Sweet Pete's was the only game in town, she used it to her full advantage. Charlsetta was lying like a dog when she told her son the dancers made a grand a night. Not after Charlestta taxed them. She made Uncle Sam say, "Damn bitch! Respect the game." The strippers had to pay Charlesetta $250 dollars a night just get on stage. The average strippers struggling to get that booth rent up every night had to subject themselves to turn a trick every now and then to make a decent profit. Charlesetta's split if they turned a trick was 70/30 in her favor. Charlesetta kept them broke and didn't give a fuck because they needed her more than she needed them. She could find a thug with a perm willing to dance for a piece of change in front of a bunch of thirsty broads at any of your local swap meets, churches, blues clubs, or Walmarts.

But there was one stripper that Charlesetta fawned and fussed over. He made Charlesetta $300,000 dollars last year working part-time. He was known as Squeeze. The first time Bodeen met the infamous Squeeze, he purposely denied the fact that he looked like him. They resembled each other in hue and height but that was about it as far as Bodeen could see.

Squeeze was the perfect visual for the word eccentric. He wore sheer clothing, Indian beads, diamond nipple rings, and sandals when he wasn't on stage. He wore a scarf around his neck and he always held one scarf loosely in his hand at all times. Squeeze was so damn conceited it was sickening. He walked with an arrogant sway and held his chin up. He would never look directly at you. He always positioned himself to look down at you from the corner of his eye. It was irritating to say the least. His hair was dyed blue to match his contact lenses. That had to be Charlesetta's idea because Squeeze already had natural light brown eyes. It was hard to detect what his sexual preference was because he always had a fine ass exotic looking bitch with him. He made people wonder where he got those women.

Squeeze took the slogan "You got to use what you got to get what you want" out of the woman's handbook and ran with it. The first time Bodeen saw Squeeze on stage, he thought Squeeze was a weirdo. He didn't dance, shake his ass, or grind on the floor like those other greasy looking strippers. Squeeze would stroll across the stage with a magic lamp in his hand. He would caress the lamp and colored smoke would waft out into the room. Money would start coming down on the stage like rain. Squeeze never picked up dollar bills off of the floor. Whatever fine bitch he had that day completed that chore. Squeeze wore a loin cloth and if you wanted to see what was under it, you had to pay top dollar. Rich white men, married couples, and enthusiasts would come from miles around just to take a peek at this man that was so well endowed.

Squeeze was the ultimate gigolo. He wouldn't even stand next to you without a least $100 in your hand. Pull off $5K to $10K and you got him for the entire night. Charlesetta would get half or more because she never told Squeeze exactly how much the high-end tricks were paying, plus she was bringing the clients to Squeeze.

For some reason or another, rich white gay men loved Charlesetta. I guess she reminded them of those big boned maids in the slavery days that catered to their every need. She would set them up in the back of the club at a special table and make sure their drinks were never empty and that all the dancers stopped by their table for a visit. Between the gay boys, dancer "taxes", pimping fees, and sales of liquor, Charlesetta was making money hand over fist.

Within a few days of Bodeen starting at the club, she gave him a 9mm handgun every night at closing to watch her back while she filled the floor safe with cash, among other things. Charlesetta always took the gun back from him once they got home. But it didn't matter. Bodeen already had two 9mm's of his own Charlesetta didn't know about.

Bodeen was paid kibbles since he had to earn his rent. He made his real money doing favors and securing the perimeter when the dancers would turn tricks in the back room. Bodeen started honing in on his craft. This was his schooling. He kept his mouth shut and his eyes and ears open at all times.

Bodeen was coming up hard and looked mature for his age but the fact still remained he was only 15 years old. In a lot of aspects, he was still a young teenager. He wanted to watch cartoons and play video games like any other kid. He just wasn't able to do those things under Charlesetta's roof. She wanted him watching *Scarface*, bagging dope, and oiling guns for fun. Deep down, Bodeen still yearned for his mother's love and guidance like a normal teenager and regardless of his upbringing, Bodeen loved Charlesetta and would do anything for her. The stories he heard from the kids in CYA and how their parents abused them made Charlesetta look like good mother. They had bones broken and some were set on fire. Some kids even said they wished they had a mother like Charlesetta. After hearing that, Bodeen figured his mother wasn't as bad as he thought.

Bodeen was still shy like many teenage boys, especially when it came to girls. From the day Bodeen woke up in the bed naked in Black Ass Bosco's arms, he was unsure of himself. But by no means did Bodeen think he was attracted to men. He was going to kill Bosco as soon as he was released from jail anyway.

But it was that incident that turned Bodeen off from sex. He hated the way Charlesetta used it against him to keep control over him. He would rather have taken the strangulation beatings again then have to deal with that *"I've got a secret that will ruin you"* lingering over his head.

Bodeen still couldn't get his mind around being "a fine chocolate drop" for the last three months because he was so used to being called an ugly black gorilla for all of his life. So that hindered his confidence in talking to women as well. Bodeen's good looks and thug tendencies made him attractive to Charlesetta's friends yet he didn't want any part of that. In fact, he tried to stay away from everything that wasn't green that he couldn't put in his pocket. But puberty was still going to occur regardless of whether Bodeen was ready or not and his hormones kicked in right along with it.

Bodeen was working one night, posted up in the far corner of the club. He could see the fat rolls on the backs of the chubby women tossing dollar bills on stage as he scanned the crowd for any signs of trouble. Through the smoke and thumping music, he spotted a cute high yellow sister drifting back toward him. She didn't look like the women that frequented Sweet Pete's at all. Bodeen knew right off the bat that she was one of the women that was conned by her friends or co-workers to let it all hang out at the strip club with them. The sight of her made Bodeen's dick hard as stone, which made him embarrassed because it was poking out his sweat pants and very noticeable. Bodeen was hoping she didn't bump into him. As she approached Bodeen, he just pointed across the room in the direction of the restrooms.

She turned to look at what he was pointing to. "I don't need the restroom. I just needed to find a place to cool out for a minute because this is not my cup of tea," she said as she dismissively waved her hand. "I tried to go outside but that evil lady at the door said there were no ins and outs. Is it okay if I just kick it here for a hot minute? Oh, by the way my name is Kimberly." She held out her hand, "And your name is?"

Bodeen tried to be cool and just pointed to the name on his jacket. Kimberly read it and said, "Your name is Security? Is that your stripper name? Oh, I'm sorry if I dissed your job but—"

Bodeen gave a shy grin, held his hand out, and told her his name. Bodeen gave her a brief introduction on what he was about and let Kimberly know in a joking way that the evil woman at the door was his mother. Kimberly was embarrassed but Bodeen made her feel at ease. Bodeen had no conversation skills whatsoever but Kimberly had enough for the both of them. She actually made Bodeen laugh the way she twisted her nose and mouth like she smelled something foul while she expressed how she felt about the male strippers.

"Ugh no, honey—it ain't nothing sexy about a nigga with a thong up his sweaty ass… now that's just nasty. And all of them either have a Jeri curl or a kitchen perm brushed back in a ponytail that's no longer than my thumb. That's just wrong. Huh-uh! Honey, I like a man's-man and the darker the better."

Bodeen was nervous. He enjoyed the company but he didn't like conversation. He was uncomfortable about revealing personal things. He also didn't want Kimberly to leave when she found out he was only 15. Kimberly was sweet and bubbly, but she had that little attitude that came with being high yellow and cute. Kimberly was only 22 but she was way out of Bodeen's league. He just listened to her and nodded for the next hour as she talked about school and her job and other things of that nature. Bodeen's good listening skills paid dividends because she gave him her phone number in the middle of the conversation. It was a blessing it happened that way because they never got the chance to part ways properly.

"Bodeen! Bodeen! I need you to get your ass up here in the front!" Charlesetta barked as she walked to the back of the club and saw her son at peace talking to Kimberly. She didn't even need him in the front but that's just how Charlesetta was.

She looked at Kimberly real funky. "The club is in there," she snarled as she pointed behind her. "This area is restricted for employees only. Yes, that way!" Charlesetta turned to Bodeen and said loud enough for Kimberly to hear, "I ain't paying you to get snatch from some pale bitch. I don't like her attitude anyway. I was about to slap that stale bitch. I cain't stand those yellow bitches; they make me sick."

* * *

They say one monkey don't stop no show, so they didn't let Charlesetta hinder their flow. Bodeen and Kimberly started hanging out together. She loved to talk and he liked to listen. Bodeen was the perfect gentlemen. It took him three dates just to hold her hand. Bodeen's behavior would have been perfect in the old days but in this new generation of freaks Kimberly wanted to know what was really going on. Bodeen didn't show any signs of being a monk or religious fanatic. It didn't help that she started hearing rumors and most were true that dudes at strip clubs were suspect. The truth of the matter was the only cherry Bodeen wanted to pop was sitting on top of Black Bosco's neck. Bodeen's thoughts were consumed with how it was going to feel to kill for the first time. Pussy was the last thing on his mind. He felt that Bosco took his manhood so Bodeen was going to take his life.

Bodeen and Kimberly came back to the neighborhood from the movies on a Monday night. They went to see a Spike Lee joint. Kimberly tried to invite Bodeen back to her place but he declined. Kimberly was irritated the entire drive back to Bodeen's pad. When they parked, Bodeen placed his hand on her knee and started to lean over. Kimberly grabbed him by the wrist and tried to kiss him on the mouth. Bodeen pushed her back in the seat. It was the same wrist Charlesetta would grab before she tied those extension cords around his neck.

But Kimberly didn't take offense to his defensiveness. She just used a different approach. Kimberly looked at Bodeen with soft eyes. She slowly leaned over to him. Bright lights blinded them before their lips met. The light was so bright it made them squint. Charlesetta pulled up behind Kimberly's Honda Accord with the high beams on. Charlesetta keyed the passenger side of Kimberly's car as she walked up to the window and started banging her diamond rings against the window.

"Bodeen! We need to talk!"

Kimberly smiled at Bodeen and said, "I'll see you tomorrow. And I'm going to get that kiss."

Bodeen was pissed because he didn't even get a chance to feel his first kiss but when he got out of the car, he noticed Charlesetta didn't look like her normal evil self. In fact, for the past few weeks Charlesetta had been looking distraught and being distant but that night it was very different. The hurt on her face had a childlike innocence about it. Bodeen became concerned. Charlesetta placed her arm around Bodeen and they walked back to her car. They drove in silence to Sweet Pete's. Charlesetta led Bodeen back to her private office. He had never been inside the office before. When she opened the door, the office was in shambles. The furniture was turned over, glass from picture frames was broken on the floor, and the wall safe door was wide open.

"What are we going to do, Bodeen? They took everything we got. We don't have a dime to our name! Lord Jesus, please help us…"

The sight of vandalism was a shock but Charlesetta actually needing Bodeen for the first time felt awesome. Charlesetta buried her face in his chest and held him tight.

When they returned home, Bodeen actually saw Charlesetta crying. She looked so vulnerable. He had never seen her in that state. He didn't even remember her crying at Sister Auntie's funeral. Charlesetta went into her room and returned with some paperwork in her hand. It was past due and foreclosure notices on the house and the club. Bodeen looked at them but he couldn't read a word on the paper. He turned a couple of pages to make it look good but he didn't have a clue. He was relieved when Charlesetta broke down and vented to him again.

"We are going to lose everything, Bodeen! The house, the club… everything if we don't pay this in two days. What are we going to do, Bodeen? I'm so sorry, baby. I tried so hard to make it right for you—I tried so hard. Your mama really needs you right now."

Rumors had been swirling around the club that Charlesetta and Squeeze were having problems. Some people were saying he ran off to Brazil with some rich preacher to get married and ice skate together. Most people were saying Squeeze found out that Charlesetta was taking him for more than half of his money and he walked out on her ass. Both scenarios were possible, but there was proof that came with the second truth. Bodeen figured that Squeeze had the place robbed to get his back severance pay. It was justifiable.

"I'm going to need you to work tomorrow night, Bodeen. We need that money."

Bodeen looked at Charlesetta. She never had him work on Tuesday nights because Sweet Pete's was closed to the public on Tuesday nights. It was strictly for high-end members only. If you drove by at night, it was padlocked and every light was off. If that wasn't enough, there was a big ass sign that said *Closed on Tuesdays*.

On Tuesdays, Charlesetta had some wild freaky shit going on at Sweet Pete's. She fulfilled sick sexual fantasies for the rich; Charlestta was doing fantasy federal prison time type of shit—for real.

Something was not feeling right to Bodeen. Bodeen looked at his mother and as bad as he felt, he shook his head no.

Charlesetta fell to her knees and started crying hysterically. She was telling Bodeen he was all she had and they were going to get put out on the streets if he didn't work. Bodeen gave in. He went into his room and grabbed his cash out of the stash. There was around nine grand. He handed it to Charlesetta. She was shocked. She didn't expect that at all. She wondered where he had it hidden. As many times she went through his personal items when he was gone, she never found that money. But Charlesetta didn't even bother to ask how much it was before she told him that it wasn't enough. She still took it though. Bodeen just put his hands up gesturing that was all he had and all he could do.

"Do you really want to help your mama?" Charlesetta asked kindly.

Bodeen nodded his head yes.

"I really need you to do me a huge favor and I'll never ask for anything from you again. I know I ain't been the best mama at times but I was just trying to raise you tough 'cuz you didn't have a daddy around. Now you know Squeeze done ran out on me and I got important people flying in to see him tomorrow."

Bodeen was never the type to speak much and he rarely spoke what he was actually thinking but he said, "Mama, if you're even thinking that, you need to get that shit out your mind 'cuz that ain't happenin'."

Charlesetta started crying hysterically again and even louder. She grabbed the foreclosure papers and shoved them in his face. She stressed the importance of losing the house and having nowhere to go. Bodeen didn't budge. He had a place to go. After he killed Black Ass Bosco in the next two days, he was going to move in with Kimberly…

Charlesetta started playing hardball.

"All right then, you selfish ungrateful black-ass nigga. I'm gonna call 555-2505 and invite that little yellow bitch over to watch a movie. Do you think she likes gay porno? You think she is going to let you move in after she sees you licking up on Bosco's nasty ass balls?"

Bodeen had never heard that part of the story before. *Did I really lick Bosco's balls?* Instead of getting mad, Bodeen felt weak, used, and unclean. Charlesetta had him.

* * *

Humiliated wasn't even the word when Bodeen heard men whistling for him when he walked out on the stage in that ridiculous costume. Bodeen was thankful Squeeze wasn't known as a twerking booty popper… well, at least not on stage. The physical scars Charlesetta left on Bodeen for listening to *Thriller* didn't even come close to the infliction R Kelly's *Bump and Grind* put on him while he walked on stage to it.

Bodeen had a partial mask on. He was not a good Squeeze stunt double as Charlesetta had thought. They may have looked similar, but Bodeen just didn't carry himself like Squeeze. But it was going to have to work because Charlesetta had too much riding on the line that night. She had every intention of her plan working because she was already plotting the next lie to keep the façade going.

He opened up his robe and his body was glistening from the grease he had rubbed all over him. Bodeen was numb as he glanced at the audience and the music thumped on.

Kimberly was standing there with a dollar bill in her hand. His heart dropped. Kimberly waited until Bodeen looked her in her eyes She put the dollar back in her purse, flipped a penny on stage, and flounced out.

That was the life-changing event right there. Bodeen was hit with what they call a moment of clarity. In flash, all the events that happened over the past few months were playing out in his head. Charlesetta was playing hardball for real. She was throwing major league pitches. Bodeen had been on the farm team long enough. It was time to move up to the Big Leagues and step to the plate. Bodeen was ready for Charlesetta to throw another curve, but he wasn't aware that she also had a mean screwball.

Bodeen left the stage. A couple of flunkies ran to his aide with towels, flowers, and refreshments to make it look like the way Squeeze would do it. Charlesetta was there to greet him backstage. She forced a juice bottle up to his lips and poured some of the liquid in his mouth. Bodeen wasn't prepared and choked before he could swallow most of it.

"Get some liquids in your system, baby. Those hot stage lights will dehydrate you. Go on now; drink it all up."

Bodeen put the bottle to his lips to shut Charlesetta's mouth. He followed her back to the office. Bodeen had to wait outside the door like he did on a regular night. Charlesetta came back out a few minutes later wearing a plantation maid costume and a scarf around her head like a ghetto Aunt Jemima.

"Did you finish that juice, baby?" Charlesetta asked and then she looked at the empty bottle and continued, "Good, I don't need you passing out 'cuz Lord knows we don't have no money for hospital bills. But shit, the way you stepped up tonight we are going to make enough money to buy our own hospital." Charlesetta busted out laughing as she held up four thousand dollars. She counted it out and gave Bodeen half.

"You see? We are in this together now, baby, just you and me, son. You got all this money in what, three minutes? That ain't shit. Now it wasn't as bad as you thought it was going to be." Her voice was sweet and soothing but then got hard. "But let me tell you something, this is real gangster shit... I mean, real gangster shit! You playin' the short con. Con men get federal time. You better recognize!"

Charlesetta's money must have been right again because she was back to her old self. As they walked back out towards the club, she started hollering. "I'm gonna to cut that waiters fuckin' throat. Consuelo! Consuelo! Where is that half a cousin of yours that calls himself a waiter? Primo, Predro or whatever his name is...He's drippin' shit all on the goddamn floor again! You better tell that short pineapple muthafucka he's going to be back to selling Chicklets. And if he thinks I'm going to be paying his dumb ass his whole $25 dollars tonight he got another think coming. I'm taking that drink out of his check!"

Consuelo just kind of tucked her chin and trotted off. Bodeen felt bad for the waiter considering drinks on a Tuesday cost $12. Bodeen was feeling bad for himself as well. He was getting a little light headed and felt a hint of nausea. The club was noticeably stuffier with it being all closed up like it was. Charlesetta detoured toward the freak room.

"I'm about to show you how to get some real money, Bodeen."

"I have to piss something awful and I have to fix this fake-ass dick. It's starting to itch."

"Well hurry up baby, and make sure you put it back on right. You need me to help you?"

Bodeen left her questioned unanswered as he walked to the restroom. Bodeen threw up and then shitted. He started to feel better. Bodeen looked at the gigantic silicone penis and thought about hitting Charlesetta over the head with it. It was bigger than a Billy club just not quite as effective. Bodeen put the fake dick back in place. Bodeen had beads of sweat on his forehead. He went to the face bowl and wiped his hands over the sweat. He turned on the water and placed his hands over his eyes. He took a deep breath and walked back out.

Bodeen kind of stumbled when he saw Charlesetta waiting for him with her hand on her hip. She looked at Bodeen's blue contacts and asked, "Bo, are you high? Your eyes are red as hell and you're acting freaky."

Bodeen shook his no and just smiled. Bodeen lost his balance again and placed his arm around her. Charlesetta had a devious smile on her face as she led him down the hallway and unlocked the door to the freak room. She went straight into character. She snatched a whip off the wall of assorted whips and chains and popped the pale naked ass that was exposed on this table designed for bondage acts.

Bodeen couldn't see his face but he had a strong British accent. He sounded like an asshole when he called Charlesetta *Mammy*. The Brit wanted to act out a slave/master fantasy and paid Charlesetta $15,000 to do it. He had the whole scene scripted out beforehand and had told Charlesetta how he wanted it to happen. The storyline was he was captured, beaten, and tortured by rebellious slaves. But instead of being killed for his deeds, he was to be raped anally by the big buck slave (who should have been Squeeze but Bodeen was now twisted in to this whole mess) for raping his mother. But as Squeeze was seeking revenge, he falls in love with the British slave master and they pretend to kill the Mother together and run off in the sunset. It was some real sick rich man's shit. Charlesetta was in character wearing a tattered dress and rag tied on her head. She was playing the part like she was trying to win a Golden Globe Award. She was striking the British cat's ass and back with that whip and showing no mercy.

Bodeen hoped she got the money first because he thought she was going to kill him. But Sir Brit loved that shit. He started begging Bodeen to ravish his anal cavity. Bodeen was acting incoherent as he was rubbing his junk like he was trying to get an erection. Charlesetta saw that the drug she slipped in his juice was taking effect. Charlesetta slipped up behind Bodeen and started rubbing his exposed balls real soft. She started moaning and whispered in his ear, "That's it... get it up, baby. You lookin' so good, baby..."

She guided Bodeen over to the pale ass crack and stepped back. Bodeen moved quickly, ripping a 9mm he had taped to the bottom of the silicone penis away and he cleaned that dude's colon for real, jack! *The Strap* and not the Strap-On made solid contact with the pink part of his butt and Bodeen blasted Charlesetta's screwball right out of the park.

Bodeen turned the gun on Charlesetta. The pistol didn't faze her. It wasn't the first time she ever had a gun to her face but she was shocked that Bodeen was smarter than she was. Bodeen's veins were still warm so he wasn't about to shoot his mother even though Charlesetta was a cold-blooded bitch.

She swung that whip and cut Bodeen right across the eye and before he could even open his eyes, Charlesetta had a 45 pointed at his face. Bodeen flashed back to where he was that little kid and she was just choking him out for no reason; he felt hurt and puzzled. There was no doubt that Charlesetta would kill him before he gained enough courage to kill her. Bodeen lowered his gun slowly and then he shot that bitch right in the kneecap.

"Aww! Goddamn!" Charlesetta yelped as she dropped her gun and grabbed her kneecap before she fell over on her side. Bodeen knew Charlesetta had guns pulled on her before, but she had never been shot. It's not like it is in the movies where the actor can get shot five times with high powered weapons and still have the courage to shoot back. When Charlesetta felt the pain from that hot lead burning through her flesh, it knocked all the sense out of her and she crumpled on the floor. Bodeen picked her 45 up off the floor. It was sweet gun. Bodeen decided right then and there he would kill Black Ass Bosco with it and let the law trace it back to his mother. Charlesetta was still gangster about hers. Bodeen had to give her that much. She started talking shit soon as she caught her breath.

"You ungrateful black son of a bitch! You must have got that from your daddy. You gonna to pay for this shit, Bodeen. Mark my words, you little punk ass bitch! When you least expect it, I'm gonna shatter your entire motherfuckin' world and let the pieces fall where they may! Punk bitch!"

He looked around the room as she ranted. Everything he needed was in there to complete the job except duct tape, which was priority #1. The first thing he needed to do was shut Charlesetta's mouth. He was tired of hearing her talking. Bodeen grabbed one of those freaky leather and metal studded harnesses with the red ball gag and strapped that muthafucka around Charlesetta's face and locked it. He grabbed the wrist and legs cuffs and hogtied her with some rope. She couldn't move. Bodeen took her keys and locked the door behind him. Bodeen walked to the strippers' locker room and took a long hot shower, got dressed, and

He walked upstairs and saw Consuelo and her cousin. He gave them instructions to clear out the club and gave each of them $100. Within moments, the music was off and Bodeen was the only one moving in the building.

Bodeen emptied all the cash registers. He sorted the money, wrapped it in a thick rubber band, and placed it inside his coat.

As he sat quietly with a fat stack of cash in his pocket, he thought over the past few days of events. Charlesetta tried to work Bodeen good on this one. She almost had him, too, but she showed her hand early. Bodeen started to figure it out when Charlesetta colored his hair. First off, why was blue hair coloring readily available two minutes after he gave in to her demands? From that moment, the whole house of cards came crashing down. Secondly, the house wouldn't be in foreclosure because it was already paid for. Charlesetta's big mouth always bragged about that. And third, Charlesetta was gangster, no doubt about that, and had the body count to prove it. There was no way she would let a hardcore nigga, much less some half-gay freak of nature by the name of Squeeze, steal all her money, and then she was going do was weep about it? Sheeeeiiit, Squeeze would have been dead before he spent a dime and she damn sure wouldn't be crying. So Bodeen started working his plan while he let Charlesetta think he was ignorant to her scheming.

Bodeen unlocked Charlesetta's private office to check on another weakness he detected in her story. The office was immaculate. Just 24 hours before, it was in shambles. The open wall safe was what tipped him off as suspect. Bodeen had listened to Charlesetta sliding heavy furniture on many of nights as he guarded the door. He knew she had a floor safe. When Bodeen saw the steel office desk that felt like it weighed over 500 pounds, he was more than sure there was a treasure in the floor. Desk built like those have been out of stock since the early 1960's. Bodeen slid that heavy desk over from both ends. He had to use all his strength to shove it out of the way. Charlesetta was a strong bitch.

But there it was. A floor safe. There were no keys on the ring that fit the lock. Charlesetta was too cheap to buy a high end safe so Bodeen shot it about five times. The hinges on the door were smoking. It came off with no problem. Loose cash covered the cash wrapped in bundles underneath it. The deeds to the house and club were in there, but Bodeen didn't bother with them but the dozen or so videotapes at the bottom of the safe did peak his interest. Bodeen packed up everything in a duffle bag and left the office.

Bodeen unlocked the first door that led to the freak room. He shot through the second door where Charlesetta was still tied up and then kicked it off the hinges. Charlesetta looked crazy as hell with that leather studded harness on her head. She looked like the World Heavyweight Lucha Libre Champion, *The Masked Hood Rat*. Bodeen untied Charlesetta from the hog tie position and kicked over her on to her back. He also loosened up the ropes around her hands and feet just enough to where she could free herself after about four or five hours. Bodeen poured some whiskey over the gunshot wound to her knee, popped the bullet out with a blade of his knife, poured more whiskey over it, and then wrapped it up real good with clean towels. Bodeen sat down two bottles of water and a straw. Bodeen took the 9mm handgun out of his coat pocket, wiped his prints off, and placed it next to the dead man. Bodeen reached his hand in the duffle bag. Charlesetta's eyes popped wide open like one of those coon actors in those racist movies of the early 1900's. She was sure Bodeen was about to kill her. That's how she would have done it. Bodeen just shook his head and showed Charlesetta the videotapes. Even with that red ball in her mouth, Bodeen understood her words, "Fuck you!"

Bodeen grabbed his bag and locked the door that led to the freak room but he left the keys in the doorknob on the outside.

Bodeen stepped from the club in to the night air. It was thick with humidity. Bodeen liked the way it felt around him. He took a deep breath and started to walk. As he took that first step, he realized he had no reason to look back. Bodeen was ready to strike out on his own.

BODEEN'S REDEMPTION

BODEEN STOOD LEANED up against the podium at the Greyhound Bus station. This was the moment he had been waiting for. He had been dreaming for years of how cold it would be to catch Black Ass Bosco as soon as he stepped one foot out of prison and blow the stuffing out of his skull before he had a chance to breathe fresh air. But Black Ass Bosco was housed way up north in Susanville, and that was too far to be trying to pull off some crazy shit, even in a fantasy.

So Bodeen did the next best thing. He knew Black Ass Bosco would be coming into San Bernardino Bus Terminal at 10:40pm. He couldn't wait to see the look on Bosco's face when he stepped off that bus and the first thing he saw was revenge gift-wrapped in a box.

10:40pm came and Bodeen was cool and relaxed. He was eating a bag Doritos. Bodeen had always looked forward to Bosco being his first murder but the fool with the British accent wound up stealing that honor.

Black Ass Bosco was well aware of Bodeen's intentions. He would get word every now and then that Bodeen was asking people around town about his release date. The incident affected Bosco as well. It bothered him so much he gave up drinking after that night. The only thing he remembered was helping Bodeen before he passed out. As long as Charlesetta had the tapes, he would never be able to convince himself or Bodeen to believe his side of the story. Black Ass Bosco had plenty of years alone in a cell to think about it and the moment of truth finally arrived.

The bus pulled up. Only a couple of passengers got off the bus and Black Ass Bosco was one of them. Bosco really looked happy to be home.

Bodeen saw his teeth before he spotted the rest of him. Bodeen crept up on Black Ass Bosco before he got his last foot off the bus. He wiped that smile clean off of Bosco's face. Bosco just did too much time in the joint to scream like he was scared even if he wanted to.

Bodeen's scowl was so evil it would crack Medusa's face. The veins in his forehead looked like they were about to pop out of his skull. Bodeen's face was tight and hard. He was biting down on his jaw so hard it sounded like the enamel was chipping off of his teeth. His lips were so dry they looked like he was eating a powdered donut. Bodeen was straining his face trying to look as mad as he could before he made his move. Black Ass Bosco had the look on his face that Bodeen wanted to see: the look of fear. And he got that. But then Bodeen relaxed the muscles in his face. He reached into his pocket, pulled out a video tape and smiled, "Now you're truly free!"

Bodeen hugged Black Ass Bosco and thanked him for taking care of him when Charlesetta beat him half to death. Bodeen really made Bosco's day when he placed $15,000 in his hand to get him back on his feet right, courtesy of Charlesetta.

For the past two days, Bodeen had been in chilling out in a hotel room viewing Charlesetta's videotapes. There was incriminating activities on all of them. Politicians, entertainers, and policemen doing some foul shit with Squeeze and some of the other suspect strippers. Charlesetta was deviously wicked. She could have made a good living extorting everyone she had on those tapes and knowing Charlesetta she was probably already doing it. Bodeen finally found the tape that had scarred his childhood. The lump in his throat was so big it almost choked him. Bodeen viewed it in its entirety. The anger that built up inside made him very dangerous. "I'm going kill…!"

But the vow Bodeen made to himself to never look back was the only thing that stopped him from going back to Sweet Pete's and burning it to the ground with that bitch inside.

Bodeen told Bosco how everything went down and how he left a clean pistol next to the Brit's dead body just to make Charlesetta sweat. The police won't tell her that it wasn't the murder weapon. So until Charlesetta and a lawyer figure it out, her mind was going to be very heavy. It was a little taste of her own medicine. After discussing Charlesetta's dastardly deeds even more, Bodeen started to realize how wickedly brilliant she really was. Charlesetta was too ignorant to realize it though. Bodeen was going to make her psychological tactics work for him. Bodeen was now the man Charlesetta raised him to be, but he had no intentions of making her proud.

"Man, you know how to play that con game well your damn self, Big Bo. The crazy ass look you had on your face had me worried as hell. I said this nigga done went berserk. You had all that white shit around your mouth." Bosco shook his head, slightly in disbelief but also in awe of how well Bodeen had played him.

Bodeen reached in his pocket and pulled out a pack of powdered donuts and offered him one. "I was straining my face so hard I fucked around and gave my own self a headache."

Bodeen and Black Ass Bosco chatted and laughed until it was time for Bodeen to jump on the midnight bus to Detroit. Bodeen didn't know a soul in Detroit. The Spanish kid that beat him up in CYA always called him The Detroit Hitman after Tommy Hearns because of his tall frame. Bodeen had a little respect for the kid so he used the name he gave him as his calling.

* * *

It didn't take Bodeen long to get acclimated to his new ruthless surroundings. Bodeen carried himself like a killer. His size, dark complexion, and quiet demeanor got him a job as a debt collector with one of the small time local D-Boy crews. Since Bodeen was an out-of-owner as well as antisocial, it took him a minute to move up the ranks. But Bodeen was content with rising slow because it was a learning process. Bodeen studied how crews and organizations work from the bottom up. He already had money so the long hours and tables scraps he was working for made him look like a true dedicated soldier to the local crew because he didn't run any side hustles.

Bodeen didn't have trouble collecting debts. He had to slap up a couple of dudes that were delinquent but he never had partake in any gunplay. And eventually Bodeen moved up. He was hired as muscle to guard the stash house. The pay was better but Bodeen was restricted to one location.

He used that dead time to master patience. Bodeen would think about all the stories he heard on the streets about players past and present that made a name in that underworld game. The Kingpins like Maserati Rick that was right there in Detroit, the notorious swaggering braggart Nicky Barnes out of New York, or the flamboyant Flukey Stokes out of Chicago didn't excite Bodeen. It the enforcers of their organizations that Bodeen admired. He liked the killers that keep dirty hands and their souls in the hotbox. Bodeen was fascinated with the stories he heard about Silk Perry, Shannon and the Young Locs on the Westside, Bobby Boyd, Pappy Mason, and Abdullah Joe. The fear that they put in the hearts of people was like no other. There were a lot of killers in the world but it was the way and style in which each man put his murder game down that made them infamous.

Bodeen heard a story one time that his idol Silk Perry spotted an enemy coming out of a building. There were potential witnesses all on the block. Silk stepped out of the cut, hit that fool in the head with everything he had in the clip in broad daylight, and just strolled off slowly with the hammer smoking. When the police and ambulance arrived, Silk showed back up at the murder scene in a different set of clothes, just to see who was snitching to the cops.

Every great artist usually emulates their idols before they eventually develop a style they can call their own.

Bodeen finally got a chance to create a little buzz in the streets. There was this despicable savage named Sheldon Bell that was a psychopath who had a penchant for murder. He was scandalous and grimy. Even if Sheldon was in a street fight with somebody he could whip easily, he would never make it a fair one. It seemed Sheldon did what he did just because he could.

Sheldon had been a bully all of his life. He grew up taking the lunch money from most of the gangsters and hustlers in the neighborhood so he only saw them as the same weak prey. The ones that tried to explain to Sheldon that they were not kids on the playground anymore met an unfortunate demise. They didn't understand that when you deal with a man like Sheldon Bell you shoot first to get his attention and then he will be more agreeable to hearing what you have to say. The neighborhood would celebrate when he got locked up and they got sick to the stomach when he was released.

Bodeen didn't know Sheldon Bell like that but he knew most bullies never stood up to hard hitters and that's what Bodeen viewed himself as. Bodeen was told to give Sheldon Bell a little package to keep him from robbing the joint. Bodeen met him and gave him the package. Besides noticing Sheldon was a little hyperactive with a nervous twitch Bodeen didn't see anything immediately threatening about him. Bodeen even loaned him his Michael Jackson greatest hits CD. Sheldon said he wanted to make a copy but he didn't return the CD the next day like he promised. He also made it known in the streets that he never intended on giving it back. The streets started talking. Bodeen decided to give them a topic worth gossiping about.

A few days later, Bodeen caught Sheldon Bell slipping one afternoon and hit him with a warm shot of dust called "Butt Naked" that was the #1 drug on the streets at that time. He threw his ass in the trunk of the car and drove over to the Fisher Building on West Grand Blvd. Bodeen called the police and the local news team and reported that there was a naked man on the roof threatening to commit suicide. As the police, media, and rescue teams arrived Bodeen threw Sheldon off of the 30-story landmark skyscraper.

Bodeen's name didn't ring out quite like his predecessors but he got the attention of Cordedius Montgomery's Organization. Cordedius Montgomery was an older hustler born in Omaha, Nebraska in 1929. Cordedius got his start as a numbers runner in New Jersey and then migrated to the Motor City sometime in the late 1940's and established it as his new home.

Bodeen was hired as an enforcer in the Montgomery Organization. He was put under the tutelage of his murderous mentors Bobby Boyd and Abdullah Joe. Since Bodeen was from the Los Angeles area primarily known as the Home of the Drive-By Shooting, Abdullah Joe established early on that they did not get down that way in Detroit.

"I don't play that across the street shit," Abdullah Joe informed Bodeen. "I walk right up on that muthafucka and put 6 to 15 in the head like it ain't shit."

Bodeen took to their teachings like a fish to water. He learned that there were thousands of ways to snatch the life out of a body without the use of a gun. Bodeen learned poisoning, ritual humiliation, and torture.

Bodeen was a model student and quick learner. While Bodeen was grateful for all the knowledge, Bodeen wanted to be better than his predecessors and go deeper. He wanted to put fear into people's souls.

With any job, there are things you like about it and things you loathe. The most important lesson Bodeen learned as he earned his stripes was there are some things that just come with the game. The more you can accept it, the better off you will be. Executing snitches and star witnesses in Bodeen's line of work is common practice and he had to dispose of a few.

In some cities, good soldiers were even terminated with extreme prejudice for just being seen having a conversation with the police. So on that note, Bodeen had a hard time in the beginning grasping the idea of working with and paying off crooked cops and politicians. But as Bodeen matured, he got over this prejudice and he learned how to find information which led to the whereabouts of star witnesses, which jurors could be turned out, what judges could be paid off, which prosecutor would fold under constant anonymous death threats, who the police were planning to raid, and how to get acquitted after shooting a good friend five times and killing him in cold blood in front of 40 people like Cordedius Montgomery did.

Mr. Montgomery was politically connected downtown and that made him virtually untouchable. Bodeen learned from a few kingpins that when you reach a certain level of the game, you have to have police and at least one politician in your pocket. There is no way around it. Bodeen was a killer and if he was ever charged, the best thing a lawyer could do for him was get him life in prison. Bodeen made some serious contacts downtown to make things disappear and they did not come cheap.

Bodeen paid his dues to the Montgomery Organization and decided it was time to leave the nest. Bodeen had a game plan. He was now standing 6'5 and weighing 275 pounds. He was ready to make his own way.

CHAPTER 20

"...LIFE WOULD HAVE definitely been different with proper guidance and direction."

Bodeen wasn't quite sure if he was ready to make a life change but he knew he had to follow all the rules of the game. Every one of the gangsters Bodeen looked up to did something positive for the community once they got set up and established. They fed people on holidays, bought kids school clothes and supplies, helped families with utility bills, and seniors with medical bills. Bodeen had only looked out for himself his entire life. He had more than enough money to live on, so it was time to give something back.

Coach, Jah, and the rest of the Student-Athletes were having fun trying to figure out a way to get back in the building without getting caught by Mother Taylor and reprimanded about her flowerbed getting trampled. Coach and the young soldiers used military tactics to accomplish the mission. It was a Black Co-op: Operation Slithery. Coach led the troops and they all lined up in a straight line with their backs against to wall. Coach whispered a command to the man behind him and told him to pass it back. By the time it reached the third kid, the instructions were all wrong. Then everybody got the giggles and was trying to cover up their mouths. Enough laughter was escaping to alarm the Vietcong. Coach went commando and dropped to his belly. He crawled until he made it past Mother Taylor's window. The kids followed suit.

Coach peeked around the corner of the building.

"Uh-huh, you're cold busted!" Mother Taylor was waiting at the entrance wearing a purple moo-moo with tube socks and house shoes on. She was holding garden tools in her hand. "Y'all thought you were slick, huh? Tried to sneak by me now, didn't you? Since you all are out here playing Call of Duty, why don't you and your boys crawl over there and fix my chrysanthemums. And while you're at it... get those weeds over there next to my Swiss chard... Go ahead, don't let me talking slow you down!"

"Aww Mother Taylor that flower bed was like that when we left. It was probably Mr. Martin's German Shepherd," Coach was playfully fibbing.

"And what was the German Shepherd doing in my flowers, Mr. Coach?"

"Chasing squirrels," Coach said with a straight face.

"You lying dog! That dog is just as old as Mr. Martin. You know Mr. Martin just got out of the hospital again?"

"Naw, what happened this time?" Coach asked with concern.

"That old senile fool bit himself on the ass!"

"What? How did he do that?"

"He flopped his ass down in the chair and sat on his false teeth."

Coach and the young lions gave Mother Taylor a courtesy laugh for her stab at comedy and then went to work. Mother Taylor had some tomato seeds and some other stuff she wanted planted as well. Coach playfully complained that was not part of the deal.

Mother Taylor begged to differ. "You shouldn't have tackled that tight head nigga into my flower bed. I was so mad when I saw him walking down the street with my daffodils stuck to the back of his ass..."

The work wouldn't have been that bad if Mother Taylor didn't have to stand over them giving orders.

"No baby, my fresh mint goes there... No. You got to use your hands right there. Don't forget to pick those weeds out of there. You got to get it by the root, but don't pull up my roses by mistake. Hey, Coach, we need some more nitrogen for the tomatoes. Go around back to the shed. I saw a big bag in there last week."

"Nitrogen?" Coach asked.

"Yeah Dad, nitrogen is the key ingredient in fertilizer. It's like a supplement for the depleted soil and it helps grow strong healthy plants," Jah stated as he shared what he learned in horticulture class.

Mother Taylor concurred, "Yeah, what he said, now go around back and go get it. If it's too heavy, get your big black buddy here to help you."

Coach was down on his knees patting down the dirt where he planted the tomato seeds He turned his head towards Mother Taylor. Bodeen was standing next to her looking larger than life. Coach stood up and he still looked small next to Bodeen. Bodeen extended his hand first. Coach returned the gesture and they introduced themselves. Bodeen then proceeded to shake hands with the children and Mother Taylor. Bodeen was polite and offered to help Coach with the bag of fertilizer. It was a good time to talk about what was on Bodeen's mind.

"Look, I want to do my part for the kids, but I don't know how to go about it. I don't know a thing about coaching kids but I can make contributions in other ways, ya feel me? But at the same time I want to help somebody I trust and is going to see that the kids get the money... I've known people to give money back to the community and it went right into some greedy-ass individual's pocket. I'm not looking to save my soul and to be true, I don't really want any publicity on this. I just want to be a part of what you're doing because I see you out here every day doing the right thing."

Coach knew a lot of guys like to talk a good game but never do a damn thing when it gets to getting out the money and really just waste time running their big mouths about how they're going to do this for the team or that for the community. He looked into Bodeen's eyes and the size of his pupils gave away the fact that Bodeen was coming down from a high other than weed. A lot of people become saints and fantasize about big dreams under the influence so Coach thanked him and told him to hit him up in the morning to see if he would show.

True to his word, Bodeen was up bright and early, narcotic free with the same passion he had for helping the children as he had the day before.

Coach invited Bodeen to hang out with him at work and while he coached so he could decide himself where he fit in and how he wanted to contribute. The recreation center was under constant threat of facing more budget cuts. The teams in Jah's football league were struggling, too. The equipment was old, the uniforms were cheap and didn't hold up, and the price to even play was entirely too much. Single parents in impoverished neighborhoods had to pay $400 for ten games of football and close to a thousand to be a cheerleader.

There were a lot of naysayers that did not approve of Coach and Bodeen's new relationship. Their story was nothing new. The good guy always catches the stray bullet meant for the bad guy in relationships like that.

But ever since he was a youngster, bad guys liked to chill with Coach to separate themselves from the negative energy that abounded in their world. Coach looked like them and talked like them, but he was on an entirely different path. Now don't take Coach's kindness for weakness. He wasn't a saint that walked around giving strange folks hugs but he was a righteous man that was doing to best he could to make a difference in this life. Coach didn't trust Bodeen as far as he could throw him but every person deserves at least one shot at redemption. For example, the most important person in Coach's life besides Jah was James the maintenance man. According to the conviction on James' record, he's worse than a terrorist. In truth, James is one of the most positive brothers you would ever want to meet. Coach gave him a shot and James made it count.

Bodeen started to admire Coach because he wasn't putting up a religious front like he was holier than thou. Coach didn't like the extra praise he received for being a single father; he was just doing his job. Coach was a good man. Everything he did was natural and from his soul.

Over the next month while Coach had his team in spring training working on strength and conditioning, Bodeen kept showing up. He made sure the kids had water, Gatorade, and fresh fruit at every practice. Bodeen purchased speed ladders, step hurdles, cones, and speed resistance chutes for the young athletes to use. For the rec center itself, Bodeen bought new computers, more sports equipment, and financed a budget to compensate tutors and student workers. Bodeen was so sincere in what he was doing, Coach even invited him over for a Pay-Per-View boxing event, against Pops Sanford's wishes, of course.

Bodeen wanted to do even more, but Coach advised him to take his time so his good gestures wouldn't attract too much attention. It was hard for Bodeen to contain himself. He was starting to dig that thing Coach called "Good Energy." It was something different. Bodeen didn't absorb too much of it though. Being at peace means being relaxed and in his line of work he didn't want to get caught meditating with his eyes closed. But playing the part of Good Samaritan was therapeutic for Bodeen. He hadn't even thought about work. It was also the perfect setting to keep Bodeen busy while he was laying low.

After executing a hit like the one in the hospital, staying inactive and off of the radar for an indefinite period of time is the only option if you enjoy freedom. Political connections can't save you once a high profile crime like that makes national news. Fortunately for Bodeen, it stayed local. Mia's toxicology report was so bad it would have brought heat, malpractice suits, and child endangerment cases to everyone involved. They swept it under the rug real quick, but Detective Andy Moretti was still shitting bricks.

Detective Moretti wasn't named as a suspect, but he was skating on thin ice under a watchful eye from up high. Detective Moretti, being of the Caucasian race, understood quite well that white people are very nosey. He knew that one of his people, not sure which one, but one for sure, would sniff around and poke in his business until they found something that was supposed to be kept secret. His Porsche and other big purchases would be under scrutiny. Detective Moretti needed to do some real police work quick, something high profile, so that any speculation about him living above his means would go away.

Bodeen hadn't talked to Detective Moretti in a month. If he didn't owe him money for the hit Bodeen probably would have forgotten all about Andy. He was the last person on his mind and he was pretty much done working with him. Bodeen even thought about letting Detective Moretti keep the balance he owed as a parting gift but he decided against that. Bodeen wanted to put it into the rec center fund he set up so he agreed to meet him.

"There he is! The big black muthafucka!" Detective Moretti laughed as he recounted the day Bodeen was first described to him by his daughter. "So you are really serious about taking an extended leave of absence and not just the normal hit man hiatus? I know some people that have some big money work for you."

"I'm cool," Bodeen stated nonchalantly.

"You took the weight of a mountain off my shoulders when you off'd that cunt wife of mine. I was shitting bricks for a minute. I thought they were coming for me with the cuffs out since my name was on the insurance policy. Shit, Mia was so drugged up they almost didn't want to pay it out. They said anybody that used that many drugs was trying to commit suicide and the policy doesn't cover self-inflicted deaths. We were lucky you shot her because if she had died from an overdose I wouldn't have received a dime. I'm not bitter about the child either. It was messy but I know your work and I know why you did it. She never had a chance. It was a mercy killing and I understand that. So enough of the past, how is the current job coming? I need this one bad. And the case has to stick. It has to be solid. I haven't brought in a case worth mentioning in years."

Bodeen gave Detective Moretti the *c'mon man* look and said, "Done deal."

"That is some good shit man! That is really great news. Now I can get these fuckers out of my life. Shit After this one I might retire with you. What you think about that?"

Bodeen shrugged his shoulders as if he didn't care one way or another. After they said their good-byes Bodeen never planned to see Detective Moretti again in life.

"...So what are you going to do now?" Detective Moretti asked before they parted ways.

"I don't know... maybe coach a kids football team." Bodeen stated with a fucked up smirk on his face.

CHAPTER 21

"JAH-JAH, GIVE THIS card to Ms. Rawls for me on the low key. I'd appreciate that son."

"Happy *B-Earth* Day? That's not how you spell birthday so I know it must have meaning behind it. You call women Goddess, Queen, Moon, and Wisdom. But how can they be Earth and Moon?"

"The moon has the same composition as the Earth. Some historians and theologians even teach that Earth and Moon were once the same. The moon, the earth's counterpart, reflects the light of the sun in much the same way that the woman reflects the teachings of her man. It's a logical theory. I have some books on the shelf breaking all that down if you want to check them out. I even have a few CD's."

"Oh yeah, I hear RZA from the Wu Tang Clan referring to women as *Earth* all the time in his rhymes," Jah replied.

"I thought Ghostface was your favorite?"

"Now Ghost is still my favorite. His rhymes help me see things on the street. But the RZA is deeper and his flow makes me want to learn more about math and science. But I still don't get why you use Earth sometimes, Dad?"

"I strongly believe that the Earth is the black woman's twin in nature. If the woman is your Earth, then she's everything!" said Coach. "When you call her your Earth, you're saying that everything you need to make life what life should be is right there in the soul of that woman. The black woman is symbolic to the earth in many ways; the earth is the only planet in our solar system that is capable of reproducing and bringing forth life.

Now based on that fact, son, how would you compare that with the black man's relation to the woman?"

Jah thought about it for a minute and said, "Just as the Earth brings forth life, or fruits of the seeds that God plants, the black woman brings forth a child from the black man. So when I call her Earth I should honor and respect her as I do the life earth has produced for us. So I don't spit on the earth, litter the earth, or mistreat the earth. Like take care of the earth and the earth will take care of you and me."

"And there it is! You're sharp, son. I should have named you Yoda. I can't even take the credit for raising you into the young lord you are. You are definitely a blessing from JAH, a reflection of the Most High indeed. Coach Love Jr. puts you in a box. Jah Love is omnipresent, ya dig?"

"You know Ms. Rawls is gonna ask me why you didn't bring her this B-Earth day card yourself. How come you haven't made your rounds to see her?" Jah inquired.

"Because those little nosey ass kids is always in our business and I noticed that they were irritating your vibe with that foolishness."

"Man, they are gonna be up to foolishness regardless. They get on my nerves about everything. Don't let that stop you, Dad. I like that my Dad is a lady's man. It's cool, mon. I just don't like when they tease me and call Ms. Rawls my mother. Now that part is not cool."

"I know. I heard them singing it, 'Whooo Ms. Rawls is Jah's new mama...' that is why I pumped my brakes. You don't need to deal with that foolishness."

"She's cool though. But what about LaTonya? Do you like her more?"

"What's with all these questions about women this early in the morning? Are you in love your own self? Does some fifth grader have your nose open?"

Jah laughed. "Those girls at my school are crazy. You just don't even know, Dad. But no. I was just asking to see how you feel about LaTonya."

"I suspect there is a reason why you are asking. If you're worried about me getting married and disrupting the flow that you and I have then you can put that stress to beddy-bye. We are doing something special, Jah and it is going to take a dynamic woman to be part of this. She will know how to adapt to our flow. And we will both know who she is when that time arrives… as for now, just worry about playing your Pokémon cards."

"How do you play Pokémon cards?" Jah laughed at his Dad's ignorance to the modern games of today. Jah was wise beyond his years and still wanted answers. "So LaTonya is not the one?"

"I really like LaTonya but I'm more in love with her fly character than I'm in love with her as a person… I think. For instance, you thought that cute girl in the movie ATL was mad hot but you were in love with the movie character named Nu Nu. Once you got past that and saw the real person behind the character was just a regular chick that likes cats that look like Lil' Wayne, she no longer did anything for you anymore. Not taking anything away from LaTonya, but I just hope she is the right one for what we are trying to accomplish here. Sometimes son, she just doesn't make me feel like she's in this with us forever. When we discuss the future, LaTonya constantly says *I*. When *I* get my so and so, or when *I* get this, or when *I* get that… it's never *we*. It makes me a little uneasy but patience is one of the keys in a relationship with a good woman, son, so we'll see. But it is time for LaTonya to step up the game fo' real, mon." Coach finished his sentence as he pulled up to the school. He looked at his son and asked, "Do you miss your mom?"

Jah sat quiet for a moment. "Yeah… well it's—it's hard to say really. I mean, I wonder what it would be like if she were here. But I've never seen her to miss her like other kids who lost a parent they have been living with all their life. So I miss Mom but in a different way."

"I feel that and hear it loud and clear, son. I'll pick you up after school. Handle your business and enjoy the day. Love you, Jah."

"I love you, too, Dad."

Coach arrived at work a little earlier than usual. When he pulled into the lot, he could see James out on the baseball diamond raking the dirt in the infield. Coach found it odd because James normally did that before game day. Then Coach saw Bodeen's truck parked in nearby. Coach was the only one with a good heart when it came to Bodeen. Nobody liked him around. James told Coach when Bodeen starting showing up, "Let that evil monster mail in a money order if he wants to help so badly. His presence is not required around here. I just don't like that eerie bastard."

"What up, Bo Diddley? You're up early this morning. Don't tell me you are going all in and walking the track with the senior citizens."

"Actually I was coming to work out on the pull up bar, but I don't think your man James likes me too much."

"You think? Hahahahaha! You're not exactly Rebecca from Sunnybrook Farm, Bo. You're a cold blooded gangster that does gangster shit."

"What's he think I'm gonna do, shoot the damn pull-up bar?"

"He's just doing the same thing you would do if the script was flipped; keeping his eyes open," Coach answered truthfully.

"Well, I can feel him on that. I am a ruthless son of a bitch but I still have rules that I won't break. I have to be this way Coach because of my profession; I compete with unsavory rats running around in the sewers. I don't have smart athletic kids in my world playing on green grass." Bodeen paused. "You know Coach, you never asked me what I did for a living or asked if some of the things you heard about me were even true. How come you don't look at me the way everybody else does?"

"I do look at you that way and I'm quite aware of your history, brotha. I'm not in the street game but I have to be aware of my surroundings. That's my job, Shotta. My concern is with these kids. I don't have a clue to what you do on a daily, but I know you hate pedophiles so I don't have to worry about the kids being fondled. I also know you are on a whole different level than the average gangbangers around here so I don't have to worry about some rivals doing a drive-by on you and the kids getting hurt in the process." Coach answered.

"I don't scare you or the things you heard about me?"

"Not one little bit," Coach answered without the slightest bit of hesitation and continued, "My faith is too strong, Bodeen. I fear nobody but the Most High JAH Rastafari! I may not be able to knock your big ass out in a street fight but I wouldn't be scared to rump with you. Now I tell you like this, if you or any man ever caused my son Jah any pain, it's a wrap and I will leave it at that. I don't mean it as disrespect; it's just the love a father has for his son. You feel me, brethren?"

Bodeen wasn't emotionally mature enough to grasp Coach's love for Jah, so he got a little pissed at Coach's statement but he let it ride.

"Well, I appreciate you letting me do a few things for the kids but

I'm gonna stay low key for a while. And if I keep doing a few good deeds, people might warm up to me. By the way, did you get the tackling bags I ordered for the teams?"

"Yes, we did. Thank you. UPS brought them yesterday. We really appreciate it. All the stuff you bought is going to last for the next five years easy."

"No problem. I got your team that new under armor they all wanted and black jerseys with their names on them. Hit me up when they deliver it and let me know everything is straight. If you need anything else you know I live across the street, just gimme the word. I like your style. You are a cool ass dude, Coach. I've never met anybody as sincere as you. You didn't judge me. Who knows? Maybe I'll coach a little team one day."

"At 6'5 300, you need to put a helmet on and get your big ass on the field and play some linebacker... Why ya bullshittin'!" Coach exclaimed as he and Bodeen laughed, slapped five, and parted ways.

Coach walked across the field to greet James. Coach already knew what he was going to say before he opened his mouth so he beat him to it.

"He won't be coming around here anymore, James. You made him feel unwelcome."

"Good...and I hope I never see that big ass grizzly bear ever again in life. If God punishes me for saying that then I will gladly accept it because I damn sure mean it. I don't like anything about him, Coach. His ass-eyes and that wide hamburger nose... he just looks like trouble..."

Coach switch hit the conversation by speaking in Patwa. "Well 'nuff bout dat bumbaclot rude boy. You still gon' keep da all seeing eye on I and I's young lord and let him nestle on foreign land until da young fiya blaze up!

"I hate when you talk that Island shit. You know I don't understand that fast gibberish." James shook his head. "Are you still bringing Jah by the house this weekend?"

"That's what I just asked you!" Coach stated, frustrated with James comprehension skills.

"You ain't said nothing about Jah... you said some shit about smoking weed in a fire eating a Crunch bar in a strange land or some shit, Mr. Rasta Man. And you better go to the grocery store before you come over if you want Jah to eat that bullshit y'all eat. We don't have tree bark and asparagus juice in my house. We eat cow until that bitch is a carcass! My kids barely survived the weekend at your house last summer."

"Bullshit, James, your kids didn't want to leave my house. Fact is, they stayed for a month!"

"That's because they were too weak from malnutrition to pick up the phone. When they made it back home, they ate up everything in the house. I asked little James if you fed them properly and he said, Daddy, are Coach and Jah Hare Krishnas? I said, why you say that, son?. He said 'cuz every time we told them we hungry, they pulled out a tambourine and told us to chant away the hunger pains. Now that's that bullshit, Coach... And while my poor baby girl is at your house starving, she remembered she had a can of Spam and some crackers left over from lunch. Your crazy ass son saw her with the Spam and threw her whole damn lunch pail out the window!! He told her pork was the devil's pumpkin pie. Ain't that some shit? The damn son of yours told my baby that she had triple China worms gallivanting all through her intestines just for having pork in her possession. He got my house all fucked up, Coach! Baby girl is running around the house crying every time we cook a gotdamn pork chop... James Jr turns his nose up and changes his accent when he tells me, I no longer chewth of the cud. What the fuck kind of animal is a gotdamn cud? *"I don't chewth..."* ain't that a bitch? Jah taught him that shit. He gon' get his ass whupped by one of these bad ass kids saying words like *chewth* in the hood. I told Jr, sit your ass down and get the fuck away from my plate... Boy oh boy, Mr. Ramadan Mon, you are raising your son to grow up crazy just like you."

Coach could tell James must of smoked a little joint because he was happy and on one. And since Coach kept laughing at his monologue, he had more.

"...And Jah? That is your son all day! He got my kids all excited for breakfast. He told 'em he was making them hotcakes, biscuits, and sausage. Man, Little Willie said he got up early, had his knife and fork ready, slapped a bib around his neck ready to dig in, and the only thing on the table was a glass of some beige shit. Jah said it was like pancakes in a shake. He said if they put their minds to it, it would taste just like pancakes and eggs. I said, they didn't have Cap'n Crunch? My son said, fuck naw, they had cereal they made from the Earth and trees and shit and no milk. Those are my babies, man, not some old muthafuckas at a convalescent home… You're a cold dude, Coach… They said you kept driving past McDonalds on purpose. They didn't even want to discuss the dinner you made so I asked what they ate for dessert. They said, broccoli… but if we put our mind to it, it taste just like peach cobbler."

Coach was on the ground cracking up. James was putting too much on it, but it was partially true. Coach and Jah ate pretty much everything everybody else did except pork and fast foods. James just loved to mess with Coach because his diet was slightly different from his. After Coach picked himself up off of the floor, James got serious again.

"After you left last night for practice, Preston came up here to see you."

"Oh wow, how's he doing since that accident? Did they ever find out who did it?"

"Accident? Ain't no accident about it. That evil bastard pal of yours did that shit on purpose. Preston is in bad shape and going through a lot of depression. He came in here drunk last night and he drinks all day now. You know he lost his scholarship to College. He has pins in his arm and foot. I know it was your new pal that did that shit to that boy."

"How you figure that?"

"That nasty-ass beast came looking for you to see if that equipment came while Preston was here. Preston damn near shit himself when he saw that big black muthafucka. Then he got pissed and hobbled out of here fast as he could."

"Damn, I hate to hear that. That liquor is gonna build false confidence in Preston and he's going seek revenge. You think Preston is going to come at him with a pistol?"

"Hell no! A pistol ain't powerful enough… Preston best bring a cannon to blow that black muthafucka into a million pieces…"

CHAPTER 22

COACH USED HIS belief in the Most High to ward off temptation and the devil's whisperings in his ear. But the Scriptures don't tell you how to deal with the devil's son-in-law. There wasn't a Psalm written to defend against him. The Devil has rules and Bodeen does, too, but Bodeen's rules were more ruthless and he followed his own agenda. Now how are you supposed to deal with a demon that the head devil can't even control?

Coach went to the barbershop to see Pops. Pops was standing in the middle of the floor with hair clippers buzzing in his hand giving one of his country sermons. His customer was sitting in the chair agitated with a tight apron around his neck. Coach walked up behind Pops, whispered in his ear, and slipped $200 to Pops' palm.

Coach walked out in a somber mood.

Pops looked at the money in his hand and then stared after Coach for a long time in silence.

Coach drove down the street with his mind heavy. There was a feeling in his gut that something wasn't right. On the corner of Washington and 8th Avenue, Coach glanced to his left and saw dozens of flowers and candles and a portrait of a young Hispanic kid that was slain from a stray bullet. The kid looked so innocent and happy. Coach had a thought that it could have been Jah on that picture and he got upset.

Coach was a gun owner at one time but after Jah was born he got rid of it because he felt it was bad luck. He didn't even like to play with guns. Coach thought back when he took the kids paint balling. Coach instructed Jah about the use of a paint ball gun like it was loaded with real bullets.

Once they started playing, Coach took it personal. Every time another adult shot a kid with paint, Coach was ready to pick a fight. The staff asked all of them to just leave.

As he sat there looking at the memorial, Coach prayed and then he knew. He called Pops back at the barbershop. Coach just told him to forget about it and he'll be by to pick up his money later on. Coach felt better immediately. The nervous feeling in his gut disappeared. Coach smiled because he just confirmed that prayer was more powerful than a pistol in a spiritual war. He felt real good about the test he just passed.

Later that night Coach and Jah were playing chess and snacking on almonds, dates and dried cranberries. Coach thought about what James said earlier and fell out laughing.

"What's so funny Dad? Did you let out one of those silent farts again?"

"No. But if I did it would smell like the scent of fresh roses on a nice autumn day," Coach replied. "James was roasting us earlier today. I want you to take him some dates when you go over there this weekend and see what he says. Are you guys just having a sleepover?"

"Yeah, and we're going to the Universal Soul Circus. Hold on a second, Dad, you just reminded me of something." Jah stood up and left the table. He returned with a packet full of papers. "You have to sign these by tomorrow."

"I know that's not those immunization and emergency cards again. Good grief, I just filled out all that stuff a few months ago."

"These are for when school starts again."

It always worried Coach when he got to the part of the paperwork that asked to give a name other than his to contact in case of an emergency. Coach and Jah didn't have anybody but themselves. Khalilah's family disappeared along with their false promises of being there for Jah shortly after she passed.

Coach decided to put James' name down. He was the only other family he had. "Jah-jah, do you have James new number in your cell phone?"

"Yes, do you need it?"

"No. I was just asking to make sure you had the new one. I'm going to put James and LaTonya down as the emergency contacts. They are the only ones that have authorization to pick you up from school if I'm busy, okay?"

"Cool, I got it. But what about Mrs. Maldonado?"

"Who in the hell is that?"

"James' wife." Jah answered as he studied his next chess move.

"Word? I never knew her last name was different than his," Coach asked but not really looking for an answer.

"Well, if you didn't know, then now you know. And check!"

"Now look at that move, son. You put me in check with your rook but the piece isn't protected. When I take it—and I'm going to take it—you are going to lose a valuable piece. Don't give up a power piece without taking one unless you got some Bobby Fischer shit jumping off over here."

"Who is Bobby Fischer? Homeboy that sings 'My Prerogative'?" Jah blurted out and laughed. He was getting more like his Dad everyday with that crazy statement.

"Checkmate in four moves, son. Do you want to sit through it?"

"I will never lay my King down until the job is done," Jah stated with confidence.

"You just don't want to go to sleep and you know its way past your bedtime. You are not the first child that thought he was slick. Checkmate! Now you know the song, *Night-niiiight... sleep tiiiight...don't let em' bite, don't let em' bite!*"

"Man I hate that song!" Jah said as he got up from the table and stormed to his room.

Coach followed Jah to his room and kept singing it. They laughed and joked around until the house phone started ringing. Coach kissed his son on the forehead and said, "Don't forget to say your prayers, son. Love you."

"Love you, too, Dad. See you in the morning."

Coach went into the living room and picked up the phone. "What's up, LaTonya? How was your day today, baby?"

"How did you know it was me? I have my phone set to private."

"Nobody calls the house phone anymore but you and bill collectors. And since it's 10pm, that narrows it down to you, my love."

"Um, from what I hear I don't think I'm the only one with your number. Who is Tammy?" LaTonya asked with a little attitude in her voice.

"Who-Tammy? I don't know what you're talking about, sugar," Coach played it off like he was supposed to, right or wrong.

"Don't act like you don't know what I'm talking about."

"I'm not acting, baby. Now is not the time for this he say/she say shit. We are better than that. So let's get down to business. I need to put you down as an emergency contact for Jah's file at school. Are you cool with that?" Coach asked.

"Of course, you don't even have to ask. I will do anything for you and Jah. I love him, too. He's so cute. And contrary to what you believe, I have your back, Coach. I'm not in stepmother mode, yet I can admit that I know I love you and want to be part of you and Jah's life. I thought long and hard about our conversation and I think I'm ready."

"You think you're ready, huh?" Coach asked.

"I know I'm ready. So do you need any help for Jah's birthday party?"

"Not really, we're going to the Grand Prix Go Kart spot off. You are coming with us, right?"

"I wouldn't miss it. Do you know what kind of gifts he wants?" LaTonya asked.

"Call him tomorrow after school and ask him. You know Jah is complex. He doesn't play with toys and shit like other kids. He'll probably want a chemistry set or a ticket to the moon or some shit."

"He is very mature for an almost nine-year-old."

"Well beyond his years."

"So am I gonna see you soon?" LaTonya asked in her sexy voice.

"Come over right now."

"I'm on my way!"

* * *

The next morning Coach laughed to himself while he was making Jah's breakfast for school and LaTonya was in the bed snoring loud like a fat man. Jah came out of the bathroom and walked into the kitchen.

"Dang Dad, who is that in your room? She sounds like a big one."

"Hahaha, that's LaTonya. That's a lesson for you, my son. Those super fine women have flaws you wouldn't believe. Sometimes it's not even fair. I had this bad honey in college. son, she was so fine she made you smile when you felt like frowning. She had a body like Serena Williams; thick as ear wax. I think something was wrong with her kidney or liver and she had to take this medication that gave off an awful foul discharge. She took her panties off and whew! It smelled like dead carnage down there. She must have had vagina dentata but I wasn't trying to find out."

"C'mon Dad! I'm eating my breakfast."

"My bad, son. I just have to cover all bases in this game called life. Anyway, LaTonya wants to know what you want for your Born Day. I need to know too."

"I don't know…maybe some clothes, oh, I want the sequel to *Midnight* by Sister Souljah *The Meaning of Love*, that book is out now. I need to know what happen to Midnight and his wife. Sista Souljah left us hanging in the first one. Oh, and I need this algebra software for my class next year. That's about it."

"You are a good son. A very, very serious young lord you are…I know I'm raising you as a young lord spiritually and a Student/Athlete mentally and physically, but I want you to enjoy your childhood because it goes by too fast. I blinked and bam, you are gonna be nine years old next week. Including flag football you are going into your fourth year of football already. Appreciate every moment of your life and don't take any days for granted."

"I enjoy life so far. I only have eight years under my belt but from what I can see I can handle it. You have me on a cool program and it's working," Jah stated and then made his first attempt at speaking patwa. "Life is cool, mon."

CHAPTER 23

"IF YOU WANT to be my #1... If you want to be my #1... let me know your future plans"

Coach rolled to work feeling like he was on cloud nine. He had the top down listening to Gregory Isaacs. Coach was thinking about the beautiful evening he had with LaTonya. She was a special woman indeed. "Oh, shit!" Coach yelled out as he slammed on the brakes and turned his steering wheel to the left. Once again, a Mexican had come out of nowhere and almost wrecked his shit.

"Sorry," The elderly Mexican said that didn't have the slightest clue about the rules of the road.

Coach was in such a good mood he straightened up his car and waved. Coach kept thinking about LaTonya. It felt good to know that she was still sleeping comfortably in his bed. Coach was thinking that maybe if he spent more time with her and made the relationship serious ,the doubts he had about her would go away.

Coach pulled into the parking lot at work. The gates were still locked. James wouldn't miss work even if Jesus told him to rest. He called James' home.

"Hello?" James' wife Jessie answered the phone sounding happy and cheerful.

"Hey Jessie, this is Coach."

"Hey Coach. How are you doing? The kids can't wait for Jah to get here this weekend."

"Is James there?" Coach asked refusing the small talk.

"Christ no, you know he leaves here at five in the morning to go to work. He probably just drove over to the 7-Eleven to get a racing form to play those horses."

"Ah. Okay. Cool. I'll see you this weekend now." Coach hung up the phone.

But something still didn't feel right even after hearing Jessie's words of assurance that James detoured to the store. He very well could be but it was unlikely. Coach left his office and walked across the field to James' lab. The door was unlocked but he wasn't in there.

Coach dialed James on his cell phone even though he never answered it. James was old school from the rotary phone days. He believed in the house phone and the work phone. The cell phone went straight to voice-mail just like Coach figured.

Coach walked back to his office and got some work done. Coach looked up from his work and noticed that two hours had passed and he still hadn't heard a word from James. Coach was trying not to think the worst but he couldn't help it. He wondered if Bodeen did something to James but he saw his white truck earlier when he left the house.

Coach decided to go to the 7-Eleven to see if James was there. As he was pulling out of the parking lot, the UPS truck was pulling in. Rolland waved his hand out of the window to get Coach's attention. Coach didn't have time to play the dozens with Rolland. He paused for a hot second. "I don't have time right now, Rolland, what do you need?"

"You have packages."

"Well, leave them in the office like you always do."

"You have to sign for them," Rolland insisted.

"That ain't never stopped you from leaving them before. Don't try to get employee of the month now."

"They been coming down on me at the job saying all my signatures look the same."

"Then use your left hand and just sign the shit and leave me the fuck alone. I have an emergency right now."

Coached walked into 7-Eleven and went up to the counter. "What's up Achmed, have you seen James this morning?

"Hey what's up Coach? Yeah, James came in this morning around 5 and got a racing corm."

"Was he with anybody?" Coach asked.

"Not that I can think of. Why? What happened?"

"Nothing... nothing at all." Coach said as he held his head down and headed out of the door.

"Wait a minute, Coach. I did see James talking to somebody outside. As James was leaving, an old red pickup truck with a lot of mattresses in the back pulled up next to his car. It looked like they were pals so I didn't think much of it"

"What did that somebody look like?"

"Oh boy. No disrespect to you or your race but he was a big black muthafucka. Like a bison."

There was only one African-American mattress collector in the hood. He was big and round, but not in height or stature. Coach dialed Bodeen.

"Grrrrrrrrrr," Bodeen answered.

"What up, man, it's Coach. I just wanted to thank you again for buying the kids those extra jerseys. It is much appreciated."

"Huh? Oh, yeah-yeah. Did they get there yet?"

"Yeah, they came this morning."

"Huh? They came this morning? Did you open the box and make sure they were cool?" Bodeen asked suspiciously.

"Yeah, man the kids are going to love them," Coach lied.

"Okay... cool... cool."

"Hey man, what were you doing out at 5 in the morning? Getting your work out in?" Coach asked.

"I haven't left the apartment all day," Bodeen answered convincingly. He added, "And Coach, you better get those eyes checked because I know the city is too small for two big pretty black muthafuckas." Bodeen laughed out loud and hung up the phone.

Coach sent a text to his student worker Jelani telling him he would give him an extra $100 to come in a little earlier and stay awhile longer. It was 1:15 PM. Jelani returned the text message and said he was on his way. Coach had less than two hours before he had to pick up Jah from school. Thinking about Jah reminded Coach to order the rest of his birth-day gifts online.

Coach ordered more gifts than he planned on but Jah deserved it. As he was entering his credit card number, Coach heard the UPS truck pull-ing up outside and assumed it was Rolland coming back for the signature. Rolland had so many infractions at UPS everyone was surprised he still had his job. There was even a clip on YouTube where Rolland was caught tossing a box filled with expensive wine glasses 50 feet into the customer's yard. Rolland got off after he proved it was a mean Rottweiler comman-deering the yard. Rolland also logged so many extra miles on his truck going on personal runs and to his girlfriend's house he had to pay a shady mechanic at the chop shop to set the odometer back. But he had an infec-tious personality and he was funny so that got him out of a lot of trouble.

As Coach was about to finalize his order, a tall slender blonde white woman dressed in the classic brown UPS short set entered the office. Everything about her said Supervisor, even without the nametag that dis-played it on her blouse. She had that supervisor look in her eyes like she couldn't wait to fire an employee for little or nothing. This was the second lady they sent in two days to conjure up something so they could rail-road Rolland.

"Hello, sir. My name is Dawn Shriver and I'm regional supervisor at UPS. I'm doing a survey on the quality of our service. I only need a few moments of your time." Without waiting for an answer, she continued, "How often do you use UPS?"

"A lot... this is a recreation center and we order equipment and sup-plies all the time. Matter of fact, I'm ordering items right now as we speak."

"Would you say daily? Weekly? Monthly?"

"Lady, I just said a lot. I don't mean to be curt, but can you please get on with it? I got things to do. I just answered these same questions the other day." Coach said with agitation in his voice.

"Are the packages left by our drivers where they are visible and can be easily found?"

Coach pointed to the big boxes she passed and obviously saw when she came through the door.

"Is this your signature?" Dawn asked politely as she could. She could detect that Coach was already annoyed by her presence. Coach knew that last question was a trap to get Rolland fired. That bitch was trying to be slick to a can of oil. Coach had Rolland's back and wasn't going to let him get caught up. Coach set his credit card down and moved from around his desk to where she was standing. He looked at his signature in Rolland's fucked up handwriting and almost laughed out loud. Coach lied and said, "Yeah that's me. I have to go, lady. Send me an online survey or something."

"So you signed this?"

"Yes!" Coach said for the last time.

"Put your hands on top of your head. You are under arrest!" Officer Shriver dropped the electronic clipboard and had a department issued 9mm Beretta pointed at his head. Before Coach could take his next breath, his office was swarmed by a herd of yellow jackets...with ATF written on the back. They were all yelling and pointing guns at Coach.

"Get down! Keep your hands on top of your head! Get on the ground! Put your hands behind your back! Get on the ground!"

Coach was not about to lay on that dirty floor for a bunch of slave overseers especially when he hadn't done anything. Coach closed his eyes and stretched opened his arms like Jesus on the Crucifix to show them that all the yelling and shit was unnecessary and he was not a problem. Coach should have known better. Police don't understand logic. All they saw was a nigger with the 'er' at the end that they either wanted to kill or lock up.

"There are 48 white men and two Uncle Toms with 50 guns pointed less than an inch from my face. What can I possibly do under these conditions? I'm not a threat. Now what is the problem?" Coach stated with supreme confidence.

"Sir, if you don't get on the ground now, we are going to be forced to take you down."

"Please do and Rodney King me if you like. I need that money. Smile at the camera," Coach replied but he was hoping they didn't call his bluff because there were no cameras in the office at all.

They used their next best trick. The old faithful good cop/bad cop routine. The good cop walked through the center of the cops surrounding Coach wearing a nice tailored gray suit. He sported a $40 haircut and Italian loafers. He had style, but the cologne he wore smelled of swine.

"All that won't be necessary, gentleman. It looks like Coach here is willing to cooperate. Put all these guns down, geez. You act like this is Bin Laden over here. Sorry about that Coach. We have procedures in situations like this. I'm Detective Andy Moretti and you are Coach..." Detective Moretti held his eyebrow up waiting for a name that went with the title and then asked again "Coach... what?"

"Just Coach."

"Just Coach? Huh. Well, Just Coach, what's the name of your team, The Bloods, The Crips, The Taliban?" Detective Moretti asked with a hint of sarcasm.

"The Inglewood Azandes is the name of the team I coach."

"I see... what do you have in those boxes over there?"

"I believe it is the new youth football jerseys and Under Armor gear," Coach answered.

One of the ATF men butted in and asked. "You believe? Weren't you the one that ordered them?

"No, sir. People make donat—" Coach was cut off by Detective Moretti before he finished his sentence,

"Do you mind if I take a look for myself?"

Coach just shrugged his shoulders. The lead ATF Agents started seeing weakness in the caseThey whispered among themselves while Detective Moretti opened up the boxes.

"Hmm, interesting..." Detective Moretti began pulling out white sheets. There were no football jerseys found. "Excuse me, Just Coach, did you say Under Armor or Under Armory? Because that's what I see over here, a fucking armory," Detective Moretti stated as he held up an assortment of high caliber automatic weapons.

Guns were drawn on Coach again. Detective Moretti walked over to Coach with his handcuffs out and began to read him his Miranda rights.

"You have the right to remain silent. If you refuse that right, anything you say or do can and will be held against you in a court of law. You have the right to an attorney..."

Coach was innocent and his cool composure reflected that... until Detective Moretti slapped the first cuff on Coach's wrist. Coach thought about being taken away from Jah and panicked. He tightened up and turned to stone. The police couldn't move Coach much less get his arms behind his back to handcuff him. One cop hit Coach in the jaw from the blind side and grabbed him around the elbow trying to pry it from his side. Coach's adrenaline was pumping so hard he hip-tossed the cop over his office desk and slammed him down to the floor hard.

Another cop slipped up from behind Coach and applied the choke-hold that was no longer legal and tried to crush his larynx. Coach was numb and didn't feel a thing. The cops couldn't subdue Coach. He was too strong. The two Uncle Tom cops saw an opportunity to show out for the white folks. The first one pulled out his taser and pressed it into Coach's ribcage until they could smell his flesh burning. As Coach was falling the other Uncle Tom cop hit Coach in the back of the head with his nightstick to help him reach the floor faster. He hit Coach four more times after he was already unconscious and was going for a fifth blow until ATF stepped in. They handcuffed Coach and lifted him off the floor. Coach had only blacked out for a second and that wasn't long enough to make him forget what was happening. Sergeant Wilburn from ATF sat Coach down in his office chair until he shook off the wooziness. He motioned to Detective Moretti to follow him out of the office. Coach looked at the two Uncle Tom cops like the pitiful excuse for men they were. Coach shook his head and said, "Bitch ass Niggas."

Sergeant Wilburn looked in Detective Moretti's eyes. "This weak-ass case smells worse than fresh horse shit stuck on the bottom of your shoes."

"What the hell are you talking about, Sarge? This is a legit bust. A black guy in a gang neighborhood, receiving guns in the mail, and using the recreation center as a front... this is front-page news. C'mon man, we both need this one."

"All right, Moretti. This case better stick. If I see any other signs of horseshit, we're done with this case and you and the State can deal with it. I don't need this as much as you probably do."

"Don't worry about it. It's solid."

* * *

"You're just a bumbuclot, butt-kissin', boot-lickin' bitch made fun bwoi! How you sleep at night?" an irritated Coach asked the Uncle Tom.

"Like this," replied the cop, snoring with his eyes closed. Then he and his punk partner started giggling like two bitches.

ATF escorted Coach outside to a police van. The parking lot was sealed off with yellow tape. There were forensic experts in protective gloves collecting samples of who knows what off of the ground. The news media was out in full force taking pictures, asking questions, and shoving microphones in Sgt. Wilburn's face. Coach was embarrassed. He held his head up high but his spirit was breaking. They shackled his feet and then cuffed those cuffs to a steel bar fixed inside the van. Coach felt every bit like a captured slave on his way to a foreign land. Coach looked out of the window and saw they already had a lectern in front of the rec center for the press conference.

* * * *

Coach was placed in a single man holding cell for hours. Everything was surreal. Coach was an avid reader of black history. He was hip to slavery, the civil rights movement, unfair and biased treatment of people with color, Malcolm X, Panthers, and all the other pro-black activists and educators. Coach knew what "the man" was capable of but he had never been in shackles and whipped. He had never been refused a seat on the bus or seen a *Whites Only* water fountain. Coach had never even been called a nigger.

The majority of the new African-Americans in society today are the first ones to say, "That stuff happened 400 years ago, get over it!" "Stop talking about the white man. You need pull your pants up over your ass, and learn to speak proper English!" Coach would be the first one to say, "That sounds good, but until you have your freedom taken from you, locked in a funky cage, stripped naked, told to open your asshole up for some strange freak to look in it, and separated from your 8-year-old son that has nobody else in the world to take care of him, you really need to shut the fuck up!"

Coach couldn't keep his mind off of Jah. He knew it was past 3 o'clock and he was out of school. Coach had never been late picking him up ever. Coach really started stressing out. Now let's get one thing clear before we move on. The condition of the jail cell, the strip search, guns pulled on him, cold cocked, and all those other ungodly things that came with being booked WASN'T SHIT compared to the pain Coach was feeling wondering what Jah was thinking not seeing his dad after school.

Coach yelled out from the cage, "I need to get my phone call please!" Coach had only heard in movies that you were allowed one phone call and he was hoping it just wasn't a line in the script. Coach was green to the system. Coach was a revolutionary that would rather die on the streets fighting for the freedom of righteous human beings. Coach wasn't trying to earn a diploma, learn the dictionary cover to cover, or win a Nobel Peace Prize for a poem he wrote from prison. He just wanted to get out of that muthafucka....quick.

"I've been here four hours and I still haven't had my phone call yet. Excuse me! I need to make my phone call," Coach yelled even louder and kicked the cage three times to make sure he could be heard. After fifteen minutes of banging on the cage door, Coach heard a guard walking toward the cell jingling his keys.

"What do you want?"

"I would like to make my phone call, please. I've been here for hours. That's all I want to do and then you won't hear a word from me while I'm here."

"A phone call is not going to help you none. It says here that you are dangerous and a threat to staff... bail is not even an option in this case. ATF just got back from your apartment and it ain't no telling what they found there. Just sit tight until they interview you."

"Sir, please, I just need to contact my people and let them know I'm okay,"

"Fuck your people!" the cop replied as he walked away.

CHAPTER 24

JAH STOOD ALL alone outside of the school gate. He barely stood five feet tall with his hundred pound backpack, almost as big as him. The other students and staff had left the school long before. Jah couldn't help but think the worst. His dad had never been late and if he was, Jah knew he would call or send a text message. Jah called his dad several times but got no answer. He was mature for his age indeed, but he was still an 8-year-old child.

The sun was going down. Jah called his dad's cell phone and then their house phone. No answer. Jah called the rec center several times and got no answer. That really got him worried because even if his dad weren't there, one of the student workers would be.

It was time to call James. It went straight to the voicemail so he called his house. There was a busy signal. He put his phone in his pocket and looked up the street once more. Everything looked bigger than normal. He felt small, scared, and alone. Jah started walking home…

* * *

Coach could feel his son's sadness and pain. Being held captive away from his son was pushing Coach to the brink of snapping. It was only the love he had for his son and getting back to him that was keeping him calm and rational.

After five hours in the cage, he was led into the interrogation room. It was much smaller than they make them out to be in the movies. There was a small table with two chairs on one side and one chair on the other. Coach sat in the tiny room for another hour with his hands and legs still cuffed from his walk down to the room.

Finally, the door opened and two ATF officers came in with Sgt. Wilburn right behind them.

"Personally, I don't think you're a major gun runner at all..." Sgt. Wilburn stated as he tossed his notepad and a file folder on the table. Coach was relieved to hear that but that feeling went away lightning quick when Wilburn continued, "...but I do think you are working for somebody that is big time. Somebody realized that you had a clean front—working with kids at the rec center—and offered you some cash to have packages delivered. Is that what I'm looking at here?"

Coach met Sgt. Wilburn's gaze but didn't reply.

"You look like a smart man. I know you went to college, so I'm going to tell you this, we don't want you. We want your boss. Tell us who you are working for and we can see about getting you a nice deal if you cooperate."

"I work for the City of Los Angeles, sir, Department of Parks and Recreation. The branch I currently work at is the Jack Tatum Center on Central Avenue where you abducted me from," Coach replied.

"Nice dodge, Mr. Fancy Pants. Are you being a smart ass? I want to know who you're moving the guns for."

Coach sat back in the chair with his mind working quickly. *BODEEN!* That snaky bastard! Coach didn't give a shit about being called a snitch in the hood for telling on Bodeen because he didn't give a fuck about that nigga but for all Coach knew, the police were in cahoots with Bodeen and he would know that Coach gave him up. Jah was right across the street from that crazy fool and Coach knew Bodeen had no mercy.

He took a deep breath. "Look. The guns aren't mine and I don't know who they came from or where they're supposed to go. I didn't even open the boxes. You did. That should have been a delivery of new uniforms for the football team."

Sgt. Wilburn wrote on his notepad for a few moments as the two ATF agents shifted nervously on their feet behind him. He opened the manila file folder and flipped through the pages.

"You don't have any family listed in your paperwork. Don't you have anybody on the outside?"

Coach was not about to let them take Jah and put him in a group home or some shelter for abused children. That was not happening. If that situation were to occur, those trumped up gun charges were going to turn into a murder for real. "No... no, I don't have any family," Coach said as he shook his head.

"If you don't have any family, then why do you have a bedroom at your apartment set up for a kid and photographs of this one young kid all over the walls?"

"This girl I used to date, that's her son. I used to coach him at the rec center. They just moved recently."

"You mean she left you? What did you do to her?"

"No, I mean what I just said. She moved because she was offered a job in Annapolis. She was a poly sci major," Coach knew Feds like that kind of bullshit talk.

"I see..." Wilburn flipped through the folder, pausing for a moment then flipping to another page. Finally, he looked up at Coach. "So you have nothing else to offer me?"

"I gave you everything I have."

"And what was that?" Sgt. Wilburn asked.

"The truth!"

* * *

A jolt of shock ran through Jah's body as he discovered the door to their apartment wide open. Their apartment was ransacked. The couch was flipped over, the TV was face-down on the carpet, all the cabinets were open, and broken dishes were scattered across the floor. Every drawer in the house was open. Jah turned and ran out of the house and flew back downstairs.

He stopped at the bottom of the stairs and caught his breath as he tried to make sense of the situation. He walked back upstairs to make sure he wasn't tripping off of what he saw. After carefully walking through the mayhem, he realized their apartment had been broken into but nothing was missing except his dad. Jah didn't know what to think. He called his dad's phone again but still no answer.

Jah sat down on the floor. The sight of the mess just made matters worse. He stood back up and assessed the room. He couldn't lift the couch by himself to set it upright but he could pick up the TV. He placed it back on the stand but he didn't turn it on. He wasn't in the mood to find out why *'Everybody Hated Chris'* that day. Not even the crush he had on the little girl who played the sister on the show made Jah want to turn the TV on. Jah didn't want anything but his dad.

* * *

"May I make my phone call now, Sgt. Wilburn?" Coach asked trying to be polite as possible though the voice in his head was telling him to reach across the desk, grab the officer by his neck, and choke the fuck out of him.

"Who you gonna call, Coach? It's gonna be big-big money to get you out on bail. And you can't possibly have that kind of money working for the City at parks and rec, unless you're doing a little something on the side. If you tell me who you're covering for, I can persuade the judge to be lenient." Wilburn paused and looked Coach dead in the eyes, but Coach didn't open his mouth nor did he avert his gaze.

Wilburn looked back down in to his folder, his brow furrowed as he shook his head slowly appearing to read something. "Huh. I must have missed this earlier." He closed the folder. "I see you're listed as a possible Muslim terrorist with connections to the Middle East and to the Irgun Hebrews, too. Now that, my man, is a threat.... and with all this crazy shit going on, every judge in the country will deny you bail. So are you sure you've told me everything?"

"So that's what this is all about? Some fuckery you are using me as a rassclot guinea pig to make your war against terrorism look legit?" Coach's voice was deep and true. "You mean to tell me, you spent billions of tax-payer dollars sending the troops across the world to be killed but all along the weapons of mass destruction were being sent right here to a recreation center in South Central L.A to someone that doesn't give a rat's ass about your wicked government or some fake-ass Arabs? You rasshole! Mi want mi phone call now!"

Wilburn stood up. "Oh? You want to play black revolutionary with me, buddy? All right then. I'll show you the real meaning of fuckery. And I'm gonna start with your life! Now tell me what I want to know, dammit!"

The interrogation went on another two hours, yet the only information the ATF got was a history lesson of why their ancestors were sent to the hills and caves of Europe and cast out of society in the first place.

Thoroughly frustrated with the dead end, the officers shackled Coach from his neck to his feet like he was Hannibal Lecter to escort him to another police van. It was dark outside. The minimal amount of traffic on the streets meant it had to be close to midnight as they pulled up to the L.A. County Jail. Coach asked for his phone call when they arrived but his request was ignored.

The cage he was placed in held about 100 inmates charged with everything from jaywalking to drug dealing to bench warrants to murder. As time slowly ticked and he stood in this mass of stinking bodies, Coach realized that stress was not just an emotional response impinging on the body and causing it to suffer; it was a real live thing. It was gray in color. There are a lot of people that know exactly what I'm talking about and if you've never seen stress in the flesh, make sure you keep it that way.

After a few hours, two guards came for him. They cuffed him out and walked him to another small interrogation room that smelled of fear and stale sweat. Two detectives came in and ran him through the same damn questions. Coach gave the same damn answers he gave before.

He truly didn't know anything. He couldn't even make anything up about the case if he wanted to. Finally, Coach was escorted to a room where he was told he would be appointed a *public pretender* if he could not afford a lawyer. He just wanted to make his phone call so he accepted who they appointed. He waited. The door opened to reveal a stringy red-haired, gray-eyed, freckled, ironing board booty, no frills-no thrills bitch with an attitude that reflected her looks. She had stacks of papers in her arms. An officer stood beside her for protection. She introduced herself as Miss Close.

Coach knew she was confused, just by her name. The 'Miss' was surely right, but nobody was trying to get 'Close' to that.

She directed the officer to stand outside of the door. She looked at Coach without humor or warmth. "I don't think we have a sexual predator here...do we?"

"Lady, I haven't been locked up long enough to even think about some shit like that. But trust a brother, that's the last thing you have to worry about. I wouldn't lay my hands on you if you had leprosy and the Lord gave me the power to heal you. Lady…"

Miss Close cut him off. "Okay, that's enough. You made your point." She began thumbing through the mountain of papers. "All right. This is serious business you're charged with. Have you read the complaint?" She shoved a stack of papers at him.

Coach read the complaint. The dark horrific details throughout it seemed to be from a dope-ass movie or bestselling novel. It depicted Coach as an evil villain that had the power to set off a nuclear explosion and destroy the world with one push of a button. It was crazy.

And while he understood the words on the pages, Coach couldn't comprehend the implications other than he knew it was some serious shit. Among the many charges, there was unlawful use, manufacture, and possession of firearms and explosives; weapons trafficking and sales; and possession and transportation of firearms, ammunition, and explosives in interstate commerce. Then there was the charge of possessing automatic weapons, including ones popular with Prohibition-era bootleggers, Nazi soldiers, and revolutionaries that had Coach dumbfounded. Plus there were charges of possession of semi-automatic firearms, short-barreled shotguns, .50 BMGs, and magazines that hold more than ten rounds of ammunition; resisting arrest; accessory after the fact; mail fraud; assault and battery on a police officer; and making criminal (terrorist) threats.

Coach set the complaint back down on the table and let out a deep breath.

"Your computer records show you make a lot of orders from your place of employment, but there is no activity from your home computer. Would you like to explain that?"

"I'm quite sure you can see from those records that sports equipment was purchased online. I am authorized by the City to purchase equipment for the recreation center. I have copies of all the receipts and they're on file with the City, too."

"I see that, but I'm more concerned with the purchases you made from work with your personal credit card. You seem to buy a lot of coffee."

For the first time since he'd been arrested, Coach laughed. "Wait a minute… you're trying to sweat me for a twelve-ounce bag of coffee that I bought with my own money?"

"Well, Coach, coffee is frequently used by traffickers when they're sending contraband items in the mail. It throws off the scent for dogs."

"I'm quite sure they don't order Bob Marley gourmet coffee from the other side of the globe to do that."

And so it went for another hour of bullshit questions from Miss Close.

Then Coach was back in another cage but it had a public phone. He lifted the receiver but didn't hear a dial tone. He pressed down on the hook several times but got nothing. Coach pressed the numbers but no tones came out. He slammed the receiver down as he eyes landed on a gray and black sign: Phone Hours 9AM-9PM. Coach lost it. He kicked the phone so hard, he knocked it clean off the wall. The loud crash got no response from the guards and no one in the cage even looked up.

He sank down against the wall.

* * *

Jah sat alone at their home waiting. He held his cell phone in his hand and his eyes on the house phone. He had called the hospitals but his dad wasn't there. And even though their home had been broken in to, Jah didn't call the police. Somehow, Jah knew that if the police got involved without his dad being there, they would take him away for sure to one of those foster homes. It was 2 o'clock in the morning but Jah couldn't sleep. He was sad and alone and wanted his dad.

A prayer for his dad to come home safe crossed his lips as he tried to stay strong like a young lion, but Jah began to cry. He cried and cried for a long-long time. He cried tears beyond tears.

* * *

Coach was shackled again for transport to the Pitchess Detention Center. They strip searched him yet again, sprayed him with chemicals to prevent lice and bed bugs, and handed him the scratchy uniform of the condemned. A wristband on Coach's arm had his name, prison number, and the letters V and D: Violent and Dangerous. He was taken to Administrative Segregation.

Ad-Seg, another slang term used for *the hole*, is for the most ruthless.

The men are considered to be so devious, they are locked in one-man cells 23 hours a day. Sometimes, inmates are housed in Ad-Seg for a day or two for small infractions; sometimes, inmates have been there for decades. It was every bit of hell without the eternal fire and brimstone.

Coach didn't know if this is what Rick James meant when he talked about it, but it was cold blooded in that muthafuckin' jail, fa' sho'! His bed was a cold steel plank with no mattress or pillow and there was a toilet and that was it. There were no lights on. When that steel cage door clanged shut, it opened up a part of Coach he didn't even know he had in him. And it wasn't anything nice. The Coach that everybody knew and loved with the pure warm heart and soul of gold was gone.

"I'm dead in here, JAH!" Coach shouted as he said his prayers out loud. "Please look after my little soldier. This is not fair to him. It is not fair at all. I will take any punishment for my wrongdoings but let my son be." Coach's voice cracked as water welled up in his eyes. "I cannot function...I cannot function like this! I'm locked up in this fuckin' cage and my baby is out there, alone with nothing! My baby—my son! He doesn't deserve this shit. This is not fair to him! This is wrong!" The tears rolled down Coach's cheeks. He cried tears beyond tears.

CHAPTER 25

"Bass drop!!
Oh! Oh! Oh! Oh! Oh! Oh! Oh! Oh!
You got a 100 dolla bill, put yo' hands up!
You got a 50 dolla bill, put yo' hands up!
You got a 20 dolla bill, put yo' hands up!
You got a 10 dolla bill, put yo' hands up!
Single ladies I can't hear y'all, Single ladies make noise,

SINGLE LADIES I can't hear y'all, Single ladies make noise!"
Detective Andy Moretti was doing the damn 'butterfly' in the middle
of the dance floor in between two thick black chicks. They were tooting
cocaine and swigging back Absolut with pomegranate juice as they cele-
brated his big bust of a gun runner. Virgil had his shirt open and the black
chicks were rubbing all over his chest. Andy was getting his freak on as he
chanted with the music, "All the chicken heads, be quiet! All the chicken
heads, be quiet! All the chicken heads, be quiet!"

* * *

On the other side of town, Bodeen was up in his apartment zooted out
of his mind. He was laid out on the floor wearing nothing but his drawers, drenched in sweat. Nearby were two empty vodka bottles. The smooth
sounds of "Love Shoulda Brought You Home" by Toni Braxton filled the
apartment. He had the song on repeat as he tried to think about the girl
he had a one-night stand with recently. But her name escaped him and his

mind kept going back to the one who he lost his virginity with, that lovely angel Angie.

* * *

The next morning the bust was in the paper but it wasn't the front page news that Detective Moretti had hoped for, only a few paragraphs way in the back of the Metro Section. But really, what did he expect? He had Coach labeled as a thug selling guns to gang members so they could kill each other. Even the fact he was allegedly using the rec center as a front carried no weight. Transgender protests and who the Kardashians were fuckin' next were the only stories drawing interest in the media. The story was on the local newscast the night before and it generated a little buzz by the people that knew Coach, but since he didn't announce he was *coming out of the closet* and wasn't accused of mistreating a dog, the news didn't travel past a ten-block radius.

Jah got off the bus at King Boulevard and Central Avenue looking for his dad. Jah walked a few blocks to rec center. It was still taped off with yellow police tape. Jah had only seen yellow tape in the movies and a body was always covered in a white sheet. Jah knew right then that his dad was dead. Tears rolled down Jah's like Niagara Falls as he ran towards his dad's office.

Jah was so small he didn't even have to lift the yellow tape to run underneath it. The door to the big building was locked. He ran around back and all the doors were locked there, too. Jah walked around the entire park twice looking for James or anyone. But just like the night before, he was totally alone.

Jah placed both hands over his face and cried so hard his head ached.

* * *

Coach had the same headache but he couldn't cry. His eyes were red with anger and his body was tensed, ready to spring. Coach decided if they were going to destroy his life by locking him in a cage and keep him away from Jah, he was going to give them an excellent reason to do so. Coach paced in the cell, waiting for anybody to look at him wrong or say some shit he didn't like and he was going to kill them with his bare hands.

He had already slung his breakfast tray clear across the tier when they tried to slide it to him in his cell with pork bacon on it. The C.O. was about to make Coach get out of his cell to clean up the mess and then took one look into his eyes and decided he didn't want any part of letting that lunatic out. Coach almost had the Goon Squad (aka Emergency Response Unit) sent into his cell to calm him down physically.

But he was looking forward to getting out of his cell for the hour they were given each day because it was an opportunity to get to a phone. The guards walked the three-level tier and counted each inmate. The words "All Clear" went over the intercom and a loud buzzer went off. Steel cage doors slid open, floor by floor.

Except Coach's door didn't open. Coach kicked on the door repeatedly.

"Knock it off, fuckface! You're in the hole for 72 hours!" a guard yelled. Coach didn't know it, but there was a rule that fresh inmates and the ones currently in trouble didn't get yard privileges for 72 hours.

"Fuck that! I need my phone call or I'll kick this muthafuckin' door off the hinges."

The C.O's took that as a threat and hit that ERU button, which caused the entire unit to go on lockdown. The inmates were herded back in to their cages as they grumbled their displeasure.

The Goon Squad, clad in black overalls, black full-face helmets and armed with shields, stomped in unison through the corridors to give the impression they were coming in vast numbers. It sounded like 60 men but there were only ten. They stopped just out of the sightline of Coach's cell and stood silent. Coach was prepared for whatever because there was no way they would inflict more pain than Coach already felt from missing his son. The goons waited six long minutes. Then just as loudly as they had arrived, they retreated without engaging. But Coach didn't feel a sense of relief or like GOD was looking over him because it is difficult to feel emotion when the heart has been hardened.

* * *

The world looked too big. The noise from the traffic, horns blowing, and people talking was too loud. Jah didn't know what to do. He didn't know how to take the bus to James' house. Jah thought about going to school and telling someone what happened. He wasn't a problem child but those teachers didn't want any extra responsibility once that last bell rang. He closed his eyes to the world around him and took a breath. And then at once, he knew what to do.

* * *

"Say, young dada!"

Coach looked around the 9x9 cage. Coach knew he was far from the point where he was hearing voices in his head but he knew he just heard someone.

"Young dada, are you all right? Talk through the vent and let me know you're cool."

Coach looked around the concrete walls again and spotted a tiny air vent above the toilet. Coach stood on the steel toilet to respond. "No, I'm not cool. I'm locked in this concrete box and my—" Coach stopped mid-sentence just in case the voice he was talking to was an informant.

"I can tell from the powdered eggs on the floor in front of my house that you haven't eaten anything. How do you feel?"

"I feel with my hands, like I always do. Now what do you want?"

"I was just checking to see if you need anything."

"I need you to get me the fuck out of here. Can you do that? If not, please let me be," Coach said frustrated.

"Listen Coach, there is no guarantee that you are going to make it out of here, but if you want to survive this shit, just do the time. Don't let the time do you."

Coach was about to snap back but he didn't like that the Voice knew his name so he stayed silent.

"Young dada, put your ear to the vent." The Voice whispered real low. "Now Coach, I know you got a son out there by himself. I can help you. I heard you praying last night and your pain was too much for *me* and I done seen it all. I can get you as many phone calls as you need. It's gonna cost you a little but I can do that for you. But to do that, Imma need for you to chill the fuck out until after dinner count tonight."

Coach didn't know if it was a setup or not but he needed that phone call. "Yeah I can do that. Say mon, how come you know my name?"

"Young dada, you're in ad-seg with hardcore criminals, the real shot callers. Everybody in here that matters knows your name and your charges. That is our job. We have to know who is who."

"Well, who are you?"

"In due time, Coach. We'll meet soon enough and introduce ourselves properly like human beings are supposed to. Just stay patient and have faith."

* * *

The airport shuttle van was out front waiting for Bodeen. He walked out of his apartment carrying a small suitcase and got in.

As the van pulled away from the curb, Bodeen thought about Coach and he laughed. Coach was a damn fool believing in all that black power, Malcolm X, *we are all Brothers* bullshit. And while he admired what Coach did with all the children, Bodeen couldn't stand when he would call him "brother." In Bodeen's business, it was every man for himself. Bodeen had been hired by black men to have their own biological brothers killed for minor shit like some pussy, so he knew there could be no real love between two niggas with no blood relation. White clients would put contracts on their parents but it was always for the life insurance money or an inheritance they couldn't wait for.

As to the "information" he gave to Moretti about Coach, Bodeen didn't feel any guilt about it. He had done worse things than that in his life and it wasn't the first time he had set somebody up to take a fall.

However, it was the first time Bodeen did it to a civilian, you know, someone not active in the street life. But it was a new era. Prisons were tired of dealing with hardened criminals; it was too dangerous. They wanted first-time offenders that were ignorant of the laws and would do their time peacefully. Coach fit the criteria to a tee... or so they thought.

* * *

Jah walked into the barbershop and everybody went silent and stared at him wide-eyed, like they just saw a spook. It was early and a weekday so the barbershop wasn't as crowded as it would be on a Saturday morning.

Shirley was the first to regain her composure and she ran over to Jah, put her big arms around him, and covered his whole body.

"I'm so sorry, baby boy. I heard what happened to your daddy. It's

gonna be all right, baby. Just pray to Jesus and everything will be all right."
Jah looked at the picture of a white Jesus at Shirley's station as he struggled
free from her hug.

Another voice said, "Don't worry, little man. Your daddy will be
home soon."

And then another asked, "How much time are they giving your pops?
You know they be stretching niggas nowadays. How much heat did they
catch him with?"

"That's enough now," Pops Sanford said. The news had hit the barbershop while the arrest was being made, damn near like they had live stream
broadcasting. By the time it was news on the tv, it was already old news
at the barbershop. He steered Jah to the back of the shop and told him
what went down the day before and that no one had seen James since it
happened. As he talked, Pops Sanford went into his locker and took out a
shoebox with a thick rubber band around it. He placed it in Jah's lap.

"I told your dad that black ass spook was bad luck! You remember
when I told him that, don't you? Bodeen's kind just ain't meant for this
California sunshine. I can't wait until he leaves this planet! Now your
father wanted me to pick something up for him a couple of days ago but
he changed his mind." Pops took out the 200 dollars Coach had given him
and gave it to Jah.

"Tell your father that this one is on me, no charge. Now get on home
with that, little man. Keep your eyes open and hey... do the right thing,"
Pops said as he ushered Jah out of the shop.

Jah felt a little better knowing his father was alive. But he had heard
older cats in the streets say that they would rather be dead than be in jail so
Jah didn't find any lasting comfort in his newly found information.

As he walked back home, Jah realized a valuable lesson about certain
people: they don't give a fuck about nobody but themselves. Everybody
knew Coach was a single father but not one adult in the barbershop asked
Jah if he needed any help or if he was hungry or needed a place to stay.
They didn't even think to ask. Jah wondered what white Jesus would have
to say to Shirley about her Christian ways.

FAITH

...the votes are in, but they ain't ours
We got these politicians running their game to regain power
While our whole black community sours
Crime rate towers, plagued by white powders
And they claim to helping us to clean up our community
But ain't no open opportunities, impunity
Is what these demons use to regulate
We keep in mind we can run but we can't hide cause the
streets we walk are never safe
Still all my shattered hopes and dreams remain scattered
Broken into thousands of pieces, smashed and tattered
But it don't matter, hypocrisy in your democracy
Is stopping me, so I'm retaliating properly
Theologically, society has got me pressured by the hate
And Heaven knows I have faith, I have faith...

—B. "Scarface" Jordan

COACH WAITED, STRESSED as he paced in his cell. As he went from one side to the other and back again, he started hearing a voice in his head. It was his favorite rapper Scarface reminding him to maintain his "faith." At 9PM, all the Hispanics that were riding together had roll call. They did that three times a day. Gang names rang out around the tier one by one on all three floors. This was their way of making sure everybody was still alive and accounted for in their cell. Coach noticed two things about this:.the unity the Spanish Cartel had was unprecedented, and there were a lot of muthafuckas named Spider.

Coach was amazed how the veteran inmates could stay trapped in concrete boxes 23 hours a day, miles away from General Population, yet still have more information on what's going on across the states, than the people currently active in the streets. And the things they invented to survive in jail were mind blowing. On the streets you couldn't pay 90% of the inmates a $100 an hour to screw in a light bulb at a regular job, but in jail they could make a damn rocket ship out of toilet paper and toothpaste. That was the sad part. There was amazing talent and skill in those cells going to waste. One of the most used inventions in ad-seg was the *kite*, aka a jailhouse telegram.

Coach was sitting uncomfortably on the metal cot. A kite slid under the cell door real smooth like. Coach didn't pick it up right away. He walked over to the cell door and looked out of the small square that was supposed to be a window. Coach saw pieces of the same kind of thread stretched out and going in different directions all across the tier. It looked like a huge spider web. The inmates were using threads from their bedspreads to create makeshift ropes. I kid you not; some thread had to be at least 300 feet long. It could hang from the third floor all the way down to the first floor and still be able to stretch across to the other side.

Coach opened the note. It had a Hispanic last name on it and a list of store items that were to be bought if Coach agreed to the terms to use the cell phone. Coach didn't have a pencil. Coach whispered in the vent to the Voice and asked if the deal being offered was fair. It was. He asked how he was supposed to reply. A pencil attached to thread slid under the door within a minute. It scared the shit out of Coach because it came under the door so fast he thought it was that famous rodent they call Freeway Freddy. Coach agreed to the terms and tugged on the thread, signifying he responded. The note slid back out the way it came in. Then Coach watched the kite as it traveled 75 yards across the room and then up three floors. And as he watched his kite disappear, Coach noticed all the activity around the tier. Not one person was visible but notes, food, phones, cigarettes, and postage stamps were being delivered, all via these little tiny threads.

Coach zoned out on watching these little kites and tried not to think about all the bullshit that landed him here.

"Rudely awaken from this bad dream
Thinking my conscience wants to tell me something good because of these bad things
(Past things) got me in the center of these mad dreams
(Flashing) homicidal thoughts of fatal slashings
Now I'm asking: explain to me these visionaries Brad seen
(Past things) sad things- killed him cause he had dreams
(A sad scene) but all I ever wanted was my mind back
Now I'm that, nigga trying to find out where his mind's at
The time that- it- took- my-self to figure out my mind's gone
My mind cracked, slide back, look at all the time gone
Rewind back, time back, understand my life gon' make these cuts that won't change
But things look so strange…"

Some of the heavier contraband scraping across the floor sounded like knives being sharpened on rocks. Some of the deliveries were knives made out of hardened newspaper. They go through human flesh like butter.

Coach went back to pacing the cell; all three yards of it. There were more thoughts going in and out of his mind than a confused Gemini.

* * *

Back in their apartment, Jah was pacing, too. He had eaten a bowl of Wheaties earlier. There was fish and chicken in the freezer but he didn't know how to cook it. The house phone rang. The ring sounded better than Frankie Beverly and Maze singing the long version of "*Happy Feelings*" in an outdoor arena. Jah snatched it off the hook.

"Dad?"

"Hi, this Carol from Consumer Card Holders with an urgent message about your credit card. Currently there are no problems with your current credit card but we…"

Jah hung up the phone, despondent again.

His cell phone rang soon after with a blocked number.

"Hello?"

"What up, Jah? How come you weren't at school today? You got locked up with your Daddy, huh? I saw it was on the news," said Jah's buddy Busby.

"Are you asking me a question or telling me what I did?" Jah asked and continued. "What did I miss anyway? Did we have homework?"

"Yeah, we have to finish those spelling words. Write each word three times, look up the definition, and write a sentence in your own words. How was jail? What was it like? What did they get you for?" Busby kept asking.

"It was terrible. You never want to go there. They arrested me for not doing my spelling words so you better get off the phone and do your homework before they come get you!"

* * *

And adapting to the everyday struggles got us stressed
Cause the fact we know we here one day and could die the next...

Coach's faith was strong but the situation he was in allowed him to under-stand why his two atheist friends chose that path. Coach was feeling like he was forsaken in the worst way, but he still prayed on it.

My last day, sad case, Heaven knows I have faith...

A small flat phone wrapped in toilet paper slid under the cell door. Coach yelled out, "JAH! Rastafari!"

He dialed the house number.

"SON!"

"DAD!"

They cried, laughed, and told each other how much they missed one another. Coach gave Jah the rundown on how he was set up. They talked for about 45 minutes. This was the best they felt in the last two days. They even had a good laugh about how Coach got a cell phone in jail. Coach didn't want to hang up from his son for one second but he had to call LaTonya and James to see if they would look after Jah so he could focus on getting out of the Concrete Jungle.

Coach called James first. He was kind of pissed that Jah wasn't there in the first place. His wife answered with a flat tone that quickly changed to fury when she realized who it was..

"James hasn't been home in two days and I know that evil black bastard you were hanging around with had something to do with it. James told you to stop bringing him around. But you didn't listen. Huh-uh. You had your own damn ideas about it. You always trying to save all those no good niggas in the hood and you sacrificed the only man who really loved you. Where's my husband, Coach? Why didn't you save him? Where is he, Coach? Where's the father of my kids, Coach?"

And with that, Coach's happiness was gone. He apologized to James' wife and hung the phone up feeling guilty and disappointed in his actions. James was a good man and this definitely wasn't fair for him and all those kids of his.

As he looked at the phone in his hand, Coach was going through the mental and emotional struggles that happen in prison they don't show in the movies because it's too hard to explain visually. He shook his head, rolled his shoulders and dialed LaTonya.

"Hello?" LaTonya answered sleepily.

"Baby, it's me!"

LaTonya changed her tone. "I've been calling you all day. Your phone was going straight to voicemail. What in hell were you doing that you had to have your phone off all damn day? And whose number are you calling from? Is this your other girlfriend's phone?"

"LaTonya, now is not the time for this silly boyfriend-girlfriend shit. They got your man locked up on some bullshit and Jah is home all by himself."

"You mean locked up, as in jail?" LaTonya asked confused.

Coach used all the discipline he had not to give her a sarcastic answer. "Yes baby, in the belly of the beast."

"How did you call me without calling me collect?"

"This Mexican leased me his cell phone," Coach answered but his patience was getting the best of him.

"Cell phone? How did he get a cell phone in jail?"

"Does it fuckin' matter, LaTonya? Goddamn! I'm in jail and Jah is home alone. I need you now more than ever and you're asking me some irrelevant bullshit. C'mon now!"

"Sorry, baby. I just—this is—well what do you need me to do?"

Coach looked at the phone like he wanted to snatch her through it and slap some sense in her head. "Something happened to James and I need you to stay at the house with Jah or let him stay with you until I take care of this nonsense."

"You mean tonight? It's kind of late, baby. Don't you have a relative's house where he could stay?"

"Are you serious? You have the nerve to hesitate about my son when I've seen you leap out of a deep sleep at four in the morning to tend to that little sissy-ass dog of yours because he was whimpering at the bedroom door. Ooh! I knew what I was feeling deep down about you was right and exact. I shouldn't have even had to explain that to a down woman. What happened to, *I'll be there for you and Jah,* and all that other sweet shit you were talking?"

LaTonya played it just like one of those typical cute self-centered saditty chicks that have no ride-or-die in them at all and remained silent. She didn't answer one question. Didn't even say a word. She was in complete silence.

"So you mean to tell me, LaTonya, you are gonna sit on the phone quiet while I'm dying inside and Jah is all alone?"

"…Well, what? –uh- I mean… I don't know… this is just…too much right now…"

"Never mind, LaTonya… you are a muthafuckin' disappointment… you jive ass broad."

He dialed Jah again.

"Dad!"

"son… we have to do this on our own."

* * *

Ten minutes later, a correction officer knocked on the cage door, looked in the cell at Coach, and said, "You can have your phone call now."

"Ain't that a bitch!" Coach said under his breath, turned over in his steel bunk and gave the correction officer his back without answering him.

He was starting to feel dehydrated. The milky colored water they had to drink didn't look right at all. Over the course of the night, Coach turned into a convict MacGyver his damn self. He made a kite and sent a message saying he was looking for some good drinking water preferably alkaline or fresh coconut. He had to be specific because the word *water* had several definitions in the joint.

After he sent the kite, Coach wondered how they were going to slide a water bottle under the 1-inch crack, but he didn't doubt they could do it one bit. They were selling pruno (jailhouse liquor) from the second floor so water shouldn't be a difficult task. But it turns out ad-seg had everything that a 7-11 did, except drinking water. Somebody yelled from across the tier and told Coach to put the bad water in a sandwich bag until the milky substance settles at the bottom. Coach tried it. It worked but he still didn't trust it to drink it. He dipped his toothbrush in it when he hit his grill but that was about it.

The next morning Coach was up at 4AM. The first thing he thought about was the Voice that aided him in time of need but the Voice was gone from the cell before Coach had a chance to thank him. Coach refused his breakfast again.

After they pulled the trays fro breakfast, Coach and about twenty other inmates were shackled from head to toe and locked to each other. They were put on the grey goose and sent downtown to court. Coach was given another Public Pretender to represent him. Coach didn't bother remembering his name or even what he looked like. The Public Pretender didn't bother looking at Coach much either. He talked while he looked through those same stacks of paperwork the ugly bitch had when he first got arrested.

"Wow, you chose the wrong time of the year to be in your profession. Let's see here. You were found with illegal firearms during elections and the Governor's campaign is the *War on Guns*. This doesn't bode well." He kept flipping through the stack of paper. "But you have no prior arrest and some of this other stuff is bullshit and I can get it dropped. If we take this to trial and you lose, they can give you up to fifty-five years between Federal and State. But if you take the deal they are offering—and it is a very good deal I might add—it would be in your best interest... you plead guilty right now to the sale of weapons and the interstate commerce charge, they will drop the terrorist threats, assault, resisting arrest, and all the other charges. They are willing to offer you fifteen years. Ten for the State and only five years for the Feds. You'll probably end up doing a little over nine total years barring you stay out of trouble. That is a great deal but it's totally up to you."

* * *

"Next up. The State of California versus Julian Hassan Love aka Coach. How does the defendant plead?"

"Your Honor, Mr. Love refuses my services and all other court appointed lawyers and wishes to represent himself..."

Judge Brown looked at Coach for a long time. He looked down at his file and then back up at Coach again.

"I want you to understand that in this jurisdiction if your concerns cannot be worked out with the attorney we have already appointed you, the courts will only replace a public defender one time, after which they will make no further substitutions."

"I understand thoroughly. A kind gesture you have bestowed on me by appointing me another Pretender, uh I mean Public Defender, but I will not require nor will I accept any substitutes. You guys have done more than enough for me already. I'd much rather defend myself so at least I can accept the outcome knowing I fought for my freedom," Coach stated and looked at the Judge.

The Judge didn't reply and seemed to be waiting for something more from Coach.

"So I enter a plea of innocent on all charges and further request that I be granted bail," Coach continued with confidence in his voice, but not really knowing what he was talking about and hoping that his inner vibe was on the right path.

"Normally, Mr. Love, you would have to notify the court in writing of your request to fire the public defender if your concerns cannot be worked out. You must include a statement of reasons, though you need to exercise caution not to reveal any confidential information which may be critical to your defense."

"Yes I'm aware of that, sir. I have the letter of request right here so you can expedite the process. May I approach the bench?"

The Judge saw that Coach was as smart as he looked, but he wasn't wise enough yet to know he should never try to make a white man look silly in a courtroom.

"No, that won't be necessary. Bailiff, would you get the document from Mr. Love, please? Thank you…"

Judge Brown scanned the letter. "Well, Mr. Love, I see you are an articulate man, but due to the complexities of this case, I would advise you not to take this into your own hands. I'm going to postpone this hearing until next month and give you time to really think of this major decision. Bail request denied." Judge Brown slammed his gavel down and excused himself from the courtroom. On his way out, he requested the attorneys come see him in his chambers.

* * * *

Jah continued with his daily program like his dad told him. To his dismay, Jah's popularity soared overnight. America's fascination with violence is a sickness. Even some of the kindergartners were in awe of the rumor spreading that Jah's dad was a gangster that owned machine guns and was selling Uzis. The things Jah heard the kids say were tripping him out. They were making him out to be a hero.

Dang Jah! Your daddy is gangster. How many machine guns he got?

My daddy got a shotgun just like the one your daddy got.

My Uncle Ray wants to know how much your daddy be selling 9mm Berettas for.

Now we see why you're always wearing all those fly clothes and Jordans! Yo daddy is ballin'

How many guns you got, Jah?

Have y'all ever shot anybody before?

All the sudden, he had friends he had never even seen before. Jah didn't think all the fanfare was necessary but it was better than being alone.

Now that he had talked to his dad, he wasn't terrified like he was two days earlier. After school, Jah walked over to Juicy's Jamaican Restaurant on Washington and 5th Avenue and ordered his favorite meal, ox tails, rice

& peas, vegetables, and fresh sweet plantains. He tore that food up when he got home. There wasn't a grain of rice or trace of curry let on his plate. He licked that plate clean. As he ate, he sifted through the mail and got his first taste of being an adult: bills. Jah shook his head just like he'd seen his father do every month.

Then Jah opened the big manila envelope from Coach. Jah knew it was coming. It was Coach's personal property, his wallet and ATM card, watch, and the gold necklace Jah's mother bought Coach before he was born. The cash was missing from the wallet but Coach never carried more than twenty bucks for the most part so Jah didn't have a hissy fit about it, plus he had enough money to live off of for a while so that was the least of his worries.

* * *

As Coach returned to the jail after court, as sick as it sounded, he was looking forward to getting back to his cell. Not only could he get away from those lames he was shackled to all day, he had access to a phone. But it didn't work out that way. Coach was moved to a general population dorm with about fifty more inmates in blue jumpsuits. There were 25 bunk beds, five metal tables for card games, and two televisions.

Coach took his state issued items over to his assigned bunk and before he could turn around to survey his new quarters, he was approached by a group of brothers. It was customary to be greeted by the blacks. The old timers believed that there was strength in numbers. The young bucks were just interested to see what gang Coach belonged to. Coach told them he was Rasta. They told him he had to claim Blood, Crip, or non-affiliate. Coach told them once again that he was a Rasta man. They left it alone. Coach wondered out loud about the use of the phones on the wall. There were three phones, but one was covered and secured with a huge padlock. A young black man with short dreads told Coach that there was a phone for the whites, one for the Mexicans, and one for the blacks. Coach didn't even have to ask whose phone was the one out of commission. He also told him that the other races might let him use their phone for a small fee but not to count on it.

Coach felt a little better hearing that. He was a people person by nature and his enemies weren't the ones that were locked up in jumpsuits.

Coach's luck shifted for the better when he found out it was store and canteen day. Coach was going to load up on items strictly for trade. Coach befriended one of the old timers and asked what the proper procedure was to get the items he promised the shot caller in ad-seg. He told Coach just to make sure he gets all the items and not to worry about it.

Sure enough, as Coach was in the Canteen line, a Mexican approached him and said, "Are you Coach?"

"That is I and I."

The Mexican handed Coach a laundry bag and said, "What's up? I'm Lil' Spider. See my homeboy over there? That's Spider. Put the shit you owe Big Spider in this bag and hand it to Spider." They slapped hands and Lil' Spider scurried on to the next person caught in the Spiders Web.

Coach loaded up his bags with the max amount of items he was allowed to purchase. Coach separated his items from the ones for Big Spider. Before he closed the bag for Big Spider, he threw in a few more items: some Top Ramen, cookies, and stamps to show his appreciation for being there when he needed him the most.

"Here you go, homie."

Coach looked up and a black dude from another dorm handed him another laundry bag.

"That's okay, black man. I already have one. But thank you for looking out," Coach said as he walked over to Spider and handed him the laundry bag. Coach turned around and the black dude was in his face still holding the empty bag.

"My bag's lookin' kinda light. Fact, I don't think I want this one anymore. I like yours better. So you take this one and give me that one," said the black dude as he clinched his fist and got ready to throw it.

"Say what?" Coach couldn't believe this fool just pushed his button. Coach was far from scared but he hadn't been in a fistfight since he was in the sixth grade.

He thought about it for a second. Coach swallowed his pride, dropped his eyes, and gave the dude his bag full of goodies and accepted the empty laundry bag the bully gave him. Then in a flash, Coach pulled the drawstring tight and wrapped it around that nigga's neck so fast he didn't know what happened. Coach was choking the life out of that fool! His lips were turning blue and his body went limp. In thirty more seconds he was going to be dead.

Coach let the drawstring loose and dropped that fool on the concrete hard. Coach flipped him over on his back so he could thrash his face with his fist. But before he threw the first punch, someone snatched Coach off and steered him back in to the crowd.

"You're blowing it, young dada. Think about your son and only your son."

Coach recognized the voice and his words calmed down Coach immediately. Receiving another charge or getting more time added on was not what Coach needed at all; now that part had him scared.

The dude he choked out PC'd up and started hollering somebody tried to kill him. The alarm sounded and everybody in the general area had to strip naked and line up against the wall. The C.O.s walked the line and checked everybody's knuckles for redness and abrasions. Coach wondered why they had to be naked to get their hands checked but it was their way of keeping the inmates submissive. Coach was glad he didn't sock the dude like he wanted to or he would have been done.

"All Clear" came over the intercom after they were kept naked and standing for 30 minutes.

"You are the Voice from the hole. I'm Coach. I really appreciate the way you looked out for me with the phone and all. Can I get you some Canteen or something for all you've done?"

"Young dada, the only thing I want you to do for me is to stay focused and get the fuck out of here so you can raise your little man right, ya dig? I don't need any more cookies and noodles. By the way, they call me Old Man Silas up in here. It's nice to meet you, young dada."

Old Man Silas was only 62 and looked extremely healthy for his age. His hair and beard was sprinkled with a lot of gray but he didn't fit the stereotype of a grandfather. The only thing old school about him was the way he wore his jumpsuit buttoned up to the neck and the Stacy Adams dress shoes he had on. Old Man Silas had a mean stroll, too. He leaned slightly to one side as he took long strides. Old Man Silas was a career criminal, but he didn't see himself that way. He preferred to call himself "one of those rebellious slaves." He only had a couple of months left to do on a parole violation. Silas told Coach how he was dating his parole officer, a little funny looking skinny broad that thought she was cute with a bullshit attitude named Ms. Parrish. He grew tired of her so she sent him to the joint for 120 days for breaking up with her. She still sent him letters every day telling him how lonely she is. Silas' story tripped Coach out, but guards and parole officers dating inmates was common practice and nothing new. Old Man Silas said he needed the break from her. She had a sexual appetite of a nymphomaniac but she wasn't really good at it. Silas squinted, looked out into space like he was daydreaming and said, "And her tongue is always coated like her mouth is dry all the time. Her breath doesn't stink but her kisses are never sweet."

Coach didn't think avoiding a sex fiend was enough to make a man want to go back to jail but he figured to each his own. Coincidentally, Coach and Old Man Silas were in the same dorm. Old Man Silas made the cat that was sharing bunks with Coach transfer his belongings to the bunk he was assigned to.

Old Man Silas led a full life and saw many things. He wasn't the stereotypical old prisoner that read every book in the prison library. He learned about life through trial and error and not hearsay. Experience was his best teacher so he was full of wisdom.

"I know you got your mind on that phone already. Use the phone for business or to talk to someone pleasant on the outside to keep you sane. Don't let that phone stress you out, young dada. Take a look over there at that fool on the phone with his hand on his head talking to his woman. He's been in here fighting a hot one for the last two years. He's all stressed out because everybody has been warming their sausage in her oven while he's been in here. Shit, everybody was fucking her all day everyday when he was on the street. That's why he's in here... pistol-whipped a nigga to death when he caught him laying the pipe to his woman in *his* bed... and they didn't even live together. How about that? Now he expects her to be celibate when he's looking at 25 to life. Boy, these cape-wearin' save-a-hoe ass niggas are something else."

"You don't have to worry about that, elder lion. I only have one focus...

well, two…" Coach mind drifted to a dark place for a second and then he snapped back and continued. "How do the phones work here, Silas?"

"The same as in the hole… the blacks' phone is out of commission for some reason or another. The Mexicans and whites will rent their phone to you for a couple of packs of noodles, but you can only use it at certain times. I hope you got a landline, but if not use, uh, 1-800-call-4-cheap, but you have to set up an account first, and then you can call people on their cells. But it will be more convenient if you get cool with one of these Keyster Kings around here that got cell phones though it's gonna cost you a little more."

"Keyster Kings?" Coach asked. He just figured it was a slang term for *the man with the magic key that can unlock hidden doors* or something like that. "Jail sure has stayed current with the times. They got computers and cell phones and shit. How do they get cell phones up in here? Do you need a special permit?"

"You really are a first timer… you're just as green as a leprechaun and the clothes on the Bishop Don Juan. You don't know what a *keyster* is, young dada?"

"Naw, I never heard of that one."

"Booty… ass."

"What you mean? Jailhouse fun boys?"

"Noooo, square," replied Silas as he chuckled. "They get paid to bring contraband in here up their ass."

"I thought that was a mule. See? I'm not totally square."

"A mule carries heavy loads up his ass and distributes them to the source. A Keyster King just keeps an item or two concealed until needed."

"Bullshit! Don't con me, Silas. I know about the drugs in the balloon up the dook shoot, but you're not about to tell me that somebody fits a cell phone up their ass. You are not about to tell me that."

"How else you think they get them in here?"

"Hell naw! They're paying a guard or something to bring 'em in."

Silas shook his head. "Young dada, this ain't an episode of *Oz*. This is central, not the penitentiary. These sheriffs are making cool money, not little struggling ass guards. See that Mexican over there with his shirt off playing pinochle? He got a phone up his ass right now. See that skinny black dude standing over there discussing business with that white boy? He got a phone up his ass right now. Watch him go to the toilet after he closes the deal."

Coach watched the black dude go into the stall and sit like he was about to shit. A minute later, he came out and he exchanged the phone for a bag of goods. Coach still wasn't convinced.

"Man, he had that taped behind the toilet. There ain't way that brother Is walking comfortably like that for some damn extra cookies. And you say amigo is sitting there on that metal seat just playing cards with a phone up his ass? What if somebody calls? How do they keep it charged? Uh-huh, I got you now," Coach stated like he knew something Silas didn't.

"Got me how? They bring the charger in the same way," Silas nonchalantly stated.

Coach fell out laughing. "Bullshit Silas. How's that possible?"

"Survival… they have the owners' manual and a bluetooth up their ass, too, if you need them," Silas stated and then he smiled and winked because he was actually joking that time.

Coach laughed out loud. He needed that laugh because he was crying on the inside.

Two weeks had passed. Coach spent most of his time in the Law Library trying to figure out the best strategy to use to beat his case before it even got to trial. Coach did an excellent job gathering evidence, character witnesses, and letters on his behalf. He would have made Johnnie Cochran proud. Coach was having a hard time locating Rolland, but he had Jah on the beat doing some PI work.

* * *

"Well, well, well… see, this is the type of shit I'm talkin' 'bout," the eighteen-year-old kid said to his friend when he saw Coach.

The kid looked familiar but he was already aging hard, and Coach couldn't match his face with a name. The kid said, "It's me, Riley Westbrook. I used to be on your Pee Wee football team."

Riley had lost his baby fat, but Coach remembered him. Coach cracked a wide smile until Riley put him on blast.

"What happened, Coach? You used to do all that talking about staying in school and off the streets and now look at your dumb ass. You self-righteous, contradictory muthafuckas make me sick to my stomach. I was actually up in here trying to remember that bullshit you was teaching us back in the day to get my mind right. And now I'm glad I didn't use it 'cause it ain't even working for you. Role model, my ass... you used to be my hero, but now nigga, I see you ain't nothin' but a sucka that talk too much."

Coach felt like shit. He let another kid down in the worst way. And there was nothing he could say or do about it. The kid was right.

To add insult to injury, the day before he received a letter of termination from his job at the rec center. On top of that shit, Jah's ninth birthday was in two days. When it rains, it pours and Coach didn't have an umbrella anywhere...

* * *

"So you really intend on fighting a case of this magnitude by yourself, huh, young dada?" Silas asked as he saw Coach trying to make sense out of the way the laws were worded.

"I don't have a choice, OG. I can't trust these public pretenders with my life."

"I have no doubt in my mind you have the skills to fight it and win, but you got caught up in that political web. They ain't gonna let you make a fool of them in their courts. Truth will not set you free when whitey is already holding the key. You need to get yourself a real lawyer."

"I thought about that. But if I use the little money I have saved and lose the case, Jah won't have a pot to piss in or a window to throw it out of. I would be playing for big stakes, betting the house, literally. At least the money in my savings will feed him and keep a roof over his head for a little under a year. And what's a paid lawyer gonna do? I've been hearing fools in here talking about they had paid lawyers and still got five to ten years."

"Listen, young dada. lawyers are some slimy reptiles—there ain't no doubt—but not all of them are poisonous. Call my man Eldee Young over at the Cochran Firm. He's white, but the only color that matters to him is green. He's already familiar with your case. Just give him a call. If you don't feel good about it, we'll keep working on it until it's right. Cool, young dada? Now go get some rest before you bust a blood vessel in your brain."

* * *

Jah woke up late on Saturday. It had been a rough week and he got some much-needed rest. Jah hustled to the living room to see if he missed his Dad's call. Jah forgot it was his birthday until he looked on the dining room table and saw the single cupcake his little girlfriend gave him after school on Friday. It was his birthday but there was nothing happy about it. Coach had told Jah to be seldom seen, act as low key as possible, and not to draw any attention to his whereabouts. Coach would be facing a serious child abandonment charge if he was caught, but he had to put all his faith into that decision. The system was not going to raise his son. It wasn't going to happen. Jah was holding up on his own. He went to the supermarket by himself, took care of the bills, and even moved Coach's car on street cleaning day.

Jah looked around the empty house. It was a strange feeling. He didn't have any presents to open or any friends to play with on his birthday. Jah put one candle on his cupcake and lit it. He sat at the empty table and looked at the fire pole dancing on the wick. Jah thought about his birthday long and hard. It was the year he was supposed to learn the knowledge and science of self and he was right on course. Jah made his wish, and I don't need to narrate what that was. Jah decided not to blow out the candle. He left it lit so his Dad could see the light and find his way home safely.

Jah cracked a wide smile when the phone rang.

"Happy Born Day son!"

"Thanks, Dad." Jah's voice was cracking as his eyes filled up with tears. "Dad… when are you coming home? I miss you here! I miss doing us. I wake up sad every day. Please come home, Dad. Please?"

Coach had never felt so hurt in his life. That would be hardest thing Coach would have to deal with in jail. There was nothing else he would face that would be worse. Hearing Jah cry was tearing Coach apart.

Coach wiped his eyes and got himself together. "I know this is a bad time to be talking about this, son, but it's important. Did you take care of the utilities and drop the rent off?"

"I knocked all that out on Thursday before I went to football practice."

"Did the manager drop the receipt off?"

"Not yet."

"Damn, c'mon Jah! I need you to stay focused. You know the manager likes to spend that rent money playing the horses and then gets amnesia when it comes to who paid. Run downstairs real quick and get that receipt. I'll hold on."

Jah put the phone down and put on his slippers. Jah had his shirt off and looked at himself in the mirror. He flexed his little bird chest and saw that those extra push-ups were paying off. He grabbed the keys and opened the door.

"SURPRISE!" Jah damn near jumped out of his house shoes when he saw his friends from his football team, the cheerleaders, and a few of his classmates at the door. Ms. Rawls and a couple of coaches from Inglewood rounded up the kids and brought everyone over. Ms. Rawls had all the presents Coach had ordered for Jah. Jah ran back to the phone.

"How are you feeling now son?"

"I feel marvelous. Thanks, Dad! This is incredible… can you call me back? I have to get dressed! My friends are waiting." Jah dropped the phone in Ms. Rawls' lap and ran off to his room.

"Have a good time, son."

"This is not your son; this is Mama, your sweet one." Ms. Rawls chuckled.

"You know, I will never forget what you're doing for us right now. I will never stop thanking you."

"Sounds good to me. I know you certainly have a way of showing your appreciation. I can't wait to be the recipient of it."

"You got that coming! Now you guys go have some fun." Coach hung up the phone feeling good, but wishing he were there.

CHAPTER 27

COACH WAS NOTIFIED that he had a visitor. It was a weekday so he knew it was the lawyer from the Cochran Firm. Coach had been locked up 43 hours shy of 30 days. Coach was preparing to be released on his next court date, but Old Man Silas knew that Coach was setting himself up for a huge letdown.

"Young dada, don't get too far ahead of yourself. The lawyer is just coming down to basically see how much you are willing to spend for your freedom. I know you ain't no cheap nigga, so don't see it as a bill; look at it as making a sacrifice, ya dig?"

"True indeed, Elder Silas, I just have to be smart about it, you know."

"No doubt... that's why I always tell you to stay focused so you can think clearly, young dada. No disrespect, but you don't handle anger very well. I understand that. You are a peaceful brother. It takes experience from being mad all the time to learn how to channel anger and aggression in the right direction. Now, do you know why I'm telling you all this?"

"Yes, sir. You're telling me my only concern should be getting out and raising Jah and not do anything to fuck it up while I'm in here."

"And what else? You know what I'm talking about. What are you planning to do when you get home?"

Coach couldn't look Silas in the eye. He knew what Silas wanted to hear, but he couldn't promise him that.

"Young dada, I'm not one that's in a position to tell a man when he should draw his pistol but don't go home and kill that man who set you up and end up back in here for life. I don't mean to pry, but who it was that set you up? I might be able to help."

Coach hesitated. He was already learning the hard way not to trust everybody like he once did. Old Man Silas seemed like a good dude but if Coach even thought he was working with those people, he was going to get him first and catch a hot one.

"This big black muthafucka named—"

"Bodeen!" Old Man Silas cut off Coach and said that name with malice in his heart. "Humph. I know that evil swine-eatin' nigga... an enforcer and reputed hit man for drug dealers and the police. He's a vicious stray dog among wolves. The devil don't even like that soul-less bastard."

Coach grinned. He had heard it before. It was amazing that jail was so fucked up it was making him miss Pops Sanford's loud irritating old country voice in the barbershop.

"Yeah, young dada, I can see where your mind is now. It is imperative that big muthafucka gets wiped off the planet. But let him die a slow death. I don't know too much about him—just what I heard in the streets—but I know the game well. Bodeen didn't last this long because he's feared and connected to police and politicians. He was serious about his profession and played strictly by the rules. Yeah, he killed over a thousand people as they say in the streets, which is false. But let's say he did. I guarantee you 998 of them had it coming. They were not needed nor will they be missed. Setting you up wasn't personal. It was a sign that he reached his peak already and he's at the stage of his career where he needs to make a transition in his life or it's all going to start coming down on him."

Coach nodded slowly.

Silas continued, "Now in your case, and this is just hypothetical, mind you, he probably owed a cop one last favor or he couldn't leave the game... and greed probably got the best of him, too. You were the fork in his road. And he took the wrong fork. There is nothing left he can get from the game. He's playing by his own rules now. Things like this happen all the time, Coach. Have you ever seen the Iceman Confessions on HBO?"

"Yeah, he was that hit man for the mob. He was a very interesting dude...a happy husband and loving father by day and a ruthless assassin at night," Coach remembered.

"What was his downfall?" Silas asked.

"His downfall was when he shot that guy that was praying. He said that was the one hit he should have never done."

"And what stage was he at in his career?"

"Past his prime!" Coach remembered that well.

"Um-hum. He's in jail for life now but that is not his punishment for those murders. Jail ain't shit to a man connected like that. What is eating his insides like cancer?"

"The day he made his family cry and he lost them."

"Slow death... think about it." Old Man Silas slapped Coach on his shoulder and sat down at the domino table.

* * *

Coach was shackled head to toe as he was escorted to his new lawyer. Coach wasn't the least bit thrilled he was just riding on President Obama's *Hope* factor. *"I sure hope he can get my black ass out of jail."*

Old Man Silas told Coach that when Eldee Young was just a pup in the field of law, he helped the late great Johnnie Cochran with the Geronimo Pratt case. Coach was happy to know there was a good white man in the world that was sympathetic to the freedom, justice, and equality of his people.

When Coach came in the room, he was released from the shackles and they were never to be put back on in that fashion by the request of Attorney Eldee Young. So far, so good! He had Coach's attention. Eldee Young was smooth, too. He was born in Edinburgh so he had that foreign swagger about himself. He knew how to dress. His suit was tailored to fit. His hair was short and neat but it was styled. He sported a full salt and pepper beard that was groomed right. The frown lines embedded in his forehead were the only indication that this tall and fit man was well into his 50s.

Attorney Young formally introduced himself to Coach and took a seat. He opened his briefcase. It smelled like good leather with a hint of marijuana. The odor wasn't strong but Coach could tell he had some weed in there before. Attorney Young offered Coach some bottled water and a snack pack of carrots.

Unlike the Public Pretender, Attorney Young didn't bury his nose in a file and talk a bunch a bullshit he didn't want to hear. He listened to Coach in detail and was impressed with all the information he had gathered for the case. A huge amount of the work Attorney Young would have done himself was already complete. It was a shame that Eldee Young was still going to charge him full price but he was a criminal lawyer and that was his job. Freedom can't be bought at a discount.

Attorney Eldee Young looked at Coach's notes after Coach finished explaining the situation. "Gathering evidence is a hidden talent you might want to expound on. Give me a call when you get out of here because I might have a job for you."

Coach beamed and even relaxed a little.

"Now let's get down to business. I've been in this game a long time. I know you are sincere so I'm going to be honest with you. If everything you have in your notes are correct and from what I've read in the police reports, this case is weaker than watered down wine. But unfortunately, you just got caught in the political web at the wrong time and that's what makes this complicated. Now if you want to get the fuck out of here expeditiously, we can play into this bullshit game, strike a deal with these bastards, and make them look like they won something." Attorney Young paused and looked hard into Coach's eyes. "Or we can take it to court and I can get this entire case expunged. And we can possibly get a lawsuit started against the state. That is going to be a long process and $40,000, just to get you started."

Coach sucked in his breath at that number.

"Now don't let the $40,000 startle you. Look at the big picture, Coach. If you win, the settlement could be range anywhere from 50,000 to a million-five depending on how much corrupt evidence we find. I can give you time to think about it if you like."

Coach had dreamed of the day he could do something great like the black revolutionary heroes of the past. He could stick it to the man, defeat him at his own game, and get paid while doing it. That would be beautiful. But the dream just wasn't as beautiful as the day Jah was born. He was real. And he got better every day. Coach had to get back to that.

In reality, 40 grand was too much anyway. Coach didn't have money like that. It took him almost six years just to save the 25 grand he had in the bank. He couldn't risk giving up all his cash with a son on the outside. The statements "*We could possibly…*" and "*If you win…*" rubbed Coach the wrong way. It didn't sound right. The tone in his voice gave him no sense of security or guarantee that he would be getting Rodney King money after the verdict was read. But the voice in Coach's head that wanted that money begged to differ. *You ain't got a job waiting for you. Take that money, fool, and buy your own park! Jah needs money for college. You can get that dream house with your own garden to grow your herb. Make bail, fight it from the outside, and get that money.*

"Eldee, with all due respect to your proposition… and your name—I knew you had to be one of those cool white dudes with a name like Eldee… I worked at a park and recreation Center in a desolate part of the City. I don't make that type of coin. I need to get the fuck out of here, like yesterday."

"I understand, Coach. Consider this option, then. Twenty grand will make most of it disappear but it's going to leave a nasty scar. I can even probably have you out of here before your next birthday if we catch a break, but no promises. You're caught up in some serious and complicated shit at the wrong time of the year. You are the poster child for the phrase 'Caught in the system.' A lot of people use that term loosely but they really don't have a clue that it is truly real."

"A black man with faith and 20 grand versus The System… whew!… fuck it. Make it happen."

"Are you sure now? You don't need time to think about this?"

Coach looked at Attorney Eldee Young like he was crazy. "Man, sheeeiiiiiittt! Are you sure you're ready for this with a question like that? What the hell you think, brotha? This ain't the Holiday Inn… this is some bullshit. If I could fold up and fit in your briefcase I'd be gone!" Coach said in a joking matter even though he was speaking all truth.

Attorney Young liked Coach's spirit and the way he healed his horrific experience through laughter.

"Man, I'm telling you Eldee Young! It's crazy up in this hell hole mon. What kind of shit are they running up in here, Eldee, for real, mon? My only line of communication is a phone that some—that makes me not even want to call home. C'mon now. What part of the game is that? And just the other day, my pinochle partner walked into the shower and came out 20 minutes later in a wheelchair. This fool went into the shower without his shower shoes and those bugs and lice started eatin' at that nigga's feet and tore his ass up! Those bugs crippled his ass... And ain't nobody want to help him up off the floor...".

Coach told a few more crazy stories that had Attorney Young laughing so hard, he was crying. Coach wasn't trying to be funny either. He was just telling it like he saw it.

"Okay, Mr. Love... Julian Hassan Love."

"You can call me Coach. I haven't used Julian since third grade."

"Yeah, that's old school. It remember it was a common name in the early 70s... Okay, now let's get down to business. I'll tell you right now that the Feds are not going to want any part of this case. It stinks to high heaven. They're trying to use the old malum prohibitum trick, which I find odd because ATF has been under fire for this behavior. They have been sticking cases based upon technical malum prohibitum on individuals who lack all criminal intent and knowledge." Eldee leaned forward on the table. "It's like this, Coach. Criminal offenses can be broken down into two general categories: *malum in se* and *malum prohibitum*. The distinction between the two is best characterized as follows: a malum in se offense is wrong as judged by the sense of a civilized community, whereas a malum prohibitum offense is wrong only because a statute makes it so. In layman's terms, it means they were pinning a case on a young individual that's ignorant about the laws and then scared into taking a bogus deal."

"Interesting to learn that," replied Coach. "So what does this mean to me?"

"It means we have to go to court and present the new evidence. Most likely, the prosecutors are going to want a postponement so they can regroup and think of something to stick on you to save face. I can request bail but it is going to be high. And know that if you come up with that type of bail money or collateral on the income you claimed on your paperwork, they are going to freeze your accounts and start investigating your assets. Honestly, this case is a wobbler already, meaning the remaining charges can be deemed weak felonies or strong misdemeanors. My suggestion is you ride it out."

"Ride It out? For how long?" Coach asked.

"I won't know until we get to court. You can be out tomorrow or in a year the latest, but no promises. Let's just see what happens in court."

That wasn't what Coach wanted to hear but he knew Eldee was honest with him about it.

"By the way, my team is having trouble tracking down the UPS Guy, uh Rolland Hammond. We tried to serve him a subpoena and he took off running and unfortunately, my guy wasn't in the best shape to catch him. His two packs of Marlboros a day had his lungs on fire. I had to give him the rest of the day off. I have one of my younger guys on him now but if you can track him down it would be most helpful." Eldee stood up and closed his briefcase. "I'll see you in court. Keep your fingers crossed."

"I'm going to cross my fingers, pray, rub a rabbit foot, and befriend a leprechaun. I'm not playing around with it!"

Coach had to get his budget together and be smart about it. After looking at all the scenarios, Coach decided to let his Dodge Challenger go. The Thunderbird wasn't an everyday car, but it was harder to sell for the money he needed.

Coach then sent a kite to Big Spider through another spider called South Side Spider to see if he could help him solve a little problem before it became a major one.

Later that evening Coach called Jah. "Coach Harvey has been taking care of you, right?"

"Yep! He picks me up and drops me off every night."

"How is our team looking this year?"

"We're gonna be tight. We have this new wide receiver named Mr. Clean. He got that name 'cause he never gets dirty! His uniform stays crisp. He's out there Moss'n Man, Dad. He is tight."

"Oh yeah, that's the kid Coach Desmond recruited that used to play basketball. I think his real name is Marcus Levi."

"Yeah, that's him. He's serious about his game."

"Is that right? How's your game looking this year?" Coach asked.

"You know I hold it down, Dad," Jah confidently replied.

"Well, keep holding down everything until I get home. Now were you able to track that lame Rolland down on his route?"

"Oh yeah. And he told me to tell you that he wants to help you but if he does they are going to find out he's been slacking off and he'll lose his job. I even offered him a nice piece of money to see if he would bite but he was acting real scared."

"Humph. I figured that. That incompetent lame wouldn't even have that job if I didn't save his ass. It's okay though. You're doing a good job son and I'm proud of you. Now I really need you to handle some big man's work for me."

"I'm ready, Dad. What do I do?"

"Tomorrow you're going to school late. A car dealer is coming to pick up the Challenger early in the morning so I can get this money so I can get the hell up out of here. He's going to give you a cashier's check for 18 grand. Take that to the bank and ask for Danny, you know, the guy with the spiked black hair and horn-rim glasses. I already talked with him and he knows what time it is. Now Danny is going to give you a check for $20,000 made out to the Cochran Firm in the care of Eldee Young. Take a cab straight to the attorney's office and give it to Eldee Young only. And make him sign for it. He's also going to give you a letter. Now when you leave the building, there'll be a Mexican named Spider Jr. driving a candy apple red Impala waiting for you downstairs. Give him that letter and then he's going to give you a ride to school and a note to excuse you for being late. Can you handle that?"

"It's a done deal. If you need more money, Dad, I can always sell my Jim Brown football card."

Coach beamed with his son's generosity. "You are a good son, Jah. Thanks for the offer, but that won't be necessary… at least not yet."

* * *

"Have you ever killed a man before, Coach?"

"No, but I know I won't have a problem doing it if it's justifiable."

"Humph. That frightens me, young dada. The reason I admire you the most is because of your love for life. You inspired me to get my shit together. This is it for me, young dada. I finally had enough. Back in the day, we went to jail for actual crimes… today they giving kids a hundred years for attempted jaywalking. It is a sad sight to see. You, on the other hand, are a rare breed. Cats like you come through the system every 50 years and inspires us to live right. They love you in here, Coach. You got the head of the Aryan Nation that's supposed to hate black people hanging with you. The Mexicans got your back; they bringing you tapes and CDs and shit. Your green-ass has done broken every jailhouse rule written and you don't even know it."

Coach shook his head and just grinned.

Silas continued. "Just promise me this one thing. If it doesn't work to keep you right, when I get out, I'll personally help you kill that big black muthafucka myself. When you get released, as soon as you step out on the street, all I want you to do is look up at the sky and take a deep breath. That's it. Because if you think you love life now, you haven't felt anything yet."

"I can promise you I will do that. Thank you for keeping me focused in this concrete jungle, wise elder. But can I ask you one question?"

"What is that?"

"Why are old wise men always named Silas?"

"It is what is, young dada."

CHAPTER 28

THE SECOND COURT date came. Eldee Young shot down every charge like a row of moving ducks at a carnival.

"How could my client be charged with out-of-state commerce when all his sports orders for the last five years have been made to the G.A.M.E. Incorporated in the City of Commerce in the State of California? With the new evidence I move to have these charges dismissed. As to the receiving stolen property charge, unless you can prove my client stole them from the evidence room of the Rampart Police Station five years ago, I move to have these charges dismissd because I have the ballistics tests showing they were used in the murder of..."

The Judge hit his gavel and asked the attorneys to approach the bench.

After they conferred, Attorney Young continued, "Unless all Federal charges are dismissed, we will consider filing under Title 42, Chapter 21 of United States Code that allows citizens who are deprived of their civil rights to sue and receive monetary damages."

The Feds didn't want any parts of that Rampart Scandal. Most of the State charges were dropped as well, but there were a few more obstacles they had to clear.

Coach volunteered to take a lie detector test but it was only admissible in court if the prosecution and defense agree to allow it, which they never do but it didn't hurt to ask. The handwriting expert that Attorney Young brought in could have cleared Coach, but the prosecution needed to postpone the court date so they could hire an expert of their own to contradict that testimony.

Even with all the Federal and most of the State charges dropped, Coach was still looking at four years but with good behavior he would be out in two. That wasn't good enough. Coach didn't like that deal at all.

"You probably would have been home no later than next week if that guy Rolland Hammond would have shown up to court."

"What?" Coach's whole body got hot and steam started to build up in his ears. "I know I didn't just hear you say what I thought you just said."

"Unfortunately, yes. If Rolland had testified, you would probably be out on bail. The testimony from the handwriting expert won't be admitted without him. That's why they are still offering deals. This case was almost closed for the most part. You would still be charged with forgery and resisting arrest but those aren't any big thing. We'll see next court date how they play it. But in the meantime, help me find your slithery friend."

Coach couldn't believe silly ass Rolland was the only thing that stood in the way of his freedom. Coach was going to have to wait in that hellhole another 30 days because of that lame. It was time to step up the game for real.

When Coach returned from court to tell Old Man Silas the good news about the case, he was gone. He got released earlier that morning. Coach was on his own now, but he didn't have a problem being alone.

Coach sent a kite to Big Spider and told him to go ahead with Plan B. It took Big Spider's people a minute to find him, but they finally caught his ass slipping and saw him working his new delivery route. It still amazed Coach how so many things can get done on the streets from inside jail. Paid professionals that worked for a law firm couldn't catch a clown like Rolland but Big Spider who hasn't seen the light of day in damn near ten years had him in the line of sight.

Coach had been in jail over 80 days already. He decided to give Rolland one more shot before he took drastic measures. Coach did like Rolland's silly ass but the love was wearing real thin. Eldee informed Coach since Rolland was considered a star witness he could very well have him arrested and detained until the next court date. Even though Rolland was fucking with his freedom, Coach wouldn't wish his experience on any man. He decided to call Rolland's mama instead.

"Hi Mrs. Hammond, this is Coach from the Recreation Center."

"Oh hi Coach! I'm so happy you are all right. Ohh, you know the park has gone downhill since you and James left. It's full of vagrants and drug addicts again. My girlfriends and I can't even walk there in the morning anymore with all those bums sleeping and drinking. You think they are gonna give you your job back?" Mrs. Hammond started talking a mile a minute just like he expected.

"I doubt it, ma'am but I'll see what happens."

"Ms. Dottie and Mrs. Majali have been worried sick about you. Mrs. Martin hasn't been walking with us lately because the corn on her left toe has been acting up something awful…"

"I'm sorry to cut you off, Mrs. Hammond, but I'm calling about Rolland."

"Oh I'm sorry, baby! I'll start running my mouth all day if you let me. Rolland is at work, baby. He doesn't get home until late most nights. I think he's been running scared because of all that police business that was going on."

"I'll be truthful. He is standing in the way of my freedom, Mrs. Hammond. Make him do the right thing and tell him to come forward," Coach stated trying to be polite as possible. And to really sugarcoat it Coach ended the conversation with, "Oh, and give Ms. Dottie and all the ladies my love, will you please?"

By Day 95, Coach was starting to panic again. Rolland's slick ass transferred to another UPS and couldn't be located. Coach's next court date was in 15 days. Jah's first football game of the season was coming up shortly after that and he would be starting the next grade a week after that. Coach already missed his birthday and that pain was too unbearable to endure again.

The entire situation was seriously causing Coach to question his faith. Coach repeatedly had to check himself because he noticed he was performing his daily prayers with an attitude. On one end, Coach felt like he had been forsaken. On the other end, Coach put the blame on himself for his spirit being in the wrong place. He didn't believe in the devil whispering in his ear. That would be giving the devil too much credit. The devil had nothing to do with it. Coach was deeply hurt that the LORD would allow Jah to suffer on his own like that. Coach named his first-born son after THE MOST HIGH so he felt that should have some kind of bearing. Coach never questioned the CREATOR'S plan but he was starting to doubt if he was going to play an instrumental part in it.

CHAPTER 29

BODEEN'S PLANNED TRANSITION in to retired life on a tropical beach wasn't heading in the right direction. Bodeen came back home from his tropical island visit two shades darker, as if that was even possible. He enjoyed the time off but he was already starting to get that itch. Somehow, sipping on pina coladas and inhaling the sweet scent of fresh Hawaiian pineapples while he looked out over a tropical paradise didn't delight him like the sight of blood and the stench of alley piss.

In fact, he wanted to quench his thirst to do more dirt. Bodeen was addicted to that power trip. *How many people could claim they are the most feared enforcers in US history? And how do you go about relinquishing that title?* Bodeen thought about those questions long and hard while he was away but he could never come up with an answer.

Bodeen flagged down a cab and got in. It was a beautiful day in Los Angeles and even in high 90-degree weather, Bodeen was feeling real cold without his heat. He didn't travel with his weapons on that particular trip. It was cool to feel naked in Waikiki, but in L.A. you best be prepared.

In the cab, Bodeen checked his voice mail. The first message was from Bobby Boyd and Abdullah Joe telling him Cordedius Montgomery died of prostate cancer. And with that little message about Cordedius Montgomery's death, it actually gave Bodeen more inspiration to stay in the game. Mr. Montgomery had defied the odds. Cordedius Montgomery had been a notorious kingpin since the 1950's and he didn't end up dead because of his lifestyle or in prison like the tragic tales of most gangsters. He died old and rich.

Bodeen had a couple of messages from his tenants. One had plumbing problems and one was late on the rent. Bodeen wasn't quite yet civilized enough to accept late rent. Bodeen didn't know what a 3-day notice was, but he bet the tenant would notice three bullets in their ass if he didn't get his money.

The next messages came from some of his clients on the east coast with big contracts on some intended targets. The economy was bad for everybody and a dollar was getting hard to come by. Even drug dealers had to lay off some employees. In those types of conditions, enforcers on the east coast tend to start ripping, robbing, and rolling on the weak dealers that couldn't pay for daily protection. This was good for Bodeen. He was needed in ten different cities. That was 200 large easy for minimal work and all expenses paid. Business was booming. He couldn't retire now even if he wanted to.

The next message was from the manager at his laundromat. Some bad ass kids stuck foreign objects in half the coin slots of the washers, plus a pipe inside the wall had burst and cost him $5,000 in water damage alone. The cost of plumbing plus the repairs drained 9 grand out of his pocket. Bodeen was pissed. He didn't even like kids. Bodeen thought to himself that if he would have caught those kids fucking up his machines he would have dished out the same punishment on them as he did that punk kid Preston that scratched up his truck, and maybe even more.

Detective Andy Moretti was bitching about something on the next few messages but Bodeen refused to listen to a word he said until he paid him that money he owed him. Bodeen didn't like the tone in his voice either. He sounded like he had an attitude. Bodeen didn't make many outgoing calls from his business phone, but when he did it was best to not be on the receiving end. He called Detective Moretti. Andy didn't bother saying hello.

"For Christ sake, I've been trying to get in touch with you. We have a problem."

"Where's my money?" Bodeen questioned, but he wasn't asking.

"What? You better check your tone, mister, and recognize who pushes the buttons around here. I can't believe you even fixed those big ass lips to speak about money after that raggedy job you were supposed to pull off.

Are you getting too old for this kind of thing, Bodeen, or are you just trying to fuck me over?" Detective Moretti stated in a heated tone.

"Don't ever question my skills, you sissy little punk. But if you have doubts about them, I can always show you up close and personal how effective they still are..." Bodeen waited for a reply, "I didn't think so. Now what excuse are you really coming up with so you can hold on to my money?"

"The gun case didn't stick, Bodeen. That crappy shit started falling apart from the start. Not only did it put me in a bad way with my friends over at ATF but I had to kiss my promotion good-bye and now Internal Affairs have been sniffing all up my ass about those stolen guns YOU were supposed to sell to the Korean Crime Watch five fuckin' years ago!...a government issued remote control timing device and blasting caps? Do you think I'm a fucking idiot? You didn't even try to make it look believable. My people on the inside say the defense is trying to locate some witness they are keeping on the hush that can fuck this whole thing up."

"So what the fuck you want me to do? I did my part just as we planned it. The nigga is still in jail, right? And he ain't getting out from under all those charges any time soon. So why you bitching about it? This ain't the first time we used dirty guns. I've been doing this a long time, Andy. I stay on top of my game. I have every angle covered. Your people on the inside ain't worth shit to you, Andy, because you're a cheap bastard. You get what you pay for. The witness is Rolland Hammond courier for UPS. He lives with his mama in a small house on 52nd and Denker. He's already a dead man walking. So like I said before, I don't know what the problem is. I want my money."

"Your money? Shit, you owe me!" Andy exclaimed.

"I don't owe you shit!"

"Yeah, you can believe that shit if you want to. If anything—and I mean anything—affects my comfortable lifestyle, you are going to compensate me royally. Think about that." Andy hung up the phone without saying good-bye.

Bodeen was hot as fish grease. He slammed his fist down so hard on the back of the cab driver's seat, it made him swerve the car in the middle of the street. He thought he hit a pothole. Tires screeching and horns blowing set Bodeen off. He grabbed the cab driver around the throat and almost snapped it like a pencil.

"Are you drunk, muthafucka?" Bodeen yelled as he tightened his grip around the cabbie's neck. The cab driver shook his head no. Bodeen let go of his grip, eased back into his seat and said,

"Well good. Don't drink and drive. That's the quickest way to die, next to fuckin' with me."

When Bodeen arrived on the block, he spotted a suspicious looking car parked in front of his building. He ordered the cab driver to slow down a bit. The car looked vaguely familiar but he couldn't quite place it. The driver appeared to be looking up at his apartment on the second floor. Bodeen cursed himself for traveling without his gun.

As the cab got closer, the figure in the car looked at their side view mirror and spotted Bodeen. Their eyes met for a split second before the mystery person hit the gas and burned rubber away from the curb. Bodeen didn't like that shit. He didn't like it one bit.

The cab ride from the airport was $25. Bodeen handed the cabbie $10 and an evil stare that dared him to say something about it.

As he got out of the cab, Bodeen looked up at his apartment to see what the mystery guest was looking at. "Oh shit!" he said as he shook his head. They had been looking at the sign advertising the 2Bed/2Bath apartment for rent that he neglected to take down. Bodeen hated civilian life even more at that moment. It was too complicated. He was more comfortable in a world where they shoot first and asked questions later.

Bodeen walked to the garage to grab his truck to go pick up groceries. He got inside and turned the key.

"Damn!" Bodeen barked as he slammed his fist on the steering wheel. The battery was dead. "When it rains it pours." He hadn't been home ten minutes and shit was hitting the fan already. Bodeen got out of the truck and slammed the door. He walked back out to the front of the building. He looked down the street and scanned the block out of habit.

"What the fuck kind of bullshit is this?" Bodeen spoke under his breath as Jah came around the corner with eight heavy bags of groceries in his arms. His shoulders were burning and the plastic handles on the grocery bags were cutting through his hands like a knife. Jah had to stop and switch the bags in his hands twice before he made it to the front of his apartment. Jah sat the grocery bags down in front of the entrance to his building and dug his hand deep into his pockets for his keys. Jah glanced across the street and spotted Bodeen looking at him. They had a standoff. Jah stood his ground and stared Bodeen down cold.

That look that sent a chill of fear down Bodeen's spine. He knew right then and there he was going to have to kill him because he recognized that cold hard stare. That was the same look Bodeen had in his eyes as a child when he decided to kill Black Ass Bosco after he was made to believe he had been tampered with and violated. Bodeen didn't like the way Jah was mad dogging him. It felt like Jah could see right through him. Bodeen dropped his eyes first. He grabbed his luggage and headed towards his apartment. Bodeen never turned around again but he could feel Jah's eyes burning two holes in his back.

Bodeen left the front door open to let some air in but then thought better of it and pushed the door closed.

He sat down on his leather couch and considered the situation. He could eliminate a potential threat in the future and get rid of Coach at the same time. Coach loved Jah more than life itself. A man like that could never live with the fact that their child died tragically and he was not there to protect them. Bodeen figured that once Coach got the news about Jah, he would probably hang himself in the cell before morning or spend the rest of his life drooling in a mental institution.

* * *

Coach sat on the edge of his bunk with a sick feeling in the pit of his stomach. It was early in the day so the majority of the inmates including all the Keyster Kings were out on work detail so Coach had no access to a phone. He lay down on the bunk and stared up, trying to clear his mind of the crazy thoughts swirling around.

* * *

Bodeen stared at Jah across the street. Bodeen always saw what the Love Family were doing because their bohemian, nature loving, let-the-sunshine-and-fresh-air-in asses always had the windows wide open. Jah wandered the through the house talking and laughing on the phone. It was a trip how much Jah emulated his Dad because Coach paced and talked on the phone the exact same way.

Out loud, Bodeen mused to himself, "Imma have to kill that lil' nigga quick. It's hot as a muthafucka outside and that fool don't even have the AC on over there."

He was going to make a statement with this murder. This one was going to secure the legend of Bodeen for centuries. Bodeen imagined what the people would be saying in the streets. *Bodeen is so bad he killed a man and didn't even have to use a weapon. He made the fool kill himself! Bodeen is the coldest killer that ever lived!*

Then Bodeen snapped out of his daydream and got to business. He didn't even consider a pistol for this job. A bullet to the head wouldn't be heinous enough to make Coach snap. This was the perfect opportunity for Bodeen to use his WASP Injection Knife. It was a cold weapon and Bodeen had been itching to use it. When you stab a muthafucka with a WASP knife, at the press of a button, the tip of the blade injects a cold ball of compressed gas that freezes all tissues and organs surrounding the initial wound. The frozen ball of gas balloons and can blow a hole in a man's chest the size of a basketball. The manufacturer says this knife will drop many of the world's largest land animals.

Now before you think this is some James Bond, CIA-issued knife, anyone can buy the standard version of the weapon with the 5-inch blade for $500. Bodeen saw it for the first time on an infomercial. Some white boy stabbed a watermelon with the WASP knife and it blew the rind off that bitch. He had to have it. Bodeen had his custom-made with a 9-inch blade with a 48-gauge gas compressor.

Bodeen took his knife sharpening stone out of the box. Bodeen sat at the foot of his bed and scraped the edge of the knife against the rock until it was sharp enough to split a diamond. Bodeen barely slid the blade across his finger and a bright line of red blood appeared. He grinned.

Bodeen peeked out of his window. It was the perfect time of the day to put the murder game down. The streets were clear. Everybody was at work that time of morning. Bodeen put the knife in his back pocket and used the tail of his white t-shirt to keep it concealed. Bodeen grabbed his lock pick and tension wrench set and kept it in his hand.

Bodeen took the emergency exit to come out through the back of his building. He stayed to the left so Jah wouldn't see him cross the street if he happened to be looking out of his window. Bodeen strolled across the street and entered Jah's building through the west garage. The lock had been broken on the security door through there for years.

Once inside the building, he had three options. There was a stairwell on both ends of the building and an elevator in the middle. The closest stairwell would lead Bodeen right to Coach's apartment door. The elevator left him without a way to see who was on the floor. Bodeen chose the stairs on the east end of the building. Bodeen walked up the stairs to the third floor. Bodeen eased the stairwell door open and took a look around. Everything was quiet and cool on that floor.

Bodeen made a right and walked down the long hallway to the apartment.. Bodeen put his ear to the door. The television was turned up loud. It sounded like Jah was watching some kids show on the Cartoon Network.

Keeping his head on a swivel, Bodeen got down on both knees to pick the locks. He placed the tension wrench in the lower part of the keyhole with his right hand and applied a little pressure. With his left hand, he inserted the pick in the upper portion of the keyhole and wiggled it until all the pins were pushed up. Bodeen turned the cylinder clockwise with the tension wrench and opened the top lock. Bodeen repeated the same procedure on the second lock. Bodeen turned the doorknob and opened it slowly.

"Stay on your knees like the good bitch you are and you better not move!"

Bodeen froze.

Jah stood behind Bodeen with his hand on a 9mm Beretta tucked in his waistband. Jah snatched the knife out Bodeen's back pocket and tossed it inside the apartment.

"Turn on your knees slowly…"

Being down on his knees made Bodeen and Jah the same height. Bodeen turned slow and looked at Jah.

"Bitch nigga, you better drop your head and keep your eyes to the floor! You're not man enough to look me in the eye." Jah had no bass in his voice whatsoever but Bodeen felt the impact of every word. Jah was serious. Bodeen put his chin on his chest and gazed downward. Jah looked at Bodeen as a pitiful specimen with his own hand rested comfortably on the handle of the pistol.

"My dad doesn't condone guns but he told me that if a time ever comes when I have to pull one all the way out, I better use it. That's the only reason you still breathing right now, you lame. What kind of black man are you anyway? It's the 21st century and you're still setting good brothers up and selling them out to the white man…that ain't gangster; that's a punk." Jah stared at Bodeen, still on his knees like a prisoner.

"I don't like you, Bodeen. Nobody likes you. Your own mother didn't even want you," Jah said in a matter of fact voice. "My Dad was the only person to look past all that and show you nothing but love. He shared the good parts of life with you that you didn't even know existed. Matter of fact, I'd say he was the only friend you ever had in your life…and you f'd him over…for what? Kibbles. My dad is a better man than I'm going to be because I wouldn't have a sucka like you around me as a friend. You're just pitiful…"

Bodeen kept his eyes cast down as Jah continued. "What is wrong with you anyway, Bodeen, seriously? You're rich, you're chiseled like an African warrior, you own property." Jah paused. "But you don't have no woman… no friends… you spend all night gettin' high… walkin' around in circles with the same nasty-ass drawers on for two days. You sit in the dark talking to yourself and answering back looking silly, like a damn clown… or you stare at the wall forgetting things you haven't even remembered yet…yeah, that's right. I've been watchin' you watchin' me!"

Those words hit Bodeen hard because he knew they were true. A sense of shame and guilt washed over him. Bodeen wished Jah would hurry up and shoot him in the head. He shifted uncomfortably on his knees.

"I want to kill you dead right now I'm not strong enough to move 300 pounds of dead weight to drag your big nasty ass down the hallway to dump your body…and anyway, shooting you would be letting you off too easy. You need to die slow and tragic so you can evaluate why it happened that way… even though you already know. So I'm gonna leave you with this you bitchness. If my pops doesn't come home in the next 30 days, I'm going to kill you where you stand. At least he and I will be in jail together.

Now I'm tired of lookin' at your sorry face. Crawl on all fours out this door right here and down those steps and hope that this is the last time we meet."

Bodeen crawled down the hallway and down the stairs until those hard concrete steps started putting a hurting on his kneecaps. Bodeen stopped and thought about it. *"Wait a gotdamn minute! I know I didn't just get punked by a little 75-pound 9-year-old…and that little bastard took my knife? Ain't that a bitch? I'm trippin' fo' real!"*

Bodeen stood up. He was tired of playing around with this kid. *"I'll snap his little scrawny neck with my bare hands."* Bodeen reached the exit door and paused. He squatted down and put his ear to the door. Bodeen could hear Jah taking the lock pick out of the doorknob. Then he heard the apartment door close shut. Bodeen decided that he would ram his shoulder into the door first so the loud noise would catch Jah by surprise. Bodeen sprang into action.

Boom!

Boom!

Boom!

Boom!

Boom!

The first shot missed Bodeen's head by a half an inch. The second one tore the cartilage off the top of his ear. Bodeen fell to his back and tumbled head first down the flight of stairs.

Boom!

Dust and debris flew into Bodeen's eyes and blinded him when Jah shot a chunk of concrete off the bottom step right in front of his face. Bodeen scrambled to his feet to get to the next flight of steps and out of firing range. Bodeen misjudged his next step and rolled his ankle. He tumbled down the next set of stairs hard. His whole body was hurting. Bodeen got to his feet but his ankle buckled under the pressure of his body weight. Bodeen limped and hopped across the street in excruciating pain. That ankle was tender as a loin.

Bodeen cursed under his breath. "These bad ass kids don't have no respect for the game today…. That damn rap music got 8-year-old good students carrying guns and shit. What part of the game is that?"

CHAPTER 30

BODEEN SAT ON the bathroom sink tending his wounds. His ankle was throbbing deeper than bass from a Chevy Impala and his ear felt like it was on fire. He used toilet tissue to wipe the blood from his ear. A big plug of meat was missing off the top. It looked far worse than Evander Holyfield's ear when Mike Tyson bit the chunk out of it in that infamous fight. Bodeen was glad he wasn't a ladies' man because it was going to be hard trying to get a fine bitch with a piece of his ear missing. But beyond that chunk of ear, Bodeen had lost something far more important. Bodeen lost that gully look in his eye. Jah had broken his spirit.

Bodeen was weak. He began to question himself. The pain shooting through his foot was giving him the answers he needed but Bodeen wasn't hip to signs and symbols.

Bodeen needed painkillers. He had some at one of his stash houses but he needed something to numb his nerves until he got there. Bodeen hobbled on one foot into his dark room. Bodeen checked to see if the curtains were closed tight out of fear that Jah could see him from across the street. He was sneaking around in his own apartment feeling embarrassed. Bodeen got a wet cigarette out of the drawer. When he lit it, he was ashamed. He kept thinking about what Jah said about his late night antics.

Bodeen put the sherm to his lip, got ready to light it, and then guilt washed over him. "Shit. I can't even get high in my own damn building." He threw the wet cigarette down on the floor and smashed it with his size 14 shoe.

"That little punk don't know who he's fuckin' with. I'm Bodeen! The

most dangerous enforcer in the history of the United States! That's right!"
Bodeen glowered at himself in the mirror and felt his vibe coming back.
"That little punk tried to take Bodeen down but I got something for his
little baby ass. And he fixed his little mouth to call *me* a bitch? Well, I'm
gonna play the part of the bitch."

He picked up his phone and called 411 to get a number.

* * *

Coach kept getting a feeling in the pit of his gut that something wasn't
right. He had conned one of the guards into letting him use the phones
by saying he had to call his lawyer. Coach called Jah several times and
didn't get an answer. He thought he was going to lose his mind. One of
the Keyster Kings returned after lunch. Coach was so desperate to use the
phone he almost snatched the phone out of the dude's ass himself.

The phone rang.

"What's up Pops? What's good with you?" Jah stated nonchalantly.

"Is everything cool around there?" Coach asked.

"Yeah Pops, why do you ask?"

"A father's intuition… so are you sure you're straight? There's nothing
you need to tell me, Jah? Don't bullshit me now."

"Trust me, Pops… I got this."

"All right, Jah. And I see that since you got a year older I'm Pops now
instead of Dad? I dig that, Pops is cool. What's going on with you otherwise?"

"Everything is cool, just holding it down and working on my
game…Oh snap! I did forget to tell you something. I'm trippin' for real,
Spider called."

"Well, which one?" Coach asked to mess with Jah's mind.

"Which one?" Jah thought about it for a second and said, "The
Mexican one…hahahahaha! Your son is slicker than most. But seriously
Pops, no joking right now. Spider said Rolland transferred to a different
UPS and they can't locate him… so what does that mean?"

"son, just pray on it…"

* * *

Bodeen's ankle had swollen up like a balloon. The pain was getting more
excruciating. It had to be broken. His shoe seemed to be getting smaller

and tighter by the minute. Bodeen struggled to make it downstairs. Sweat was pouring off of his forehead like a fat man in 90-degree heat. By the time Bodeen made it to his truck, he was exhausted and out of breath. He sat for a moment and then turned the ignition.

"Gotdammit! Fuck...Shit!" Bodeen slammed his fist on the steering wheel after every curse word. He had forgotten the battery was dead. Bodeen called AAA. He sat waiting, his whole body trembling with pain.

AAA finally came and jumped his truck back to life. Bodeen put his truck in reverse but had to slam on the brakes and put it back in park. "Muthafucka!"

A Buick had him blocked in as the driver, Mr. Willis, was taking his time trying to carefully park. He was in his late 60s and one of the last of the old school blue-collar workers. He had the same job for the past 45 years and never missed a day's work until his hand got severed in a freak accident. Now he was late in his rent to Bodeen.

Bodeen was so mad he jumped out of his truck and hobbled over to the Buick. Bodeen took out his faithful 45 and pressed it up against Mr. Willis nose.

"Where's my money?"

"Young man, what is this all about? There is a proper way to settle this business. I sent you a letter telling you they put a hold on my disability check until they received the paperwork from my doctor's office," Mr. Willis said, confused and scared with the gun pointed at his nose.

Bodeen did remember getting a letter. It could have been written by hand or in Braille but results still were the same: tossed in the trash unread. He continued to stare at Mr. Willis.

"Now look here. I've never been late a day paying my rent my entire life until I got hurt. Shouldn't you give me a three-day notice at least before you start pulling guns out? If this is how you do business, young man, I'll pay you what I owe you and move to another building. This is ridiculous."

"Old man, I don't care about yo' sad-ass stories. I want some of that change I hear jigglin' in yo' pockets."

"That is my knee hitting the keys in the ignition. You got me nervous. I'm not lying to you, young man. You can see my hand for yourself." Mr. Willis showed him the bandages around his hand up close.

"Look, I just got back from the pharmacy. Here is my pain medication right here, if you don't believe me."

Bodeen snatched the bag out of Mr. Willis's hand and ripped it open. He had that good strong shit. Bodeen snatched the old man's keys out of the ignition and opened his trunk. There was a tire iron in the otherwise empty trunk. Bodeen snatched it up and started wailing on Mr. Willis.

Bodeen threw Mr. Willis in the back of the trunk and slammed it shut. "This here is gonna be your new home until your check comes and I get my money." Bodeen shot three air holes in the trunk. He wanted Mr. Willis would have enough oxygen to live so he could cash that check when it came.

Bodeen opened the pill bottle and chewed two Vicodin tablets dry with no water to wash them down with.

The adrenaline flowing thru Bodeen's body felt good. Punking Mr. Willis felt even better. He had almost forgotten about the throb in his ankle. Bodeen was back and he wasn't taken any shorts. Bodeen had a smile like the Joker and said to no one in particular, "Next up…Rolland Hammond. Let's see what Brown can do for me."

CHAPTER 31

THE STREET RUMBLED like an earthquake was hitting. The roar of the engine and bad muffler could be heard blocks away. The high-pitched squeaking brakes coming to a stop was loud enough to pierce an eardrum. The distinct sounds are an indicator that the UPS truck is near. The sound of a metal door sliding open and then slamming shut moments later comes next. Then appearing from behind a cloud of truck smoke dressed in a snug fitting brown uniformed short set was the lame named Rolland Hammond.

Rolland was happier than a punk in a pickle patch the day he was called in to the main office and told he was being transferred to the Thousand Oaks branch. He couldn't stop grinning. Hell, he even skipped like a schoolgirl out of the office that day.

Rolland's new route was easy and stress-free. The air was so fresh he could taste it. He didn't have to contend with the hustle and bustle of L.A. No horns honking at him; no risk of getting a ticket by double parking when he dropped off packages; no more rude customers; and there were no more vicious dogs. And even better, Thousand Oaks certainly did not have dog shit all over the sidewalk.

In Thousand Oaks, the people were friendly and the traffic flowed smoothly. On Rolland's new route the residents didn't even park on the street. They had nice big houses with driveways and garages. Rarely did he even see a car parked on the street.

On his first day there, Rolland looked around the neighborhood in awe, like he was in the mystical land of Atlantis. He was acting like he'd never seen a two-story house before. Rolland was thinking to himself as he looked at the well-manicured lawns and perfectly groomed children and their mothers driving in expensive SUVs to the park *"Boy, these white folks sure do live well out here."*

But even though he loved his new route, Rolland hated that he was hanging Coach out to dry. Coach was the sole reason Rolland still had his job when he vouched for his character and work ethics to the supervisor. He loved Coach, but Rolland knew he would get fired for sure if UPS found out he was the one who really signed for the package in a high profile case. Rolland figured there was really nothing he could do. Coach needed more than a witness to testify about a signature. He needed the damn Dream team and the late great Johnnie Cochran to get him out of that mess.

Besides, Coach wasn't the type of man that would want him to miss work and a day's pay coming to court anyway is how Rolland continued to justify his yellow-bellied behavior.

Rolland stepped off the truck and looked at the box. SIGNATURE REQUIRED. "Damn!"

Even though he didn't have to walk through a gate with an evil pit bull guarding the yard, Rolland wasn't quite used to Caucasian culture so he did what most silly Negroes would do and Tom'd his way around Thousand Oaks. In his own hood, Rolland strolled with style and swagger, a sense of ease and familiarity permeating his vibe. But out in Thousand Oaks, Rolland walked up on his toes with a bounce in his step looking like a sucka. He was swinging his free arm with every stride. He had on a thick belt that was pulled so tight around his brown shorts, he looked like a sausage squeezed in the middle, even though he wasn't a fat man.

Rolland walked into the yard bouncing like he had springs in his shoes. He started smiling before he even got to the door. Rolland pressed the doorbell and took a step back. He stood on the porch with his shoulders square and back straight. He rang the doorbell for the second time.

"Who is it?" a feminine voice asked from the other side of the door.

"It's UPS, ma'am!" Rolland answered with a big cheese eatin', Kool-Aid smile on his face.

The door opened. Rolland felt like a damn fool for doing all the brown nosing and the person wasn't even white. He even felt like a bigger fool when a big black-gloved hand came out from behind the door and snatched him by the front of his brown shirt.

"Get yo' silly ass in this house!"

Before he could even react, a pillowcase was thrown over his head, a voice told him he was a stupid muthafucka, and then he got socked twice in the forehead extremely hard. Rolland was tied up and thrown head first into a closet. His workday was over.

Bodeen looked from behind the floral curtains and checked the street. Something about this Rolland job wasn't feeling right. Leaving a body in Thousand Oaks was not ideal.

Bodeen was posing as a special investigator. He paid the homeowner in Thousand Oaks days before to use his house for police business. Bodeen told him he was on a stakeout. In reality, Bodeen ordered a package and had it sent to that address.

As he continued to scan the street, he began to wonder if Detective Moretti was setting him up.

But it didn't make sense. They agreed when they first started working together to keep their business open so they could never be tempted to snitch the other out. With the information they kept, one couldn't roll on the other without implicating themselves. Bodeen and Detective Moretti kept personal records of their various dirty deeds, photos of the bodies of the victims and dead informants they dropped together, political documents, and surveillance reports on every known major narcotics dealer they dealt with across the country. Bodeen put the thought out of his head.

He limped across the street to his white truck. He stopped for a second and looked at Rolland's UPS truck. Bodeen thought about taking some items with him but then he decided against it. Bodeen shrugged his shoulders, accepted it as another day at the office, and got into his truck. He was ready to get out of Thousand Oaks anyway. He didn't blend in too well in that city.

CHAPTER 32

BODEEN WAS UPSTAIRS with his bags packed. He was taking the red-eye flight to the East Coast a little after midnight. Bodeen had been hired for his services to control or take out the young gunners that had been rippin' and robbin' the dope boys. Due to the bad economy, a lot of gangsters and kingpins had laid off some of their muscle, runners, and lookouts. It made a lot of grimy enforcers turn on their employer. It also opened the door for stick-up kids to rob at will. Bodeen knew some of the enforcers that were preying on the weak. He actually found it amusing. He didn't see anything wrong with cashing in on it as well. Bodeen was needed from Detroit to New York. He needed those jobs to build his ego back up more than he needed the money. His gully attitude and confidence were still shaken from the incident with Jah. His cold hard heart was just a shell ready to shatter at any moment. He felt as if Jah put a root on him and he didn't like it one bit.

Bodeen was in an unconscious state and still couldn't find rest, though he was laying down in bed. The clock read 9:10pm. The cab would be arriving to pick him up in less than an hour. Bodeen dreaded getting to the airport hours early because of that damn terrorist threat security shit, but it was kind of humorous to Bodeen that he was worse than the a terrorist and yet he got on the plane with ease.

He got up, put on his shoes, and made a final check that he had his travel weapons and FAA permits to carry them. That Federal LEO license cost Bodeen a huge chunk of change when he bought it from a friend of Detective Moretti's but it was worth every dime. Bodeen thought he heard a car pull up and wondered if it was the cab. He was still hesitant to peek out of the window ever since the day Jah embarrassed him about his late night freak show in the window. Jah was getting on his last nerves, too. Ever since that day, it seemed like every time Bodeen looked out of the window Jah was across the street staring back at him. It was creepy. Bodeen glanced out the window again and saw Jah had his bedroom light on

"This is some bullshit! I called them and yet Child Services still ain't picked that little punk up yet! What kind of world is we livin' in that don't see about an abandoned kid? That's a damn shame!"

But his aggravation over Jah running free was quickly forgotten as he noticed a car door open outside his building. It was the mysterious car that had been parked in front of his building when he returned from vacation. Bodeen grabbed his pistol. The driver was wearing something on their head that looked like a turban. Bodeen immediately thought Detective Moretti sent one of his Taliban friends on the government's payroll to come take him out.

Bodeen took the emergency exit that led to the garage. Bodeen stooped low and placed his body in between a parked car and the wall. He stood up and placed his back against the wall and began to inch slowly so he could get closer to take a better look at the perp. The trespasser was standing on the sidewalk holding a huge brown box, looking upstairs at Bodeen's apartment. The big box blocked Bodeen's view of their face. His first thought was they put a bomb in that muthafucka, no question about it. Bodeen patiently waited.

The mystery guest began to walk slowly towards Bodeen's downstairs apartment. Turban Head stopped, looked upstairs again, and proceeded to the front door. Bodeen watched as the muthafucka looked all in his front windows downstairs. Finally, Turban Head sat the big box down and rang the doorbell and waited for a few seconds, then rang the doorbell again. Finally, ol' Turban Head tested the doorknob and it was open. Bodeen had a bad habit of forgetting to lock the door downstairs. That habit came from spending too much time locking himself upstairs getting high and now it came back to bite him. The perpetrator just stuck their head inside the door and took a quick look around. They reached their hand in the leg pocket, pulled out an object, and placed it in the box.

That must be the detonator! Bodeen thought. The person slid the box inside the apartment, closed the door softly, and began to step backwards slowly from the apartment.

"I think you left something that belongs to you." Bodeen pushed the back of their head with the gun and walked them back toward the door. His first choice was to get the hell up out of there before that bomb went off but Turban Head had him curious.

"Pick it up!" Bodeen ordered.

Turban Head reached down and grabbed the big box.

"Now step back out here and get a good look at the last person you gonna see on earth."

"I thought you loved me? I came back for you!"

It was Angie's voice. He dropped his gun to his waist. His heart started to get fluttery and his head was tingling on the top. He wondered if she would still as beautiful as ever but he was scared to look at her and ashamed for what he did. But he was still madly in love with Angie. All those lonely nights of dreaming about her was finally about to pay off. As she turned to him, he said, "Baby, you really came back to me!" Bodeen closed his eyes to kiss her.

"Nigga, please! You too ugly to be Michael Jackson!"

Bodeen opened his eyes.

Charlesetta was staring at him wearing the same turban Angie had on.

Bodeen woke up from the nightmare sweating and tried to shake it off. Even though it was a dream, Bodeen's poor heart was wounded. Feeling rejection in his dream was almost worse than that heinous evening. It felt too real. The jittery feelings that came with the flashbacks of that night were also recurring more often when he wasn't zooted off the wet bomb. The face of the first victim Bodeen killed popped in his head once in a while. The rape was haunting him, too.

Bump, boom!

Bodeen flinched. Now that sound was real. It was not part of the dream. It sounded like somebody just kicked the shit out of the door downstairs. The sound of glass shattering spooked his ass because the brick came through the window right behind him. Bodeen dove out of his chair and hit the floor hard on his belly. He reached over to the coffee table and grabbed his pistol. Bodeen jumped to his feet and ran to the staircase to get to his downstairs apartment.

But Bodeen's bad ankle gave out by the fourth step. Bodeen's big ass hit about four walls with his hand and shoulders trying to keep his balance and it still didn't prevent him from falling. He rolled over immediately and popped back up. He held the handrail as he jumped three steps at a time on one leg to make it downstairs quick. Bodeen bolted to the front door.

"Gaaaaaaaaaa-damn!" Bodeen yelled as he hunched over and went to one knee slowly. He closed his eyes and took in a deep breath. The pain that hit him made him forget all about that bad ankle. An object had been placed across the whole doorway. It was hard and stationary and it caught Bodeen hard across both shins.

As he looked around, he saw the car that had been creeping and parking in front of his apartment burning rubber as it hit the corner. It was the same car that was in his dream. It didn't freak Bodeen out like it should have because Bodeen knew in his gut it was Andy Moretti testing one of his new minions. He had seen that tactic before. Bodeen got to his feet and paused.

He looked down and there was a huge black duffle bag partially open still sitting in his doorway. Bodeen hesitated. Andy Moretti was a ruthless son of a bitch but he's not going to blow up a building in a residential neighborhood...or would he?

Naw. Probably some poisonous snakes or a box full of hungry rats, Bodeen thought. That was the kind of shit he and Moretti used to do together when they were trying to make a statement.

He didn't even bother looking in the duffle bag. He grabbed the bag by the handles and hurled it against the side of the building with brute force. The bag hit the ground with a thud...

As soon as the bag hit, loud crying came from the duffle bag that sounded like... a baby? Bodeen forgot all about his theories and rushed over to the duffle bag. He unzipped it the rest of the way. He looked inside.

It was a beautiful baby girl. She was perfect. Bodeen got scared quick. It wasn't the type of fear he knew existed in death. This feeling was fear of the unknown, a new life. Bodeen stared at her. She was buckled up in a baby carrier. He lifted her out of the duffle bag. Blood streamed down her face from the cut over her eye when she hit the wall. Bodeen immediately rushed in the apartment with the baby. Bodeen took the baby in the bathroom and cleaned the blood from her face. It was a nasty cut. It hurt Bodeen more to look at it. The baby stopped crying soon after he cleaned her up and held her in his arms.

Bodeen knew it was his immediately. She had all his features. Bodeen thought Angie was something special to look at but his little girl was far more beautiful. She had Bodeen's dark complexion, broad nose, and full lips. She had long thick curly locks that were soft as silk. The natural sparkle in her eye twinkled like a shining star and she had the cutest smile Bodeen had ever seen.

Bodeen knew who the mother was. It was the chick he had relations with when the Heavy Hitters were in town shaking down Alonzo. She had the same curly locks and similar smile as the baby. The chick actually liked Bodeen and wanted to make love to him but at the time his mind was still clouded with thoughts of Angie so he didn't even bother remembering her name.

Bodeen held the baby in his arms and rubbed the back of his hand gently across her forehead. He kissed her on the nose and said, "Daddy loves you so much."

The baby flashed her sunshine smile and grabbed Bodeen's finger.

"Daa.. daa….. daa!"

Tears fell from Bodeen's eyes like a waterfall. He even wet the baby's face all up. Bodeen played with his daughter until she was worn out. He placed her on his chest and she slept there the entire night. Bodeen didn't want to sleep. He didn't care why the mother put the baby on his porch. He didn't even think about it.

CHAPTER 27

RING!

"Pops, I've been waiting for you to call. We have a problem."

"Every problem comes partnered with a solution. Run it down to me, son, so we can get it fixed," Coach replied as calm as could be, though he could feel a stressful day was approaching.

"When I came home from practice last night there was a letter on the door from the Department of Children and Family Services. It was saying that a child had been reported to be living here alone and if one or both of the parents doesn't contact the office by noon tomorrow, they will be back with the proper authorities."

Coach closed his eyes as a wave of nausea washed over him. Coach didn't want to think about the pain he was going to unleash on the person that removed his son from his home. But he did think about it and it was ugly. What Coach and Jah didn't know was that Children and Family Services had already been to the apartment on several occasions since Bodeen snitched them out. GOD and having a good daily program was the only reason Jah was still safe. Every time they stopped by the apartment, Jah was either at football practice or over at one of his teammate's houses. They would miss him every time by minutes or less.

Coach gave Jah some instructions hoping it would buy them some extra time.

"I got this, Pops. I love you."

"Love you, too, Jah." Coach hung up the phone and stared off in to space, his mind spinning with all the problems.

With Rolland missing, the lawyer saying he may be looking at a year in prison, and now the State was trying to take the best part his life away, it was a lot to handle locked up. Jail was so fucked up even the kindest gestures came with a price. One of the black Keyster Kings saw the worried look on Coach's face and offered him a joint rolled in tainted Bible paper to relax his nerves. It was just what Coach needed…but not under those conditions.

"What's that brown mark right there?" Coach asked.

"Oh, that ain't nuttin' but a little piece of hash."

"You are lying like a son of a bitch. That's a little piece of your ass!" They both feel out laughing because it was true.

Coach continued, "Bumbaclot! How you gonna offer me a joint with a doo-doo stain on it, brother? You a cold-blooded muthafucka. If this ain't jail, it's got to be hell."

"A little poo-poo ain't ever hurt anybody…think of it as if it were skunk weed. Don't be so ungrateful. I'm helping you."

"Helping me? Brother, you're frustrating me! But I did need that laugh. So I am grateful for that…"

As the Keyster King strolled away, Coach thought, *Man, I need to get up out this bitch with the quickness.*

* * *

"Thank you so much, Doc. Are you sure that's enough money?"

"It's more than enough. I've never known you to be this generous before. Did you find religion?" the Mafia doctor replied.

"Nope, not religion. Something better than that…so you're sure everything is okay, Doctor?"

"She's going to be fine. That's a tough little girl. She has your genes. Now you need to wear that foot brace I gave you, too."

After the doctor left, Bodeen stayed up. It was 4am. He had called the doc at 3am because he had to get the baby's eye mended. Bodeen cringed every time the doctor stuck the needle through her soft baby skin to stitch her eye up. She required eight stitches right above her eyebrow. Bodeen was in more pain than the baby. She didn't even cry during the procedure.

Bodeen had to jump into fatherhood from ground zero. The mother left him with nothing but the baby to start with. There were no diapers; there was no formula, no Gerber Baby products, not even a toy for the baby to play with. The mother left no birth certificate or social security card.

The only thing they left was a note that read, Her name is Mika and pronounced as (Mee-kah).

Maaaan, it took Bodeen damn near four hours to read the baby's name. This big grown ass man was standing in the middle of the living room floor, holding the little piece of paper with both hands, using phonics to sound out a four-letter word.

"Mmmm…. I… Iiiii… Mmmmm- Iiiiii…. MmmIiiiiii-"

Every so often Bodeen would look up from the paper and look around the room like the furniture was going to help assist him with the word or something.

The baby even had a look on her face that was saying, "Damn, daddy spit that shit out!"

"Kkkkk ah Kkah… PpahPaaa… rrrrrrrr… rrrrrrr… Ohhhhhh… nnn-nnn… pro-noun-ced oh… pronounced…"

He sat down and kept looking between the paper and his beautiful daughter. "Oh! I get it now, Mee-kah…that's her name Mika with an I but sounds like an E. I was wondering why she would write her last name inside those curved things."

Bodeen didn't know when the baby's birthday was. He counted on his fingers, not because he couldn't count—that was one thing he did very well—but just out of habit, and thought back.

"Let's see. I lost my virginity 20 months ago. Met old girl three months after so that was seventeen months ago… A pregnancy last 9 months… hrm. So that would make Mika about six or seven, maybe eight, months old."

Mika was a good baby. She grinned and played with Bodeen's nose.

The first time she cried Bodeen didn't have a clue what to do. He started to regret that he crossed Coach and Jah. He had needed their help now more than ever. Bodeen was seconds away from walking across the street and apologizing to Jah so he could help him.

Bodeen didn't know what Mika wanted to make her stop crying but it didn't take long to find out once the smell of baby boo-boo burned the hairs out of his nostrils. Bodeen's knees buckled.

"Goddamn! What was your mama feeding you, baby girl? Goat meat and possum sandwiches? Whew!"

Mika started laughing at Bodeen. Her smile and that luminous twinkle in her eye lit up the entire room. It was at that very moment Bodeen manned up and handled his business like a true parent. There were no markets open at that hour to buy diapers so Bodeen made some. He cleaned Mika up real good and applied some cocoa butter to her bottom. Bodeen had a pack of fresh white t-shirts. He grabbed those, a pair of scissors, and some safety pins. He cut the cloth, shaped it into a perfect triangle, measured it next to the baby by sight, and made some nice cloth diapers. They were a perfect fit.

He was showing all the signs of being an overprotective father. I already feel sorry for the first boy that has to ask Bodeen's permission to date Mika when she got older. Since the car seat had broken when he threw it the night before, he just strapped Mika in the back seat and put pillows and bubble wrap all around her.

They went to Target to get diapers. Bodeen didn't know what to get. Bodeen went down the row looking at the pictures of the kids on the packages. Bodeen picked Mika up and held her next to every package of diapers trying to compare her size to the one on the photo. Bodeen became frustrated and started ripping the Huggie packages open until he found the size he was looking for. He bought ten boxes. He put the diapers that he ripped open back on the shelf. Bodeen was still Bodeen. Even a blessing like Mika can't totally civilize a nigga like that overnight.

Next up was Babies R Us. Bodeen tried to clean out the entire store. Bodeen grabbed the most expensive car seat equipped with a cup holder for $700, a $999 Ferrari stroller, two play pens, a high chair, bedroom furniture for the baby, and it took a whole second cart to carry all the stuffed animals for decoration. Bodeen was proud of the way everybody complimented him on how beautiful and happy Mika was. He even got a couple of phone numbers from the ladies that were admiring them.

The next stop on the list was shopping for clothes. Bodeen put Mika in her new stroller and walked around the mall proud with his chest out for two hours before they even began shopping. Bodeen asked the cute sales representative to help him pick out the clothes for Mika. Bodeen bought 25 outfits, all the same size. The sales lady tried to explain to him that Mika was going to outgrow most of the clothes before she got the chance to wear them all, but Bodeen wasn't listening. Mika was his baby girl and he was going to worry about tomorrow when it came.

The last stop was Toys R Us. Bodeen bought every toy Mika pointed to or looked at. By the time the day ended, Bodeen had dropped $19,000 in cash without blinking.

But while he was busy stocking up to be a father, he took time to talk with the mothers he saw shopping. He asked questions about food, immunization shots, and things of that nature. The good mothers shared information from their soul and from experience and from the knowledge that was passed down to them from their mothers. The mothers Bodeen didn't trust were the ones that kept telling him to go online. It had nothing to do with his reading level. They just didn't have the same passion about raising a child as the old school mothers.

Bodeen never imagined he would really be living the good life. All the money and materialistic things he bought in the past were nothing compared to the few hours he spent with Mika. The sparkle in Mika's eyes shined so bright it made the diamonds in his Rolex look dull. This was what life was really about. This is the life Coach wanted for him and Bodeen now had it.

* * *

Jah was in the apartment chilling doing his day-to-day routine. It was still early in the day but he had his dinner cooking so it would be ready when he came home from football. Jah made Jamaican oxtails, rice and peas, plantains, and steamed broccoli. While that was cooking, Jah fixed a bowl of Wheaties with strawberries and bananas. He sat on the couch and turned the channel to the NFL Network. Before he could even focus in on the program, there was a knock at the door. Jah wasn't expecting any company. Jah put some bass in his voice and asked who it was from where he was sitting.

"It's Mrs. Johnson from the Department of Children and Family Services. I need to talk to you, please."

Jah cracked the door open just enough to get a good look at Mrs. Johnson. She fit the image of a typical supervisor. Mrs. Johnson was a tall, light-skinned black woman with wide hips. She wore brown polyester pant suit and flats. She had a pair of eyeglasses hanging around her neck and her name badge pinned to her chest. Mrs. Johnson wore cheap perfume that was already turning sour.

Jah hoped he could shake her before his cereal turned soggy.

"Yes ma'am, may I help you?"

"Hi, you must be Jah. Are your parents home? I need to come in and talk with them."

"My parents are in the bed sick today, ma'am. It wouldn't be wise to come in. They have the Swine Flu that has been going around. I caught it at school and passed it on to my parents. If you have a business card, I'll be sure to give it to them."

"Are you okay, Jah? Are you happy here? Is there anything you would like to talk to me about?"

"I'm fine, ma'am. Why would you ask that? I have the best dad in the world, a roof over my head, healthy food in my belly, and nice clothes on my back. Unlike the previous generations before me, I am actually having a happy childhood."

"My, you are very articulate and so well-spoken," Mrs. Johnson stated in a saditty manner.

"I'm not sure if I should take that as a compliment, Mrs. Johnson. They said the same thing about President Obama, and two weeks into office the same people were ready to impeach him. So what does that really mean?"

"Excuse me?" Mrs. Johnson was taken by surprise.

"Don't con me, Mrs. Johnson. You're not here to help me. You came to hurt me. The only reason you are here is to break our family apart...but it's not gonna happen so you can get that out of your mind. My father is raising me well. You see it for yourself with this brief encounter with me. Now if you would kindly excuse me I have to get back to my Breakfast of Champions before they get soggy. I'll have my parents call you soon as possible. Have a pleasant day, Mrs. Johnson. ONE LOVE!" Jah flashed a quick smile as he closed the door without giving her a moment more to speak.

* * *

Mika became Bodeen's whole world. He rearranged both of his apartments to accommodate his baby girl. Bodeen decorated the baby's bedroom on his own. It was extra girly. Bodeen painted the room pink and had plush pink carpet installed. The furniture was white with pink accents. He got pink and white curtains for the windows, too.

Mika also had two playrooms, one for the big toys like the victorian playhouse, jungle gym, and stuffed toys. The other playroom was used for dolls, board games, Legos, and books. It was better than Sesame Street and Disneyland.

It was a sight to see Bodeen's big ass crawling around on the floor with Mika, playing with Fisher-Price toys and baby dolls. Most of all, Bodeen loved coloring books. He loved to use crayons and it challenged his skills trying to stay inside the lines. Yeah, Bodeen was really getting into fatherhood deep.

So deep, in fact, that Bodeen got rid of all the guns and drug paraphernalia in the apartments. Bodeen chose life over death and found a new high that was so good he didn't want to ever come down. Bodeen opened all the drapes and windows in his apartments wide. He didn't care who was looking; he wanted the world to see. For the first time in Bodeen's life, everything was right. Mika was the light that led him from a dark place.

Every day was a new adventure. Bodeen and Mika went to petting zoos, the Long Beach Aquarium, fed ducks at the lake, amusement parks, beaches, neighborhood parks, and museums. They took trips to Santa Barbara, Solvang, San Diego and Catalina. They did all that in two weeks' time and they were just getting started.

Bodeen's dark past was only fourteen days behind him but he felt as long as he stayed on the straight and narrow he would be light years ahead before it could catch up to him. He was able to cherish the small things that he forgot or never knew existed.

One night as Bodeen held Mika in his arms, he had a revelation that blew his mind. Bodeen realized that he hadn't truly smiled since he was a child. He hadn't laughed in years…and he had never truly been happy a day in his life until Mika arrived. But none of that mattered because Mika was worth the wait. He was blessed with Mika at the right time. Bodeen was in a new place where the sun shined every day. It would be awhile before Bodeen became a reflection of the sun, but at least he was now standing in the light.

CHAPTER 34

IT WAS 4 in the morning. It looked like fog but that would be impossible because it was indoors. Coach realized it was the gray cloud of stress hovering over the dormitory.

Coach had to get up that early for his big court date. This was it. Coach was optimistic about a positive outcome. Without Rolland, Coach was going to have to do at least a year in the pokey or maybe more. Every time Coach seemed to have a charge beat, the state prosecutors made up new ones.

At the request of his attorney, Coach was able to wear civilian clothes to court. Coach was Versace down to the socks. He wore a dark gray slim fitted Versace suit with a dark deep purple shirt underneath. He had onyx and diamond cuff links setting the suit off something lovely. He had on black Italian loafers with soft gray eel skin accents. Coach was so sharp the inmates were asking him if he was going to court or starring in Ocean's Eleven. The guards even had to bow down. Coach was clean…for a minute. (END OF LILY EDIT)

The State believed that with an expensive outfit like the one Coach had on he needed some jewelry to set it off. They gave him some silver bracelets for his ankles and wrist and fucked the whole outfit up. They escorted Coach and 49 other inmates in orange jump suits to the bus for court. It was only 4:30am and Coach's court time wasn't until 11am and time was moving so slow. Coach waited in several different holding cells until Attorney Eldee Young arrived.

Eldee Young was looking sharp as well. Eldee was sporting a Tailored to Fit Sharkskin Suit, a Royal Blue Silk Shirt with the wide collar, and dark blue alligator shoes, custom made. The face on his Gold and Diamond watch matched his shirt. His salt and mildly peppered beard was glistening like it was just conditioned. Eldee Young was a cool dude but he was still a lawyer. Personally, Eldee Young really liked Coach and he knew the system was railroading him. Eldee Young didn't get into law to fight justice; he was in it for the money. Eldee Young would defend a mass murderer and get him off if the price is right and there is a hole in the case. His motto was "If Right is wrong and wrong is is not right, if the price is right I'll take that Wrong and I'm gonna make it right." Eldee Young compromised his Soul so long but he explained that to Coach. He told Coach that he didn't see right and wrong. The God he worshiped said, "Every Man deserves a fair trial…" He stood by that and that alone. Emotions and principles couldn't be involved, just law. Coach couldn't do anything but respect it- He didn't like it but he respected the fact Eldee Young was honest about it.

Attorney Eldee Young pretty much told Coach what he already knew; without Rolland he was through. The deals the Prosecution was offering weren't appealing one bit. The four years with half time was still the deal on the table and the Prosecution wouldn't budge. Attorney Eldee Young also informed Coach that if they took the case to trial and lost he would lose 10 years of his life and his money. Coach was in a lose/lose situation but it was up to him on how much time he wanted to lose. If he took the deal he would lose over a year. If he took it to trial he would have to fight it for a year. If he lost the trial he would get 10 years…depending on the circumstance. It could be more or it could be less. Coach wondered if the Judge was going to be named Monte Hall. The Judicial System was saying "Let's make a deal," with a bullshit prize behind curtains 1, 2, and 3. Coach had no faith in the judicial system. Everyone in the court knew he was innocent but Coach would have to plead guilty to something in order to be free, and for them to save face. It didn't make sense to Coach.

The only logical choice was to put his life in GOD's hands or the man's hands. That made it an easy decision. Coach said,

"No Deal!"

"Boom, boom, boom!" The knock on the apartment door startled Jah. He said to himself, "This broad comes every time I'm eating my Wheaties.

Just because I eat the breakfast of Champions is doesn't necessarily make me a winner." It was a shame that Jah was only 9 years old and never been in contact with the law but yet he knew that was a police knock he heard at the door. Jah did exactly what he was supposed to do too. He didn't answer the door. They knocked on the door and rang the doorbell repeatedly. Jah thought to himself, "Damn they are worst than the Jehovah's Witnesses." Jah remained silent. He crept into his bedroom and peeked out of the window. He saw a government issued vehicle outside that looked like a police car but it wasn't the LAPD. Jah watched the car from his window for over 45 minutes. Mrs. Johnson and huge white guy in a khaki colored uniform finally left… they returned an hour later.

Coach was seated in the court room next Attorney Eldee Young. Coach looked into the devilish eyes of the Prosecuting Attorneys. Coach spotted Detective Andy Moretti and three other cops he vaguely recognized from the day he was arrested. There was also a young black girl seated near them that Coach had never seen before. She was acting as their star witness. Coach was concerned as well as Eldee Young.

"What is going on here Eldee?"

"This is the session when the Prosecution presents any witnesses or new evidence to strengthen their weak case." Eldee Young whispered to Coach. "I expected them to bring some detectives but who's the black girl?"

"I and I don't deal wit dem jezebels sire." Coach blurted out by accident but it was loud enough for the girl to hear.

"Ahh I see they have a few tricks up their sleeve so we are gonna have to dazzle them with a little bit of magic of our own. Do you have a rabbit in a hat?" Attorney Young tried to make light of the dark situation.

Coach looked at Eldee Young with a very serious look on his face. Coach told him respectfully yet he was very firm,

"Man, I am not in a joking mood right now… Not right now brutha… not right now."

The Bailiff's voice carried across the courtroom,

"All Rise…. this court is now in session… The Honorable Judge Rob G. Wapner presiding.

Judge Robin G. Wapner entered the court and took her seat.

"You may all be seated." Judge Wander stated. She spoke eloquent with evil undertones.

Coach looked at the hard faced woman and just shook his head in disgust like it was already over. Racism wasn't a factor. The white Man will be the first to tell you, it ain't nothing worse than an ugly white woman with power. The judge was in her mid to late 50's. She wore a short hairstyle parted down the middle. She had a narrow face, wicked pale green eyes that lacked luster, a sharp thin nose, and a rat mouth. Her lips were so thin they didn't even touch when she began to speak.

"This is case number 75B01-0703-JL-0509, in the matter of Julian Hassan Love aka Coach. Present in the court room today is the defendant and his attorney, the deputy prosecutor, and...."

Back at the apartment Jah was getting a little perturbed with Child Services hanging out in front of his building. Jah was supposed to be going school shopping with his friends and they were slowing his day down. Jah's intention was to catch the metro link to Kendrick's house and hang out until his mom came home from work and then she was going to take them to the mall. Jah couldn't sneak out of the building without being seen. Jah watched Mrs. Johnson downstairs asking the neighbors questions. mother Taylor was the only one that had something to say to those people but there was no telling what she could be saying. It could go either way depending on what mood she was in. Jah anxiously waited until they left again.

The judge asked the state to present their case. Coach could see firsthand why so many people of color have no chance in a court of law. They spoke in a language that is hard to understand. They spoke indirectly and used a lot of penal codes and laws instead of talking straightforward and rational for anyone to understand. Twenty minutes in, the Prosecutor started to sound like Charlie Brown's teacher to Coach,

"Womp- womp- womp womp!"

After each witness told their lie, the Judge asked the defense if they had anything to present in rebuttal of what the state presented.

Attorney Eldee Young got up to make his case and explain to the judge and why Coach Julian Love should not be found guilty.

Attorney Young stopped talking mid-sentence and stared at the mystery witness for a long time. The mystery witness was a piece of work. She claimed to have had relations with Coach. As soon as Coach heard that he whispered to Eldee Young, "That ras clot Bitch ain't ever seen my Shaft in her life mon'." Coach whispered it a little too loud and got a few giggles. He even got a chuckle out of the Bailiff. Whoever schooled that jezebel of a witness did a pretty good job. She knew where Coach lived, where he worked, his birthday, and what kind of car he drove. By the time she was finished she made it seem like Coach was a dangerous arms dealer.

Eldee Young said,

"You say you have been with Coach for six months and I'm not going to argue that fact. It's obvious you know so much about him. I find it strange that you say so many bad things about my client and his mother says so many good things about you. Could you do me a favor and point her out to the courtroom?"

The star witness only panicked for second. There was only one elderly black Lady in the courtroom sitting directly behind Coach crying so that made the lie easy to tell. The fake witness pointed to the elderly lady.

"That is her right there."

"Interesting... That is all... Your Honor this witness is obviously lying because that is not my clients mother the witness pointed out because that is my mother Mrs. Rosemary Young...Hello Mother." Eldee Young stated and waved at his Mom. Detective Moretti was pissed off. He stormed out of the court room cursing under his breath.

Eldee Young began chipping away at all of the other trumped up charges one by one until only a couple were left. Attorney Young used documentary evidence that consisted of the original documents words, numbers, and figures, Coach and Jah put together months before. The Prosecution took an hour to present their case whereas Attorney Young kept everything short and sweet.

"Your Honor... I will keep this simple and use the Best Evidence rule on this matter... Original document must be produced; there are no exceptions —no evidence shall be admissible other than the original document itself, I'm holding the originals right here in my hand so I have no idea what the Prosecuting Attorney is presenting to the court... They are relevant to the fact in issue, so I would like these documents to be exhibited, examined, and viewed by the court..."

Eldee Young returned to his seat. Coach was still mesmerized by the magic he performed. Coach whispered in his ear,

"I thought you were white from Edinborugh?"

"Named Eldee? I'm Creole from Edgard. Ssshhh keep that on the low." Attorney Young stated and smiled.

The state got one last chance to argue their point. During this point, the Prosecutor kept reminding Judge Wander of all evidence that was entered into court that supported their side.

* * *

Jah was happy Child Services finally left from in front of the building. That was a close call. Jah missed the Metro Link he wanted to catch originally. The next one would be coming in 30 minutes. Jah made sure he had his money in his front pocket and he grabbed his keys. Jah looked out of the window once more to make sure the coast was clear.

Jah locked the apartment. Before he took the stairs, Jah stopped to admire the patchwork he did covering the bullet holes in the door a few weeks back. It was good but it wasn't perfect. Jah rubbed his hand over it and took the stairs. Mrs. Johnson and the Officer were waiting in the stairwell.

"That's the child." Mrs. Johnson stated as she pointed to Jah. "We need to talk to your parents now or you will have to come with us."

Jah needed to buy some time. He had to think quickly on his feet.

"My Dad just walked to the store. He'll be back in a minute. Would you like to come in and wait?"

"I was just gonna suggest the same thing." Mrs. Johnson stated so she could get a good look at the apartment that was labeled a sewer in her reports.

Jah knew what Mrs. Johnson was up to so he volunteered to give them a slow tour of the apartment. The inside of the apartment looked better than Mrs. Johnson's house and it was much cleaner. The Officer just played his part and didn't say much. Jah told entertaining stories about the exotic houseplants in the living room. The Ming Aralia and Red Velvet Polka Dot Plants kept their attention. Jah only told those stories so Mrs. Johnson could see his scholastic and perfect attendance awards on the wall just above the plants without having to point them out.

Jah took them into the kitchen and offered them beverages. He opened the refrigerator wide so Ms. Johnson could see the beautiful assortment of fruits and vegetables. Just like a typical supervisor with a bad diet, she looked passed the healthy items and said,

"Where's the meat? I don't see any spam or beef jerky." And then she had the nerve to roll her eyes and speak under her breath, "Make a note that the child is being starved to death."

Jah just stared at Mrs. Johnson with a puzzled look on his face. After more than an hour passed, Jah had nothing left to show Mrs. Johnson. Mrs. Johnson's feet were starting to hurt and she was ready to leave as well. She said,

"Jah, I'm sorry but you are gonna have to come with us until we talk with your parents. As a minor you need a guardian here 18 years or older to watch over you. Technically your parents are not supposed to leave you in the house unattended even to go to the store. I am led to believe that you are living here alone."

Jah already had more than enough time to think about his next lie. He just hoped that it worked. Jah spoke in his most polite voice.

"I do have a guardian Mrs. Johnson. When my parents are at work or not at home, I stay with Mother Taylor on the first floor. That's where I was headed when you stopped me. I just came up here to get my video games to play with."

"Well If Mrs. Taylor can confirm that she is authorized to be your active guardian then I will leave you in her care until I talk to your parents. If they don't call me by the end of the day we will have to come back and take you with us understand. Now let's go downstairs and talk with Mrs. Taylor." Mrs. Johnson stated like she didn't really care about Jah one way or another. She was ready to go lunch.

* * *

"The state rests your honor…" The Prosecutor stated as they concluded.

Judge Wander said,

"The defense may now present their witness."

Coach put his head down in his lap and rested his elbows on his knees. He was feeling pretty good up until that point. Attorney Eldee Young got up and spoke,

"Your Honor, Our witness has seem to uh, vanish mysteriously and we ask that-"

There was a loud noise at the back of the courtroom. The sound occurred outside of the doors but everybody in the courtroom jumped because of the loud boom. The Bailiff responded to the sound. He ran behind the Judges Bench and hovered over her using his body as protection. The double door flew open and a voice with a Spanish accent in a the far distance said,

"Get your goofy ass in there dawg!"

Coach turned around and all he saw was Rolland Hammond rushing in through the door and into the court Room from a hard push somebody must of given him. Rolland was wearing his UPS uniform so tight he looked like he had on Brown Biker Shorts. The force from the push had Rolland a little off balance and when he got to the seating area he had the nerve to say,

"Sorry I'm late... What's up Coach?"

Coach didn't know whether to be happy or mad. He just looked at Rolland and said,

"Sit your goofy ass down and be quiet before you get choked."

Rolland said,

"Why? What did I do?"

Attorney Eldee Young continued like the interruption didn't happen.

"Well then. This is our witness, Rolland Hammond, the courier that delivered the alleged weapons to The Jack Tatum Parks and Recreation Center and he is willing to testify that is his signature on the receipt in question and he, Rolland Hammond forged Coach's signature. We have the Prosecutors Handwriting Expert to verify this as well as results from a polygraph test also provided by the Prosecution to prove it..."

Attorney Young continued to present strong evidence to clear Coach of all of the major crimes against him without saying he had been set up and bamboozled. The Assault on a Peace Officer charge lacked imminence. Once the Cop testified that they pulled their weapons on Coach before he was flipped to the ground hurt his case. Eldee Young proved the officer in question had no reason to fear for his safety with 49 guns already pulled on Coach at close range.

"My Client would have had to been provoked… What other reason would he have to slam one peace officer to the floor with 49 guns drawn on him other than self defense…we have evidence that proves this… We have evidence that proves that… We have evidence that will clear my client of charge number… and under penal code…The Defense Rest."

Judge Wander asked the state for any argument but they didn't have one. They were stuck. The Prosecutor asked,

"Your Honor may we approach the bench?"

* * *

Jah couldn't believe that Mother Taylor didn't vouch for him. She kept trying to use Religion and the Bible to justify her actions. She was just scared of authority point blank. She kept saying the same old bullshit,

"He is a good boy, not like all these other bad kids around here but I can't say I'm his guardian because it's just not right. He and his Daddy live upstairs that's all. My Bible says "Thou shalt not lie,' and I go by my Bible. And my Bible says to obey the law because I go by my Bible and my Bible says…"

Jah was taught to respect his elders but his father also taught him a lame is a lame no matter if they are young or old and he looked at Mother Taylor and said,

"You need to stop going *by* your Bible and go *IN* your Bible Ms. Taylor"

* * *

Attorney Young sat down with Coach after a long discussion with the Judge and the Prosecuting Attorney. He stated in a calm manner,

"I have good news- with the new evidence, the prosecution had no choice but to move to have all the major charges dismissed by the judge.

But As I explained to you before, you were caught up in some Political Bullshit from up high. The state has to save face. They need something.

They want you to plead guilty to Penal Code Section 470 Felony Forgery. Remember when we talked about the "Wobbler?" He waited for

Coach to give him a look that assured he remembered the conversation. Then he proceeded to explain again.

"They identify the crime of forgery as a "wobbler" in California because the prosecution has the discretion to prosecute it as either a felony or a misdemeanor. A felony forgery offense is punishable by imprisonment in state prison for 6-16 months. They are willing to offer the minimum of 6 months and a strike but only if you to agree to promise not to file a wrongful imprisonment lawsuit against the state or any other charge thereof."

Coach was tired of it all. He was still going to have to plead guilty to a crime he didn't commit. He got frustrated and asked Attorney Eldee Young,

"SO WHAT THE FUCK DOES ALL THIS MEAN? Speak to me straight up like you use to talk on the streets of New Orleans. 6 months-16 months- wobblers, strikes with no violence, when can I go home? That is all I want to know with no extras... please!"

"Well as your lawyer I have to explain these details; it is the law. Now by pleading guilty to Penal Code Section 470 Felony Forgery and agreeing to prison for minimum of 90 days and not to exceed the maximum of 6 months. The state of California is willing to grant half time since this is your first offense..."

Coach just cut him off and said,

"Three months and it's over? Fuck it! I'll take the deal."

Attorney Eldee Young and the prosecution huddled up to agree on the terms. Both lawyers approached the bench. Judge Wander began to speak, In the case of the State versus *Julian Hassan Love aka Coach

I have been asked by the Prosecution to dismiss Penal Code 12020 weapons charges... Penal Code Section 240-248 dismissed, Penal Code Section 12040... Penal Code..."

That shit went on for about an hour. Finally Coach plead guilty to Penal Code 470. The Judge looked at Coach as if he should be sorry for what he didn't do. She took off her glasses and asked Coach,

"I would like to know Mr. Love how you feel?"

"*Bitch I feel with my hands like I always do!*" It took every ounce of strength Coach had left in his body not to say the first thought that popped in his mind. When he did answer it wasn't any better but he was smooth.

"How do I feel? How do I feel? I feel that this is some bogus bullshit. I know it's some bullshit, you know it's some bullshit, and everybody up in this muthafuckin' courtroom knows it's some bullshit!" Coach was so cool the way he delivered his statement the Judge didn't even bang the gavel.

After Coach agreed to the deal he sat down with Attorney Eldee Young and said,

"So what happens now?"

"Well since my services here are no longer needed I'm leaving."

"What about me?" Coach asked.

"What about you? Attorney Young replied.

"Please stop side talking me man." Coach pleaded.

"What? You got 6 months. You did 90 days already…that's half-What? I don't know what you want me to say."

"You mean since I already did 90 days- that counts as the half of the 6 months? So wait are you telling me… so that means-"

Eldee Young cut Coach off and said,

"Yes Muthafucka, you are free. So take your ass home unless you want to ride back to jail and tell everybody goodbye. And this is not your lawyer talking this is Eldee Young New Orleans finest baby! Right On!"

Sheeeeeeeeeeeeiiiit Coach was so happy he almost *came* in his pants. He shook Eldee Young's hand, gave him a hug, and then almost pushed him down on an accident. Coach couldn't wait to get the hell up out of there. Dumb Ass Rolland looked at Coach with a sad puppy dog face and had the nerve to say,

"What about me?"

Coach grabbed Rolland by the back of his brown shirt collar and they high tailed it fast out of those courtroom doors and out of the building.

Coach took a deep breath when he got outside. Old Man Silas was right. The air had never smelled so clean and fresh in his life. The sky was so beautiful. Coach reached out and grabbed some sunshine and rubbed it on his face.

Baby Spider III was outside waiting in the car. Coach introduced himself and they slapped hands. Baby Spider III said,

"What's up homes, you made it." He stopped and looked at Rolland next to Coach and said,

"Not this stupid fucker again. Your boy is a goofy muthafucker. We couldn't wait to get him to court and out of our house."

Coach cut Baby Spider III short,

"First of all, I want to thank you and all the Spiders for helping me through this bullshit- and secondly, this lame ain't my boy." Coach couldn't resist and punched Rolland in the gut with a nice easy shot when he wasn't looking. He caught him right in that soft spot too. Rolland couldn't breathe or move for a cool minute. Coach opened the car door and pushed Rolland in the back seat.

Baby Spider III said,

"You should've punched him in the face dawg. This fucker never stops talking dawg. He eats like a motherfucker too dawg. If my Uncle Big Spider didn't have love for you homes, he wasn't gonna make it to court. My old lady was ready to shoot him dawg. We tried to be nice and let the fucker watch TV you know... he gets on the computer while my old lady is in the kitchen cooking and was he trying to add her as a friend on facebook and shit. He was sending messages to her friends telling them to "meet me at Baby's Spiders house- I'm his Cuban primo from out of town. Ain't that some shit dawg...I locked his dumb ass back in the closet for the last three days cause he wouldn't shut up."

Coach wanted to hold it in but he had to laugh. Coach told Baby Spider III to take the 10 Freeway and get off at the Western Exit. Baby Spider III said,

"I know homes; I've been to your pad. Your son is cool as hell dawg- unlike that fucker back there. What are we gonna do with him?"

"Drop him off on the way." Coach answered and winked. Coach turned around in the car seat and looked at Rolland.

"Man, what the fuck were you running for all that time rasshole?"

"Man I didn't know what was going on. The police was coming to my house and to my job...man you know how it is. I was scared."

"Of what? All they needed was to verify your signature."

"Is that all they wanted?" Rolland asked.

Coach bit his bottom lip. He refused to talk to Rolland until it was time to drop him off. Baby Spider III pulled onto the 10 Freeway. Coach saw the spot he was looking for.

"Pull over right there." Baby Spider III pulled the car over between the Hoover and Vermont exits. Coach yelled at Rolland,

"Get yo' goofy ass out and hit that pavement!"

"Right here on the Freeway? C'mon Coach at least drop me off at the exit. These cars are moving too fast. This is dangerous."

Coach opened his car door and got out. He reached in the back seat and snatched off Rolland's shoes and threw them as hard as he could in the middle of traffic on the other side of the freeway. Then Coach pulled Rolland out of the car by the back of his Brown shirt and tore it a little bit. Rolland said,

"C'mon man this is my good work shirt."

Coach got back in the car and closed the door. Baby Spider III peeled out and drove off. Rolland stood there looking just as goofy as he wanted to be. Rolland made himself believe they were just playing a prank and they would be coming back to get him soon.

Coach looked over at Baby Spider III and asked,

"You got some beats up in this ride?"

"You know it dawg...I'm gonna hit you with that Roy Ayers baby... Light that shit up Dawg, you're home now!" Baby Spider III replied, as he turned on the music loud.

"Dippy Doooo, Run, Run, Run Dippy Dooooo, Run, Run, Run

"Awwwww shit! Roy Ayers turn that shit up player!...Cause you been mean to me! And I've been good to you... And I've been oh so strong! Heyyy ya ya haa haa! Whooooooooooo this song is cold!" Coach exclaimed as he sang along and bobbed his head with the song.

Coach was so happy to be out of that damn jail cell and it showed. His high pro glow was electrifying. In one more mile, a right, 5 long blocks and a left turn, he would back for his young lion.

...HEY YA YA HAA HAA

Jah didn't want to cry. He fought back the tears but he was emotionally upset. Mrs. Johnson let him grab a few things out of the apartment and then escorted him downstairs.

Jah saw the neighborhood handyman Rock and wished he had said that he was his guardian instead of Mother Taylor. He would have stood on it like a Rock, no pun intended. Jah tried one last attempt to buy some more time or try to escape to Kendrick's house for a few days.

Jah yelled out,

"Kidnap! Rock they are trying to gaffle me up man. Help me!"

Rock ran over to Jah with a huge wrench in his hand but he pumped his brakes when he saw the big white man in the uniform. He wasn't even a real officer. He didn't have a gun. Rock's punk ass was so scared he started encouraging Jah to give up,

"Just go on with those people now little man. They know what's best for you. You'll be all right. Foster homes ain't that bad, I'll tell Coach they took you."

Mother Taylor was looking out of her window the entire time doing nothing but being nosey.

Mrs. Johnson snatched Jah by his arm and told the officer to cuff him. Coach and Spider III hit the corner. Coach had the car door open getting out before the car even came to a complete stop. Jah was elated.

"DAD!" Jah pushed Mrs. Johnson off of him and did a swim move to get passed her like she was an offensive lineman. Jah leaped in his father's arms. Coach held Jah tight with his eyes closed. He didn't even realize he tear'd up a little bit until he opened his eyes back up. Coach missed his young lion so much the feeling to have him back was overwhelming.

Mrs. Johnson tried to ruin the moment. Coach cut her off quick. Coach spoke under his breath directly in Mrs. Johnson's ear so she wouldn't feel too embarrassed.

"Listen Bitch, I saw you grab my son. On any other day it would have been bad for you but I'm in such a good mood right now I'm gonna let it ride Sista so please let me have my moment." Coach tried to be smooth as he could under the conditions.

"Excuse me?" Mrs. Johnson asked with extreme attitude as she placed her hand on her wide hip.

Coach couldn't believe this broad was trying to take him to a dark place.

"I know you heard me lady. Don't kill my vibe." Coach stated without looking at Mrs. Johnson or raising his voice.

"Are you the child's father... uh Julian Love?"

"*No I'm his mother…* of course I'm his father and a proud one at that. What do you really want ma'am? I have some pressing business right now."

"We have a complaint here that says you are abusing and neglecting your son and living in an unsafe environment- and it is my job to check into this matter."

"Did you check?" Coach asked.

"I saw the apartment."

"Wait a minute; you were in my house without my consent?"

"Well um, uh…" Mrs. Johnson started to stutter. She didn't expect Coach to switch up on her like that.

"Listen Ma'am, I don't know who you are or what you want and I apologize that I had to be curt with you but I've had a long day and it's not even noon yet. Come by later I will give you permission to do whatever you need to do but right now please let a brother be."

"Well it's not that simple Mr. Love. If we feel the child is in danger we must remove them from the home until we further our investigation."

"Look at my son. Do you feel that he is in danger?"

"According to these reports… Yes I do believe he's in danger." Mrs. Johnson stated. She didn't hear a word Coach said.

"Lady, I'm gonna tell you like this one time, if you even think about taking my son from me one more time nobody is leaving this block…"

Mother Taylor had the gall to yell out of window,

"Just do what the lady says Coach… we don't need any trouble out here…"

Coach never took his eyes off of Mrs. Johnson and he pointed back directly at Mother Taylor with his right index finger and said,

"Bitch!…Don't speak out of turn!" He lowered his hand real slow still looking stern into Mrs. Johnson's eyes.

"Hey Dawg do you have a problem that needs solving? I'm real good with numbers. You know 9, 12, 22, 32, 45…" Baby Spider III asked Coach as he got out of the car and opened the trunk of his car.

Coach continued to stare at Mrs. Johnson. He looked in Baby Spider III's direction and then at Mrs. Johnson again and asked,

"So do we still have a problem that needs solving?"

Mrs. Johnson was terrified. The tarantula and spider web tattoo's covering Baby Spider III's entire body made him look menacing. Mrs. Johnson shook her head no. Coach wasn't a bad guy he was just serious about his life. Coach put Mrs. Johnson's nerves at ease.

"You look hungry Ma'am. Why don't you come upstairs and let me fix you and your buddy something good to eat."

"Thank you Mr. Love I appreciate the offer but I have to decline... you guys don't eat anything but chickpeas and fava beans. I want something that taste good and unhealthy"

Coach fell out laughing. He went into his pocket and gave her a $20 dollar bill.

"I can dig that. Well go and get you some beef on me... and get some vegetables to go with that burger too now. Take care."

Baby Spider III pulled two CD's out of his trunk.

"This is a welcome home gift for you dawg, enjoy."

Coach looked at the CD's and his face lit up.

"Aww man, this is that real shit... what you know about Dynamite Dave Soul?"

"WTDK dawg, that's all I fuck with."

"*A Tribute to Roy Ayers Parts I and II*... I love the stories Dave Soul tells about the music and the artist...thank you man, I appreciate this along with everything else your Familia did for my little man and me. I'll never forget this as long as I live-That was righteous!" Coach sincerely stated. They slapped five and hugged. Baby Spider III shook Coach's hand for a second time and placed another gift in his palm.

"...Just a little something extra to go with the Dynamite Dave Soul Classics to help you ease your mind... Jah my main little homie show me some love... come by the pad soon. Stay down with the black and Brown homie, One Love!" Baby Spider III said as he hopped back in his Cutlass Supreme to leave.

Coach's crazy ass put the black Power Fist in the air and said,

"La Raza~"

CHAPTER 35

BODEEN WAS FEELING so good he thought the telephone ringing was church bells going off in his head. The house phone never rang and He hadn't even bothered charging his cell phone. Bodeen's voice sounded delightful when he answered the phone.

"Good Afternoon."

Former Detective Andy Moretti thought he had the wrong phone number for a second. Bodeen had been either grunting or silent for so long Andy forgot what his real voice sounded like.

"Good Afternoon? For whom? My afternoon is not going good at all."

"Who is this Andy? Man, I'm sorry to hear that. It is such a nice day outside too. How's everything been? How are the kids?"

"Are you serious or are you fucking with me, high on that shit?" Andy stated agitated.

"You should learn to relax and enjoy life sometimes Andy. The last few times I've talked to you Andy, you have been upset and constantly complaining. You have beautiful kids Andy- you have plenty of money, young fine white girls all over you, fast sports cars, and you still find the time to bitch about everything. Why don't you take your daughter to see Madagascar in 3D and eat some bon bons and cool out?"

"What in the hell? Did you find religion or something?"

"Nope, I didn't find Religion… it's something even better than that?"

"Well I don't give a fuck what you found. I'll piss on what you found. The case didn't stick Bodeen."

Bodeen tried to hold on. He wanted to make the conversion to square life peacefully. Andy was bringing that old thing back.

"So what in the fuck you want me to do?" Bodeen asked.

"It is what you didn't do asshole. What the fuck happened with the Rolland guy? He showed up in court."

"Are you serious? Wow! That cat Coach is special for real." Bodeen stated not talking to anyone in particular. He started laughing inside from amazement. Bodeen let Andy in on the humor.

"You know Andy. I admit I had the wrong idea about you. I thought you flipped on me. I waited in that house in Thousand Oaks for 10 hours on that joker Rolland to arrive. He made a stop three houses down from where I was posted, and he never came back out... I told you that dude Coach was sharp. He's special and highly favored... the blue moon. We lost that one Andy. Just chalk that one up, we can't control the unknown occurrences."

"Well it's not that easy to just chalk it up. I got suspended from the job indefinitely without pay. That stops both of my incomes. No respectable drug dealer is gonna pay protection fees to an out of work cop. It could be up to two years before this shit clears."

"I wish I could help you but I'm out of the game. I thought about what you said. I'm getting old. I'm not sharp anymore. I let a square outsmart me. I'm taking your advice and shutting it down." Bodeen expressed. He told Andy a bunch of lies to get him off the phone but it wasn't that easy.

"Don't con me you black motherfucker. I told you that you were gonna have to compensate me for every dime I miss if I lost my job."

"I should be asking if you are the one that's high. Andy I ain't paying you shit. I don't owe you shit. You're a civilian now Andy. You weren't shit before and now you are worse off than that. I'm trying to change for the better but I'm much closer to my past than I am to my future. And you know better than anyone how I get down. So don't go there."

"You are gonna pay for this Bodeen one way or another when you least expect it- And when it happens- I want you to know now- it was me that did it...nigger, with the er."

Normally Bodeen would have chocked the life out of Andy Moretti before sunset but he couldn't stay mad now. Bodeen brushed off Andy's threat like lint on a coat. Andy was nothing without that badge.

"Hi baby girl. Are you crawling in here looking for your Daddy?"

And just like that, Bodeen never thought about Andy Moretti again.

* * *

Coach was feeling so good to be home he was standing in the mirror smiling and Pop-Locking. Thinking about Jah and Jah only while he was locked up Coach didn't even realize how many little privileges he was missing. Using the restroom alone- in peace, never felt so good, being able to hold the remote control to the TV in his hand again felt warm and succulent like a woman's tender breast, the window- oh my god-being able to look out of a window again was like seeing GOD face to face- The Brother on the Cream of Wheat Box- Coach Saluted him for achieving greatness...it was really that deep. The overwhelming feeling of appreciation was something else.

"Jah-Jah! I'm home young lion bless up, JAH Rastafari! Babylon will not keep I and I down." Coach shouted in jubilation.

"I don't know if you want to talk about it but how was it in there?" Jah asked politely yet he was interested.

"It was fucked up! It was the worst place on earth. That is it in a nutshell son. As far as getting into detail, it is kind of hard to explain unless you experience it but you don't want to do that. We were all in the same place but everybody's journey is different- For me, jail overall wasn't shit but wasted time. The hardest part was missing you son. Nothing else really mattered."

"I feel you. I'm glad your home. I missed you Pops."

"I missed you too young lion. You handled your business like a true Warrior. I'm sorry you had to give up some of your youth and become a man overnight."

"It was gonna happen eventually Pops. It happened for a reason. I'm cool with it. You are here and you are safe." Jah explained with maturity.

"Unbelievable son, what else has been going on around here otherwise? What happened to the stairway outside? It looks like somebody bit a chunk out of it."

Jah never lied to his Pops. He didn't have to. They were tight like that. What made it even more beautiful was Coach never gave him a lecture on lying like most lying parents do. "I don't care what you do just don't lie to me... I cain't stand a liar." Coach put that weak technique to sleep. Coach expressed honesty and he explained to Jah the importance of it. This situation was different and worth lying about. Jah knew if he told his father about Bodeen even crossing on their side of the street he would probably kill him. There was no telling what he would do if Jah told him Bodeen attempted to kill his only son. Jah couldn't risk his father going to jail providing that information. The only problem with that was Jah didn't know how to lie to his father. His eyes got big and he started stuttering,

"Umm...who- what? What stairway... the one outside?"

"Naw, the Stairway to Heaven the O'Jays sing about, you know which one I mean son. Well maybe somebody chopped it off with that custom Wasp Knife I saw in the kitchen drawer. Are you sure everything was cool while I was gone Jah Lion?"

Jah looked away and put his head down and nodded,

"Cool Mon!"

Coach knew Jah was lying but he didn't stress the issue he just used a different angle.

"What's up with that rasshole across the street anyway? Have you seen that punk?"

"Awwww man!" was the only words that could came out before Jah busted out in an uncontrollable laughter. Jah got so hysterical he couldn't even finish the story. He could not get a half a word out to save his soul. Jah's laughter was so contagious Coach started cracking up and he didn't even know why he was supposed to be laughing. Tears were coming out of both of their eyes. Coach was dying to hear what was so funny.

"What happened Jah? It must be crazy?" Coach asked.

"Man Pops. To truly appreciate it the way I did, you have to see it for yourself."

"I don't want to see that punk no time soon or I will be in jail for real this time." Coach expressed sincerely.

"Don't even worry about it. That dude is the least of your worries now

Pop. Trust your son when I tell you this." Jah stated and started laughing again.

"What happened did he get Religious?" Coach asked.

"Nawww Pops, something better than that- all I can say is, the only thing Bodeen is missing is a sweater, some wack sneakers, and a song about the neighborhood."

"No shit...." Coach said astonished.

"No kaka-poo!"

* * *

Later on that night Jah fixed dinner for his father. He fixed a Customary African Kings Fish, Rice & Peas, Carrots, Cabbage, Squash, and festival bread. For dessert they had fresh mango shaved ice with mango ice cream on top. It was the bomb. Coach was blown away. Jah lit the red, yellow, and green candles. Jah put on a classic Live Jam Session with BB King and Jimi Hendrix recorded at the Generation Club from 1968.

"Damn young lion what have you been doing since I've been gone."

"Sssshhh, just living Pops- just livin'." Jah expressed like he had the whole world on his shoulders.

Coach and Jah ate well and listened to the blues. Coach sipped on a Bob Marley energy drink while Jah knocked down shots of Gatorade. They talked and laughed together for hours and had a good time.

Around 2 or 2:30 in the morning Coach's house phone rang. Coach and Jah were still up listening to music and talking about everything under the sun. Coach wasn't alarmed. He was expecting a call from a cutie pie so he could see what that other welcome home feeling was all about, ya dig. It was actually OG Big Spider calling from the hole in Pelican Bay.

"What's up Carnale' how does it feel to be back at the Barrio?"

"It feels like a fine Virgin lying naked in a bank vault full of money that's all mines!"

"Ha ha you sound happy as a motherfucker Vato, Gotdamn. I'm glad everything worked out Carnale'. Are you getting your head right and letting your mind free?" OG Spider asked.

"I'm on top of Cloud 9 with butterfly wings on Big Spider. Where have you been? I was calling you like crazy for the last week."

"These Pinche Puta's like to bounce me around because I have too much influence. Pinche Pendejos just make the Clicka stronger. I'm up in Pelican Bay now. I had a feeling you were stressing out. I told my little primo to call your son and tell him we kidnapped that goofy fucker from UPS but he got into with his old lady that night and forgot to call. I heard you left that goofy fucker on the freeway ha ha ha that was cold Carnale. He's a Pandejo but he was still likeable."

"Yeah, I like Rolland's silly ass that's why I didn't punch him in the face. He called me about 4 hours later and asked me when I was coming back to pick him up. I had to send a cab to rescue him off the freeway, man that fool is crazy. But on a serious note I don't know what I can do to possibly repay you. Do you need any money?"

"No Carnale', I'm already a multi millionaire with life in Prison. Hahahaha Imagine that... You already paid me enough, trust me."

"How do you figure that OG?" Coach asked.

OG Spider hesitated for a minute and then he proceeded.

"A few years ago my son played on your football team."

Coach figured it wouldn't be hard to remember the kid because he averaged one Chicano kid on his team a season.

"Oh Yeah what is his name?"

"Tona."

"Tona! Oh! That was my little Aztec Warrior; The Sun God. That was my little Partner. It broke my heart when his Mom said they were moving to Bellflower. Your son is football player for real. What's he up to?

"...He's doing good... but- but I can't bring myself to talk about it right now Carnale... you feel me.

Coach could hear Spiders voice crack just in those few words.

"To make a long story short- you know I'm committed to this life and wasn't there for my little man but you were. All he talked about was Coach and the things coach told him. He would come in the house with his chest puffed out and say, "Coach said "I'm not a mortal man- I'm an Aztec God; The Patron of Warriors. I'm a true descendent of *Tonatiuh the Aztec sun god. Tonatiuh provided warmth and fertility but in order to do so, he needed sacrificial blood. Coach told me that every time I hit the quarterback and draw blood I'm making that sacrifice.*" That was all he talked about was Inglewood football.... Man (sniffs nose)...so all I want you to do for me Coach is keep doing all the good things I heard about you in the streets. They say you do shit from the heart and not for money and recognition. Oh but you know what? I do want to ask you for one more favor?"

"What do you need OG?" Coach asked.

"I got a little primo that wants to get into that football shit too. He never played before so I don't know how good he is."

"That's cool, how old is he?"

"I think the little vato is nine."

"That's even better. He can play on Jah's team. I'll Coach him up. He'll be cool. What's his name Lil Spider Jr the 3rd?".

"Fuck you Carnale', you got jokes dawg. His name is Rudy."

"You got it. Tell him to be at Darby Park tomorrow at 5 o'clock sharp."

"Thanks Carnale', My Familia loves your son too Carnale'. They call him The Baby Face Wise Man. My nephews said Jah came over and brought his playstation and about 20 games. They said while they played Jah sat in the big chair drinking coffee and worked on the crossword puzzle in the back of the TV Guide dawg."

"He's serious like that. Even when he does play video games he uses probabilities and statistics to figure it out and shit. He's a heavy little dude and I love him to death. But seriously, Thanks for helping me to get my life back Big Spider I mean that shit brother."

"Yeah man you sound sincere. That's why I did it in the first place. Hearing about Vato's like you keep me going in here. It's not always about a color... it's about being around good motherfucker's man. You see I'm supposed to be in here Carnale'. I'm no good for the streets. But I don't like seeing good people get fucked over that didn't have it coming to them."

"I heard somewhere the black and Brown didn't get along."

"That is Political Media bullshit. You know they do that shit to turn the city's attention off of the fucked up shit they are doing. We already talked about that remember? We just have to get the youngster's that's buying into that bullshit they read on the computer to chill the fuck out. But don't think for one minute that those pinche gueros want to see us unite. You see the magic that happens when we work together. If you were the guilty man that pushes the buttons wouldn't you be scared?"

CHAPTER 36

A YEAR AND some change flew by. Getting acclimated back to the life Coach was comfortable with was proving to be more difficult than he imagined. Coach lost his good job at the wrong time. Unemployment in America was at an all time high. The economy was in shambles and a dollar was getting harder and harder to come by. The Felony that was now on his record, made Coach leery and sick to the stomach when he filled out a job application and came across the deadly question, *"Have you ever been convicted of a felony?"* Coach finally felt what James had to deal with before he hired him back in the day and it wasn't a good feeling. Coach was starting to wish he didn't sign that affidavit saying he wouldn't sue that state. He was starting to need that money real bad. Coach always put the thought out of his head because that was broke talk. If he wouldn't have come home when he did Jah would have been caught up in the system and no amount of money was worth that. Coach and Jah had to live off a tight strict budget. They were making it without stressing about it so far but the savings account was getting a little lighter every month.

Coach caught a break and treated it like a blessing when he found out he was eligible for an Unemployment Check. He had never been unemployed before. The EDD Check along with a little change in his savings helped them out tremendously.

Living on a budget didn't stop the progression of life. Youth football was the saving grace during these hard recession filled times. Coach put together a team that was so exciting and good he it made the jail incident became a thought way in the back of his mind. His football team healed that wound. Coach and Jah left the Inglewood Azande's and joined the Snoop Dog football League. They joined a team called the Greater Crenshaw Bears. They had a wicked squad. Jah led a defense that didn't give up a first in 10 games. The opponents netted minus yards. They beat teams every week 40-0. They would go on to have a couple of undefeated championship seasons and become one of the best youth football teams in the history of the sport.

Coach concentrated on the brighter side of life. His money was short but mentally, physically, and spiritually he was holding on. Coach decided to drive up to Noble Drew Ali Park on La Cienega and get a workout in. He saw Mother Taylor downstairs picking the weeds out of her flowerbed. Coach and Jah used to help her do the dirty work but she lost those privileges. The vibe wasn't the same. Coach would nod in her direction and acknowledge she was there but he wasn't speaking to Mother Taylor yet. Coach was disappointed in her. He kept his antennas up around her and when Coach finally spoke he refused to call her Mother. Coach nodded and said,

"Taylor."

"How long are you going to stay mad at me Coach?" Mother Taylor asked.

"That was a year ago Taylor. Why do you keep bringing that up? I told you before that I'm not mad at you; I'm disappointed in you. I just don't agree with what you did. I don't respect it and I can't accept it."

"I'm an old lady and you know you really hurt me Coach when you called me those names."

Coach laughed as he remembered that moment,

"I apologize again for using you in the moment. I wasn't calling you a Bitch, per say. But the timing was so perfect I had to use it to my advantage to put that Child Service lady on notice. It was not personal at all but it was Cold Blooded wasn't it? Beeaitch! Don't speak- Coach was about to relive the moment but Mother Taylor cut him off.

"Yeah nigga I know what you said you don't have to act it all out again. Well I'm sorry too. I shouldn't have let those people try and take your boy away."

"I'm not tripping Taylor, I understand, truly I do."

"Well if you ain't trippin' why are you still calling me Taylor? I hate that name and the way you say it. You make me sound like a man." "TAYLOR!" Mother Taylor mimicked Coach in a gruff man's voice.

"When you change your state of mind and your last name to Teresa I'll gladly call you Mother… until then Peace Taylor." Coach walked off laughing knowing he would strike a biblical nerve.

"Well since we're talking again, when you get back I need you to help me pull up these weeds!" Mother Taylor yelled as Coach was leaving but didn't get the response she wanted.

Coach wasn't lying. He wasn't angry with Mother Taylor or LaTonya or any of the other people that didn't step up to the plate while he was away. Coach didn't put the burden on them by saying, "You know who your real friends are in time of need." The truth was they didn't know how to handle the pressure. When Coach thought about it and put himself in their shoes he realized they were not built for overcoming adversity. It wasn't a knock against them. They were just stronger in different areas of life. Coach's heart would have been wounded something awful If Gerry was in town and didn't step up to help or somebody like James because they know what time it is. They would look out for Coach without hesitation because they were the only family he knew.

Coach hated to leave Jah alone during his foul trial but that was a risk he had to take and the best possible thing for him. There wasn't that many people who would follow the Love Family's Program.

Take Mother Taylor for instance. Mother Taylor worshipped white Jesus only because he was white, gave all her money to the Reverend, and then ended up stealing some of the good food she was supposed to be giving the homeless and keep it for herself so she wouldn't starve. Coach couldn't put Jah's life in Mother Taylor's hands when he was away. It was not a knock on her lifestyle but Coach needed to separate from those old sharecropping ways and live righteous. Shirley from the Barbershop was another one. She was a cool sister but her only focus was trying to hold on to a man and she was having trouble raising her own kid's. So Shirley would have been no help to Jah. Coach wasn't trying to raise a kid. He gave birth to a god. That concept alone is hard enough to try to explain to the average person on the street. As far as LaTonya went, even though Coach knew she wasn't built for adversity, he was still disappointed in her actions. She was better than that.

The life Coach chose to live is based in spirituality not a man made religion. Coach had never seen OG Spider a day in his life and that man did more for him inside a cage than Mother Taylor did from inside her church. So go figure that.

Coach was a forgiving dude except when it came to Bodeen. That fool had no passes coming. Coach wasn't going to forgive or forget. Coach had seen real gangsters before and Bodeen wasn't it. Coach didn't want karma to come back on Bodeen until after he got his hands on him first.

Coach enjoyed a nice work out at the Park. It is one of the better ways to relieve stress. He decided to stay at the park until it was time to pick Jah up from school. Coach started reflecting on his life. He thought he knew what his purpose was in life but now he was having doubts. Coach always looked in the mirror when things went wrong and never laid the blame on the next man. Coach knew he was making a difference. He left a positive impact on everybody he came across. The trial Coach was going through was bigger than him. When he lost his job, the kid Jelani lost his job and his place of peace. The Student Athletes no longer had a place to practice and stay out of trouble. The kids no longer had a safe place to go and be surrounded by other children with the same mindset that wanted to achieve greatness. Iron wasn't sharpening iron. That hurt Coach more than anything. It was frustrating to see celebrities on TV pretending like they love the children and not doing a damn thing for them. Not one of them could help the park survive for four months. The biggest slap in the face Coach had to take was watching the abundance of pedophiles running Park and Rec Centers across America and they continue to just move along on the upside of life with no consequences. A Brother like Coach comes along that does the right thing with the kids and it's taken away behind some bullshit. Something was definitely wrong with that picture. Coach couldn't wrap his mind around that. It wasn't about life being fair it was about life being what it was supposed to be, righteous. Coach believed that life should be balanced like the Universe and not leaning to one side all of the time. Coach believed in GOD'S plan but he just wanted to be a part of it. It's nothing wrong with that.

As Coach was sitting down questioning his spirit, a little girl about 4 years old snatched away from her mother and ran over to Coach. She smiled and gave him a big hug and then she said,

"You're a nice man," and the little girl ran back to her mother. The mother put her hand over her chest in shock and said,

"I'm sorry sir she has never done that before. She never goes to anybody not even her own father."

"Don't be sorry at all. She is a blessing. I needed that and she recognized it." Coach answered and then looked at the little girl "Thank you young princess you made my day, bye bye."

"Bye-Bye Lion King!" The little girl said and giggled.

"JAH! LOVE!

Coach needed that bad but at the same time it still made him question his faith and his purpose. He had the god given gift to make people feel good but he no longer had an outlet to fulfill his duties. It wasn't meant for Coach to walk up and down the street with a megaphone reciting Psalms. That wasn't his strength or personality. He wasn't a leader of men. He wasn't a motivational speaker. He led by example.

Coach reflected on his time in jail and had to laugh about it. He was in there doing everything wrong. Silas was right. Coach broke every jailhouse rule written. He sat down to eat at the table with the Aryan Brotherhood because he was engaged in a conversation with one of the Nazi's about the Raven/Steelers Rivalry. If it were anybody besides Coach a full out prison riot would have jumped off. The Brotherhood didn't even know how to react because Coach was the first black man to ever sit at their table in history. One of them whispered to Coach and said,

"Hey man you are cool and everything but I don't think we're supposed to sit like this. It's not me just jail politics."

The relationship he had with OG Spider was not supposed to happen. Coach wasn't an extraordinary muthafucka but people just liked him. Coach was in jail but his mind was free. He didn't see inmates stabbing, raping and killing each other when he was locked down. He was able to come home with funny stories about things that happened inside a fucked up place. That part of the journey was now over but the question that continued to burn inside of his head since he returned home was "What happens next?

Coach picked Jah up from school and they decided to drop the top and ride to the beach. They drove up the PCH until they arrived in Pacific Palisades. Coach found a nice spot overlooking the beach and they posted up right there. While Jah was knocking out his homework Coach looked out into the sea. He performed a couple of Yoga Meditation exercises. For some reason the song "Be thankful for what you got," popped in his head. Coach smiled and took a deep breath.

There was Wild Cactus growing near the edge of the cliff. Coach decided to wash his hair with it. Over the past year Coach decided to grow his Dread Locks in the traditional way. Coach went back to the car. He opened the trunk and got an empty ½ gallon water bottle and the WASP knife Jah took from Bodeen. Coach searched the trunk looking for an old shirt to strain the Cactus Juice. He couldn't find one. Coach looked at Jah. He had on 3 T-Shirts. Coach walked over to him and sliced one off of his back. That WASP knife was no joke. Coach cut down 3 huge cactus leaves in one swing. He scraped the prickly needles off with the edge of the knife like they were dead skin. Coach placed the cactus in the t-shirt and covered it up. He used the handle of the knife and pounded on the cactus like a hammer until it was smashed. Coach Lifted the T-Shirt and started to twist it like a wet washcloth. He strained the Cactus Juice into the water jug. Coach poured it in his hair. He shook his head real hard. This was the best method to rid the dread locks of any grease at the root of the scalp or any lint from the pillow lodged in the lock.

Coach had witnessed the Elder Rasta's clean their locks in that fashion. They didn't school Coach on how to perform the ritual but they opened up skills that were already in him. He was genetically predisposed to Island life. His skin color and smooth texture, his faint accent and easy transition to speak in Patwa brought out a lot of questions about Coach's upbringing he would never be able to answer.

After Jah completed his school lessons he and Coach went on a light two-mile jog in the sand. Jah would have much rather run sprints at the sand dunes because a light jog meant a quiz was coming. Coach liked to exercise the mind, body, and soul. Most of the quizzes were fun to Jah.

Coach always added something to make it sound exciting. It was just getting over the initial hump of taking a quiz outside of school that bothered Jah. It was kind of like doing laundry. Even though the machine is doing all the work we still hate it… but then love it when it's all said and done.

Jah actually set himself up. Coach was just enjoying the jog. As they were running along the beach Jah said,

"It seems like the ocean just goes on forever."

"Forever? Forever would be infinite. How can it go on forever when we are on a planet with land and water? We don't live in Atlantis we live in South Central L.A. where the crips and the bloods play. Who said that?

"ICE T" Jah stated and shook his head.

"What is the total area of the land and water on the planet Earth?"

"196,940,000 square miles." Jah answered.

"What is the area of the Land?" Coach asked.

"57,255,000 square miles." Jah answered.

"What Ocean are we looking at?" Coach asked.

"The Pacific Ocean and it covers 68,634,000 square miles." Jah stated with ease.

Coach taught Jah those actual facts when he was 3 years old. He started off playing the point and name game with Jah like any other parent. "Nooose, Eyeeeesss… Doooog… Cat… Sun…Moon…Stars…" And Coach just kept adding on to it over the years little by little,

"Sun, the Sun is the center of the Solar System; it gives light that brings life to the planet, 93 million miles from the planet earth. It brings positive energy and cancer to the enemy. It is also symbolic to the black Man…"

Jah took to it like fish to water because he loved science and mathematics. Coach spoke to his strength. If Jah was into History and English Coach would have used a different approach. He would have given Jah the same lessons in story form, used pictures, and taught him how to do research. Jah asked his Pops,

"Pops, remember the discussion we had about life on other planets?

"Yes Indeed. That was a cool one." Coach answered.

"You told me why we are symbolic to the Sun but you never told me how the other planets characteristics relate to us."

"I thought you would have gained an understanding once I laced you with the Knowledge, (the planet and where it is) and the Wisdom (what the planets functions are)….So let's make it interesting. I'll break it down for you again and you tell me what person that Planet reminds you of, ya dig."

"Let's do it." Jah said full of excitement.

Take Mercury for example. Mercury is a swift planet in orbital velocity and always on the move just like somebody with a hyperactive personality that uses lots of adrenaline. The type of person that finds it very difficult to calm down, they are always on the go. Who has that characteristic that we both know?"

"Pops Sanford!" Jah stated and laughed.

"Now take my favorite." Coach started talking in a smooth player style.

"Saturn: Its significant feature is its Rings, which consist mainly of precious metallic and icy debris, you know, that cold blooded shit! Ya dig, It also has a myriad of satellites and it is one of the greater spectacles in the Solar System because of its flamboyancy. Saturn is like the Charismatic Fly brothers and sisters that garner a lot of attention- However the deepest challenge is how to address all the attention that is given to them when there so many beautiful stars often times managing all those women- uh, I mean- managing all those *planets* may lead to collisions between the various satellites."

"That is you all day Pops, hahahahahaha. I knew it was you because you put all the smooth extras on it. I love you Pops. What about Shirley?

"Jupiter! I know you saw that big booty. Jupiter is the most massive of the objects in the Solar System."

"I believe that." Jah concurred.

"The majority of Jupiter's constitution is hydrogen, methane, and ammonia gas. Its appearance may be menacing because of its size, but in a reality, it's just a lot of hot air." Coach concluded.

"That's real talk." Jah agreed.

"All right last one, and let's get up out of here. Some people have that type of personality that is frozen, which is similar in constitution to the conditions on Pluto. Pluto is the farthest observable planet from Earth. It takes Light a lot longer to reach them, and when it gets there, it is not very Bright or clear to them. Who is that?" Coach asked seriously.

"That chick that took you out two nights ago… Where did you inherit that bill?" Jah clowned his father and fell out laughing.

"You were eavesdropping weren't you? You little slick rascal. Well you must have heard me calling her Pluto. She thought I was calling her by the Cartoon Dogs name Pluto, which in turn she thought I was subliminally calling her the B-word. That was not the case at all. I explained to her that I was just comparing her to the planet; the one that is so far out of touch with reality, a cold dull personality, and even if Moses came to her with the sun in his hand she still wouldn't see the light."

"Where did you find her?" Jah asked curiously.

"I didn't find her, that fool Cheeba laid that burden on me."

"The fly dancer cat?"

"Yeah, that crazy fool. I was hanging out with him and Preeshay at the jazz joint. I should have known he was up to something because all night he kept saying "She's a cold piece of work.""

Coach and Jah returned to the pad. Jah could see that his father's spirit was cool but his mind was heavy. Jah lit some candles around the house to keep the vibe relaxed. He sliced some fruit and placed it on the table. Jah put on Stephan Marley's "Inna Di Red" and put the CD player on repeat. Jah stepped out of the room and let his Dad get his head right. The gesture alone made Coach feel like a new man. Coach closed his eyes and listened to the lyrics.

"I didn't get no sleep at all last night
My shoulders were as heavy as lead
I felt something was just not right
I had to roll a little spliff for my head…"

JAH the Light and Jah the reflection of the light relieved him of his worries instantly. Coach felt real relaxed actually. He was in the mood to have some fun. Coach called his play cousin Mellow and his son young Ju Ju and invited them over for a classic game of Monopoly.

Coach met Mellow as a youngster in school. They were friends for about two weeks before they realized they lived two doors down from each other. They use to tell everybody they were cousins when they were little and that's what everybody knew them as so they kept the lie going thru adulthood.

Mellow was smooth around the ladies but when it was just the fellas he talked loud like a sports analyst. He loved to debate, over-talk and dominate a conversation. Gambling was his true hustle so Monopoly was right up his alley. Mellow was wide and stocky and he wore big truck jewelry. His son Ju Ju was tall and skinny. When they walked through the door together they looked like the number 10. Mellow started talkin' shit as he and Coach hugged each other.

"Look at this shit. Every time I come over here you got it looking like the Reggae Sunsplash up in this bitch. Why you got it all dark up in here living off candlelight? Are you and Jah in here praising a head of Lettuce? You ain't mystical and deep-you're just cheap. You just hate to give that white man his money don't you? I ain't gonna be sitting in here with men in the dark. Turn on some lights up in here… and I bet you about a hundred household bugs take off running across the floor."

"Ain't that a bitch? I know your thick neck ass ain't talkin' shit. Your head is so big it looks like you should be doing aspirin commercials. Now go sit down some place sausage nose and enjoy the vibe." Coach hollered back.

The game got underway and they were all having a ball. Mellow was fussing at his son Ju Ju for buying the cheap properties and all along he was cleaning his father out.

"C'mon son! Why would you spend money on a nice hotel in an impoverished neighborhood on Baltic Avenue? I saw that street on American Gangster, it was desolate as hell."

"Land is the base of freedom. And you just landed on it so free yourself of my $450." Ju Ju laughed and rubbed his finger together until his father gave him his money. Mellow was broke but he kept coming up with hundred dollar bills to pay his debts. He was an excellent cheater. Jah was controlling the bank so they were amazed on how he kept pulling it off.

Coach rolled the dice and moved his Top Hat six spaces and landed on Chance. He flipped the card over and it told him to Go to Jail- Go straight to that ungodly dungeon-Do Not Pass Go-or collect any money in the process.

Mellow said,

"Boy you still ain't learned your lesson yet have you? While you're in jail make me a grilled cheese sandwich with an iron and some newspaper... Speaking of that- how come you didn't call me when you got caught up in that twist? You know Jah could have stayed at my house with JuJu."

"I didn't know your number by heart. This cell phone era made remembering numbers a thing of the past, I just found you again last week at the park."

"That doesn't mean a thing. Fools in jail can find a man quicker than an investigator." Mellow spoke the truth.

"Now that's real talk. You ain't lying at all." Coach agreed.

"I know...what's up with that fool that set you up?" Mellow asked.

"He lives right across the street and I haven't seen a peep out of him in a year. That shit is crazy!'" Coach answered.

"He's living? Man I would have dropped that clown soon as I got home."

"In due time brethren, the heathen's of Babylon will fall Ras."

"Now here you go with your Harry Belafonte accent. Do you see an Island and pretty girls sipping on Martini's? This is the Island of L.A., niggas are drinking 40's out here acting like animals and a 9mm is the best tranquilizer on the market to calm the savage beast. You use prayer to protect you from the devil. You use a pistol to protect you from the beast."

"Hey Coach, where are you from Jamaica?" Ju Ju asked.

"Naw, he's from the Bahamas right Pops?" Jah answered but not really sure because Coach never talked about it. It was not that Coach had a terrible upbringing but he knew just as much about his childhood as everybody that was sitting around the table. Coach wasn't ashamed so he shared what he knew.

"You are close son; it starts with a "B" but not the Bahamas. I was told I was from Barbados. Supposedly my mother got pregnant by some cat from the States, I don't know what he was doing over there but it is what it is. I think he was out of East Oakland."

"That figures... that's why you look like Ziggy Marley with a Pimp Cup." Mellow chimed in. Coach laughed as he pictured what Mellow said in his head, and continued the story.

"I don't know what Mom's situation was. I don't know if she was poor or young or what but she put me on a plane and sent me to America to live with my father so I could have a better life."

"How old were you?" Jah asked.

"I don't know. I was still an infant and not sure how many months old I was at the time." Coach answered.

"That was the best thing your Mama could have done for you. You don't want to live in Barbados. It's poor as a muthafucka out there. You'll be sittin' around there eating Wish Sandwiches all day. I Wish I had a piece of bologna for this dry ass bread. You cain't even get squirrel meat to bar-be-que out in that bitch. That land is dry as hell with no habitat." Mellow's crazy ass cut in again. Coach laughed and said,

"Man I think you just love to hear yourself talk. What are you a thick neck archeologist? Barbados is the 51st richest country in the world." Coach responded.

"Yeah, I know it is...out of 52. I saw that shit on the National Geographic Channel; they are about 40 years behind. They just heard RUN DMC's first album over there last week."

"The singer Rihanna is from Barbados and she's fine." Ju Ju told his Dad and Mellow just threw his hands up as if to say, "There it is I proved my point."

"Anyway," Coach tried to finish his story. "Moms put me on a plane to come live with my father but he never showed up."

"Dang, that's cold blooded. So what happened next?" Jah interrupted.

"If you listen with your ears instead of trying to be my hype man I can finish light bulb head. Now—"

"So you never saw your mother again? Ju Ju interrupted Coach and asked.

"Naw he didn't but I saw her last week doing the Choppa City Juke dance after she scored that touchdown. She got me 13 points in my Fantasy football League." Mellow interrupted with his corny Mama jokes. Coach replied,

"Just because you'll never be the man your mama was don't let it derail you from your mission in life... Now listen and you might learn something...like how to wipe that white shit out of the corners of your mouth… Now- the Stewardess that was assigned to watch me on the plane didn't know what to do when my father didn't arrive. The information she had on him was bogus. Now I'm not saying this to sound arrogant, just stating a fact that fits the story. Since I was so cute and an Island Baby the Stewardess decided to keep me and kept it hush-hush."

"So if you were an ugly baby you would have been fucked?" Mellow stated in question form

"Not really- actually being cute was gonna get me fucked. The Stewardess met a lot of weird people traveling and it was big money to be made in the black Market for Cute Island Baby's. She was gonna sale me to the highest bidder. I wasn't gonna get lucky enough to be placed with a nice white family and grow up to become a star athlete, and then Hollywood makes a movie out of my life. She was trying to sell me to some freaky rich couple from France and make me a sex slave or some bullshit. The stewardess had a roommate named Lily-Ann."

"I remember that bitch. She had a long chin." Mellow remembered.

"Yeah, her…but let me get to that part Murphy Lee. I don't need your wack ass adlibs. Um, Lily-Ann or Lily White- that was the name she used on the streets. She was a High End Prostitute. She found out what the Stewardess was up to and she wasn't having any parts of it. The two broads got into a fight and Lily took me with her cross country." Coach concluded and went silent. Everybody waited and waited for Coach to finish the story but he never did.

Jah asked his Dad,

"Is that it? What happened between the ages of 1 and 20?"

"Y'all didn't say that. Ju Ju asked me where I was from. I didn't know you wanted to hear my entire Autobiography. Well honestly, I don't remember anything when I was a one year old. But I know from 2-5 years old I had two jobs. I worked as a sharecropper in the morning, you know I tended to the crops, and at night I worked on the railroad with some Chinamen."

Ju Ju's eyes opened wide in astonishment.

"Are you serious Coach? Man you grew up hard."

"Don't believe that shit son. The only crops he ever tended to in his life are those ugly ass daffodils in Mother Taylor' flower bed." Mellow answered.

"No seriously I don't remember much from maybe 1 to 5 years old except one event. All I remember clearly was the day we moved in with this Pimp Dude for a few months…he was so fly. He didn't wear all those clown suits with the loud colors and his hoes didn't look the part either. They looked like mothers and School Teachers. They wore nice dresses and spoke eloquently. The Pimp's Name was North Star. What was his motto? Um, "if you need some guidance in your life" no-no-no-no- it was "if you're lost-look for the North Star to lead you in the right direction" or some shit like that. We weren't with North Star that long but he left an impact on my life. He was a good dude and he taught me a lesson I never forgot. I remember he had 5 of the finest hoes I had ever seen in my life. He had Rolls Royce's, a Mansion in Vegas, and he gave all that up without blinking to raise his sons and be a great father. I had never seen a father play the role of the mother especially a diehard pimp. I remembered he treated me the same as he did his sons and he loved me but he adored them… as he should have. Two of his hoes stayed with him and became his wives and they ran his businesses. Lily's dumb ass didn't like working at his strip clubs as a legit waitress so she chose Geraldine as her pimp and we moved in with her."

"Well shit, living with Geraldine was like having a father in the household. That Bitch looks like James Earl Jones with fucked up French Braids. It could be the middle of July and Gerry will be walking around the streets in dress shoes and jeans and a long sleeve shirt."

"I know that's right. I remember when Gerry trained you to be a Tailback. She had you nice too."

"I remember. She was always the Quarterback for both teams when we played football in the streets. She was a load to bring down when you tackled her too." Mellow reflected on the good old days.

"And you better tackle her from the back because if those church shoes kicked you in the shins it was over." Coach added.

"Gerry had the thickest hands I've ever seen on a woman. They were swollen like she punched meat all day. She should have been named Abdullah the Butcher… but that's my girl and I love her to death." Mellow stated with love in his heart as he reminisced about the days he lived two houses down from Gerry.

"Yeah, remember when Dubie passed her a joint and saw her hands and said she had Penis Fingers! We were rolling like a muthafucka... But anyway, yeah mon' that's my life story. Gerry raised me from say 5 until I was 15. I got a job at the Fox Hills Mall and met this older chick that liked to look after me. I moved into a single at 16 and been on my own ever since. After that I grew a pair of wings and became the fly cat you see before you today."

"Fly my ass. Where is Geraldine at anyway turning some young broad out at the gay parade." Mellow's crazy stated.

"Her old ass is probably Pimpin' in DC. I believe she's been there for the last year I think. I haven't talked to her in a good minute. Hey tell the truth Mellow, when we were 14, you hit that old coochie back in the day on the side of Tee Tee's house didn't you?"

"Did Gerry tell you that?" Mellow asked showing his guilt.

"No she didn't– but you just did– hahahahahaha." Coach yelled out as he put Mellow on blast. They all fell out laughing. Mellow had to laugh too because he was cold busted. His first piece of pussy was dress shoes Gerry.

"Didn't you take her some flowers or some shit?"

"Man, she slapped them roses to the ground and said,

"Nigga if you want to get a piece of this get them bullshit flowers out my face and bring me back a muthafuckin 40 of Old E!" Mellow confessed and laughed so hard he dropped the Monopoly Money on the floor that he was cuffing under his sleeve and hiding in his hand. Everybody saw the wad of Monopoly money drop and pointed to it. They couldn't stop laughing. Mellow was a true gambler that liked to win by any means necessary. He brought the extra Monopoly Money from his personal board game at home.

The father and son Tandems played Monopoly and told funny stories until about 3 in the morning and they had a good time.

* * *

Meanwhile directly across the street, Bodeen and Mika were inseparable. Bodeen stayed up late a lot of nights just staring at his baby girl and watching her sleep. He couldn't believe he had such a beautiful baby under the conditions in which she was conceived. Bodeen had a one-night stand after the club. He didn't know the condom came off because he had never used one before. Bodeen didn't even remember the mother's name. It didn't matter. Bodeen was happy with the results. As evil as Bodeen was back then he thought his kid's head would be spinning in circles and spitting green shit out of its mouth like in the Exorcist.

Bodeen and Mika had a big day in the morning. They were going to dress up in their best outfits and have a tea party.

Mika was the total opposite of Bodeen. She represented the good in Bodeen he didn't even know he had. Mika was over two years old now. She was walking and talking and had Bodeen wrapped around her finger. Mika was extremely sharp. She didn't speak in simple sentences; Mika spoke in full paragraphs. She was reading and writing better than an English Professor. You know Bodeen was proud about that. Mika was intellectually sharp and her lady like qualities was too much for a two year old. If you looked up the word Little Lady in the Dictionary it would just be a picture of Mika. Bodeen always dressed her in the nicest outfits. Mika had unbelievable manners. She sat upright with her legs closed at all times. Mika would step to the side and let Bodeen open the car door for her before he picked her up and put her in the car seat. Bodeen didn't teach her any of these things. Mika was born that way.

Bodeen was also very honest with Mika. He told her that Daddy use to be a bad man until she came into his life and changed all that. Bodeen didn't even realize how much he learned about fatherhood from watching Coach. He translated everything he was teaching Mika from Coach's blueprint whether it was being honest with his child or to developing a daily program.

Bodeen wanted to approach Coach and apologize but he didn't know how. What could he possibly say to Coach to make him feel better after what he put him through as well as Jah? Sorry just wasn't enough. And now that Bodeen was a father he couldn't imagine being away from Mika for two seconds. Bodeen had a thought one day that hit him very hard. If he was Coach he would have killed the man that set him up and took him away from his daughter. So on that note, Bodeen just tried to avoid Coach as long as he could until he figured out the right thing to do.

Later on that morning Bodeen and Mika were seated at the plastic table dressed in their finest threads. Bodeen was too big to sit in the plastic chair so he had to take a knee. Mika requested that Bodeen wear a nice suit and ascot. She wore a cute white sundress, a pair of white gloves that were too big for her hands and a big white and pink rose tulle tea party hat with fresh roses. Mika ran the show. She taught Bodeen how to drink his tea with his pinky finger up.

Jah was up in his room across the street. He was looking for something and just happened to glance across the street from his window and saw the action that was going on in Bodeen's apartment. Jah shook his head in amazement. Jah thought about calling Coach into the room so he could see it but he decided against it. It was already inevitable they were going to run into each other sooner than later. Sooner came within the next hour.

Bodeen and Mika had reservations for a champagne brunch on a small yacht in Marina Del Rey. Bodeen always took the side door that led to the garage to avoid conflict but for some reason they walked out through the front door. Bodeen was feeling so good he thought why not.

Coach and Jah were walking outside of the apartment on their way to the K1 Track to race Go Karts.

Coach and Bodeen's eyes met for the first time since the incident. Coach reacted, bolted across the street, and jumped on Bodeen before Jah had a chance to tell him to keep his cool. Coach started choking Bodeen by his ascot. Mika was standing behind Bodeen when they first walked outside so Coach didn't even see her. It wasn't until Coach got ready to punch Bodeen in his face he heard a sweet voice say,

"Please don't hurt my Daddy. Don't hate him anymore."

Coach stopped when he saw Mika. He actually felt really embarrassed that he was acting like a savage in front of the young queen. Mika humbled Coach and did what her own dad couldn't.

"Daddy is sorry for what he did to you Coach he just doesn't know how to say it yet. He was a bad man but he is good now." Mika stated with sincerity in her voice. She ran over to Coach and leaped in his arms. She gave him a kiss on the cheek and said,

"You are Coach and that is your son Jah. And my name is Mika." Mika pointed them out and pointed to herself. She showed Coach more than his share of love so she stretched her arms out and reached down for Jah to hold her. Mika kissed him on the cheek. Jah held her in his arms not really sure if he was doing a good thing but it felt right.

"Will you be my big brother and walk me to school when I'm old enough to go?" Mika asked Jah.

Jah didn't know what to say to that. He looked at his Dad for the answer. Coach kissed Mika on the forehead and just walked back across the street alone to think about what just happened. Coach even left Jah standing there holding Mika. Bodeen sat on the porch with a little minor scratch above his lip. Coach fucked his ascot all up. It was all twisted and wrinkled around Bodeen's neck. Jah waited until Bodeen dusted himself off and got his wardrobe back in order. Jah sat Mika down and told her it was nice meeting her and goodbye for now. Jah didn't even look at Bodeen. Jah just turned around and gave him his back. He walked across the street to meet with his Dad. Mika kept waving and saying bye-bye to Coach and Jah.

Coach and Jah got in the car.

"What the hell was that son? How come you didn't prepare me for that?" Coach asked in astonishment.

"I told you he changed his whole game Pops. That was crazy right. I had to let you see it so you could get full shock value. Were you shocked?" Jah stated still amazed as well.

"I got electrocuted. For a demon he was sure blessed with a beautiful young goddess. Are you sure it's his baby? Coach raised his eyebrows while he asked the question.

"I don't know. She has his nose and a few other features but not his personality. Do you think he is sincere this time? It seems like it to me." Jah stated truthfully.

"Man, fuck him. He knows how to apologize. It makes me think he used that baby and told her to say those things because he knows I love kids. And I don't want to think like that about Mika, ya dig. It's terrible but I have to watch all his angles. Now he's got me confused. My mind is all over the place. I don't like this shit. You know she is the only thing that got me off his ass. The fool was big too son, and strong, good lawd... Hell no I don't think he's sincere. But then again everybody can change I've seen it before. Shit I don't know son... I can't play the good Samaritan this time- that is what got me twisted in the first place. A real gangster would have apologized and broke bread when I came home. Even if he didn't feel comfortable approaching me, he was supposed to send word and a nice package through a 3rd party. That's how the game works son but only if you are true to it. That fool is fraudulent. But you know son- just to be fair and sincerely honest-I will no longer wish anything bad on him now that I know he has Mika. And I will be man enough to admit that I know his love for Mika is sincere and she will turn his life around in due time no question. She is special indeed. But me, I have no more love for that dude... not now... not ever.

CHAPTER 37

LIFE CONTINUES TO move on. Some people as they tend to get older become wiser and healthier. There are some that just let themselves go. And then there are the ones that fear getting older. They want to hold on to the past; scared to let go of the days of yesteryear. They won't even allow themselves to see that life gets better as long as they stay on course. They are moving forward in life but walking backwards. That was the case with former Detective Andy Moretti.

Andy had 99 problems and Bitches were 95 of them. His troubled rebellious teenagers were two more problems. The indefinite suspension from the force was still lingering plus the stress that came with problems 1-98 equaled to 99.

Andy almost had his job back until a couple of his un-loyal officers that he groomed from the Rampart Days snitched him out as one of the pioneers. Andy had been long gone from that division before the infamous scandal took place so it was only speculation but Andy's track record was so suspect, the department just kept him away until further notice. Andy would have been okay if he weren't still trying to maintain his rock star lifestyle. There is always employment for out of work cops as private security for celebrities and politicians. Those jobs barely covered Andy's overhead at home so it was nowhere near the amount of money he needed to maintain his Porsche, Boat, Beachfront Condo, and freaky 18-year-old girls that loved cocaine and pills.

Andy's life was consumed with pink late notices, foreclosures, repossessions, and tax debt. Andy needed money bad. He knew Bodeen had plenty of it and he wanted some. Andy had been plotting to get piece for the past two years. He had to take his time. Andy didn't have any more loyal friends that he could trust helping him take that kind of money especially from a Man with a reputation like Bodeen's. Andy had to pull off this job on his own. The job was proving to be difficult because Bodeen was a homebody now. Bodeen didn't calculate every move like he used to, so Andy couldn't track his schedule. The streets were quiet. Andy asked around and Bodeen hadn't been active in the underworld at all. Word was Bodeen was off the radar not only in Los Angeles but across the states. That further let Andy know Bodeen was relaxing on a nice sum of money. Andy had the heart but he didn't have the skill to face Bodeen up close and personal. Andy had developed a 30-year habit of saying, "Freeze," with a Beretta in his hand of course, and the suspect usually gives in to the command with no resistance. Bodeen would kill him on sight before he formed his lips to make the 'F' sound.

The time that passed between their falling out was going to be Andy's best advisory. It had been over a year and Andy was hoping Bodeen had put his guard down by now. Andy finally came up with the Master Plan and he intended on executing it to the fullest.

CHAPTER 38

THE HEAVY HITTERS were burning the candle at each end. When Cordedius Montgomery died from cancer Bobby Boyd and Abdullah Joe became the most sought after free agents in the game. They were the best muscle money could buy. After working for a true old school kingpin like Cordedius Montgomery, it was hard to dumb down to the level of the small time gangsters that tried to employ them. When Cordedius was alive he was the man and everything in the street went through his organization. He controlled it all. After his death hundreds of chump-change making hustlers sprang up and started setting up shop on different corners across the city. Cordedius Montgomery was wealthy, politically connected, played by the rules, wore tailored suits, and most importantly he knew how to keep his organization under control. Mr. Montgomery never underpaid or overpaid his organization; it was just enough so they would always need him. Along with all the extra quirks that came from working for a Kingpin of that stature, it was a pretty good job and it came with medical benefits. The young crews setting up on the corners weren't even at the level of when the Heavy Hitters first started out in the game. The new crews did everything wrong. They had no connections political or major product. They didn't know how to dress. Wearing their pants sagging off their ass wasn't anything new but they took it too far. These youngsters today that have a waistline no bigger than a pencil are buying size 48 pants extra long. They walked around holding up one side of their pants up with one hand. They even run from the police like that. Some of the more popular Pushers were making real money but it wasn't kingpin paper.

The Heavy Hitters were wise grown ass men that learned all the tricks of the trade from their elders. They knew some old school tactics the youngsters were too arrogant to sit down and listen too. Bobby Boyd and Abdullah Joe had a fierce reputation and the young dealers that were making enough money to hire them tended to excel faster than the competitors.

There were too many crews and not enough territory and that equaled war, bloodshed, and hostile takeovers. If a dealer employed Bobby Boyd and Abdullah Joe they didn't have to worry about another crew trying to take over. They didn't have to worry about getting robbed. The dealers that didn't hire them now had to worry about the Heavy Hitters taking them out.

Bobby Boyd and Abdullah Joe exploited the fact crews needed them to make a name in the game and used it to their full advantage.

Bobby Boyd and Abdullah Joe played the short con and the extortion game on all the young dealers that weren't wise to their clever tactics. They had all kinds of old school trickery that always enabled them to skim some cash or product off the top. It was so easy to them it became boring. To keep the game interesting, Bobby Boyd and Abdullah Joe decided to make the streets think they had a falling out and stopped working together. They played the con out to a tee. They were very patient and let the heat buildup gradually. First they started out saying foul things about each other in the streets until the rumors created a little buzz. They let the rumors in the street predict what would happen next. They gave the people what they expected to see. One day they had a heated argument at a local Barbershop where they had to be separated. To put the icing on the cake, they had a shoot out with one another in an undesirable after-hours club where the people with the biggest mouths frequent. Once the word was on the street it instantly turned into, "Who do you think is gonna win between Bobby Boyd and Abdullah Joe?"

It played out just like The Heavy Hitters knew it would. They were the Puppet Masters pulling the strings and now it was time to collect. Working separately they could cover more territory and keep more crews active. Even though The Heavy Hitters were equally dangerous some dealers feared one more than the other because of something they may have heard in the streets or something they may have seen one do and not the other.

So this is how it worked. Bobby Boyd would put the lean on a dealer that feared Abdullah Joe a little more than him. Bobby Boyd would extort the dealer for protection fees, which were 50 grand at the time. He also took money off the top during transactions he supervised and everything else he could in a boisterous and aggressive manner. Bobby Boyd made the young dealer hate him but he also made the youngster enough money that he still needed him. So now Abdullah Joe comes along. He's smooth, cool, fair, and feared more than Bobby Boyd on that particular side of town.

Abdullah Joe puts the truth in the young dealer's ear that Bobby Boyd is a greedy thief, he's over-charging him, and he's taking side money on the deals that the young buck is brokering.

"…And you know that I know what I'm talking about because we were partners for damn near 30 years. Our names are stuck together like Jack and Jill… and he is Jill. Now don't get that wrong, Bobby is no bitch but he likes to spend money like a bitch, you hear? That's why I stopped fucking with him. That stealing shit is not cool. We were tighter than brothers. So if he fucked over his own brother, his family -what do you think he's doing to you?" Abdullah Joe would say convincingly. He would wait for the young fish to bite and then reel him in.

"This is what I will do for you young soldier cuz I like your style and I want to see you come up in this game. You are different from all these other little punks out here. Give me 40-grand- just a flat rate annually and I'll take over as your muscle and get that thieving nigga Bobby off your back. As far as hits go if we need to take it there just pay me by the job."

After hearing that good deal the young hustler jumped on the proposition immediately. Bobby Boyd was charging them 50 grand every other month or sometimes whenever he felt like it. Abdullah Joe was thought of as the better killer and he came at a cheaper price. Abdullah Joe was hired and Bobby Boyd was fired.

The Heavy Hitters outwitted all those young bucks out of their cash and split the proceeds in half. The Heavy Hitters played the "good cop/bad cop extortion con" until the fires at the end of the candle met in the middle.

The Heavy Hitters outsmarted the young bucks with old tricks but they weren't the wisest. That's why they were muscle and enforcers and not kingpins with all the knowledge they possessed. They had two weaknesses. For one, they didn't save any money over the years. The money came in and it went out. They were killers. They had to live in the moment because tomorrow was not promised in their profession. They didn't expect to still be living until they were 40 years old. Professional killers working for drug dealers really don't plan for the future.

The second mistake they made was underestimating the Young Hustlers they conned and extorted. The Heavy Hitters were too set in their ways and didn't bother keeping up with the times. The Young Hustlers weren't clever but they weren't stupid either. It took them a minute to get wind something fishy was going on and a while longer to figure it out but they were on the Heavy Hitters ass now. Those Young white Tee Shirt wearing thugs were wild, dangerous, and they ran in packs like bloodthirsty wolves. Unlike the Heavy Hitters, Bodeen, and other OG Killers that made a name in the game by dropping bodies for business, these youngsters came to the table with guns blazing and they would Uzi up the whole block for fun. Their motto was "WE" WE went down to so and so… and WE LIT that Muthafucka Up!"

Before the Heavy Hitters knew what hit them they had bounties on their heads in every state they worked in back east. The price was getting so high to take them out Abdullah Joe and Bobby Boyd wanted to set up a con and fake their own death just to collect the bounty. They just didn't have anybody they could trust to pull the fake trigger and be willing to split the money.

Bodeen would have been the perfect candidate for a con job like that they thought. He was feared more than them because of the way he executed his victims and he did it alone. He was an independent contractor with no loyal ties to any crew.

The Heavy Hitters hadn't spoken to Bodeen on purpose in two years because he didn't show up for Cordedius Montgomery's Funeral. Bodeen didn't call and give a reason for his no-show. He didn't even send flowers or a card. Bobby Boyd and Abdullah Joe took that as the ultimate disrespect. Cordedius Montgomery raised Bodeen and gave him a job when he was wandering around Detroit looking for guidance. Mr. Montgomery put food in his stomach and clothes on Bodeen's back. The least he could have done was send a telegram. They felt Bodeen owed Cordedius Montgomery that much.

The Heavy Hitters didn't have a clue that Bodeen was living in an entirely different world. In their eyes Bodeen wasn't bred to live a normal life and that's why he was so effective as a killer. Bodeen couldn't be strayed away from the game because he found religion, love, or family.

To be perfectly honest, Bodeen just forgot about the funeral. Death was the last thing on his mind. Bodeen was experiencing what life was all about. Bodeen appreciated what Cordedius Montgomery did for him as a teenager. He was a better parental figure than Charlesetta had ever been. Mr. Montgomery was the perfect man Bodeen needed to become the dominant force he turned out to be. He was partially responsible for his success but that was then. From where Bodeen's head was now, he looked at their history from a father's point of view and he wondered what did Cordedius Montgomery really do? He taught him how to kill, extort, con, gamble, and survive in the streets. He didn't teach him about life, love, and family values. Bodeen remembered that Cordedius Montgomery just showered his family with money and gifts. He didn't have a relationship with them. He never took his son to ball games. Once Bodeen realized he forgot the Funeral he was content with it. He figured Cordedius Montgomery didn't need any money for the funeral; he was rich. He didn't need to see Bodeen one last time; he was already dead. Bodeen felt he made the right choice but in the underworld it was the wrong decision.

The Heavy Hitters were hot as a firecracker on the east coast and it was best to lay low out west. Their money was funny by their standards and it wasn't worth the risk trying to get the currency, jewels, and cars they left behind.

The Heavy Hitters previously had a discussion about the money Bodeen stole from that stash house a couple of years back. They laughed about it. It was no big deal to them then. They were rolling in the dough at that time. They were going to keep that money and hide it from Bodeen if he had not found it first. So since they never had it in their possession they didn't take it as a loss. The only question mark was they never knew how much it was Bodeen really stole. If they knew Bodeen hit the jackpot they would have killed him in the house with Alonzo.

Bobby Boyd and Abdullah Joe didn't travel out west with the intention to do Bodeen harm. That was not in the plan. They came in peace. Their intention was to pull off the new con but once they contacted Bodeen and he didn't want to roll with the plan to collect the bounty money, that's when they decided that they were just going to rob his ass simple and plain.

The Two killers respected Bodeen but they didn't fear him not one bit. They had already killed ruthless men much deadlier before and Bodeen's reputation didn't mean shit. He was just another nigga in the game to them. They trained Bodeen and the student was no match for both of his masters.

CHAPTER 39

COACH WAS HOLDING on and keeping his spirits up the best way he could. He wasn't happy but he never showed it. He refused to be the black cloud that came in the room and killed the vibe because of his depression. Coach couldn't stand to call or see a friend that was doing well complaining about everything under the sun. *"I'm sick of this job (that pays 80 grand a year)…my feet hurt (sittin' on their ass all day)…my back hurts (never lifted anything heavy ever)… I'm sick of my kids I'll be glad when they leave the nest (the nanny is the one raising the kids)…It looks like I'll be at the Benz Dealer for the next two hours getting my car serviced, this bullshit is stressing me out…"*

Coach never complained in front of his child about how broke he was. He just told Jah "things are gonna be a little tight until I find another job," and he left it at that. It was getting close to damn near 2 ½ years now but Coach stayed true to his Faith.

Coach may have not complained about how life was treating him but he vented to other people who were in the same position he was in from time to time. Coach and his rational thinking friends agreed that life was not fair according to science. They believed in natural balance and universal order. If 10 million lame asshole Americans that take life for a joke can consistently be successful, it is only fair that at least one person that takes life serious got a shot at being successful. They didn't want handouts or a million dollars; all they wanted was a fair shot. That's not too much to ask but it is so difficult to achieve. Like the great James Brown sang, *"I don't want nobody to give me nothin'-open up the door- I'll get it myself."*

Coach was tired of hearing, *"America is a great place to live-"* *"If you put your mind to it you can be anything you want-"* *"Go to College and get a good education-"* *"I want to Thank my Lord and Savior Jesus Christ because this BET Award wouldn't be possible without him."* Even though ALL that is true, there are still millions of people those philosophies just don't work for. It is not their calling.

Coach thought about Bill Cosby and his classic rant when he blasted and talked down to the black community about their ethics and level of education. Coach loved him some Bill Cosby but he was hurt by what he said. Coach was everything Bill Cosby was claiming he should be. Coach knew how to speak articulate. Coach pulled his pants up. Coach went to College and graduated with academic honors. And he still didn't have shit to show for it. He didn't have a pot to piss in or a window to throw it out of. Coach was so tired of the appointed so called leaders talking loud and saying nothing. Education is very important. Coach took the time to learn about certain brothers like Bill Cosby and his Boule' Society friends long ago from the school called Knowledge of Self. These Boule' Cats most notably Booker T Washington, W.E.B. Dubois, and a few other current caricatures of that nature are put in power by rich philanthropists to keep the black community in check. They are given a little money and allowed to start black Schools but they have to use a European Curriculum. Most black Schools don't teach a black Curriculum. The Boule's have the tendency to talk down to people less educated than them. They don't use uplifting positive words and inspire them about life. They say things like,

"We, as black folks, have to do a better job...they're standing on the corner and they can't speak English. I can't even talk the way these people talk.... You can't be a doctor with that kind of crap coming out of your mouth. In fact you will never get any kind of job making a decent living... Parenting- Correctly parenting. That's what it's about. You got to — you got to straighten up your house. Straighten up your apartment. Straighten up your child."- Bill Cosby

Well Coach and a lot of other black People have done exactly what Bill Cosby is preaching and have nothing to show for it but a 50 thousand dollar student loan steadily adding interest and no job to pay it back. Coach was tired of hearing everything that didn't sound like coins. Coach took all of his College Degrees and Academic Awards off the wall and smashed them in the trashcan. He was no longer proud of them. All the hard work he put in didn't amount to shit. They were just a piece of paper in a picture frame.

Coach actually put himself in the position that he was currently in by befriending Bodeen so he had nobody to blame but something had to give. So finally after two years of searching, Coach finally got a job 27 miles out of Los Angeles. It was the worst job on the planet earth but Coach had to do what he had to do. Pride was no longer an issue. Coach along with all his A's and his Bill Cosby encouraged College Degree was working as a Custodian Cleaning the Infected Stool and Blood of Dangerous Quarantined Mental Patients for slightly above minimum wage. It was awful. They facility provided Coach a thin paper apron, thin paper shoe covers, and the cheapest latex gloves on the market. The Mental Patients were infected with AIDS, Malaria, Chagus, the Drips, Meningitis, Herpes Zoster, and every other transmissible fungus that can kill your ass. The Mental Patients were crazy but they weren't fools. They knew what they were diagnosed with and they had no problem launching a handful of infected shit in your face because you refused to take them out to the yard for a cigarette. They bombed Nurses with sandwich bags filled with piss that would burn through skin like acid. The difference in these patients from the ones that were born mentally handicapped is that this was their choice. 95% of the patients were the ones that pleaded temporary insanity in court. So instead of going to jail they came to that facility. Coach vouched from day one that jail wasn't even that bad compared to that shit. There is a chance of survival in prison. The mental hospital was so fucked up every patient was going to be discharged with their mind permanently damaged. There is no chance of a full comeback. The Patients thought they were being slick and beating the system but the system fought back and destroyed them for the rest of their life with medications that were no good. The patients loved to smear feces on the walls too. Coach's job was to clean all that shit up. That was only the half of it. Coach had to keep his head on the swivel and his eyes open at all times. They should create a reality show called "When Mental Patients Attack." In a split second the Mental Patient you would least expect would stab a staff member in the neck with a plastic fork just because they didn't like the way their neck looked that day.

The Patients Rights Rules was more golden than the Constitution of the United States. Coach witnessed Nurses getting Aids infected Blood thrown on them over a cigarette and end up suspended or fired because the Patient said the Nurse provoked them to act that way. The Management then has this huge investigation and witness reports to determine if a Crazy Muthafucka that has a history of violence, lying, and murder, plus several infractions for throwing contaminated blood and stool is telling the truth or the suspended Nurse in question. 99.99% of the time the Patient is always right.

Coach felt kind sorry for 1% of the patients that were placed in the facility by their rich parents as a teenager because they were the rebellious children at home. They usually came from large wealthy families and they were the first ones in the house to get bad grades or experiment with drugs. Funny style parents like the ones Coach met at the facility didn't have a clue where they were taking their child. The facility Coach worked at was called a Rehabilitation Center but it was far from it. It was a guinea pig factory that tested humans with mind controlling medications. The Parents just read the ad that said *Rehab and we also treat chemical dependencies.* Their kid would walk in that spot just needing some attention at home and never make it back out the same again. It was sad.

Coach hated that place with a passion. The smell in there was ungodly. There is no possible way a person can be healed in a place that smelled like that. The other employees besides a couple of cool ones were nothing but modern day foot shufflin' slaves that snitched all day long. It was truly ridiculous.

Jah didn't like Coach working there either. He told his Dad he would rather they be broke than watch him work at a ratchet facility like that. It wasn't good for the spirit. Jah was so right.

Coach thought about what Jah said every day as he toughed it out at the job for the next week. Coach looked around the dreadful facility. It wasn't a Hospital at all and they should have been charged with slander and perjury for calling it such. Coach had to get around the fact that those people locked up in the facility weren't patients. They called them Residents instead of Patients. They didn't need to be cared for and healed. They chose to be and wanted to be sick non-functional evil residents that loved their meds, Folgers Red Coffee, and cigarettes.

Coach was fond of one resident in particular named Victorio because he always kept himself clean. Victorio asked the Management if Coach could be his counselor and mentor. They agreed. Everything was cool until Victor volunteered to tell Coach why he had been in that ungodly facility for the past 20 years. Victorio said,

"I got caught making love to my two year old niece and I've been in here ever since."

That did it for Coach. They weren't paying Coach enough to care for a man like that and treat him with love like a real patient. It wasn't right. It was like giving Mouth-to-Mouth Resuscitation to Lucifer to keep him alive if he was dying in the gutter. Coach didn't want to be accountable for nothing of the sort. Coach tried to get fired but those bastards wouldn't let him go so he quit.

When Coach quit his job he was no longer eligible for Unemployment Checks. That hurt him bad. The last of his savings was also gone. Coach was 5 months behind in his rent and all his bills were in the red. If Coach didn't have Jah, his health, and a good spirit, his life would have been totally fucked up.

When Coach first left the So Called Rehabilitation Center he needed a break. He didn't know there was a place that existed that was worse than jail. The first couple of weeks out of work again were cool. Coach caught up on some TV shows that he had never seen when they were on the air originally but a man can only watch so many reruns of *"Everybody Hates Chris"* before he loses his mind. Coach also realized how much the show "Good Times" made him unhappy. Coach used to love that show as a kid but as a broke adult it made him depressed.

The story that really got Coach was the one when some Bank Robbers in Los Angeles that were being pursued by the police said fuck it and started throwing the money in the streets. Coach was making a payment on the gas bill to keep it on with his last $20 dollars just two miles from where the bank robbers were letting it rain on the poor people in the streets. When Coach got home that day and saw it on the news he got sick to the stomach. Coming up on a good fifty dollars would have been cool. The young bank robbers throwing money out to the people was the good part. That sad part was the amount of unemployed people in the streets that day that needed that money.

Coach put on a nice suit. He had another job interview but he wasn't pumped up about it. He was getting sick of pumping himself up with hope just to be let down. A friend of Coach informed him about this low budget insurance office that needed a file clerk and someone that would be able to handle light phone calls. Coach had taken that route before and the results were always negative. Coach was told for the first time in his life that his degree made him over-qualified for the position. Coach had always thought that was a myth. The other challenge was the online applications. Coach was likeable. The jobs he had in the past were because of his personality, people skills, and work experience was last on the list. Fortunately he was an excellent dedicated worker. Online Applications and non-formal interviews took away the integrity and pureness of job competition. Companies think they are saving money by hiring inexperienced clowns but they go downhill fast.

Coach grabbed his briefcase and threw his blazer over his arm. As soon as Coach stepped foot out of the front gate Mika was smiling, waving, and yelling out his name.

"Coach! Coach! Hi Coach."

"Hi Princess I see you over there glowing like a halo. Coach waved and replied.

For the past year since Mika introduced herself Bodeen always stepped back and let his daughter have her moments with Coach and Jah. Some days when Mika really wanted to spend time with Jah Bodeen would go in the house and give them plenty of space. He would observe their activities from the window.

Life is amazing sometimes. Bodeen didn't even realize how much he learned about child rearing from studying the Love Family while he was setting them up for ruin. Bodeen knew Mika needed people like Coach and Jah in her life. He still hadn't found the words or the courage to step to Coach and try to heal the wound. It would have been useless anyway.

He triggered a mean streak in Coach and it was going to take some time. At the present moment Coach wouldn't piss on him if his ass were on fire.

"Where is Jah?" Mika asked.

"He's at school young princess."

"I'm going to school now too Coach. It's called Pre-School. I have three new books. Do you want me to read them to you?" Mika asked so innocent and sweet.

"Wow, what books do you have? Do you have that new book by Legendary called "Dubie the Hustler"?

"No Coach, that's for big kids." Mika hit Coach with her little fist playfully and laughed.

"What about Confucius?…Message to the blackman? The Secret Relationship between blacks and Jews Part II?" Coach teased Mika.

"I don't know what books those are Coach…you're funny. I have Harry Potter Books."

"Wow, you can read big books like that already? You know Harry's real name use to be Hiram Powers until the white man changed it. He wore an afro and a red black and green dashiki. He didn't wear bifocals he wore stunner shades."

"No he didn't…you are so funny Coach."

"How old are you now Mika?"

"I'm three years old."

"That is great. Jah was very mature like you at three. I'm gonna have to stop calling you princess and change your name to young queen."

"I like that name." Mika stated like royalty. And continued,

"So can I read them to you now?"

"So…you want to read all three of those encyclopedia sized books to me right now huh Mika? That is so sweet but I don't have the time young queen." Coach replied trying not to laugh.

"Where are you going?" Mika asked like she was Coach's wife. He laughed and answered,

"I have a job interview ma'am. May I get your blessing?"

"Of course you have my blessing. I hope you get the job. I love you Coach, you are a nice man."

"I love you too young goddess you have a pure soul."

As Coach walked away Mika asked Bodeen,

"Daddy what is a soul?"

"I couldn't tell you Mika. Daddy lost his Soul a long time ago…"

Coach walked into the office that was no bigger than his living room. Coach had to sign in. He took a seat next to some people that were interviewing for telemarketing positions. Coach was the only person that was dressed for success. Everybody else had on jeans and sneakers. Coach didn't have and a problem hiring a kid with tattoo's and his pants sagging' off his ass when he was the boss as long as they were proficient and got the job done. But the job description stated that it was a suit and tie environment but Coach didn't see it.

Coach was called in for his interview. He knew he was in trouble when he saw an old railroad water cooler made out of steel in the corner of the office. An 18-year-old intern that thought she was the President of the Company interviewed coach. She was a regular old white girl that talked in a fake accent. The stale smell on her clothes let Coach know she shopped at thrift stores and wore the clothes straight off the rack. She was the type of person that refused to listen to anything logical. Coach wanted to choke some sense into her.

"I see you graduated with honors. That's great…. I see you worked as a Park and Recreation Director for 7 years. Oh I see you also worked at our Corporate Headquarters, Nationwide State Farms…for three years. You were floor supervisor for the clerical and office administration department. That's good. You know this is a clerical position you're applying for right?"

Coach didn't know if she was making a statement or asking a question.

"Yes Ma'am."

The intern looked on the second page of the resume and held it away from her body like it was contaminated and said,

"You failed to list any other job experience."

Coach wanted to say "Bitch if I go back any further I'm gonna be in diapers." So he decided to politely say,

"That is 10 years of experience Ma'am. I was in school prior to that."

"Oh I see. So you've only had two jobs in your life?"

"Basically unless you want me to add the summer jobs I had at the mall in high school."

"Oh so you did work prior to this. Why didn't you list it?"

"Those jobs are irrelevant. I was 15 years old."

"I need you to list that job on your resume and any other job you failed to mention. You know honesty is very important when you work for insurance companies, take that into consideration."

Coach just made up some bullshit information. The store he worked at closed down years before. The Intern looked at the resume like it was still incomplete.

"I don't see any File Clerk Experience on your resume."

Coach couldn't believe the bullshit coming out of this broads' mouth.

"Ma'am I began my career as head Supervisor of Office Administration. That includes secretarial and file clerk duties."

"I know what an Office Supervisor does but that doesn't negate the fact that you weren't the file clerk. Your resume says Supervisor and Director of Parks and Recreation. Your job duties didn't include filing and answering phones."

"Miss, I hired and trained file clerks and secretaries on how to do their job."

"I'm aware that you have experience hiring and training File Clerks but it still doesn't negate the fact that you were not "thee" File Clerk yourself per say. Times have changed since you've worked in an office like this. Will you be able to adapt to the newest techniques?"

"The newest technique to filing?" Coach asked and looked at the old beat up aluminum file cabinets and said, "I'm positive that I can adapt to the new techniques ma'am."

"I see you didn't list any phone skills. The job description clearly states experience in answering light phones."

"I was a Director, I answered phones all day."

"I understand what a Director does but that still doesn't negate the fact that you don't have experience answering light phones on the job."

After it was all said and done she told Coach that she would hold on to his resume and call him after she made her decision. Coach was mad he negated to put his foot in her ass before he left the office.

Coach drove home looking at the gas gauge and praying he had enough petroleum to get him home. Coach thought about selling his car but he wouldn't get the right price from a classic auto dealer. Coach would probably get just enough to pay his back rent and bus fair to get home. As much as it hurt Coach he even had to ask Jah to sell some of his rare football cards. The economy was so bad card collectors were bidding way below the market value anyway. People were starving out there and a Jim Brown football card with cheese doesn't taste good between two pieces of bread.

Coach had no other alternatives. James was the only person Coach could borrow that type of money from but he was gone GOD rest his soul. Coach could have borrowed it from several sources but he didn't want to be in debt like that to his black friends. It's not a negative but Friendships are tested for some reason in situations like that. Borrowing from a standup individual is fine and dandy but borrowing from several sources with no income coming in is ugly. Uncontrollable circumstances just seem to happen when it's time to pay it back. Coach didn't know what to do. He even had to prostitute himself to a pain in the ass chick he didn't even like because she brought them groceries and kept a little change in his pockets. Coach felt like taking a long drive but he didn't have enough gas to do so.

When Coach arrived back at the apartment the dreaded moment he had been anticipating had come. The Notice of Eviction from the Marshall stating they had three days to vacate the premises was tacked to the door.

Coach's stomach knotted up faster than a black woman with a bad perm after she jumped in the pool. Coach started thinking fast instead of thinking straight. He was going to sell his car so he would have enough money to put the furniture in storage and stay at a Motel. Coach didn't even bother going in the house. He hopped back in his car and went searching for boxes.

Coach stopped at the Barber Shop first. They always had big boxes in the back. Coach ran into Pops Sanford. Pops saw the look on Coach's face and said,

"Boy you look like a pregnant Possum... Angry- ready to scratch and attack!"

"Even though that was funny I'm not in the mood for your Share Cropper Sayings today Pops Sanford my mind is heavy."

"Like a fat man with an elephant on his back. I can see that clearly. Are you still having trouble finding a gig?"

"Pops it's worse than that. Can I get those boxes over there?"

"Damn, that is bad. And all this happened because of that big grizzly bear. I tried to warn you that he was the evil storm coming. But you are the Sunshine Coach; the blessing that comes after the storm. This is what I want you to do. Take this money I'm about to put in your hand, put on one of those fly outfits you like to style in, and take Jah out and have a nice meal in a fancy restaurant on me." Pops concluded sincerely.

Coach didn't bother looking at the amount of money Pops gave him. Coach was just grateful that he offered. It was probably no more than $25 dollars because Pops Sanford's idea of a fancy restaurant was Panda Express.

Coach loaded his car with boxes. He drove to the local supermarket and grabbed a few smaller boxes. Coach went inside the store and stole some duct tape. Coach didn't want to do it but he had to do it. He needed every dollar he could muster up.

When Coach left the market an ugly hard faced broad in a pretty BMW tooted her horn at Coach. Coach walked over to see what was on her mind.

"Damn nigga you kind of fine what's your name?" The Broad asked.

Coach could tell in the first 3 seconds that he wanted nothing to do with her. She looked liked trouble but once she brought up the word money it stopped Coach in his tracks. Coach still made up a name because he didn't trust the way she looked.

"My name is Billy."

"Damn Billy you sure are sexy. My name is Charlesetta. Do you want to make some money?"

"Who doesn't want to make some money? What do you have in mind?" Coach replied sounding interested.

"I own the largest Male strip Club in L.A. You could make $500 a night easy. How big your dick is?

Coach laughed at the idea and declined.

"That's not my thing lady, but thanks for finding me sexy."

"Well listen honey, take my card and call me if you want to make some money in other ways too... you feel me. Shit, call me if you want to make some babies with your fine ass. You from one of those Islands or something huh?...ohh I want to Ssssssss your- um let me get out of here before I get in trouble.... Call me."

Coach shook his head and walked away. He put her card in his pocket and visualized himself making love to Charlesetta. Coach cringed and said, "Damn that bitch kind of looked like an ugly version of Bodeen. That's not a good look."

When Coach returned, Mika saw him unloading the empty boxes out of his automobile. She had been standing in the window downstairs waiting for Coach to come home so she could read her books to him. She saw all the boxes and yelled across the street,

"Are you gonna make Jah a Club House with those big boxes Coach?"

Coach was so distraught Mika couldn't even brighten his day with her angelic face. Coach didn't mean to but he answered Mika with sarcasm in his voice.

"I'm gonna build a regular House... Me and Jah are gonna be living in one of these boxes soon because of your punk ass daddy." Coach checked himself when he saw the sad look on her face. Mika didn't care what he said about her father she was hurt because Coach barked at her like it was her fault.

"I'm sorry young Queen I did not mean to snap at you please forgive me. Its stress young queen and stress will take a man out of character sometimes. The truth is we have to move soon." Coach apologized and explained.

Mika became extremely sad,

"No don't go. You can stay over here. We have two apartments."

Coach was so desperate he would have jumped on that offer if Bodeen presented it to him. As long as Coach had a rent-free roof over his head he had enough hustle to get back on his feet in a major way.

Bodeen heard Mika's offer as well but he didn't act on it. He felt bad about Coach's situation but he didn't give charity. He chose to sulk instead. Bodeen also hurt Mika because of his selfishness. She genuinely loved Coach and Jah.

Coach saw Bodeen in the window and waited for him to come clean.

"I don't think that would be a good idea young queen." Coach expressed very disappointed.

"I don't want you and Jah to go Coach." Mika stated and started crying.

The look on Mika's face was far worse than facing the eviction. The Eviction would eventually go away but that look of sadness on Mika's face would be embedded in his mind forever.

Bodeen even had to walk out of the room before he teared up. Bodeen's past was catching up and hurting his daughter. He vowed that after he cut her eye that she would never hurt again. Bodeen had to do something. Andy Moretti soured the relationships with most of Bodeen's political figures but he still had a couple under his belt. Bodeen didn't want to back-slide but he called some of his old connections on the inside and bribed one of the judges to give Coach an Order to Show Cause (OSC) and a Stay. An OSC court Document signed by the judge was the only thing that could delay the eviction until the issues raised by the tenant are addressed on a hearing date set by the court. Bodeen paid for the latest date possible. If Coach accepted it, it would give him a good six months of free rent to get back on his feet. It was the least Bodeen could do. Mika was so proud of Bodeen she made him a heart out of red play-do and presented her first gift to her Daddy.

Bodeen still didn't want to face Coach so he left his kind gesture anonymous. Coach would receive a certified letter in the mail in a day or so informing him about the extension.

CHAPTER 40

"DADDY CAN YOU read this book to me?"

Bodeen was completely embarrassed. Mika needed him and he couldn't be there for her. He felt helpless. Bodeen didn't want pity or sympathy. Bodeen wanted to learn how to read. The good thing about Bodeen was he never hesitated to give reading a try. Bodeen picked up the Book and stared at all those words. The font was much smaller than the words in Mika's Dr. Suess Books. Bodeen tried to play it off,

"Are you sure this book is for kids Mika?"

"Yes Daddy, its Hiram Powers. We have the DVD's." Mika stated as she used the black name for Harry Potter Coach told her about earlier.

Bodeen looked at the name Harry Potter and really got confused.

"Hiram-mmm..." Bodeen looked at the letter Y at the end of Harry. Hiram is with an M...He just figured the M was silent. He was so confused. Bodeen kept staring at words. He was excellent at memorizing phrases he overheard. That was how he got over all those years. Bodeen remembered the characters from the movie version so he decided to adlib,

"So Hiram told the evil Sorcerer, "Say 'what' again! Say 'what' again! I dare you! I double dare you, Mother Hubbard! Say 'what' one one more darn time!"

Mika had read the book already and she didn't remember seeing anything like that. She let Bodeen read on.

"Dig it, magic peddler. We're out here building a new nation for Sorcerers. It's time for you to start paying some dues, Wizard!" said Malfoy. Then Ron Weasley said,

"I ain't givin' you jack! I'll tell you what you do, you go get a Magic Wand and all those Sorcerers you keep doin' so much talkin' about get Wands, and come back ready to throw down, then I'll be right down front killin' sorcerers. But until you can do that, you go sing your marching songs someplace else. Now we're through talkin'."

Mika didn't go for the con game. She never watched Superfly or Pulp Fiction before but her Daddy didn't fool her one bit. Bodeen just flipped the words.

"What are you reading Daddy? That's not what it says on that page."

Bodeen gave the con one last effort,

"Uh, I'll be back?"

Mika had a curious look on her baby face. She asked Bodeen in her sweetest voice,

"You don't know how to read Daddy?" Before Bodeen could feel ashamed Mika added, "It's Ok Daddy I will teach you! I learned to read using Phonics. Let's start with the A sound. There is the Long A sound and the Short A sound... Aa... Aa..."

Mika was so patient with Bodeen his reading fundamentals began to develop quickly. Once Bodeen mastered the sounds of the Alphabet, he started from the beginning and began to work on words with the A sound in them.

"A-ah-at... -Mm-a-ck the Rrr-a-t...Mack the Rat- A-a-Mack Ssat on 'A' Can-... The Ants Ran to the Jam-Mack had a Pan- Mack had a Fan- the Ants ran and ran..."

Bodeen and Mika spent all day studying the alphabet from A-Z. When Mika took her nap Bodeen kept reading Mika's baby books until he damn near had them memorized. Bodeen was gradually getting better and better. Bodeen approached reading books like it was a new toy. He started reading billboards, traffic signs, even Playboy Magazine for the articles and not the pictures. Bodeen still couldn't transfer the words to paper if he needed to write a letter. He still had trouble spelling certain 'EI' 'IE' words and words with silent letters. The shots he took to the head as a child when Charlesetta abused him had a lot to do with it but Bodeen wasn't aware that was his problem. He just continued to work on it.

* * *

Mika was the light that took Bodeen out of darkness literally. He cried tears of joy when he read that the name Mika means Shining Star. It all started to make sense. The mother brought Mika into his life for a reason other than looking for child support payments. She brought him life' -a life that he never knew existed. It would be a long time before Bodeen's soiled soul would breathe life but at least the first seed was planted.

* * *

On one particular evening Los Angeles was hit with an Earthquake and Thunderstorm. It was one of the worst in years. The wind was ripping Palm Tree Branches off at root and they were falling down scratching the hoods of parked cars. The raindrops were so big it sounded like small rocks were being thrown at the window.

Bodeen was sitting in his reading chair sipping on tea and looking for a good article in Ebony Magazine to read. Mika was in her room sleeping. Bodeen actually found an article on Adult Illiteracy. There were 774 million people worldwide that couldn't read and 32 million were in America. As Bodeen started the paragraph on why so many American's were illiterate without having a disability, Mika let out a loud terrifying scream and started crying. Bodeen sprang out of the chair in a worrying rage to see what was wrong. Mika was sitting up in the bed terrified. The loud thunder going off like a sonic boom made it an eerie scene. Mika was screaming her head off yet she was still looking like she was half asleep. Mika was having a terrible dream. Mika wasn't scared of the thunder and lightning nor did she fear the dark or the Boogey Man with a big 6'5 300 pound Daddy that was a killer. That particular night something was different. Mika was crying hysterically. Bodeen picked her up in his arms and carried her in the living room.

The weather outside was terrible but it was perfect conditions for a fool that was up to no good. In this case it was two fools that were up to no good. The Heavy Hitters Bobby Boyd and Abdullah Joe had been in town scoping out Bodeen's apartment building for the past couple of days. They called Bodeen several times on his phone when they arrived in town but it always went straight to voicemail. Bodeen hadn't returned their calls even after they left a coded message they always used in the past that meant imperative. The Heavy Hitters had been staking out the apartment but hadn't seen too much activity besides the houselights going on and off throughout the evening. They knew Bodeen kept his money upstairs in a safe. Their plan was to ease in the building and catch Bodeen slipping as he was coming out of his 2nd floor unit. From what they remembered about Bodeen he also liked to get high upstairs in the dark for hours. From the time they had been watching Bodeen he hadn't been upstairs one time or left the apartment. They saw Bodeen walking around downstairs having conversation alone. They assumed he was talking to himself. They weren't surprised if he was talking to himself. That was normal for a killer that liked PCP. The Heavy Hitters were more alarmed that Bodeen had sissy colored sheer see-through curtains covering his windows instead of blinds. They figured West Hollywood finally got the best of him. The Heavy Hitters started to question his sexual tendencies. They had never seen Bodeen alone with a woman before. Pussy was never a priority with him. The Heavy Hitters made a joke or two with their theories about Bodeen's sexuality but it was time to get paid not to play.

It was cold outside but the Heavy Hitters had plenty of heat. They didn't want to kill Bodeen but they knew it would be inevitable. The Bodeen they knew didn't value his life more than his money. He wasn't going to let them just take it. Muscle was a different breed. They were protection. They didn't get robbed. Bobby and Joe personally carried two guns a piece on a church day. They slept with guns and even fucked women with a gun in their hand. Enforcers normally got killed over something their boss had done and in the midst of protecting them the muscle might get smoked in the process. Real Hustlers like to keep good muscle alive and hire them for their organizations.

The Heavy Hitters trained Bodeen so they would have to proceed with caution. They had four guns out, locked loaded and ready to go. They eased along the side of the building. Bodeen had a reading light on in the apartment so it was extremely easy for the Heavy Hitters to see inside. They looked inside the window to see what Bodeen was doing. A bolt of Lightning streaked through the sky and hit a nearby Power line. All the lights in a 2-mile radius went out instantly. It was pitch black outside.

The Heavy Hitters couldn't even see their hand in front of their face. They could have sworn they heard a baby crying when the lights went out but the wind was whistling so loud outside it was hard to tell. Within Seconds Bodeen started lighting candles inside of the apartment one by one until they generated enough light for the Heavy Hitters to see everything Bodeen was doing. They stayed low and watched him through the window.

Mika was obviously shook up from the nightmare she had and along with experiencing her first loud thunderstorm and lightening knocking the power out was kind of frightening for a young three year old. Bodeen was a little terrified because he had never seen Mika cry like that. Bodeen asked Mika

"What is wrong Mika? What was that bad dream about?"

"You didn't love me anymore and you left me all by myself in this big ol' room- and it was dark-and these bad dogs came in barking real loud and started biting my legs."

Even in a dream Bodeen was ready to confront the dogs biting his baby girl and chop them up into Korean Bar-b Que. Bodeen tried reading one of Mika's favorite books to her and make her proud of his progress but she wasn't interested. Bodeen decided to do something he had never done for anyone but for Mika he was willing to do any and everything to make her comfortable. Bodeen went into Mika's playroom and came back holding her miniature keyboard in his large hands. Mika didn't have the traditional plastic piano where you hit certain notes and toy animals pop up in the back. Bodeen bought her some shit Cameo would use on stage... just a smaller size. Bodeen hit a couple of keys and started a familiar melody that he previously programmed inside the keyboard. Bodeen looked at Mika like she was the last breath keeping him alive and just belted,

"There will be no darkness tonight, Lady our love will shine,

(Lighting the light) Just put your trust in my heart, and meet me in Paradise,

(Now is the time) Girl, you're every wonder in this world to me A treasure time won't steal awaaaaayyyy…"

Bodeen hit a note so sweet when he sang the word *Paradise*, Mika kind of jumped back and her eyes popped wide open. She had a look on her face that said, "DAMN DADDY !" Bodeen had an unbelievable vocal range.

His Tenor and Baritone skills were impeccable but his falsetto notes were mind blowing.

"So listen to my heart, Lay your body close to mine
Let me fill you with my dreams- I can make you feel all right
And, baby, through the years... Gonna love you more each day
so I promise you tonight, that you will always be the lady in my life..."

(Bodeen singing all Falsetto) "Stay with meeee...I want you to stay
with meeee...I need you by my si-iiiiiiiiiiiide...
(Baritone) Don't you go nowhere!"

(Always the lady in my life) you're my lady and I love you, girl

Bobby Boyd and Abdullah Joe saw the whole performance unfold and still couldn't believe it. They were looking at each other in the pouring down rain in disbelief. Bobby Boyd and Abdullah Joe didn't say a word to each other; they just stared. Finally they just got up from their crouched position and walked away laughing their Asses off. Bobby Boyd was tickled pink and asked,

"Did you just see that shit mayne or am I trippin'?"

"Brother, I was about to ask you the same thing. What the fuck was that?"

"I don't know mayne but that nigga sho' sounded good. I was ready to throw my draws on the stage mayne." Bobby Boyd said astonished.

"Man, that muthafucka sounded better than Michael Jackson on his own shit!" Abdullah Joe exclaimed.

"Who are you tellin'? We actually sat there in the pouring down rain until he finished the whole damn song with our mouths wide open... Mayne, that big black muthafucka was blowin'. Did you hear Bodeen hitting those falsetto notes like Eddie Kendrick's mayne?" Bobby Boyd asked.

"Hell yeah I heard it. Man that fool should have been a singer." Abdullah Joe suggested.

"Shit it's hard to market a big black muthafucka that looks like Bodeen mayne." Bobby answered.

"It worked for Nat King Cole and Biggie Smalls."

"You got a point mayne... Bodeen sure has a beautiful daughter. How did he pull that off?" Bobby Boyd asked.

"I don't know. I thought he was a Gay Blade for a minute. I'm kind of proud of Bodeen. I've never seen him look like that." Abdullah Joe said sincerely.

"I agree… so what you want to do about that money? I'm not even in the mood to rob mayne." Bobby Boyd asked.

"Let's think of something later… I'm still in too much shock to deal with that shit right now." Abdullah Joe stated still in disbelief.

"You ain't the only one main…. *She's my lady… do do do do- do do doooo…* Man, he was killin' that shit!"

Abdullah Joe and Bobby Boyd got back in their vehicle singing Bodeen's version of "Lady in my Life" and drove off.

CHAPTER 41

COACH WAS IN the apartment packing up all their items in boxes. Coach was putting a rush on it. The Marshall didn't come with the padlock on the day he was supposed to. Coach was glad about that because he wasn't even close to being finished. Coach signed for the Certified Letter that came from the court but he never opened it. He figured it was just the official Eviction Notice and he didn't want to read about any more bad news.

Just the day before, Coach was called for a job interview with the L.A. Avengers Arena football team. Coach hadn't even applied for a position with the Avengers so he knew it was a blessing. Coach was feeling great about the opportunity. He could be around sports again doing what he enjoys. Coach didn't care if they started him out in the mailroom. In a work environment with equal opportunity Coach wouldn't have a problem moving up the ladder into a position he desired.

Coach arrived at the Avenger Headquarters inside the Staple Center. Coach felt like he was on top of the world. The only problem with being that high up is the long drop down. The position they offered Coach was the Avengers team mascot, a fraudulent superhero named TD. The Costume was a Trojan Gladiator in a football jersey and Huge Red Shoes. Coach didn't get the job. He didn't have two years of experience as a mascot on his resume.

That was just the tip of the iceberg. A couple of hours after the interview Coach got in the car to pick up Jah from school and it didn't start. The engine was revving up slow like it wanted to start up so Coach assumed the battery was low. One of the neighbors gave Coach a jump but it was the same result. That only meant one thing. It was the Water Pump. A new Water Pump with labor was $750 bucks. Coach just added that to his collection of bills.

Coach continued sifting through paperwork and old pictures. He was separating the junk from the things he needed to keep. He was looking at Jah's Baby pictures and tripping off how fast time flew by. Jah was already in middle school. It was crazy. Coach looked at a picture of Jah's mother and realized how much he missed his best friend. The memories, sweet-sweet memories...

Coach was feeling like a hoarder. The trash pile he created was way bigger than the stack of memorabilia he wanted to keep.

Coach carried 4 plastic trash bags full of old papers and receipts downstairs. As he walked out of the back of the building to the Trash Bin Coach could hear horns honking and an angry black woman's voice cursing somebody out. Coach looked to his left and saw one of his Border Brothers trying to maneuver an 18-Wheel Big Rig truck down the narrow residential street. It made no sense whatsoever. The black lady that was driving toward him had no room to get passed the wide truck. Coach had his own problems to deal with and their minor conflict was the least bit of his concern. Coach tossed the trash bags into the Bin two at a time. One of the bags hit the edge of the bin and a couple of pieces of trash fell out onto the ground. He wasn't a litterbug regardless if he was being evicted or not so bent down to clean up his mess. Coach saw something that looked extremely odd. It looked like a leather strap that wasn't torn or worn under the bin. Coach moved the mass of smelly metal back a little and spotted a brand new Louis Vuitton Duffle Bag behind the trash bin. It felt like it was tucked back there on purpose. He slid the bag toward him. Coach pressed the side of the bag with his fingertips before he opened it. He wanted to make sure there were no body parts or something that felt mushy. With the bad luck he'd been encountering, the last thing Coach wanted to do was stick his hand in a bag filled with shit. That would really fuck his day up. Coach had seen Dog Lovers do more outrageous things than putting doo-doo into a designer bag before so he wouldn't have been surprised. Coach felt both sides of the bag. He unzipped it.

"Whooo Shit!" Coach exclaimed. He snatched that bag up quick and got the fuck up out of there.

"JAH! JAH BLESS! Yes Mon! Yes Mon! JAH BLESS! Wooo hooo!" Coach was so excited he almost died from a heart attack. His heart was fluttering and his hands were shaking. Coach was overwhelmed with adrenaline. It took a while before he could calm his nerves down but he finally got a grip on it when he arrived at the Park and Rec Center where he used to work. Coach caught the bus. He got extremely nervous as he wondered what would happen if the people riding the bus knew he was carrying what they needed just as much as he did. Then he got scared. In the midst of all the excitement, the nervousness, and jitters, Coach could still hear a voice in his head that said, "Stay focused and be smart."

Coach arrived at the park. It was raggedy as hell. Coach went back to James old office. Before he went in Coach said a prayer for James and his family and apologized for what he got them involved in. Coach also promised James in prayer that he would make sure his kids were going to be taken care of financially.

Most people have shared the same dream of wishing they had a million dollars at least once time in their life. Coach realized that it is very important that when you wish for something to include the specifics as well, ie, *"I wish I had a million dollars and a money counter to go with it"*. Now that may sound selfish and inconsiderate and trust, Coach had no complaints about it but counting 2.5 million dollars in cash by hand is a lot of hard work and it takes a very long time. But when it was all said and done, it is also a very good problem to have.

Coach calmed his nerves and played it smart. He wasn't about to go out and make a large purchase like a Rolls Royce or a new house the next day. Coach just took out enough money for his back rent, water pump, and a little for his pockets so he and Jah could be straight. Coach had a gut feeling that somebody might come looking for that money sooner or later. It didn't look like bank robbery money because the bills were too old and they weren't separated in neat stacks. It was bundles of cash bound in rubber bands and each stack was a different amount. It looked more like buy money for a major drug deal. Coach felt like he was treading in dangerous waters. He was swimming upstream in a downhill world.

Coach didn't know exactly *what* he was going to do with the money but he could tell you what he *wasn't* going to do and that was turn it in to the police. For some odd reason Coach thought about Florida Evans from the show *Good Times* and what she would have done in that situation. He laughed at the thought of giving it to the police.

Coach camouflaged the rest of the money and stashed it in several different secret locations James built in the back just in case somebody got lucky and found a secret spot, they couldn't get it all. James still had his life insurance documents and other relics hidden in there. The police didn't find any of the valuables. James was a genius. Coach also found out some freaky shit about James he didn't want to know. James saved all the pull-outs of the monthly Playmates in his Playboy Magazines. Coach loved to read the Playmates hobbies. They were some adventurous hoes. They all liked Mountain Climbing, Scuba Diving, Horseback riding, Kayaking, juggling on tight ropes, and they all had Master Degrees in Science and Chemistry. Coach tried to spread the picture open to see what the girl was working with but the pages were stuck together. Coach immediately slammed the box down and ran to the sink to wash his hands. After Coach quarantined his hands and secured his small fortune, he went back to the apartment and tried to act like nothing special happened. It was hard to fight that feeling.

CHAPTER 42

COACH STAYED LOW-KEY for a couple of days. He didn't spot any suspicious characters in the neighborhood looking for their lost treasure. Even though the streets were quiet it didn't encourage Coach to go out and do anything that would cause attention. He moved with extreme caution. When he paid off his debt Coach went to nine different Check Cashing locations spread out across the city, and bought small money orders. He cashed the money orders, took the clean money, and purchased Cashier Checks from the bank. Coach wasn't taking any chances. He was going to do whatever he had to do not to bring any attention to himself and hold on to that money.

Coach left the house to see if there was any word on the street. He went to the Barbershop of course. Since his Dreads were locked and he had no use for a barber anymore Coach had to think of something clever to justify his reasons for being there without Jah. Pops Sanford was there so all Coach had to do was sit back and let the conversation come to him.

"What's up Rasta Boy? Where have you been out in the ocean trying to catch fresh fish with just a net?" Pops Sanford asked when he saw Coach with his dread locks out.

"I was with your Mom's shooting' marbles so if you wonder why her knees are dirty she wasn't out doing what she is known for so relax."

"Why are you always coming in here talking about my Mom's and you're smelling like a curry rabbit and some weed? You got everybody in the barbershop high and hungry."

"Man I don't have time to be messing around with you and your old yearbook photo face. Where's Herman?"

"You ain't heard?"

"Heard what?" Coach asked.

"I don't think he's going to be working here anymore." Pops Sanford sadly expressed.

"He's not gonna be working here anymore?" Coach asked with an astonished look on his face.

"He's gone." Pops Sanford answered and put his head down.

"Gone? Stop talking to me in riddles you black ass Leprechaun and spit it out."

"I thought you heard?" Pops asked.

"Heard what?" Coach answered by asking.

"Man, some crazy shit went down." Pops began to explain.

"Some Crazy shit went down? Like what? Coach inquired.

"Crazy like two cats with their tails tied together. Where have you been brethren? I thought you would have known first! Have a seat Rasta Boy and get an earful of this…"

Pops Sanford's version of the story had more holes in it than a machine-gunned crumpet with stigmata. So let's rewind this story back a few days.

It wasn't hard for Bodeen to recognize the talents Mika was blessed with. He enrolled her in the Assata Shakur School for Gifted Students. It was a sister school of the Freedom Home Academy in Chicago. The school was incredible. The age range was from 2 years old to 6th grade. Mika was 1 of 40 kids that were learning 3 languages, advanced reading, math, and consciousness. They were learning about parts of the heart and lungs and what their functions are. They studied Yoga, Nutrition, and Exercise to compliment what they learned. They just didn't have basic test like matching the Capital to the State; they learned about the entire planet. The Educators working at the school made it challenging and fun to learn.

From the time Mika started attending the school Bodeen never left her sight. Bodeen was very over protective but he was more intrigued with the curriculum. Bodeen learned from Coach to recognize the child's strengths and build on them. Mika liked everything about school except finger painting and physical education. Mika was too much of a little lady to get dirty out on the yard.

Mika and her classmates were learning new spelling and vocabulary words. Bodeen just learned how to spell his own name correctly and here he was watching a four-year old child mastering words like amorphous, anomaly, apocryphal, and austere. Bodeen's first thought was, *"These kids don't know how to use those words."* The four year old begged to differ and used the words in sentences.

"A Bird that can fly is an anomaly." "To impress his friends, Raheem invented apocryphal tales of his adventures." The four-year old stated as he read the sentences from the chalkboard.

"What does apocryphal mean?" The Educator asked.

"Apocryphal means... uh, doubtful, questionable... not quite certain if it's true."

"That's very good young brother. Who would like to go next?"

Bodeen marveled at the way all the children were ready to jump out of their seat for a chance to go next. Bodeen remembered when he used to hide in the back of the class while they recited their ABC's.

Bodeen was lured away from the lesson by a repeated phone call. He stepped outside of the classroom so he wouldn't disturb them. Bodeen was notified that the Laundromat he owned was burned down in a fire. He chalked it up as a loss. He really didn't care. He had been losing money on it from day one and was in the midst of selling it to some Arabs. The next part of the conversation is what had Bodeen a little perturbed. The Owner of the Chinese Food and Donuts Take out next to the Laundromat wanted Bodeen to pay for the damages that occurred to their place of business. They wanted $47,000 for Fire Restoration Damages and cleaning fees. Bodeen cancelled the Fire Insurance on the Laundromat months before. That money was going to have to come out of his pocket. Bodeen just reached an out of court settlement with Mr. Willis to drop the assault and kidnapping charge and that put a huge dent in his pocket also. Bodeen no longer had Andy Moretti around to get him out of that ordeal. He was past the days of killing so he gave Mr. Willis a nice start at a new life. Bodeen had to shell out close to $200,000 dollars to Mr. Willis.

Now this Chinaman wants another $47 g's. Back in the day Bodeen would have eliminated that debt and became the new owner of Bodeen's Chinese Food, Laundry and Donuts. He was a legit businessman now. He had to settle his disputes in court and he hated it.

Bodeen needed to drive over and check on the property. He didn't want to take Mika over to the Laundromat and subject her to inhaling the toxic smoke but he never left her under someone else's care before. He trusted the Instructors at the school but Bodeen already decided he wasn't going to leave Mika unattended until it was time for her to attend kindergarten.

Bodeen waited until the Spelling Lesson was complete and asked the Educators if Mika could be dismissed because of the emergency. Bodeen didn't want to leave because the class was going to learn how algebra is applied to everyday life. Bodeen along with millions of other Americans were always curious about that and he was about to miss his opportunity.

He took Mika out of class and they headed over to the Laundry to see the damage.

"Look Daddy your store was in a Forrest Fire." Mika stated as she pointed to the soot and ash that used to be a Laundromat. Mika was repeating a sentence she had overheard on a television commercial and for the first time Bodeen didn't want to hear her voice at that moment.

Mika said,

"I sure hope you had enough insurance to cover the damages."

Bodeen looked at Mika through the rearview mirror and clinched his jaw real tight to prevent him from saying something he didn't really mean. Mika continued to speak her mind.

"Look Daddy, your store messed up Mr. Kyun's restaurant too. You may be liable for those damages as well."

"Mika! Will you shut up! I can't even hear myself think!" Bodeen yelled as he got out of the truck and slammed the door as hard as he could. Mika's bottom lip started to pooch out slowly as the tears welled up in her eyes.

If Bodeen had seen that sad look on his baby's cute face it would have devastated him. Bodeen left Mika in the truck while he tried to decipher which Korean words meant *"You Big black motherfucker,"* as Mr. Kyun cursed him out repeatedly. Bodeen didn't understand a word he was saying but he could tell Mr. Kyun wanted to fight. Mr. Kyun was all up in Bodeen's chest area raising his closed fist and acting hostile. He towered over Mr. Kyun. He wanted to slam his big fist down on the top of Mr. Kyun's head and break his kneecaps. Bodeen started to speak to Mr. Kyun like he was in a Kung-Fu movie.

"A Moth that lives to close to the flame will soon find his ass on fire so mool jom joo-seh-yo Pabo."

"Phuck You won-soong-ee"

"There it is right there. You just called me a Nigga in Korean didn't you?"

"No. We don't say N-Word in Korea. I call you monkey...that's betta, yeah?" Mr.Kyan sarcastically asked.

"Uhl-mah-yeh-yo you asshole" Bodeen stated.

"$47,000."

When Bodeen told Mr. Kyun he would pay for it and gave him 5 grand out of his pocket to shut him up, Mr. Kyun transformed into all smiles and nods.

"Ahhh Thank you sir thank you sir... Ahhh yeah- you not monkey-you big strong man yeah, thank you sir. Let me give you donut for baby ok..."

Bodeen didn't know why he waited for a donut glazed with soot and smelled like smoke. He was just going to throw it away. He wasn't about to feed his baby any of that bullshit Mr. Kyun was selling if it was fresh off the farm. When Bodeen first bought the joint there were a lot of mice in the back. When Mr. Kyun moved in, they mysteriously disappeared without the help of traps or exterminators.

Bodeen tossed the dozen of donuts Mr. Kyun so kindly gave him in the garbage when he got back outside. Bodeen walked to the truck and got in.

"Sorry it took me so long Mika. I didn't want you inhaling those bad fumes... Mika? Mika?? Mikaaaaa!!!!"

There was nothing in the back of the truck but an empty car seat. Mika was gone. Bodeen became hysterical.

"...So after the altercation between Bodeen and Mr. Kyun, he just passed out and fainted in the street. Bodeen busted his head wide open when he hit the concrete. The people at the hospital had a hard time keeping him calm once he came to. He had to be strapped down and heavily sedated. Shirley over there thinks Mr. Kyun put a Toxicodendron shot in his stir-fry. But I think he had some big money stashed in that Laundromat and it burned up with it. What other reason would cause a Big Muthafucka like that to faint in the middle of the street? The Beatles weren't perform-ing…He didn't have a stroke or heart attack- that nigga fainted…" Pops Sanford continued with his version of the story.

"Damn when did all this happen?" Coach asked.

"A few days ago… I thought you would have heard since you live so close to that black Bears Cave… That fool was out of his mind. They said when he came to he just started screaming and speaking in tongues… what was he yelling Shirley?…Um Michael? Or it was -Ma-Kayla…or Mika- Knowing him was probably high off that PCP and he finally flipped out.

"So what does all that have to do with Herman not being here? Coach asked.

"Oh, that's the crazy part. Well you know Bodeen is crazy as a bag of cats and that fool is looking for some money that was taken from him. He thinks somebody stole it and set his Laundromat on fire. So this fool has been after anybody he sees that bought something new. Herman bought that new Lexus and Bodeen wanted to know how he bought it on a Barbers Salary. We all know Herman had been saving for that car for three years but Bodeen didn't want to hear it nor did he believe it. He tried to gun Herman down right out there in front of the Mexican tire shop… yes he did. You see I'm wearing the same clothes I had on yesterday. I don't need that fool shaking my pockets. I hope you still have that package I gave you."

"What package? Ahh rasclot, I never got that package, you gave me the money back remember? That was like two years ago."

Pops didn't want to get Jah in trouble so Pops stuttered his way out of it,

"Huh? Uh, oh yeah that's right… I did. Well keep your eye on that fool he's crazy." Pops concluded.

There were still pieces of the puzzle missing in the story. Coach couldn't link the money he found to the cash Bodeen lost in a fire. Coach kind of wished it were Bodeen's money that he found. That would be a Big Payback, James Brown style. Coach was looking for information about his hidden treasure. He wasn't interested in what happened to Bodeen. Coach wouldn't have batted an eyelash if Bodeen had burned up with the

Laundromat. Coach didn't wish anything bad on Bodeen but he wasn't rooting for him with pom-poms in his hands.

Bodeen looked directly at the sun and it was pitch black. It would be acceptable if he was looking at the world from the dark side of life but he wasn't. Bodeen was standing upright on the square in triple darkness. His light and life were taken away from him. Bodeen cursed GOD and vowed to kill the devil when he got to hell for not staying loyal to his offspring.

Bodeen had to be hospitalized, strapped down, and sedated in a hospital bed for two days. Bodeen still had minor traces of PCP in his system from years of abuse so the hospital assumed he was having what they call a flashback. Even though he cried for Mika and yelled her name all hours of the night, the hospital staff never once asked who the person was he called upon. Bodeen got a grip on himself when he realized he lost two precious days under the heavy medication and checked himself out of the hospital.

Bodeen got back to his apartment and it felt empty. He felt lost. He wanted to sink into depression but it wasn't an option. It didn't take long before Bodeen received a phone call saying Mika had been kidnapped and she was being held for ransom. The kidnapper had the nerve to use that goddamn auto-tune to disguise their voice.

"It's about time you woke your big ass up. I'm not a baby-sitter and this little smart mouth bitch is starting to get on my nerves…now let's get down to business. You haven't worked the streets in three years but you're living comfortably so that means you are sitting on something of value. I figure you got about three million in cash and assets and I want 2.5 of it or I will put the light out on your shining star."

Bodeen's pain and fear disappeared immediately. It was replaced with anger and revenge. Whoever this fool was that crossed the line played right into Bodeen's hands. Hustlers and Kingpins were always getting one of their kids, wives, or soldiers in their organization kidnapped and held for ransom. He was always the man that was hired to orchestrate the transaction. Bodeen was the best at making a kidnapper wish they never got into the profession.

Bodeen and the abductor made arrangements to drop off the money. Bodeen used their knowledge of him being in the hospital against them. He conned the kidnapper into believing he was unable to drive because of the heavy medication. Bodeen arranged for the money to be picked up behind a trash bin in a designer duffle bag. Bodeen agreed that he understood the demands and the consequences of what would happen to Mika if he did anything heroic.

Bodeen hung up the phone. He walked over to the closet where his past was securely padlocked. Bodeen opened the door. His black Leather Coat seemed to smile at him like it missed being clung to his body. His arsenal of weapons didn't look as friendly. They were ready to get back to work. Bodeen got what he needed. He went into the bathroom and looked into the mirror. His eyes told the story. The old Bodeen was back.

The methods of violence that entered Bodeen's mind were borderline demonic. Killing Mika's abductors quickly with a bullet was not even an option. Cruel, gruel, and inhuman torture was what Bodeen agreed upon. He was ready to take it there. Bodeen was not playing. He wanted to make whomever did this feel it. He even decided to employ the Heavy Hitters and put them to work. Bodeen walked over to the phone and placed a call.

CHAPTER 43

"HEY MAYNE WHO were you on the phone with all that time? It better not be any problems with that money we need to go pick up." Bobby Boyd stated angrily.

Abdullah Joe hung up the phone slowly and had a puzzled look on his face. Bobby Boyd stared at him waiting for a response. It took a minute to get the words out but Abdullah Joe said,

"You are never gonna believe who that was on the phone."

"Listen mayne, I ain't in the mood to play guessing games with you fool. My only concern is where we are gonna pick up that ransom money so we can get rid of that whining little bitch in the other room." Bobby Boy stated in an evil tone.

Abdullah Joe shook his head and said,

"Naw Man, the ransom money situation is already straight. We pick that up at the Shoobie Doobie in an hour. But that's chicken change compared to this Bob. That was Bodeen on the phone."

"What? Mayne you bullshittin'?" Bobby Boyd acted surprised and continued, "What was that about?"

"Bobby, he was laying down some heavy shit on me. He needs us for some real serious business. He's talking a hundred large just for reinforcement."

"Oh that means he's about to get sick with it, huh?" Bobby Boyd questioned.

"Barbaric!" Abdullah Joe simply replied.

"So are you gonna let me know what's happening or do I have to read through that thick skull of yours? Bobby Boyd urged Abdullah Joe.

"Man, I'll tell you about it on the way. He wants us at his apartment ASAP, that's an acronym for as soon as possible." Abdullah Joe stated and laughed.

"Fuck you and that's an acronym for fuck you. So what are we gonna do about this ugly broad in the other room mayne?"

"Brother, I couldn't care less what you do with that buck-toothed mole rat. I'm upset we got to the point where we're taking penitentiary chances that carries a life sentence snatching up low level drug dealers kids for pocket change. Her punk ass Daddy couldn't even scrape up 20 grand for his own kid. We had to make a deal for seventeen." Abdullah Joe stated truthfully.

"We got desperate. Shit happens when your money gets funny mayne." Bobby Boyd explained the reasoning why they were doing rookie jobs again.

"You ain't bullshittin' Bobby. Wipe the room down and they can pick that sickly looking kid up here. And please go give that bitch some oatmeal or something that's gonna stick to her ribs. Every time I look at her I feel like singing "We are the World" as homage to the starving children." Abdullah Joe joked but he wasn't laughing.

"Bodeen came through right on time mayne? I almost feel a little guilty that we were about to rob his ass." Bobby Boyd stated as he left and closed the apartment door.

"I love it when you get sentimental," Abdullah Joe said tenderly mimicking Bobby.

"Well let me have a kiss… on the ass, you jive time Mutha…"

"Man, Let's Bounce!"

CHAPTER 44

BODEEN BROKE EVERYTHING down to Bobby Boyd and Abdullah Joe shortly after they arrived at his apartment. Bodeen had a short list with the top suspects and potential abductors names on it. Coach topped the list. Bobby Boyd and Abdullah Joe were also in the top five but Bodeen crossed them off the list once he saw their reaction when he explained to them what happened. Honestly, as grimy, rotten and, ruthless as the two heavy hitters were, they wouldn't have ever taken Mika from Bodeen. The scene they witnessed between Bodeen and Mika was too beautiful not to mention priceless. That was one line they would have never crossed.

Bodeen lit a cigarette. He needed something to cope with the stress that came with Mika missing. He wanted to get high again so bad but that sherm stick would have taken him straight to the deep end. The Cigarette didn't do him any good at all. Bodeen's system had been squeaky clean since Mika had come into his life and that funky smelling nicotine had him nauseated as hell. Bodeen wiped the sweat that broke out on his fore-head and stood in the middle of the living room giving instructions while the Heavy Hitters sat and listened.

"Keep your ear to the street and check to see if anybody in the game has made any big purchases. Matter of fact, If you see anybody that has bought anything new, especially in this neighborhood- in the last 48 hours- and hey I don't give a fuck if it's a pair of cheap canvas no name tennis shoes from Payless, come down hard on their ass with extreme prejudice, you hear me. Now I got all the bills marked..." Bodeen talked out of pure instinct and the conversation tended to jump from what they were going to do to what happened the day of the kidnapping. He continued,

"...And then I placed it across the street behind a trash bin so I could see them clearly from my upstairs apartment window when they came to get the package.... A damn Mexican driving an 18-wheeler blocked my line of sight when his truck got stuck on this narrow street... I didn't see anybody show up and they said the money never got to them," Bodeen concluded as he showed the Heavy Hitters what to look for on the bills.

CHAPTER 45

BODEEN WENT ACROSS the street to face Coach alone. Bodeen proceeded with caution. He didn't have the best track record when it came to his sneak attack skills against the Love Family. Bobby Boyd and Abdullah Joe trailed Bodeen and acted as a safety net. They could see it in Bodeen's eyes that he wasn't the same dude that would kill at will. He definitely was going to perform a devious murder upon the person that was fool enough to kidnap his baby girl but Bodeen no longer had the heart to kill for sport anymore.

Bodeen decided against the sneak attack and approached Coach like a man. He knocked on the door. Coach looked into the peephole. He opened the door and stepped out into the hallway. He closed the door behind him. Bodeen looked Coach right in the eye and said,

"Did you do it Man?"

Coach looked at Bodeen. The sadness he had in his eyes affected Coach spiritually. He actually felt guilty... for a second. Coach replied,

"As much as I want to do something real bad to you, you know your damn self I would never harm your little princess as a retaliation tactic. So with that being said, I pray Mika will be protected but as far as you and I are concerned, I think it's best for you to get fuck out of my face... quick!"

Bodeen looked at Coach and he knew he would never kidnap Mika but he had to see it. Bodeen was a broken man. His sincerity was inevitable when he spoke from his soul,

"Would you help me please?" Bodeen asked without consciously knowing what just came out of his mouth. He was even shocked but since he put it out there he carried on,

"I know I fucked your life up and I'm not in the position to ask something like that but I need you…somebody, I just… I just don't know what to do." Bodeen concluded.

The traumatic journey changed Coach. He developed a cold-hearted side that he wasn't pleased with. Stress and anger is a very wicked combination and it got the best of Coach over the last year.

"I don't know what you need me to do. You expect me to trust you now. You got nothing coming from me you Ras Clot informer. I just told you once and this is the last time I'm gonna repeat myself. G'wan and get the fuck out of my face."

"The man asked you for his help and you just gonna shit on him like he's the ground beneath you." Bobby Boyd spoke with attitude in his voice as he came up the stairs with his gun visible for Coach to see.

Abdullah Joe came from the other direction with his pistol in his hand. He didn't need to say anything. Coach looked at that 4-5 and heard him clearly.

Bodeen was in no shape to get gangster so Bobby Boyd took the lead.

"Say Bodeen, I don't like this dude's attitude mayne. I think we need to teach him some manners. Some of that good old Detroit Hospitality, you feel me? You know how we used to do it. A Hot Ice Pick poking thru his nuts will make a nigga give up his mama. I got the tools in the car. Just give me the word mayne."

Bodeen hesitated for a long time. He said,

"Give him a pass." Bodeen looked like a broken man.

"A Pass? Fuck a pass. This dude knows something I can feel it. I've been in this game a long time and I got a gut feeling. He may not have kidnapped baby girl but he knows something about it… he knows something about that ransom money too. I'm not wrong about this cat mayne. I might not be 100% Correct but I ain't wrong either. I'm telling you, put him under the guillotine and he's gonna tell us something mayne." Bobby Boyd stated trying to encourage Bodeen to do the right thing.

Coach was known for showing his emotions on his sleeve and he had animated facial expressions when he was under pressure. Coach was trying to keep a poker face but it was hard to do because he wasn't a poker player.

"Yeah this dude knows something. I can feel it too." Abdullah Joe spoke with confidence.

"You can feel it to huh Mayne?…Yeah, bro he knows something… Say Bodeen didn't you say you marked the ransom money? And without hesitation Bobby Boyd pulled his pistol from his waistband and said,

"Check this fools pockets mayne!"

Coach was a nervous wreck. His mind started racing a mile a minute. He had $200 dollars of the ransom money in his pocket. People always say, *"You should always go with your first mind!"* But that was bullshit. The first thing that came to Coach's mind was to lunge at Abdullah Joe and disarm him of his weapon. That wouldn't have been too smart. Coach would have gotten his ass shot off listening to that first thought.

"Pull everything out of your pockets mayne… and don't do anything that's gonna put your son in a position to be raised as an orphan. You see us. *We* are the results of Foster Care and No father in the home…but we still turned out all right hahahahahahaha…." Bobby Boyd stated as he sarcastically laughed at his own joke even though it wasn't intended to be funny.

Coach was sweating bullets but they were not the kind of bullets to stop these cats in their tracks. Coach wasn't nervous for his life but at the same time he wasn't ready to leave earth yet. He just kept saying to himself over and over again, *"I'm not about to go like this. Jah will not come out of the house and find his Pops laid out in this filthy ass hallway leaking blood. No sir!"* Coach had no doubt they would kill him once they saw the marked bills in his pocket. If the situation was reversed Coach would have killed Bodeen without question if he had Jah's ransom money in his pockets.

Bodeen didn't do or say much but he was definitely curious to know if Coach had his baby kidnapped for ransom for what he did to him. Bobby Boyd dug his big hand in Coach's front pocket. Coach felt violated like a punk and didn't like it at all. Coach had two pistols pressed against his head so there was nothing he could do about it. Bobby Boyd had his hand in the wrong pocket anyway and came up empty. Coach didn't want to experience that punked feeling again so right before Bobby Boyd stuck his huge hand in his other pocket Coach closed his eyes and said a quick prayer. Abdullah Joe pulled another gun out with his free hand and was pressing the barrel of the pistol in the back of Coach's neck hard. Bobby Boyd lowered his pistol when he felt the money in Coach's pocket. Coach braced himself anticipating a blow to the back of the head once the money was discovered. Bobby Boyd didn't pull the money out of Coach's pocket. He actually let it go and took a step back. Coach knew his faith was strong but sometimes the power of prayer ain't no joke, and it could be a bit overwhelming. Coach opened his eyes. The first thing he saw was some Easter Sunday Shoes looking like they just got shined. They were standing on point behind Bobby Boyd and Abdullah Joe. Coach knew it wasn't Jesus because he wore sandals. This savior was wearing Stacy Adams with the Biscuit Toe. It was Gerry holding two 45's with a toothpick hanging out of her mouth.

"What's really hood fool? What the fuck is this bullshit Coach? Y'all got guns out on my baby boy? Oh these fools got to go!" Gerry stated before she got ready to pull the trigger.

"Slow your roll Gerry!" Coach said in a low cool tone. Shouting would have startled Gerry and caused her to lick some shots off. All three of those dudes would have been dead in the next few seconds if Coach hadn't intervened.

"Who are these country looking muthafucka's?" Gerry asked as she relieved Bobby and Abdullah Joe of their weapons and continued.

"Whoo you got that Remington 1911! And look at here; you got that Heckler 45 ACP… Damn this gun is sweet! Oh- You gots to come up off that homeboy! You don't need this much heat in sunny California anyway." Gerry put that gun in her pocket and tossed Coach the other one and continued.

"Y'all need to get up on outta here,…go on now!"

Woman or not Bobby Boyd knew he was facing somebody that was seconds from blowing his head off. They would not win that day so Bobby Boyd said the best thing he could to save face before they walked away.

"Those are some really nice Stacy Adams you got on mayne."

Gerry didn't even say thank you. She just used her 45's and shooed all of them out of the building.

Gerry had a quirky look on her face when she spoke to Coach

"Hey man, those were some real killer's right there. What the hell are you into?"

"Yoga and Acupuncture." Coach answered sincerely.

"Well muthafucka you need a new Sensei or something cuz that Chang Chong shit ain't working in the hood. You need some gangster rap and a pistol up in this bitch fucking with them type of niggas. Sheeeeiiat"

"Give me a hug girl. Damn it feels good to see you. I heard you got put in a twist in D.C. When did you get out of the joint?"

"I just got out of that vile place this morning. I haven't even seen my parole officer yet. I heard you got caught up in some bullshit awhile back and that broke my heart I couldn't be there. So I had to come see you first Pookie Pie" Gerry stated using the nickname she called Coach by when she missed him a lot.

"Hey Homie wasn't lying though, your Easter shoes are sparkling like chandeliers. You just got them shined at Chambers on Slauson?"

"You know it… I hope you got some grub up in the crib. I'm hungry as a muthafucka."

"I got some fresh Kale and some, um…I got some mango, watermelon, and coconut cut up already."

"No Meat? What kind of bullshit is that? I want a Porterhouse Steak, with some Eggs, Grits, and some Toast. I want some shit that's gonna stick to my ribs. I just got out the joint and you offering me some goddamn Rabbit Food. I can't stand you organic gluten free muthafucka's…"

Coach took Gerry and Jah out to eat and they a cool time vibing, laughing, and talking about everything under the sun. The energy they gave off illuminated the entire restaurant.

CHAPTER 46

COACH DIDN'T KNOW what to think. His mind was heavier than a baby's diaper that hadn't been changed in three days. Coach couldn't leave Mika out there for those savages regardless of what he thought about her punk ass daddy. He felt bad about the way he talked to Bodeen in his time of despair. Even if Bodeen deserved it Coach just wasn't comfortable being nasty and evil. It bothered him.

Jah walked into the room and saw the look on his Dad's face and said, "Man, what's wrong with you, Pops?"

"I'm in a Moral Dilemma son. It's serious, jack!"

All Jah said was "Dang," and he walked back to his room. The tone in which Coach delivered the answer accompanied by the heavy look on his face was enough for Jah to know he was too young to deal with it.

Coach thought of a thousand and one scenarios about how he could help get Mika returned safely. Voices were going in and out of Coach's head for the next two days…

What are you gonna do about that money?

But that's Mika not Bodeen

But he fucked your life up man! You have to give THAT MONEY BACK!!!

You are home

You made it

Jah made it unharmed

Do The Right Thing

What is the Right thing?

?????????????????????????????

Visions of Mika smiling at Coach

Visions of Mika showing unconditional love to Jah

You HAVE TO GIVE THAT MONEY BACK!!

Mika doesn't' deserve that.

If you return that money now those dude are going to kill you fool!

You have Faith.

YOU HAVE TO GIVE THAT MONEY BACK FOR MIKA!!

If that beautiful baby gets hurt you will never get over that.

Is the money worth all the pain that will come with the agony if that baby gets hurt or worse?.

What about your pain? Your pockets are hurting. You pride is hurting. Hunger pains. You don't have a job! You don't have a pot to piss in. You need that money fool. You don't have shit!!!!!

Everybody deserves a second chance

Maaan, Fuck Bodeen!
Mika deserves to have her life and you're holding it.
Without that money you will be homeless
Think about what you are doing
What if that was your son?
What should I do?
What you gon' do?

???

Your Faith will bring you thru
WHAT IF GOD IS BUSY?
Faith could have also brought you that money…you prayed for that too you know that money was your blessing fool!!!

You made it through the storm

Coach's mind was so heavy-He thought hard every second of the day until he finally came to a conclusion and made his decision…

"I'm keeping this money, Fuck the dumb shit!"

CHAPTER 47 "THE HUNT"

"BREAST WITHOUT NIPPLES are pointless.... A Man with a head up his ass can't see for shit!!" Pops Sanford was raining country quotes on Coach like a hail of bullets. Pops Sanford was so upset Coach thought his brain was going to hemorrhage. Pops Sanford did not want Coach helping Bodeen by any means. Pops Sanford did have one quote that resonated with Coach. *"If you put your ear to the pavement long enough the streets will start talking."*

The Hunt was on. Coach had to help search for Mika. He felt like it was his obligation. It had nothing to do with the money at this point. It was strictly about Mika. A gifted child with a natural glow like she had must be special. Her smile alone gave Coach the energy to move on when he was at his lowest point. Coach would never be able to enjoy that ransom money if he knew something happen to that beautiful baby girl because of him.

Like Pops Sanford stated previously, "If you put your ear to the streets long enough they will eventually start speaking." Coach received a lot of data but trying to decipher what information was valuable was the hard part. Bodeen had so many enemies it could have been anybody that kidnapped Mika from the police to his own Mama. Coach decided to concentrate on the clues that were oft repeated throughout the hood. It seems that the majority of the gossipers believed this crew of hooligans that specialized in collecting ransom money kidnapped Mika. These cats' morals might have been twisted but the business they created was very lucrative with minimal risk. They were kidnapping Kids, mothers, and Wives. Not even the hardest, I-don't-give-a-fuck-killers wouldn't hesitate to pay a hefty ransom to get their mother back. From what Coach heard on the streets this crew got their start when they caught one of their rival foes that was making a little noise in the game coming out of a store alone. They were just going to smack him around, beat him up and rob him but as a joke they decided to kidnap him just to see what would happen. Those dudes ended up getting a $50,000 ransom for a peanut head drug dealer in Oakland that wasn't worth a damn to nobody. From that moment on, they figured they could get top dollar for someone the dealer really loved. Once they got the swing of things they wouldn't make a move for nothing less than a 100,000 thousand. As more time passed they started playing for Big Stakes and started hitting million dollar targets. Coach knew a lot of grimy villains in the neighborhood but he didn't have enough street stripes to find some cats at that level. He was a community Activist not an underground kingpin. It was such a long shot Coach didn't even bother with that lead.

Next Coach had to enter a dark place. The Child Sex Trade was a cold vicious game. Coach saw some things that made him cringe and he was barely scratching the surface. That was a world Coach couldn't even enter if he wanted to. He didn't want to know what was going on and glad he didn't know. Coach had to break down and give thanks to the MOST HIGH for blessing him with Gerry. He was destined for that wicked cycle in the child sex trade as an infant before he was redirected and put on the right path. Gerry gave him a fair shot at life.

Coach needed time to think. He realized the underground wasn't his territory and he needed some help. Coach decided to call Gerry and he told her they needed to talk. Gerry informed him they she had some business to take care of in West Texas and was driving there in the next couple of days. Gerry suggested that Coach should take the trip with her and just get away from the pressure for a minute and clear his head. Coach jumped on the opportunity. A cool road trip with Gerry would be nice.

CHAPTER 48

THE SUSPECTS WERE narrowing down or were they? Bodeen could have attracted an enemy seeking revenge at any point of his life. It was very hard to tell in his line of work. Bodeen suspected that Detective Andy Moretti was the demon that caused his heartbreak. Anybody could have been Bodeen's enemy but Andy Moretti was the only man he knew that was sick enough to do something like that to him. Bodeen heard through the grapevine that Andy Moretti was doing awful since he was suspended from the job. Being broke and doing bad is definitely a motive for revenge. Bodeen didn't even have to dream about what he would do to Andy if he were the silly one that took Mika away from him. It was already pre-ordained. Killing Andy was the last option; suffering was the first and letting him live without sight or limbs was a close second. There were other devious methods that rounded out Bodeen's top ten of torture that would disfigure him but Andy would still be breathing.

Bodeen found that locating Andy Moretti was not going to be simple as it used to be. Andy's house was seized by the Bank and sold in an auction. Andy was also being investigated about the murder of his Wife and mother to his kids. Andy Moretti now had one step up on Bodeen because his whereabouts were unknown and he could reach out and touch Bodeen whenever the time was right.

Dealing with the stress of not knowing what was happening or who was doing god knows what to his baby girl all came to a haunting reality when he received that first package at the door. Bodeen already knew what it was. He has left them a time or two when he was trying to get his point across that he was serious about collecting his money. Bodeen didn't see it as karma coming back. His spiritual side hadn't yet grasped that concept. Bodeen saw it as the rules of the game. 4 days had passed and Bodeen didn't have that amount of money they wanted any longer. Bodeen was dealing with a professional kidnapper; not a babysitter. After three days, body parts start being removed, packaged, and shipped daily to expedite that ransom money. Bodeen had no fear opening the box. He had already made up his mind that any fate Mika suffered he would endure as well. Bodeen opened the box and just like he assumed it was his baby girl's finger. Bodeen closed the box and tears fell from his eyes instantly. Thinking of his Mika being cut up was too much for Bodeen. The pain was unbearable. Once Bodeen had no more tears left to shed, he went into the kitchen, grabbed his knife, laid his hand on the bread board and chopped his index finger clean off. Bodeen didn't shed one tear and he didn't feel it at all.

Bodeen's life was in a downward spiral and when matters couldn't have been getting any worse the next package arrived at his front door. Bodeen's Heart fell out of his body when he saw the baby ear that was severed off of Mika. This time there was a sarcastic note that accompanied the package that read, "Can you hear me now!"

Bodeen's emotions were on a roller coaster ride, sulking, anger, revenge, and fear. He was able to deal with those nervous jitters but it was his incompetence that he could not stomach. He was his daughter's protector. Bodeen had to make it right. Whatever Mika suffered Bodeen felt he should be dealt the same fate. Her problems were his problems. Her pain was his pain. Bodeen looked in the mirror at the ear Jah shot a chunk out of. He used his left hand and stretched his ear out by pulling the lobe. He placed the sharp blade of his knife against his ear and began to slice it with slow even strokes until a bloody ear was left dangling in between his fingertips.

CHAPTER 49

COACH AND GERRY hit the road. Coach needed this little get away to clear his head. A nice road trip with some good music playing is the cure for a lot of life stresses. The trip also gave Coach some time to analyze Gerry's day-to-day routine. Even though Gerry raised Coach the early years of his life he never truly paid attention to what she did for a living. As a kid that was the least of his concerns. Also, when a person loves an individual unconditionally it really doesn't matter what they do anyway. They are only going to see the good in that person. Besides a few broads she turned out and a little weed she peddled, Gerry never brought her business home from the streets.

After a day of watching Gerry, Coach still didn't know what she did and he still wasn't concerned. It didn't take deep thought to see Gerry wasn't this phenomenal hustler. She was just a broad that did what she had to do to keep a roof over her head, some money in her pocket, and some nice men's dress shoes on her feet.

Rio Rancho New Mexico- the City of Vision, West Texas. Once again Coach had known Gerry damn near his entire life and had no clue of what kind hustle she could possibly have in this town. Coach stayed in the car by choice when Gerry handled her business. Coach wasn't nervous one bit but Gerry liked to do business with those hard luck looking muthafucka's and he just didn't want to be around that type of energy. Gerry also had a couple of broads she checked on out there that either looked lost or was looking for a way out. Those bitches were torn up. Gerry had the nerve to Mack to one of those bitches. Coach was sitting in the car cracking up as he was watching the scene unfold. Coach was thinking, *"Gerry could have saved that Mack."* That bitch was doing so bad she would have done anything Gerry told her to do for a hamburger and small carton of milk.

As they traveled through towns that Coach never heard of and will never see again in life, he started to take it all in. Gerry was right. The road trip was exactly what Coach needed. The thoughts that clouded his mind like a fog began to dissipate and everything was slowly starting to become clear again. This was the first time Coach allowed his mind to rest in a couple of years. It felt pretty good. Coach's life test was no joke. He stayed in good spirits but mentally it was heavy for him. He saw that the trial did make him stronger, sharper, and a better person but he still didn't like that shit. Coach had put the incident far behind him but he couldn't control a flashback popping up in his mind every now and then. He didn't need any more reminders. The lesson was learned. Coach was ready to move on. He didn't have one flashback or bad thought the entire trip. Laughing with Gerry and at Gerry's crazy ass lifestyle was definitely the cure that was needed.

Coach lit his first spliff of the trip. The vibe was finally right. The air was fresh and this area called the Bosque that was full of cottonwood trees was gorgeous in a spiritual sense. Coach was taking it all in… and then it dawned on him that he hadn't even thought about that money in two days. Coach thought about it. He started smiling like a muthafucka. Gerry saw him grinning and thought he was high because that was the first joint he had in a while. Coach had a big smile on his face but he kept his mouth shut. He didn't tell Gerry about the money yet. She would be too worried about him. When the time was right he was going to lay it on her.

Coach spotted a cool Motel called the Rancho Inn. He was in need of a hot shower and he wanted to crash in a nice bed before they returned back to L.A. It would also give him a moment to ponder about his future plans. Gerry wanted to stop at bar and get a little taste before they turned it in. She spotted a bar off the highway and pulled over.

"What kind of bar do you have me at Gerry? Can we ever do something modern? If your spots were classics it would be cool but everything you do is played out. It's not timeless. This bar probably has hay on the floor."

"Just kick back and let me sip on some Yack… what the fuck you gon' drink Vodka and Spinach juice? Oh I forgot you don't drink huh? You square ass health freak... Hey Coach, hey Coach, There you go- right over there, look. Go cut down a piece of that cactus and have the bartender pour you some cactus water from the earth in a glass." Gerry clowned.

"G'wan and get out of here with that foolish talk mama you crazy." Coach stated as he laughed at what Gerry said.

"Have you called and checked on Jah?" Gerry asked as a family member would.

"Yes Indeed. My young lion is marking his territory at Ju Ju's house. All is well." Coach stated with pride as he talked about his little big man.

Gerry stared at Coach before she spoke again. She didn't want to change the mood but something heavy was on her mind.

"I don't know if it's your dreadlocks or what but as you get older your accent comes out more. Do you uh, ever think about your biological mother?"

"For what?" Coach answered nonchalantly and before he was about to tell Gerry what she needed to hear the bouncer checking ID distracted them.

When they entered the bar the music was loud and it was full of Mexicans. It wasn't the kind of Mexicans Coach was use to like Big Spider. These Mexicans looked like Texans.

They wore cowboy hats with spurs on their boots and expensive belt buckles. There were a few white dudes sprinkled in there that was probably truckers. Coach saw a host of disheveled looking women in the bar that would start to look like glamorous queens once the men got real drunk. There were two black dudes in the joint and Coach was one of them. The way the other brother was seated Coach could only see him from the back. He was definitely a dude Gerry could relate to. He was an older man going through a middle-aged crisis but from yesteryear. He had a Luster Silk Perm combed straight back into a shag. The Shag part was crimped at the ends. Four drunken ivory complexioned women surrounded him. He was only hugged up with one but real flirtatious with the other ones. Coach could tell the dude was no playboy. He looked exactly like a trick that just came into some money and he couldn't wait to fuck it off on some silly shit.

Coach shook his head as he and Gerry looked around for a seat. As Coach walked past the area where the loud black dude was trying too hard to be the life of the party, he was taken back for a second. Minus the arrogance in the dudes laugh, it kind of reminded Coach of James and it made him kind of sad. James was his friend and he missed him dearly.

Gerry wasn't fooled by the Tricks transformation. She caught up to Coach with a light trot and said,

"Hey Coach, ain't that your boy from the Rec Center over there cooning for those white women with his hair all whipped up? Hahahaha, that fool looks silly as hell. He must have just came into some money and don't know what to do with it."

"You know good and damn well that ain't James. He would never be caught out there looking as ridiculous as that lame over there." Coach stated and obviously irritated. His voice began to crack a little bit as he continued,

"...Plus Gerry, you didn't know this but James passed not too long ago... he was killed behind that bullshit I got caught up in." Coach concluded while getting kind of teary eyed. He felt ashamed but he kept it together.

"No disrespect intended baby boy but that's one hell of a clone then. I know that laugh anywhere." Gerry stated as she respectfully held her ground. Gerry was hood and didn't give a fuck. She yelled James name out across the bar as she started to walk in his direction. Coach followed her so he could apologize to the man for what was about to happen. Coach couldn't see the tricks reaction when Gerry called him by James name but Coach would have paid money to see it because the after effect was priceless. Coach was hoping he was looking at a Ghost because James turned whiter than the women he surrounded himself with when he saw him and Gerry.

Coach was angry but he was hurt more than anything. His emotions were so mixed up he didn't know how to react. Coach clinched his fist so tight his knuckles turned white. Every voice going off in Coach's head was telling him to punch James hard right in his face. Coach's conscious warned him against it. The effort it took holding his fist back kind of wore Coach out and it took a toll on him mentally and physically.

The best James could have done in his current situation was either fess up or shut up. James could barely get a word out. A man that once spoke so articulate started stuttering like he had a speech impediment. That could only mean one thing; he was about to lie his ass off.

"Uh C-Co-co-Coach, uh uh, um um, you-you- uh, you- you- uhh, and then, that's uhhh, you- you- ohhhh fuck it, are you gonna kill me tonight?"

"It's a very strong possibility!" Gerry said calmly but with deadly intentions.

"No way, I wouldn't even give you the satisfaction of letting you take the easy way out. You got to feel this! No Sir...does Jessie and kids know about this?" Coach asked frustrated.

"Jessie she had her hand in it, but the kids don't know... they would be thoroughly disappointed in us if they ever found out." James confessed.

Coach was disgusted. He remained cool until he thought about his little man.

"But my son, my son man, Jah, your Godson...you left my son out there for the system to raise him. There is no forgiveness for those actions. It's more or less about me at this point. How could you do some shit like that to Jah? I hope you got something out of it so I can at least see why you sold me out."

Gerry showed her pistol resting in her waistband. James started speaking without stuttering.

"Well *your boy*," *he emphasized Bodeen being Coach's boy to try and take some of the weight off of his own ass.* "...Your boy showed up at my house in that white truck. He had some white cat that looked like a hipster but smelled like police deliver a package and message. He told me that I could either wake up tomorrow a rich man or I wouldn't wake up at all and to make the choice. He said I had to leave immediately and never look back. He laid 250,000 dollars on me man. I have never seen that type of money before. I mean c'mon man- $250,000 to leave town and start a new life. I was able to start my own landscaping business and I finally feel free. And Honestly, I didn't know what they had planned man, they didn't tell me nothing- by the time Jessie told me what happened it was too late. I still have over a hundred and fifty thousand dollars of that money left over. You can have it all. Please just don't kill me."

"I don't want your money sucka. The best punishment for you is I'm gonna let your kids know what type of punk ass daddy they have. I can guarantee you that! A man with principles like you will never feel comfortable with a pocket full of money walking around in shame. That perm can't disguise what type of man you really are underneath it." Coach stated and walked away from the table.

"Sheeeiit he might not want that money but I do! Oh-You know you gots to come up off that homeboy!" Gerry stated with quickness and a look in her eye that meant business.

CHAPTER 50

BODEEN WAS ON the hunt. He had no choice but to rediscover his past. That was the only way he knew how to get the job done. He was subjected into doing some bad things that he was no longer proud of at this stage of his life but he was determined to find Mika and whoever got in the way at that moment, oh well. Bodeen hunted down everybody with a kidnapping jacket and put serious pressure on them. He shook cats down for money that he knew was innocent but he had to do it. Bodeen overplayed himself quick. Once the word hit the streets, and it didn't take long, that Bodeen was on a rampage everybody started laying low. Bodeen got the information he needed but he didn't get it from the streets. Bodeen set his sights on Andy Moretti. He was the only one left.

Bodeen's resources were limited. The people that could easily lead Bodeen to Andy would stay loyal to the Detective so they were of no use. Locating Andy's dealer or one of his hookers was Bodeen's best shot and he hoped they would be disgruntled. Bodeen went two for two out the gate. It was just as he thought, with the condition Andy was in he couldn't possibly be paying his dealers and hookers on time and for a little bit of money they lead him straight to Detective Moretti.

Bodeen found Andy with his pistols ready to shoot but it was no use. Andy Moretti was a walking corpse already. He looked awful. He was in no condition to do anything but commit suicide. Bodeen had seen many men of Andy's status in his day hit a that brick wall when they were looking for a way out. Bodeen saw the belt hanging from the ceiling in Andy's rundown Motel room full of vodka bottles and drug paraphernalia when he located him.

Andy Moretti was the last piece of the puzzle. He would no longer be on earth from what Bodeen saw in the room. Bodeen was confused now more than ever. Who had his baby girl?????????????

CHAPTER 51

A DAY AFTER they got back to town Gerry told Coach to met her at the Pool Hall on Gage and Central. It was across the street from the oldest black Historic Masonic Lodge in California. Since masonry is also associated with secrecy Coach's curiosity was automatically drawn to it as he wondered what went on inside that old weather tattered building.

Coach walked into the Pool Hall. It was just like he imagined. It was Dark and smelled like cheap arm pit liquor. The California law that states smoking his prohibited inside public buildings didn't apply at this joint. Central Ave no longer had the swag and swing that Coach read about in those Easy Rawlins Mystery Books he loved so much but you couldn't tell him that. Coach was so proud to be on the Central Avenue where the greatest artist, jazz players, and bluesmen once congregated. He felt that he was standing on Holy Land.

The Wood on the Pool Tables was scratched something awful, the felt material was shabby, and the pool sticks were sticky but there were brand new blue cubes of pool cue chalk laid out on every table.

"Coach!" He heard somebody call his name. He looked around and it was hard to see in the dimly lit smoke filled pool hall. Coach looked toward the floor and saw a needled toe shoes cutting through the cloud and knew it was Gerry approaching him. She was looking good in her brand new khaki suit. Coach laughed at the fact that every time hard faced thugs got groomed up they always looked shiny like they used Vaseline to moisturize. That money she took off of old James was making her glamorous...by hardcore thug standards.

"W'Sup Pooks? I'm mad as hell you are going out of your way to help that punk muthafucka that got you caught up. But on the real-When I was in the joint- I read that Nelson Mandela became best friends with the man that got him locked up for 27 years. I could never do no shit like that myself. But it shows me you got a soul of gold Coach.

"Who do you think I got it from? You raised me Gerry. You raised me. You did that!" Coach sincerely stated and giving her the credit.

"Damn, picture that... an old Butch broad like me, who don't even have her own life together raised a man that's doing some Mandela Shit.

"You are far more than that to me. You are my Mom's, in my Pops Shoes, my beautiful Queen, and my Blessing. My situation could have been fucked up but you gave me life. You are the only mother I know but even better than that, you're the only mother that I want and need. I love you unconditionally and always know that."

Gerry wiped the tears from her eyes and hugged Coach tight. She slipped a card in his pocket and said,

"Be careful Pookie Pie If something ever happens to you again I'll lose it."

Coach patted his pocket where the card was placed and said,

"I got you watching my back so I feel very secure. Thank You... Moms."

"Get on outta here baby- you got me all emotional around all these criminals up in here, boy ya making me vulnerable."

"What are you about to get into?" Coach asked.

Before she answered Gerry looked around the pool hall real slow and took a puff of some very good top shelf herb.

"I got this new hard head bitch I got to deal with that needs some disciplining and then I'm gonna take her to buy me some new shoes."

"Some more Church Shoes?"

"Naw brutha, some Gators! I'm steppin' my game up fo' real."

Coach left the pool hall smiling. He loved him some Gerry. She didn't need to use sermons, religion, strict rules, or violence to raise Coach into a good man. All it took was pure love. Coach started to reminisce about how fun it used to be growing up in a house with a woman that looked and acted like your favorite uncle.

When Coach drove up to his building Bodeen was standing outside just looking out into the atmosphere at nothing. Coach walked up on him. They stared at each other for a long time. Bodeen was a broken man. He looked a mess spiritually but mentally he still looked determined. There were bandages where his ear used to be. His hand was also wrapped where he once had five fingers. Coach reached into his pocket and pulled out the card Gerry gave him.

"Faith and this card will lead you to your baby girl. One without the other would be useless. You make the choice. Bless up!" Coach made his peace and turned around to leave.

"Coach!" Bodeen called out and extended his handshake. He looked Coach in his eyes with sincerity and said,

"Thank You Man."

Coach nodded his head and turned again to leave. Bodeen's grip became tighter around Coach's hand and prevented him from leaving. Bodeen looked at Coach as if he could see through him and added,

"And by the way... you can keep that money. You and your son got that coming"

Coach was speechless. All he had was the *how did you know* look on his face.

Bodeen let go of his tight grip and smiled before he said,

"I was a contract killer Coach... My job required that I know everything."

Coach heard Bodeen and had a good sense of what he meant but he was still marveled by it. Coach stayed very low key about his newfound fortunes. Bodeen eased his thought with a little advice.

"...it's your body language. You're an honest man and a good dude Coach so all that love you have in you... it shows. I got two words for you Coach, "Poker Face." Bodeen smiled turned on his heels and walked away.

Coach stood in the street baffled. He didn't know what to think of it. As Coach thought about the event that just took place he discovered something even stranger that would bother him for a long time. Bodeen still never apologized. Coach didn't think about it long. He smiled so big the corners of his mouth almost touched the back of his ears. Coach had pep in his step as he walked across the street. Before he got to the entrance a feeling of extreme happiness just came over Coach and he jumped as high as he could with his arms stretched out and clicked his muthafuckin' heels in air... That's how happy he was! Coach just kept pumping his fist all the way to his apartment. Coach and Jah were ready. Let the new journey begin.

LAST CHAPTER....

BODEEN DIDN'T HAVE the money or an elaborate plan. His mind was already made up. If Mika was disfigured, raped or hurt in any such way that she would find it difficult to overcome in life, Bodeen was going to kill everybody in the room including Mika and himself without hesitation. Bodeen stopped for a moment and decided to try that thing called Faith that Coach hipped him to. It was only one problem. Bodeen didn't know to apply faith or what to do with it. He couldn't pull it like a trigger. He couldn't twist faith around Moretti's neck. Bodeen still questioned his faith because he still didn't have it yet. Bodeen decided to act just using gut instincts.

Downtown L.A., a few blocks away from the Garment District, Bodeen was kneeling on the roof of building across from the address Coach gave him. Bodeen looked through his binoculars. He spotted a recognizable figure inside the Loft. Bodeen wasn't shocked one bit by what he saw but he was pissed off that he let himself get played like a poot-butt. If this was a cartoon Bodeen would have morphed into a lollipop with Sucker written across his forehead. He just shook his head at his incompetence.

Andy Moretti was inside the Loft sitting on a futon watching television. Andy still looked bad by playboy standards but he was groomed compared to when Bodeen had seen him last. Andy Moretti taught Bodeen well but as he learned the hard way he didn't teach him everything. Andy played an old con on Bodeen that he wasn't hip to. Bodeen knew he had to proceed with extreme caution until he figured out how this con was so supposed to play out. He learned long ago to look at all the possible angles when the con is being played. Other than that little bit of knowledge right there that's all Bodeen knew about that game. He was going to have to figure it out on the fly and that's not smart. A con is planned in advance and any move Bodeen made was already suspected and a countermove would be waiting to put his lights out forever. Bodeen was known for fucking with his victim's mind but the con man has the ability to blow your mind and make you wonder what in the fuck just happened?

From where he was positioned Bodeen wasn't able to see any other parts of the loft and locate Mika's whereabouts. Bodeen had to act on instinct. In most cases Bodeen would have temporarily cut the power and bypassed the low-level loft security cameras but Andy Moretti taught him all those tricks. It would be a dead give away. He wasn't in the mood to be clever or in the mood come up with a brilliant idea to get to Andy Moretti. Bodeen wanted his Baby girl. Everything else was a hurdle in his way.

Bodeen said Fuck it and made his way down the building and across the street. He saw a side entrance that would be accessible once he picked the lock. The area was dimly lit and the darkness played out to be Bodeen's best friend. Being a Big black Muthafucka had its advantages. Bodeen made his way along the wall with ease. He didn't even have a shadow. He orchestrated his way into the building. He ran into another obstacle when he saw the heavy-duty loft doors. A simple gunshot would not be able to blast the locks off the door. Bodeen didn't want to risk picking the lock so close to danger because his track record had been tainted in that department after Jah shot that plug out of his ear. He could faintly hear the television but he could clearly hear the hard sole shoes of Andy Moretti as he walked across the concrete floors of the loft. The sound was going in the opposite direction. The Loft doors might have been made from hard steel but the windows on those old downtown building was older than water. Bodeen jimmied the window and jumped his big ass through it. Bodeen made it to his feet and immediately took a shotgun blast to the stomach that put him on his ass. Andy Moretti was standing a few feet away from the fallen Bodeen. The barrel of the shotgun was still smoking. Bodeen just suffered a few buckshot's. He wasn't badly injured but he didn't let Andy know that. Andy Moretti put the shotgun down and pulled out his police issued Beretta. He walked slowly over to Bodeen with extreme caution.

Bodeen was a paid killer and capable of anything. Andy ordered Bodeen to disarm himself. He picked up Bodeen's weapons and frisked him for more.

Bodeen kind of expected the worst by walking in a trap but what he saw next completely blew his mind. Mika walked out of the back room perfectly healthy. Her ear and finger was completely unharmed.

"Hi Daddy, look my Mommy came down from heaven just to see me."

It was Angie. Bodeen didn't know how to react to it. He was stuck like his PCP days but in a good way. Bodeen was so confused he didn't know if he looking at a ghost or not. She was still very beautiful but anyone that saw her before knew her heart had been hardened and her soul had been scarred. Angie had developed dark circles under her eyes since their last encounter. Angie did not exude happiness. Bodeen could hear the pain in her voice when she spoke.

"I thought seeing you suffer would help make me forget about the past but there is not a day that goes by I don't think of that horrific night you ruined my life. I prayed and prayed from the moment that I found out I was pregnant that it was the Blessing that my murdered husband left for me so I could be content to move on. That is the way it is supposed to work out right? When Mika was born I immediately knew this was not my husband's child. I have never in my life doubted my faith until that very moment. I didn't give birth by Immaculate Conception and this was not my husband's blessing. I was cursed. Not just because her father is an evil demon but the fact that Mika is not you, and I will never be able to love her as a mother should. As beautiful as she is I cannot look at her face without seeing you and remembering that night. The pain is unbearable. Mika spirit is so strong she helped renew my faith. There is no doubt Mika is a Blessing but she is your blessing Bodeen. As much as I want to I could never love her like you do. You turned your life completely around and that alone will never make me question my faith ever again. That was a miracle if there ever was one, Good Lord. But the mental scars are too deep at this point in my life to forgive you. That is not my job. My job is to tell you- only because of Mika, that Faith is something you should consider. I'm gonna leave it at that."

All kinds of flashbacks started hitting Bodeen at once. *The Nurse at the Hospital-…The Strange Cars following him and parked in front of his crib.*

She was even working at the Funeral Parlor as a Pathologist when Bodeen first hired LeRon. That is how she was able to send the packages containing the body parts. Bodeen just kind of turned his head to the side and cracked a smile in disbelief. Angie was good. She used his best strategy against him and fucked his mind up! He didn't see that one coming at all.

"Are you done going down memory lane with all this sentimental bullshit. This story does not end happily ever after. I want my fucking money!" Andy interrupted.

"Money? What Money? That wasn't part of the deal." Angie expressed in confusion.

"You're right because your part in this is over. I'm the hero in the last chapter." Andy confessed

"You used me as a pawn?"

"No not a pawn- more like a knight or rook- hell even the Queen because you were a powerful piece...to a much weaker opponent. To me a Queen is just a bitch with fancy moves so ultimately; you're just like all the other pieces, So Yes... technically I guess I did use you and now the King is the only one standing.

"Boom!" Andy lifted his arm and shot Angie her right in the forehead. The thud when her skull hit and bounced off the concrete floor was a very eerie sound that would always haunt the ones that heard it forever.

"She didn't want to live anymore. Her life was miserable. I did her a favor. You fucked her life up Bodeen. I found her hiding in the basement when I went to the horrid scene you left behind out in Redondo when I had to clean up your shit. I would have never believed it was you until she told me it was a big black motherfucker and I took her away from the scene before anybody witnessed her. After I saw the mess you left... after I heard what you did? I knew you were getting weak. Not weak as in soft but you started showing all the signs of Hit man burn out. You started making mistakes- beating up old men... getting shot by a child that could barely hold a gun, I mean my god man... you're done! I want that money you have saved up and I want you to turn over the deeds to those pieces of property you own. You are not gonna need it. Its better I have it than the government right?"

Bodeen looked at Moretti with vengeance in his eyes. Even with three guns Moretti still felt uncomfortable by Bodeen's evil stare. Andy didn't like it at all. His countermove was cold blooded.

Andy grabbed Mika by her beautiful locks.

"You killed my unborn child and think karma wasn't coming back to get your ass." Andy Moretti started speaking out of his head.

"You ordered the hit" Bodeen spoke the truth.

"I know and that's why I'm here because Karma wasn't coming for you so I came… You know, it actually feels good to see you sitting there suffering and shivering every time I shake this little pickaninny by her head" Andy said and let out a sick laugh. He was a high. Bodeen could tell. Andy said,

"I want to see your see face when I place this blade to this little bitches neck!…Aww look at you, you look pitiful. How many times have you put that look on a poor souls face before you killed them? I feel like taking this knife and slicing this bitches throat as slow as possible… Whew you should have a saw your face that time! I thought you were shitting on yourself."

After mentally torturing Bodeen and Mika for the next 30 minutes, Andy finally said,

"You know I'm not gonna kill either one of you. Bodeen I got the evidence that you killed my pregnant wife- I got the murder weapon, I got a written statement from this murdered mother before her untimely demise that you kidnapped this little girl. You are gonna jail for the remainder of your life. If you think you can include me and take me along with you think again. You are not that smart. I have blood samples showing how much PCP you keep in your system- no judge will ever believe you. This arrest is gonna get my job and my life back."

Andy Moretti looked at Bodeen with a wicked smile on his face and took out his phone and said,

"You should have never fucked us over."

When Andy Moretti said "Us" Bodeen automatically assumed he was referring to himself and Angie. That Andy Moretti was just full of all kinds of surprises. Bodeen didn't know he was going to unleash the Creature from the black Lagoon.

"Come here baby. This is my baby right here!" Andy Moretti squeezed her ass and kissed her on the mouth. Bodeen looked up in shock! It was his mother, Charlesetta... still looking like a hot mess as usual.

"Soon as I call my boys in blue this chapter is a wrap!"

The Call to the cops was never connected... two bullet wounds was placed to the back of Andy Moretti's head as he began to dial 911. Andy fell face first on the concrete floor of the loft. His nose and front teeth shattered on impact. Blood splattered everywhere. Bodeen looked up in shock.

Charlesetta looked at her beautiful granddaughter for the first time in her life. "Get over her little girl..." Charlesetta looked her up and down not showing any emotion whatsoever.

"What's your name?

"Mika" The child answered politely.

"Miko?" Ain't that a boy's name?"

"No Ma'am Mika."

"Oh, sound like you said Miko to me. Who is that nigga over there?" Charlesetta asked referring to her son.

"That what? I don't know what that is ma'am but that's My Daddy right there...Hi Daddy!"

"Hmphf, you love your Daddy huh?" Charlesetta asked in funky monotone.

"Yes Ma'am, I love him very much, please can I go hug my daddy he looks hurt."

"What? No you cain't!! Charlesetta answered Mika's question and then looked at Bodeen and continued.

"Payback is a bitch ain't it Bodeen? I told you I was coming back to get your black ass. I ain't gonna ever forget what you did to me... I am your mother! I raised you! How could you do that to me? I hope you rot in hell with gasoline draws on for what you did to your only mother.

But... as a favor to somebody that's sweet to me, I'm gonna do the right thing." And for the only time in his life Charlesetta sounded like his mother,

"I do owe you that much... Go on and raise your baby girl right. Do everything I didn't do. Go on little girl. Go be wit yo Daddy!"

Mika ran and jumped in Bodeen's arms and hugged him tight. Daddy

I missed you so much. On her way out the door Charlesetta heard Mika say,

"Who was that lady?"

"Mika that's Your…" but before Bodeen could give his mother her rightful title, Charlesetta looked back at her beautiful granddaughter, and then she looked at Bodeen with no type of gleam or happiness in her eye whatsoever. Her face was frowned up and grotesque for no reason. Bodeen knew what she was thinking. *I'm looking too good to be called somebody's grandmother!"*

Bodeen answered Mika.

"Remember when we watched that movie the Wiz together? Well that's the Wicked Witch of the West."

"She was mean. It looks like you've been in a storm Daddy are you hurt?"

"The pain has gone away… literally. I'll be all right."

"What happened to your ear?"

"Sacrifice baby girl sacrifice."

"You have Faith now like Mommy said?"

"No doubt about it!"

"What are we gonna do now Daddy?"

"We are gonna live happily ever after."

"That's how all the good stories end."

EPILOGUE

A BRAND NEW custom Chrysler 300 waited like a chariot on the curb. Charlesetta tried to open the passenger side door but it was locked. The window rolled down. Charlesetta tried to use her best sweet baby voice and said,

"Did I do good, Daddy?"

"Bitch! You want some form of congratulations because you finally did something to help your son for the first time in your sorry little life? It's about damn time. I don't believe you fixed your mouth to say some silly shit like that around me. You know what, Charlesetta? I don't want to hear you talk for the rest of the night. Use them cracked chapped lips for what they do best, bitch, and hop to it!"

Charlesetta ran around to the driver's side of the car and waited for the nod to open the door. Charlesetta opened the door and dropped to her bare knees on the concrete.

Two feet came out of the car with a pair of brand new Mauri alligator shoes on and they stopped to rest on Charlesetta's thighs. Charlesetta kissed the toes of each shoe and then she guided them back into the car making sure they never touched the ground.

"Now get yo' triflin' ass in the back seat and keep that mouth shut!"

Gerry looked down at her new Gators with a grin. She had diamonds on fingers and watches on her arms. She had a pocket full of money, the deed to a new house in Baldwin Hills that she now lived alone in, and was the sole owner of a male strip club. Gerry put her custom Chrysler 300 on 20-inch rims into drive and headed toward Figueroa… stylin'!

THE END

ALLAH this Blessing was Amazing! No matter how deep and dark this journey got I kept seeing the light. All Praises Due! Now it's all on me to Stay True. The God!

SON! There was no greater feeling than riding this one out together. "The Bond between Father & Son is a Fabulous One!" Let's Go! Let's Go!

Craig D Frazier & Colin Sutton The Roots of this Literary Tree I didn't *Give it Up* and y'all *Turned me Loose* and this is coming from your Soul Brother *Straight From the Lip!*

Bear Grass the Man that *is* always there at the exact time I need to get my paper right and puts me in position to achieve my family dreams. You earned your wings on this one. And now we both can take flight! See you at the Top!

The Super Director Adam J. Hardy thanks for sharing some key and pivotal moments with your Cutty and opening my 3rd eye that allowed me to see the Visual for the Cover.

And Last but not least Mr. Quentin Tarantino Whooooo Boooyyyy you know you gots' to fuck with Me! Recognize Nigga L-E-G-E-N to the Muthafuckin' D! I Got Cho Azz!!